GW01071948

TWITCHER

By Andrew Osmond

To Alison,
Hope you enjoy your
next trip to Lundy

Andrew

Minnow Press

2001

Published by
Minnow Press

© Andrew Osmond, 2001

ISBN   0 9539448 0 8

1 3 5 7 9 0 8 6 4 2

British Library Cataloguing in Publication Data
A catalogue record of this book is available from the British
Library

Printed in Great Britain by Antony Rowe Limited,
Chippenham

For
Henty
With
Love

Author's Note

This novel is entirely a work of fiction. The names, characters and incidents portrayed are the work of the author's imagination. Any resemblance to actual persons, living or dead is entirely coincidental. The Lundy section of the book is inspired by happy times spent on this beautiful island, and although the geographical locations may be factually accurate, the descriptions of the characters in this book, their conduct, and their work procedures, are not based on the actual post-holders, either current or past. And finally, an apology to birders. Although I have tried to adhere to accuracy as regard to bird descriptions, behaviour and habitat, I realise that I have taken one or two liberties for the sake of the story. I hope that die-hard twitchers will not be too over-critical. And now, if you are still emboldened to read on, I hope that you enjoy the tale.

Prologue

To Whom It May Concern.

This may be the only chance I have to communicate to you. I think my life may be at risk and I don't think I have very long before they find out. If you are reading this now I have been proved correct in this belief. Everything else you will hear will be told to you by murderers. Believe me about this if nothing else. Everything. That is why I write this testament - to shine as one ray of truth through a darkness of deceit.

It was only last night that I discovered the truth myself. Now I can marvel at how I could have been so blind. So stupid. It was only last night that I finally found out what happened to my wife. I discovered the pages from the journal under his bed, quite by chance when I was looking for something else. Should I have read them? Of course, I wouldn't have, except that I saw her name. In black and white. In front of me on the page. And then I was lost. Curiosity is such a powerful instinct. But even now, I wonder if I wouldn't have been better off if I had just put those pages back unread. Except it is not true what they say, that ignorance is bliss. Ignorance was killing me as surely as my life is finished now.

Part One

A Lesson in Ornithology:
The Cuckoo and the Peregrine

Listen to the furthest sound. Close your eyes. Keep totally still. And listen.

At first there is nothing. Or perhaps just the faintest rustling of the leaves and the branches if the wind is particularly strong. But then out of the blackness, awareness grows. Like eyes adjusting to the darkness, so hearing becomes more and more acute. Reaching out further. Crickets chirping in the long grass, like the rhythmic rasping of a bow across a string: a symphony of insect jazz violinists, some playing close at hand; some answering from far away. The buzzing of a honey bee, lost in a field without a flower. The whisper of the breeze through the reed beds, and the faintest of splashes as a fish surfaces in the pond with a ripple and a water boatman skims across the shallows in a shimmering heat-haze of movement. The constant low hum of traffic on the dual carriageway; the purr of powerful performance cars, the heavy rumble of laden lorries, and the noisy misfirings of an ancient motorbike. And further still, a car horn sounds, jarring in the housing estate beyond the woods. Somewhere high overhead, an aircraft. Or perhaps a helicopter? And a dog barking. A big dog, with a deep, angry bark. And then a Cuckoo. Out of the cacophony, so distinctive, that rich, gurgling call. Like froth building up into bubbles in the throat. That unmistakable two-tone siren. Cuck-oo. Cuck-oo.

The herald of spring. The European Cuckoo is a bird that, like the most disrespectful of infants, is heard but not seen. It is a secretive bird, plain in colouration, a master of disguise some might even suggest, happy to pass unnoticed amongst its own kind, universally shunned by the rest of the avian community, forced to exist in the murky fringes of bird society. Not without reason: it has some fairly unpleasant habits. Indeed, its very first instinct, only hours after birth, is the basest of them all: murder.

Still blind and naked in the nest; the first touch of air feeling chill after the days spent in the warm, secure cocoon of its protective egg; alone in a prickly, itchy basket of twigs and moss, except that is for the scratchy little fleas and bugs that hop and crawl across its bare, goose-bumped flesh, and the newborn powerless to prevent them; the first to hatch, it senses the presence of other eggs around it, vague shapes containing the fluttering heartbeats of its kin. Or its rivals? The effort required is immense: each unborn egg must be rolled, slowly, painstakingly, one over another, up the sloping sides of the nest, and then the manoeuvre repeated as it so often rolls back, one by one, each smooth, round egg, until the very last one has been ejected from the nurturing cradle to fall, cracked and useless on the ground below, and the panting, exhausted hatchling can rest, lonely as is its destiny, but master of its domain, all competitors eliminated, waiting for the return of its surrogate mother.

The cuckoo knows it is a bird eat bird world; a constant battle to keep one jump ahead of the opposition. Relax, just for one minute, and it will be overtaken, and the arch-parasite will become cuckolded itself. Don't ever be fooled into thinking that birding is a gentle pursuit: it's life and death out there.

Ornithology has a long history. It could almost be said, dating right back to the very first life on earth. Was it not Darwin's study of finches on the Galapagos Islands that helped him formulate his theories for *Origin of the Species*: the theories for life and evolution itself. Academically, ornithology emerged as a distinct scientific discipline from the all-embracing subject of natural history during the nineteenth century, although as a result of the great age of exploration during the previous century and the ensuing plethora of new information about previously undiscovered and exotic bird species, it was already being recognised as a subject in its own right from a much earlier date. It was during this time that one of the inspirational pioneers within the field, John James Audubon, wrote his *Ornithological Biography* detailing patterns of bird behaviour, and also published his 435 prints of bird illustrations, which brought the excitement and magnificent variety and splendour of the bird world to a much wider public. Audubon societies, dedicated to the conservation of birds and bird habitats, exist in hundreds of cities around the world to this day.

In England, the ornithologist's enthusiasm for observation and classification, spilled over into the 'Victorian Leprosy' of collecting. The pseudo-scientific term oology was coined for the practice of egg collecting: a mania which was to have a severe detrimental effect on the population of many rare native species. The taking of wild birds' eggs has only been illegal in Britain since 1954; nowadays though, since the introduction of the Wildlife and Countryside Act 1981 it is illegal merely to possess or control the eggs of wild birds. Egg thieves can be punishable under provisions, WCA 1981, section I(5)(a) disturbing a bird; section I(1)(c) taking eggs from a nest; section I(2)(b) possession of eggs. Chapter and verse.

Peregrine eggs: now that is a prize. The first, documented record of a sighting of a wild Peregrine Falcon was on the island of Lundy. It seems rather appropriate.

To see a Peregrine Falcon take out a pigeon in mid-flight is a sight of beauty. Plunge-diving, faster, faster. Eyes locked on like a Cruise missile on its target. Co-ordinates set. Faster, faster. Steep vertical bank, turning out of a bright burning sun. Sweeping lower. Wind rushing past. Ground rushing closer; looking through the eyes of a killer. Speed, power and accuracy combined in perfect destructive harmony. Wings swept backwards. Feathers streamlined; points trailing. Co-ordinates locked. Steeper, steeper. Faster, faster. Impact.

A dull thud: the sensation of flesh striking flesh. Bones jarring, as the force of the collision moves up from the feet, through the legs, to be absorbed by the bulk of the body. Talons lock on and sink deeper, finding little resistance to their razor sharp edges. The perfectly controlled free-fall dive has changed into a wildly erratic spiralling somersault: the two birds locked together in a head-over-heels earthbound plummet, like a panicking skydiver who has lost control over his descent. Pull the rip-cord. Suspend the motion.

A rush of air upwards. Equilibrium regained. The frantic bating ceases as the pigeon hangs limp, life relaxed, and is then dropped to free-fall like a rock, until springy heather and hard earth provide a final resting.

With its wild snake-eyes ever watchful the raptor, one foot across its victim's neck, stands proud. And still. Like a big-game hunter of old, posing for a photograph beside a recently shot trophy. Panting slightly, like a champion prizefighter basking in the glory of victory, its humbled opponent prone before it; chest feathers puffed and full, it savours the moment of triumph, and the whispered plaudits of a hushed audience of heath and air. It bobs, once then twice, sticking its rear up into the air, before stooping to pluck nonchalantly at the pigeon's plump breast with its hard thick beak, sending a flurry of downy feathers into the air, like a scene from a childhood bedroom after a pillow fight. The falcon is not so hungry that it can't take its time to prepare its meal as it should be eaten: plucked and clean. Stabbing deeper, reveals the first white of skin, followed by red of blood and gore, and black of liver. And for the first time, a lack of self-control? The dagger-beak rips in quicker and more impatiently through yielding flesh, and trickles of blood run down the pigeon's plumage and trail away to leave brown stains in the soft earth. A gristle-bound string of innards hangs from the falcon's mouth, the feathers of its head and neck are wet with sweat, and its dark moustache is matted with congealing filth. The snake-eyes swivel, glassy and unpredictable, before returning once again to contemplation of its unfortunate Prometheus. An efficient killer knows no mercy.

Man has always been envious and greatly admiring of this skill, and has attempted to harness this lethal potency for centuries. Falconry is one of the oldest recorded sports. Submissive falcons, wearing hoods and tethered with primitive jesses, feature in art of the middle and far east dating back as far as 2000BC. The practice came to Europe via the Babylonians, Greece and later the Romans, and was a favoured sport of kings in Britain from the Middle Ages until the seventeenth century, when the introduction of firearms began to make the practical side of the activity redundant. King John was known to have a particular love for falconry. In England, there was introduced a hierarchy of men and birds - the Laws of Ownership - where each bird of prey was allocated a rank, and no man could hunt with a bird allocated a higher rank than himself. In such way did the falcon gain its nobility. A Peregrine, though, free on the wing, unfettered and unbroken by man, needs no artificial hierarchy to prove its status.

This Peregrine can not be caged. It will always know what it means to be free.

Part Two

The Case is Closed

'The case is closed.'

'Thank goodness. Does this mean that I might get a first decent night's sleep in months, without having to hear you constantly boring on about the bloody Twitcher?'

'Boring?'

'Boring.'

'Yes, of course. The case is closed. Nothing more to be said.'

'Good night then.'

'Good night, darling.'

David reached across to the light-pull, checked, thought, reached again, and then swung himself out of bed and crossed to the bookcase by the door.

'You don't mind if I read for a few minutes, do you? I still feel on a bit of a high after today. Not really tired, you know. Or would you prefer the light out?'

Diana half raised her head from the pillow and looked through sleepy eyes to where her husband stood facing her. He was still a very handsome man she thought - perhaps a little grey was beginning to show at his temples now that he had his hair cut so short, but this was hardly surprising given the stressful nature of his work. His body was still very fine though, hard and muscular, and not showing any signs of the middle-age flab or beery excesses that most men succumbed to. He even looked good in pyjama bottoms. It was just a shame that she felt quite so tired. Lights out please. She gave her husband a look that could with a great deal of imagination have been taken to mean 'No, you carry on and read for as long as you like' and slumped back into the isolation of the downy softness.

David crossed back to the bed, book secreted behind him.

'Ten minutes. That's all. I promise.'

Ten minutes turned into twenty turned into one hour as the spell of the novel made time blur. Pages turned with increasing rapidity as the plastic numbers on the teasmade's clock clicked over signalling each relentless passing minute. Diana's breathing changed from noisy exasperation to gentle regular somnolence.

The book was eventually closed with a resounding

thwack of finality which broke the magic spell of tranquillity that had held the room in respectful hush. Diana's head first jerked and then she bodily sat up as the book was forcibly cast down landing centrally on the bedclothes.

'You know, that really wasn't very good.'

'What?'

'That book. Really not very good.'

Another look - this one unmistakably meaning 'And did I need to be woken up to know this?'

'It started off OK. A young woman's body was discovered in an old quarry in the middle of nowhere, but the people who discovered it were a man and a woman, who were ... well, how shall I say, up to no good, and who shouldn't have been there, at least not together that is, and this of course throws them into a dilemma as to what they should do - report the body, or pretend they have never been anywhere near the scene, and let someone else make the gruesome find.'

'David, please.'

'No, hang on, this part was quite gripping. So anyway the bloke persuades the woman, against her better nature - since it was him that was the married one and had the most to lose, you know the kind of thing - to just forget the whole incident, but, of course its obvious that the whole affair is going to come back to haunt them, and that this is only going to be the start of their problems Well, the body is found shortly afterwards, and in the course of their enquiries - as the old cliche goes - the police turn up evidence at the murder scene - because murder is what it turns out to be - that leads them to the other woman, you know, the one that wanted to report it in the first place. After that, though, it all became a bit too far-fetched, too many coincidences, you know. It turned out the married man had been having it away with both the woman that was arrested and the young woman that was discovered in the quarry. And do you know what else?'

'I'm really not interested.'

'Well the chap at the centre of the mystery just goes missing. And do you know the reason why they couldn't trace what had happened to this Pimpernel Lothario? It was because ... no, I'd better not tell you, in case you might want to read it yourself. I wouldn't want to spoil the story for you. You don't think you will? No, well it really wasn't very good. No, but it was because he was the policeman who was investigating the whole thing in the first place. I guessed it quite early. Obvious really. The old bent copper twist. Nothing like that ever actually happens. If there's murder been done, look to the lover, is what I say. That's what it always comes down to. Husband, wife, mistress, partner, jealousy and murder.'

'David, please. Don't you get enough of this in real life. Do I have to hear about you solving fictional cases as well as actual ones now? Just go to sleep.'

'Do you know, he even ended up killing his wife right at the end of the story. Quite ridiculous. I really think I could have done better than this myself.'

'What?'

'This book. I think I could have written a better story. Take this Twitcher case ...'

'No. Not again.'

'No, really. The Twitcher case. That would make a good story. Perhaps even a film. Kate Winslet would be good for the lead. And how about Nicholas Cage for me?'

'Believe me it's a swap I make in my dreams every night.'

'Sorry? What was that?'

'David. Write the novel. Make the movie. Just shut up and turn off the bloody light.'

Part Three

Recuperation

Chapter One

Doing bird. It's a strange expression. Rhyming slang so I've been told. Bird-lime. Time. The beaks, too. That's what they call the magistrates, or the police. It's not really me, though, this kind of talk. Perhaps I had better revert back to my own voice if you want me to tell you a story.

Prison is not what I had expected. And I mean that in both senses. It was not where I had expected to end up, and it was not how I had expected it to be having got here.

I had seen all the films: Steve McQueen in *The Great Escape*; Dustin Hoffman in *Papillon*; Clint Eastwood in *Escape from Alcatraz*. And it was nothing like any of them. Bouncing a rubber ball in the sweat-box wouldn't block out the ceaseless noise: the non-stop prattle of harshly spoken voices and the hum-drum rattle of knife-edge nerves. The sound of wasted lives. And looking weak and intellectual finds you only bullies, never a protector. As for escape! Escape to where? To what? Escape implies freedom, and that is something I do not remember. I am no more a prisoner now than I have been this past year.

There is the *Birdman of Alcatraz*, of course. Burt Lancaster. Or Robert Stroud to be more factually accurate. I have always been fascinated by him. Not that he is a role model I ever aspired towards. Convicted of murder in 1909 in Alaska, he was sentenced to twelve years imprisonment on McNeil Island, before being transferred to Leavenworth Jail after attacking a prison worker. Worse still, at Leavenworth Stroud stabbed and killed a prison warden and was sentenced to death by hanging, only to be reprieved at the eleventh hour and his sentence commuted to life imprisonment. It was during these years at Leavenworth that Stroud developed his interest in birds. It was as it was with me: when everyone else deserts you, the birds alone remain. No, perhaps I am over-romanticising my past. Anyhow, Stroud used his incarceration to study avian diseases and wrote two detailed books - I have seen one in a library - *Stroud's Digest of the Diseases of Birds* and *Diseases of Canaries*. At one stage it was reported that Stroud kept over two hundred birds in his cell. I doubt that that would be allowed here. Stroud was eventually transferred to the fortress prison on Alcatraz Island where he was kept in solitary confinement until his death in 1963. Every day on Alcatraz he fought for the right to be with his birds, to no avail. I find it ironic that I should end up in similar circumstances to him. I hope that my history will not pale in comparison. It is still early days. I am not yet completely familiar with my new environment. But I think that it has potential. I have started keeping a notebook again of my sightings. I wasn't sure if I would be allowed to, but they are not inhuman in here, and I have been able to buy quite a decent A4 pad and a biro. Not ideal, of course. Not quite what I had been used to. But, with time. It is still early days.

From my cell window I have spotted only twelve species so far, which is altogether poor, but the view is rather restricted and frankly not prepossessing to either bird or beast. In the very far distance there are some trees and a small patch of green, which I think must be close to the canal, but in front of this is nothing but flat, corrugated rooftops and large warehouses and a mechanical alien landscape of soaring steel cranes and the motionless hulks of disused gasometers. It is much better out in the courtyard, where there is a small garden and five trees. There are some old rooks' nests in the highest branches. I look forward to seeing if they return to them later on in the year. We are allowed into the courtyard quite often, and some prisoners work in the garden, which I hope to do eventually. I find it quite difficult without my binoculars - to make a positive identification that is. I'm fairly sure I've see other birds, but I've not been convinced without my binoculars that I have identified them correctly, and so don't want to mark them down in my notebook. It is important to be accurate, otherwise it is all a bit pointless.

Chapter Two

The only noise in the small interview room was the mechanical whirr of the tape recorder, interjected by a rhythmic click as the spooling tapes hit upon a regular interruption. Whirr, whirr, click. Whirr, whirr, click. The noise was becoming hypnotic. It was getting warm in the room too. Whirr, whirr, click. Whirr, whirr, click. The two reels turned smoothly in the machine, roughly the same amount of magnetic tape wound around each side, slowly revolving. Round and round. In perpetual motion. Whirr, whirr, click. It was enough. The break was over, it was time to carry on.

'Please continue.'

'I moved in with my brother when it happened. After a couple of nights on the street that is. I think it was only two nights, it may have been three: I was in a bad state and don't really remember. I just knew I had to get out. After one day I didn't know where I was. Two days and I didn't know who I was. Three days ... well thank God, he found me. I still don't know how he did. We'd gone our separate ways, you know ... afterwards. Maybe someone saw me and told him, or maybe it was just chance and he happened to be passing by that way. I don't know. I don't think it was fate or providence or anything, because I don't believe in any of that. And I don't think it was that strange telepathic link that some people talk about that is supposed to bond twins together, because I don't believe in that either.

'We are twins though, although not identical, is what they used to joke. When we were younger we never really had a lot in common, perhaps we were both too fiercely independent; too keen to establish our own sense of separate identity. I know at age seventeen he left home and I didn't see him again for several years. He never did say where he went to or what he had been doing during that time. We did reestablish contact again, but just an odd letter, or a card at Christmas, or a postcard if I went abroad, nothing more. And an occasional meeting. Very occasional. Normally if he rang me out out the blue. Normally when he wanted money. Until more recently that is. A couple of years ago he came back.

He'd got himself married. Moved back into the neighbourhood. He didn't seem to have a regular job, but they got by. He'd taken up with some of his old friends again. It was nice, it was like a new beginning for us both.

'Postcard from abroad. I'd forgotten about that until just now. It seems like a different lifetime ago. I travelled quite a lot. I wasn't always like this. I went to India. For three months. And once to a friend's wedding in Australia - all that way for just one week. And several times with work, of course - Frankfurt mainly, but once to the States, although it was too brief to see anything. I had been planning to go back there that summer.

'Spring it was when he found me, April it must have been. I was half-dead with cold, so he told me. And hunger. And shock. Delayed, you know. The cold and the hunger were quick to put right. The shock was something different. It came on like a lengthening shadow; an icy numbness starting in my toes. As I left the flat; as I closed the door never to return, turned my back, went down the stairs, out of the front door, into the street, already its fingers were clutching at my feet, making me stumble; making each step seem like a mile, each second seem like an hour. I watched myself walk past one row of terraced houses, and then another, and then another, all alike. And the shock clung around my waist, weighing me down, tenacious. Gripping tighter. Squeezing. Like an old man's desperate arthritic embrace. A cold terror in my stomach, waiting to bubble ever upwards. Another slow-motion street, and as if I walked through mud, the darkening stain of shock seeped higher: its touch chill upon my chest, yet my back dripping wet with sweat. More houses, and a road I did not recognise. Lost, but where was I going? Just away, outside. Anywhere. I sat before I fell, and the rising wave of anxiety swept into my head as though it had found an empty chasm; a void waiting to be filled. My ears were deaf; my eyes were blind.

'This is where I was discovered: slumped in a little-used alleyway between a row of two-up two-down houses and the wooden fence of a builders' yard. Trying to be optimistic, even then, in that state, I must have had some sort of sense of self-preservation; some notion that things would improve, or at least change: I had chosen a quiet spot, one in which I wasn't disturbed or molested, slightly under the shelter of a tree that overhung the fence, slightly protected from the cold by a carpet of litter on the ground. I must have curled up and slept.

'With a rush of air my hearing was restored, and I sat and listened to the silence. So too was my sight, even though I looked and did not see. I knew how it was to be lost in a daydream; my parents had used to laugh at me when I was small at how I would disappear into "a world of my own". But this was different, this time I was conscious and there was nothing but blankness. Everything had changed. Now there was nothing worth opening my eyes to. The only thing I remember being conscious of was that it was still daylight, but whether the same day, or the next, I did not know.

'He had been speaking for some moments without me being aware. It was not until he took me by the arm and tried to lift me that my cocoon of isolation was shattered and my focus retuned to the real world. He said my name, and I let him lead me away. He has been leading me ever since. Him - it's ironic, when it should have been the other way around.

'He said, "What if the police had found me, what then?" He seemed quite concerned about that. He pulled at my clothes and said, "What were you thinking of wearing these?" I wanted to tell him that they were all I had. And he kept saying, "How did I get right out here?" Out where?

'I had walked for miles. Without realising. I was in a part of town I had never visited before, never had call to. The walk back was something of a dream too. I recall street name after street name, all unfamiliar: harsh black names on little white signs, each spelling out so clearly to me, "You do not belong here". In my weakened state the journey seemed to take an eternity. I wanted to stop and sit down again, to find a corner and hide, but my brother kept pulling me to my feet; increasing our speed when I could only imagine slowing it; lifting and dragging me forcibly when my legs would not support me and my feet hung useless and weary. I asked my brother why he didn't fetch his car, and he said that he didn't have one. And why we couldn't catch a bus, and he said that he had no money. And why he couldn't get someone to help, and he said there wasn't anyone. And he was right. We didn't pass a single other person on those streets that evening - I thought it strange at the time, one small spark of cognition that had been working clearly.

'It was dark when we arrived. I had seldom been to where my brother lived before, at least not to this new house. He had moved around a lot, even since coming back, and I hadn't recognised the name as we turned into the street, opened the gate, walked up the drive, and came in through the front door. I remember a big white number five newly hand-painted on the gate, a short driveway of cracked paving and mossy blotches, overgrown with spiky shrubs and stunted, sawn-off trees, and a key turning in a lock to signal home.'

Chapter Three

'I moved in with my brother when it happened. In a room on the top floor. And that is where I stayed for the next thirteen months. And three days.

'Quite a large room: I'm still not sure how my brother was able to afford to rent it. He said that he had "an arrangement" with the Jeffries. He had the room next door, although I never went in there and the door was always kept closed. I'd guess it was the same size and shape as mine, but I don't think I ever once so much as saw in far enough to see the colour of the wallpaper, or whether it had carpet laid inside, let alone see as far as the back wall. There was also a kitchen, but my brother tended to do most of the cooking. And a bathroom and toilet separate, when it would have been more sensible for them to be combined.

'I always think of mine as a very light room, but I am sure that this is only because I was always at the window looking out. In actual fact, I think it was quite dingy, now I think back to how my own place used to be in comparison. At the time, we neither of us seemed to care or to notice. The window was my life-line to reality. That and the stories my brother used to tell me when he came back home each evening.

'For the first few days, though, I recognised reality as something purely to run away from, not as the precious commodity it is, which should be grasped and clung on to, forsaking all others. I had a lot of reeducation to undergo on the topic of what was important in life and what was not. I am only thankful I am better now. I am only thankful that my brother was such a patient teacher.

'I would lay on the mattress in the furthest corner of the room for hours - days to start with - on end. Looking up at the ceiling. Tracing the path of the cracks from the lintel above the window, straight across to where the bare bulb hung limp from its flex, fanning out to form a mosaic of fine lines in the plaster above my head. I tried to trace each individual crack to its source, but I would follow one only for it to fork and split in two, and follow the fork only for that too to split and diverge, like roots from some great tree, reaching out, trying to find something firm to cling on to. In the same way, so too was I. Staring upwards until the light from the window faded and darkness filled in every crack.

'That first day after I arrived my brother stayed in all day. I was dimly aware of the sounds of crockery in the kitchen, of the lavatory flushing, and of a radio playing very quietly in the distance. Not music, talking. Low and quiet. He brought me food in twice, but didn't stay and chat - actually I don't think he talked at all. When it was dark he brought an extra blanket and laid it over me, even though I was too hot already. I ate and I slept and I counted the cracks in the ceiling and physically I felt stronger.

'There were no curtains at the window - not then - and I remember waking with the light and hearing the pigeon for the first time. Right outside the window I could hear it coo-ing, signalling the start of a new day as proudly as any farmyard cockerel. I couldn't see it from where I lay, just the shadow of the fluttering of its wings as it flew off. The house was silent. My brother had already gone out.

'Quite a large room, as I say. Above my mattress, on the wall, hung a cheap reproduction of Millet's *The Gleaners* in a fussy chipped gilt frame. I remember thinking, that would have to be moved. I never have been able to stand anything above my head where I sleep. Damocles Syndrome, a partner used to joke, before we split up. The door was at the foot of the mattress and opens on to a large porcelain vanitory unit. It is very poor planning really, since the door bangs into the sink if you open it too quickly, or push it too far ajar, and a large piece had already been chipped out of the basin. Not then, but later, the Jeffries complained and said that we would have to make good the damage. My brother argued that it had been done before he arrived, but to no avail. I don't think damage to property is covered by "the arrangement".

'Beside the sink was a huge free-standing wardrobe - very ugly, in a dark stained wood. It had a crenelated top, which made it look like an over-sized castle on a chess board. On top were some boxes of games and two jigsaws. There was a tiny key in a lock in the right hand door. I opened it one day that first week but it was empty inside. Except for some thin lining paper on the floor. The carpet fitted wall-to-wall and was an energetic pattern of dark yellow and russet swirls, like a raging fire. In the daylight it burnt warm; in the dusk it smouldered drably like a near extinguished flame. From the position of my mattress on the floor I could see that it didn't hide the dirt as well as one would have supposed.

'I can't remember where the desk was to start with. I just remember the job I had moving it over to the window, so that I could sit and look out. It was solid and dark like the wardrobe, but where the wardrobe carried its bulk with the austerity and awkwardness of a severe maiden aunt, the desk glowed with the warmth of a favourite jovial uncle. I liked to keep it clear of clutter, but it is always all too easy to lapse into untidiness. The armchair beside my mattress was very soft and deep and not very suitable for sitting up at the desk, but one day my brother turned up with a small, hard-backed kitchen chair which was just right, and which slid away right underneath so that it didn't take up any extra space in the room. There were some shelves too, in the corner next to the armchair. They were empty when I arrived, but full of my books by the time we left.

'On the whole I have happy memories of number five, King Street.'

Chapter Four

'The Grouses lived at number eight. I used to see them most mornings in their front garden. Bickering. Other than my brother they were the first human voices I heard after arriving at number five. Them and the Shags. They lived next door.

'I never had any desire to go out. I suppose I had lost my confidence; wanted to shut myself off from everything, out there. From a world that had once been as far flung as Australia, as populous as India, as busy as New York, my reality had shrunk to the size of four rooms - three of them little used - a view of a street, five houses and a small wooded corner of the cemetery grounds; and a horizon that stretched only as far as two roads distance, where once it had reached to the stars. And beyond.

'My routine was fairly fixed too. Wake with the light - whatever time I woke my brother had already left the house - breakfast, coffee, toast and marmalade at the kitchen table with the radio on listening to the morning news; watch from the window; lunch, normally a sandwich in my room, although sometimes there was cold quiche or something left from the night before; read, or doze a little, and then watch at the window until I saw my brother coming home. Sometimes it was dark by then. My brother would then make supper for us both, which we'd eat off our laps in my room, while he told me about his day. And about the birds.

'He had always been keen on birds, even as a young boy. He would talk about ornithology at an age when other kids were barely stringing together two syllables; would speak incessantly and eloquently about birds at the same time his peers were peppering every sentence with four letter words; and was still chatting about tits and shags at a time when most other youths' minds were conjuring up far cruder images for those words. Back then, I had been one of the many to have mocked him - it was a time when we were each of us discovering our separate personalities, each defining our place in society, and my place was firmly with the "in" crowd, not with the dorks who had yet to discover that there was life outside of "O" Level Biology class. Me and a friend of mine, Brian Stamp, one day we hid ourselves behind a hedge that separated the far end of the School's grounds from the road that led to the park and the woods beyond and, concealed, showered my brother and one of his group with stones we had collected from the driveway. I never saw if we hit him or not, but I heard several cries and the sound of breaking glass, and later that evening, when he arrived home, the binoculars that he used for bird-watching were smashed. He didn't know it was me at the time. I have told him since, of course, but he said not to worry, because they had already been broken from when he had tried to climb up to see into a nest and had dropped them from a tree.

'My brother was something of an embarrassment to me in those days. I laugh to think about it now. He is actually an hour or so older than me, I can't remember if I mentioned that before. You would never have known that then, though. People were always commenting how mature I seemed; how self-assured and confident. My parents used to say how they wished that he would "grow up"; get a girlfriend; stop spending so long in the woods and think about what he was going to do with his life. I wonder what they would say now. In hindsight, I think perhaps they would be rather disappointed in the both of us. He would talk about those school-days quite often as we sat down to eat each evening. His memories are so different to mine: tales of bullying and fights, and fear - fear, I think above all else. He would speak about the dread of the alarm clock sounding each new weekday morning; of feigning illness and of our parents never letting him get away with it; the walk to school, fatalistic as to the executioner's block; and of the wooden desk in the front row of form 3D, target for every pupils' taunts and worse: chewed up pellets of paper sticking on the back of his blazer, and spit, sticky and matted in the back of his hair. And once a dart that stuck into his shoulder. I guess I saw his pain, but chose to turn a blind eye. I was young: it was easier to join the bullies than oppose them. I don't offer that as an excuse though. In the same way, that I don't offer it as an excuse now.

'The birds were an escape for him then. As they became for me later. In their world he was accepted as an equal. The rooks did not look down upon him from their lofty nests and sneer, and the Blackbirds didn't chatter about him behind his back, nor the starlings huddle together in whispering groups to mock and do him down. As it was for him then, so it became for me now in my second floor eyrie. A touchstone on reality, made to come alive through my brother's evening stories and from my window on the world: King Street numbers three through twelve.

'Of course, I didn't call them the Grouses at first. Back then, I wouldn't have known the difference between a black grouse and a capercaillie. All I recognised was the sound of squabbling voices and the sight of an elderly couple in the front garden opposite. He was a tall man, bald-headed, very thin. Skeletal, except for a strange pot-belly which seemed to be trying to make a permanent escape-bid from between the buttons of his tightly-fastened tweed waistcoat. I never saw him wear anything but a three-piece suit, not even an overcoat in the winter, or a macintosh in the rain. She wore a hat. A ghastly tea-cosy in the cold, and a large misshapen piece of green fabric when the sun shone. I decided she had no hair. I don't know if they argued the same inside the house, or if it was purely a spectator sport, but they never ceased to maintain a constant back-and-forth bickering banter as soon as they stepped outside of their front door. With my window closed I could only make out the sound of their voices, but when summer arrived and with my window open to let in the fresh air, odd snatches of conversation used to disturb my morning peace.

"It was there last week. I don't know what you can have done with it."

"What I've done with it!"

"Who else? You were always the same. Remember that butter dish that went missing. That turned up where I said it would, didn't it?"

"Butter dish? What's that to do with anything. What I'm saying is it's not there now. And I know I've not had it."

"Are you saying I have?"

"I'm saying it's not there now."

'Or.

"What did you want to go spilling it for anyway. That stain will never come out. You know how it was with that chocolate."

"'That came out.'"

"'Not properly, it didn't. You can still see a mark. If you hold it close up to the light.'"

"'And who's going to do that?'"

"'You never know. Anyway, I know.'"

"'Chocolate's different to coffee anyhow.'"

"'Not so's you'd notice, the way you spill them both.'"

'And.

"'1976.'"

"'No, it was 1977.'"

"'No, '76. '77 was coronation year.'"

"'Coronation! What are you talking about. '52 was coronation. '77 was silver jubilee.'"

"'Silver jubilee, that's what I meant.'"

"'Then why did you say coronation?'"

"'I meant silver jubilee.'"

"'Huh.'"

"'Anyhow it was 1976 that Ted died.'"

Chapter Five

'I remember waking with the light and hearing the pigeon. Right outside the window I could hear it coo-ing, signalling the start of a new day. I couldn't see it from where I lay, just the shadow of the fluttering of its wings, passing over my desk and across my blanket as it flew off. I presume it was always the same one. Its routine fixed as rigidly as my own.

'Routine has always been an important part of my life. I know what you're thinking, particularly now, when it is enforced upon me, but it was just the same when I was at work. 06.30: alarm clock rings. 06.45: shower. 07.00: breakfast. 07.15: leave flat. 07.23: bus to station. 07.48: train to Euston. Second from last carriage. Middle section of seats. By the window. Facing.

'Every morning, the same set of faces. The man who read his newspaper - *The Times* - and wouldn't move his feet to let me pass; the young man with a mole on his cheek who was forever suppressing hiccups and fidgeting uncomfortably; the woman on her mobile phone two rows back, who wanted the whole carriage to know how wonderful the wine-bar was last night; the two men who bored each other - and me - one talking about his son's school football results, the other about local council policy; the young woman with attractive legs and knows it, who read a weekly trash mag and fiddles with her hair; and the man with the vacant eyes which reflected my own familiar image back to me.

'I would sit in silence, half-annoyed that no one took the trouble to register my existence: the newspaper is never put down upon my arrival to share a thought, exchange a compliment, pass the time of day; the mobile phone is not turned off to make sure that I am OK, that the world is treating me well, that I am not falling down between the cracks in life's pavement; and the trash mag is not discarded to enquire if my daily railway presence doesn't hide a deeper despair. I would sit in silence, half-dreading that someone will.

'Blur of tree and field and houses, and station signs - not stopping - flashed by too fast to read. Jump, as passing trains, so quick, so close, made the windows rattle and the young woman gasp and look up from her book, smiling embarrassed. "Tickets from Watford please" and "The next stop is Harrow and Wealdstone". Two jolts at Willesden and the smell of baking from the McVitie's biscuit factory. Hope for no "incident on the line" at Camden, and then stop, inexplicably - 08.08 - at the sign that reads "Euston Station 1 mile". Vacant eyes would shuffle through his rucksack, get up and stand by the automatic doors. An optimist.

'08.12: "You are now arriving at London Euston. Please make sure you take all your belongings with you". 'Escalator down. And down again. Northern Line, southbound, City line. Rush of air, sliding doors, "mind the gap", people off, people on. King's Cross. Angel. Old Street. Moorgate. 08.27.

'Round Finsbury Circus, down Blomfield Street, left along London Wall, right into Bishopsgate. Leadenhall Street. 08.41.

'Electronic doors. Starch, white-breasted security guard: "Good morning". Elevator up. Illuminated red, level six, ping. Key in my door. Look at my watch. 08.44. Early. One minute of my own time for reflection.

'A passing line of strangers on the escalator, some talking, some smiling, some larking, most staring, blank-expression, unseeing, into the void of the immediate future: the here-and-now of public transport and work and routine. A procession of posters - Go Bilbao from £80; Dillons recommends Wilbur Smith; Go Faro from £120; Pregnancy advice ring us. Now.; Go Milan from £80; See *Rent* at the Shaftesbury Theatre - advertise fleeting daydreams of freedom. Momentary mirages of leisure and far-off places to fill the empty space. And the sound of music. A busker playing his clarinet, and the tinkle of loose change mingles with his melody. What tune had he been playing? 08.45.

'It is strange what constitutes freedom. I had always thought it was money. That every minute spent working and every pound building up in the bank bought you a vital extra second of freedom. That freedom was an elusive quantity that had to be earned and strived for. It was that minute before 08.45. It was the time after 17.30. It was the weekend. It was two weeks in the summer in the sunshine. It was those precious years between retirement and death, however many, or however few you were granted. For most in here, freedom is the daydream of the nine-to-five. Not for me. 'Freedom is a clear conscience. For the first time in years, I am free.'

'It had been Gershwin that the busker had been playing. *Rhapsody in Blue.* I remember it now, from the film *Manhattan.* The long drawn out rising warble of the first bars. The resonating floating reed of birdsong, ever more frantically striving to drown out the low rumble of the world below. 'Most of us are trying to be noticed. Some are the loudest on the train. Some are the first in to work each morning. Some are just singing sweet songs to find a mate. Ornithology is different, my brother explained this. It requires going unnoticed. Unseen. To observe and not be observed. Silence and patience. You have to have time. At an upstairs bedroom window at number five, King Street, it was the ideal recuperation.'

Chapter Six

'It was my third morning of looking at the Blackbird in the tree that I first saw the woman in the bedroom opposite. The man with the greased-black hair and neatly clipped moustache had just parked his shiny pale blue Escort in the same spot as the previous morning: behind the motorbike - under wraps - that never moved, and with enough clearance, so that the Grouses could get out of the driveway if they chose to - if they had a car to get out.

'She was naked - from the waist up at any rate - standing, looking out of the window. Not at me, not at anything in particular, just standing and looking. And swaying. Slightly. Back and forth, as if moved by a slight but steady breeze. Slowly, slowly, she swayed a fraction faster, rocked a little firmer, her hands now supporting her, palms face out, pink and fleshy, where they pushed flat against the cold glass pane. Her mouth opened slightly, and a gasp of breath misted the window about her face, fogging the scene, as her eyes rolled back and she twisted her head around; her torso still rigidly facing forwards, outwards. Defiant. Or supplicant? I didn't see the man, not then, just his hand, clasping around her left breast, squeezing tight, drawing her around, pulling her back into the darkness of the room.

'When I next looked, the Blackbird had flown away.'

'My brother never talked about his wife. I could see that he was hurting. I could see that he missed her. I never mentioned her either. I thought he would talk if he wanted to. I didn't think it was down to me.

'It was one thing we had always both had in common: relationships. We were neither of us very good at them. Be it my string of early lovers or my brother's solitary coupling, neither brought a mate for life, or anything - at least, I know it's true in my case - more than the briefest moment's happiness. Laura. I've always thought it a nice name. My brother's wife.

'I think the only married pairing in King Street, numbers three through twelve, were the Peacocks. They were a very smart young Indian couple with two very smart young children, who lived at number twelve. Next to them, the house is split into three flats: Craig Cuckoo at the top, Scarlet Ibis and her daughter underneath, and in the basement the seldom seen Mr Nightjar. And next to them, directly opposite me, the Grouses. Brother and sister. Bachelor and spinster. The Shags could surely not be married, not from the sound, through the walls, of their energetic - and frequent - union. And next door in the other direction, number three stood empty, an estate agent's For Sale board long since kicked over, half buried in the tangle of undergrowth that once constituted a "desirable, south-facing" front garden.

'Then there was Polly Plover. I didn't know about her. She lived at number nine. She passed by every morning at quarter to ten, pushing her pram in front of her along the pavement; each day swerving slightly outside number seven to avoid the uneven paving slab that the council have still not fixed; blond bubble perm bouncing at every step; smiling, always smiling. She saw me at the window and waved up to me on the second morning after I arrived at number five, and included me in her good humour with a widening grin and eyes to match. That day, I just huddled back in the shadows, pretending I had not been seen, and watched her pass by from the corner of the window, until I could no longer see her as she walked off the edge of my world's extent. Later, I would wave back. Every morning at quarter to ten. And once, just once, returning back the same way, at half past one in the afternoon. I didn't know if she was married then: I had never seen a Mr Plover, although I could only see the path of number nine and not the house itself, so maybe he leaves home in the other direction. I couldn't tell from that distance if she was wearing a wedding ring or not - not that that is much of an indicator these days. Perhaps through my binoculars ... I used to think. Or would that have been just too rude? I never looked, in any case.

'The binoculars were a present from my brother. As were all the books. He said I couldn't be a serious ornithologist without them. I am still really grateful to him. Most of the books looked rather worn and I was sure he had bought them second-hand, although some were his own personal copies because his name was pencilled neatly in the top right hand corner of the first page, along with a date underneath - the date he bought them, I presume. He was very meticulous in his ways. The first book he gave me was an old paperback edition of the *Collins Field Guide to the Birds of Britain and Europe.* Pages seventeen through thirty two were missing. Finches mainly. I read it cover to cover, laying on my back on my mattress. It was a diversion from the cracks in the ceiling. At first it was just so many words on a page; pretty plates, facts and figures. It was the pigeon that made the difference. That morning, I remember waking with the light and hearing the pigeon. Right outside the window I could hear it coo-ing, signalling the start of a new day. I couldn't see it from where I lay, just the shadow of the fluttering of its wings as it flew off. But this time it was different. It wasn't just a pigeon, it was a Feral Pigeon. And it wasn't just coo-ing, it was making a three-tone warbling note, diminishing to a throaty wooo. And now I wasn't just content to watch its passing shadow fly across my blanket, I wanted to see the bird. To really see the bird. I know what you're thinking: "it was only a pigeon", but as my brother had often enough admonished me, "everything has its place" and "everyone has to start somewhere".'

Chapter Seven

'The man with the greased-black hair and neatly clipped moustache had just parked his shiny pale blue Escort in the same spot, behind the motorbike. He carried a rather battered brown leather briefcase, and he always made a point of returning to his car after having taken a few bold steps away, to recheck that he had locked it securely. He always had.

'Scarlet Ibis's daughter sat on the front steps of number ten, mechanically picking off leaves from the bush by the front door and dropping them down in a thin shower to the basement where Mr Nightjar lived. Despite her bright, colourful clothes and the pretty braids in her frizzy black hair she looked a sad child. Her eyes were downcast and the vitality of youth had been squeezed out by a too early experience of the pressure of adult reality: childhood dreams and innocence are not accounted for in the income support. I never once heard her speak, either to raise a petulant cry or a joyful laugh. Her depression was a prison and she was too young to be allowed to hold the key. So she waited for her mother to return to let her in.

'The birds were my escape - still are. I wanted to tell her about them, but at the same time I knew that it was pointless. The joy of watching a Robin sitting proud on a garden fence is no substitute when what you really want is a new pair of Nike trainers to keep up with your friends at school. The sight of a Pied Wagtail flitting back and forth, so erratic and unsure, pales in comparison to the bold graphics of Lara Croft defeating wolves and dinosaurs in Tomb Raider III on a Sony Playstation. And a Blackbird and her fledglings are no company, when it is only one errant mother that can take away the feelings of loneliness.

'Number ten was the house I watched most. Not out of nosiness - no, really, I assure you. But because of the large silver birch tree that was growing immediately outside. And all of the birds it encouraged. The Blackbirds made a nest that first year. Unusually for them, quite high up in the sparse branches, where it was plainly visible from my bedroom lookout. Very precarious in a simple V-fork of two sky-bound limbs. Distinct, against the white bark and black knots. I watched the female sit for one week, two weeks patiently, incubating an unseen hoard, until one day in late-spring four clamouring little beaks announced themselves to the world, just barely visible above the nest's rim of twigs and moss. Two further weeks to fledge and, I privileged, witness to the first tentative attempts at flight, before one day I rose to find the nest abandoned and all its occupants gone. My first Jay was in that tree too. I've seen many other since of course, but the first is always something special. And a Green Woodpecker. Probably my favourite bird, if I was pushed to name one. That, or the Great Crested Grebe, perhaps. Not that I am likely to see either from in here.

'Scarlet Ibis didn't return until after four that day. The man with the greased-black hair and neatly clipped moustache who always parked his shiny pale blue Escort in the same spot had already returned and driven it away. As had the roofer, who had parked his van - Rick's Roofing, No Job Too Small - in the Grouses' driveway, while he had been doing a minor repair to the guttering. And the Grouses had gone out, sister and brother, Tuesday afternoon, Bingo I imagine. It had all been a dreadful mix-up: much gesticulating, waving of arms, hand to the forehead, "Whatever has happened, why aren't you at school?"; hugs and kisses; "So sorry, so sorry, I forgot it was a half-day holiday". The key is produced and waved in an exaggerated fashion and with a guiding arm around her shoulder Scarlet Ibis's daughter was led inside.'

'The estate agent was a jolly-faced young man. Big and burly like a rugby player. He would look at the broken post and battered For Sale sign in the garden of number three, fail to disentangle it from the web of weeds that held it pinioned down, pricking his thumb into the bargain on a thorn and then suck on it theatrically, examining it with an expression of hurt concentration. He drove a red and white Citroen 2CV, which he always parked badly, facing out into the middle of the road as though he was expecting to have to make a fast getaway. He was working late that night. The prospective buyers arrived at 18.15 and were gone again by 18.22: a young couple who stood on the pavement long enough to wave the little red and white car out of sight before bursting into laughter.

"'Did you see the colour of the kitchen?"

"'What about the colour of the bathroom."

"'Oh, yes. And the bath. It almost made me want to be sick. How did they describe it." She drew out a single A4 sheet of paper from her shoulder bag. "Here, 'characterful, although in need of some minor renovation'."

"'I think they meant gutting."

'They laughed again, screwed the estate agent's blurb into a tight ball and added it to the increasing pile of debris in the "desirable south-facing", before walking off, hand-in-hand, down King Street. That was farewell House Martins.'

Chapter Eight

'Not everything was as routine in King Street as perhaps I have made out. Actually you'd be surprised at the number of "incidents" that occurred. The day Mr Nightjar arrived home drunk was particularly memorable. I had been watching a wren popping in and out of the hedge at the front of the Grouses' garden through my binoculars, when a sudden darkness passed in front of the lens, momentarily blocking the view. I looked up and there was Mr Nightjar, standing - leaning - at the Grouses' gate, supporting himself on the wooden post. I don't think I had ever seen him in daylight before; I probably wouldn't have recognised him then, except that he was wearing the same long grey coat he always wore when he went out in the evening. He took two uncertain steps towards the road, and then immediately two back again to once again grasp the security of the gate. He must have caught the latch as he did so, because instead of providing a firm support, the whole structure swung inwards, depositing Mr Nightjar in the left hand flower border leading up to the Grouses' front door. I remember thinking it was a good job the Grouses were out. I'd seen them leaving - three-piece suit on, tea-cosy pulled down - first thing that morning. He lay still for quite a long time. Strange thinking back on it, I never once thought that he might be in trouble, or in need of help, he lay so still and peaceful. I don't know who reported him, but the police car turned up about an hour later. Two uniformed constables - would they be any other rank? - got out. One bent beside him, while the other said something into a walkie-talkie. Mr Nightjar was all right. He must have told the policemen where he lived, because they lifted him between them, one on each side of him, his arms around their shoulders, took him down the steps next-door, and left him in his basement abode. The same one was still talking into his walkie-talkie when they both came back up, and then they said something between them which made them laugh, before driving off. I didn't see Mr Nightjar for almost a week after that. And then he was back to evenings in his long grey coat. The left hand flower border was a further source of bickering between the Grouses. '"What have you gone and done standing on that for?"

"'Standing on what?'"

"'The marigolds. They're all trampled down. Can't you watch where you're treading.'"

"'Me? I've not been near them. They're your precious marigolds. You take more care of them.'"

"'Fat use taking care of them, if you're going to put your great feet all over them.'"

"'What have I just told you? Perhaps it was that roofer in his van?'"

"'Huh. Roofer.'"

'The cemetery was a constant source of activity, too. Last respects so seldom seemed very respectful. I used to watch after dark for owls, but never saw one. A few bats: fluttering silent silhouettes, black against the gloaming background of streetlights and humanity. One night two lads climbed over the cemetery wall - not difficult, for it was not very high, even though there were pieces of broken glass embedded in the stone and concrete to try to prevent out-of-hours intruders. Opening my window, I could hear them laughing, their voices unnaturally high, excited by their daring. A sharp scrunch of folding metal and a clatter, as a tin can, quickly followed by another, was kicked, conversion-style, in a looping arc back over the perimeter wall to land, one on the pavement, one in the road. More laughter, and a flash-torch switched on, then off, then on again, its beam illuminating like a light-sabre, cutting a bright pathway in the night air. I could follow the path of light and make out the two shadows that trailed troll-like behind it, as they trod cautiously around tombstones and took care not to stumble over the thick clumps of long grass and uneven hollows that comprised the "natural" eastern border of the graveyard, before circumventing the trimmed flower beds close to the church's side door. There was a sound of muffled banging, a whispered consultation - sounding unnaturally loud out of the clear, still darkness - and then a resounding crash and a splintering of timber, followed by an oath and the sound of running footsteps. The torch-light had disappeared, but simultaneously two black wraiths appeared tall above the cemetery wall, clambering over to land on the pavement in an undignified heap, before dispersing into the night.

'The vicar was out next day examining the damage. I heard him talking to someone else about "needing a new panel" and later on he was down on his hands and knees by a gravestone, a damp sponge in his hand and a bucket of soapy water beside him, scrubbing away energetically. I suppose I should have reported what I'd seen, but sometimes you just think, why bother.

'I felt sorry for the young girl in her school uniform. Monday, Tuesday, Wednesday, Thursday. The same time - 08.30 - each morning, she would be waiting at the cemetery gates. Anxious look at her watch. Five minutes pass. Tug at the hem-line of her skirt; straighten down her blouse with her hands. Ten minutes pass. Walk up one way then back the other. Fifteen minutes pass. Another glance at her watch, a last long look up the road, and she shoulders her bag again and is gone. Friday: the end of the week brought with it the end of hope, a dab of tears, and realisation. He wasn't ever going to be there. A week of making excuses ends in humiliation not a secret tryst. What different scenario had she imagined each previous evening for that following morning? I'd done the same so often myself. Plans. Worked out minutely in my head: and I'd do this, and then they'd do that. And did they ever? And did I ever? He'd be waiting at the gates before she arrived. She'd see him in the distance, looking anxiously at his watch, straightening his clothes, tidying his hair. She'd walk slowly, nonchalantly, not to appear too eager. He'd be good-looking, pale blue eyes, with a wave of long fair hair that he constantly had to flick back to stop it falling in front of his eyes. Seventeen years old, with a car of his own, newly bought by his dad. He'd start the conversation: tell her how nice she looked, ask her where she'd like to go later. She'd say meet me after school, by MacDonald's in the town centre, the one up at the end of the High Street, not the one by the pond. She'd say she had to go now, school starts in ten minutes, and he'd offer to walk part of the route with her. She'd meet a friend on the way - Lucy Turner - who'd look on enviously, and who would tell her friends later, "Guess who I saw ...?". As it was, she would be glad that there were no onlookers as the pin was finally stuck in her dream balloon. Except for me and Mrs Grouse that is, the twitching curtains of suburbia.

'Polly Plover was talking to the postman. She might not have been so friendly if she had passed by two minutes earlier and witnessed him pissing in the alleyway between the cemetery and the Grouses' side wall. The postman was looking into the pram and jiggling with the mobile that hung on the hood above the baby's head. I imagined drops of urine dripping off his fingers anointing the unfortunate innocent's brow. Polly pointed back towards her house and the postman shuffled through the letters he was carrying in his hands and then shrugged and opened his arms wide: "sorry, no mail today". They shared a final word and both laughed, before the postman pushed back the gate to enter number ten, and Polly continued on her way along the street with a quick wave to me as she passed. She had taken to crossing over the road and talking to the postman quite regularly those days.

'My brother received very few letters. I received none.'

Chapter Nine

'Craig Cuckoo was a distraction. I admit. It was very hard to concentrate on birch-life and to keep my notebook of sightings accurate and up-to-date, when Craig was "entertaining". As he so frequently used to. I found myself recording the comings and goings at the top floor flat, number ten, King Street, almost as thoroughly as my daily journal of birds.

'June 6th

'09.45. Green woodpecker. Quite a small individual. Rather dull dark red crown, unusually dark green back and wings, and grubby chest and rump. Perhaps a rather old bird. Spotted low down on the trunk of the birch outside number ten. Stayed completely motionless, probably resting, for four minutes, before making one long trilling cry and then flying off over the gardens opposite and disappearing behind the houses. Not an individual I can recall seeing previously.

'July 14th.

'12.05. Brunette. A very young woman, very petite. Dark navy beret and matching jacket, with a spiky rubber rucksack - very trendy. Probably French. Spotted examining the house numbers along the street very closely, almost turning into the Peacocks' driveway, before boldly marching up the front steps to number ten. Perhaps short-sighted, but too vain to admit it. Seen leaving again at 14.15, minus beret. Not an individual I recall seeing previously.

'August 9th.

'09.25. Chaffinch. Only a fleeting glimpse, but I am pretty sure of my identification. First seen in flight, where its pale wing bars were very distinct. Flew into the thickest foliage at the top of the birch tree but was momentarily able to make out the pink-brown breast, pale blue crest, and short, wide beak quite well through the binoculars before it flew off again. I couldn't follow where it went too. None too common around here. May be the same bird I saw feeding on the ground in the Grouses' front garden on the 10th June.

'August 10th.

'19.30. Redhead. Quite statuesque. Full figure, large-breasted, very straight-backed and dignified. About forty years old. Simple red dress and light red sandals and startling red

lipstick emphasising already full lips. No bag, no jewellery. Long even strides. Knocks three times, doesn't use the bell. Seen leaving again at 20.35.

    'August 18th.

    '19.30. Redhead. Definitely the same one as last week. This time wearing a dark shawl over a dark green dress. Same habits as observed last week: knocks three times and then enters quickly, without a look back. Seen leaving again at 20.35.

    'August 25th.

    '19.30. Redhead. A regular visitor. Looked up towards the top floor flat upon opening the front gate of number ten and waved to someone at the window. Still knocks three times. A creature of habit. Today, wearing a dark green jacket over a white blouse and long floral skirt. Seen leaving again at 20.35.

    'September 2nd.

    '18.10. Flight of Canada geese. Heard loud honking sound long before I saw them. Flew from the north appearing very low over the top of number five and onwards - probably to the reservoir - over and beyond number ten. Classic V-formation flight pattern of fourteen individual birds, although one was straggling slightly at the rear of the right hand fork. White chin strap markings and light breast feathers particularly visible in flight on each bird. A lovely sight for a balmy late-summer evening.

    'September 13th.

    '17.35. Oriental woman. Early-twenties, or perhaps even late-teens. Long, lustrous black hair and a small round face. She walked with small clipped steps as if her ankles were tied together. Or perhaps her denim shorts were too tight? Dark blue T-shirt, so short it showed several inches of flesh around her navel with the promise of it riding up even higher to expose her flat boyish chest. Carrying an open wicker basket, stuffed high with fresh produce, vegetables, eggs and milk. One egg rolled out and smashed on the front step as she entered the house. Not seen to leave.

    'September 24th.

    '09.15. Collared dove. Slightly smaller and much less scraggy than the normal feral pigeons that are always around.

Kept its distance from the other birds all busily pecking at a kebab that someone had dropped on the pavement. Breast, body, and wings almost pink in colour with a distinct black band around the back of its neck. Walked several yards down the pavement before quickly taking to flight.
  'October 14th.
  '16.20. She was naked - from the waist up at any rate - standing, looking out of the window. Not at me, not at anything in particular, just standing and looking. And swaying. Slightly. Back and forth, as if moved by a slight but steady breeze. And Craig too. Standing behind her, his face, half in shadow, just visible beyond her shoulder. For one moment our eyes met across the divide of the street and he held my gaze, steady, at the same time undistracted from the rhythmic motions of his auto-pilot body, before the curtain swept across, drawing a barrier between that which is real and that which is purely imaginary.'

Chapter Ten

'It was Polly Plover who drew my attention to the seagulls. She was holding her baby - a girl I'd guessed, dressed all in yellow, coat, scarf and bonnet - outside of her pram, twirling her around and around in her arms, and pointing up to the sky, trying to draw the child's eye to the swirling mass of birds in the air above. She saw me looking, smiled, waved, and pointed up to the sky for me to follow her gaze too.

'Storms at sea, that's what they always said when you saw seagulls inland, in the towns, in winter. We took a hovercraft to France once, the four of us, my parents and my brother and me - we were only little then, six or perhaps seven. It was the first time either of us had been abroad. The crossing going had been fine: calm, smooth sea and a clear blue summer sky, although once the hovercraft got up to speed the spray and sticky salt residue splashing up from the water blocked out any view through the tiny pebble-glass windows. In Calais we saw chickens in cages at the street market, and a noisy wedding celebration in the main square. We looked at sticky cakes through the window of the patisserie and we ate chips - not as good as back home - bought from a van at the side of the road and served in a cardboard carton. My mother bought squidgy plum tomatoes from an old woman sitting on a stool in front of her shop and my father bought four hundred cigarettes from a duty free store. My brother and I between us bought a wooden sailing ship with Calais written on the side and Made In China written on the bottom and I said "merci" to the man behind the counter, because my mother told me to. The blue skies turned to grey mid-afternoon and the wind became stronger and colder. One by one the bodies on the beach departed, and the expanse of sand that had earlier looked so full of summer, became empty and alone; each golden grain drained of its warmth and colour, each new wave dancing in agitation at the change it saw. The hovercraft's engines hummed, and it rose up on its cushion of air and skimmed across the sand with a confidence that no one shared. Through the porthole I remember seeing a lone seagull soaring effortlessly, white wings stretched wide, England-bound, before the shimmering spray once again confined us all. I envied it the simplicity of its flight.

'My brother had been sick. It was the first time I had not known him leave the house first thing. I had gone in to the kitchen to make some toast and listen to the 11.00 news on the radio when I heard him in the toilet, vomiting. At first I had thought it was an intruder, so accustomed had I become to having the house to myself during the daytime. He opened the toilet door and I saw him, ashen-face, glance in my direction, before staggering into his bedroom and closing the door behind him. I heard the sound of the lock turn from the inside.

'There was no bread, just two crusty rolls, which stuck in the grills of the toaster and would not pop up automatically. One half I had to throw away because it was too burnt and black. I had been planning to knock on his door to see if my brother could be tempted to eat something, but the clicking lock had suggested all he wanted was privacy, and half a charred roll seemed a meagre offering to present. I decided the blackened roll need not be wasted, and fishing it out from the pedal bin I took it back to my room and threw it out of the window, where it landed in a bush beside the path, a meal for some hungry bird to discover later.

'The Peacocks were taking their car out of their drive. It was always a difficult manoeuvre with so many parked cars in the street obscuring the view. Mr Peacock was behind the steering-wheel with the two young Peacocks strapped in the backseats. Mrs Peacock was standing in the middle of the street, looking anxiously first one way, then the other, before beckoning her husband forward. Bit more, forward, forward, turn a little. Stop. You're rather close on this side. Back again. Hold on, there's something coming. Forward, forward. Final turn of the wheel before Mr Peacock leant across to open the front passenger door and Mrs Peacock scooped up the trailing hem of her sari and got on board.

'The radio had been talking about a murder. It had been on the news. It had taken place sometime late last night although the body had only been discovered this morning. The police were not yet prepared to release any details other than to say that the victim had been a young female student, and to warn the public to be vigilant and take sensible precautions if walking out late at night. It was confirmed that Detective Inspector David Sutton - strange how things work out isn't it? - would be leading the investigation, and that further information would be released as soon as the victim's next-of-kin had been notified and the time was appropriate.

'I remember thinking, thank goodness it hadn't happened anywhere near here.'

Chapter Eleven

'My brother had been around to complain to the Shags. The noise was becoming intolerable. I think he only became aware of it during the three days he was confined to bed and was forced to listen to them all day long. I don't know which noise was worse, their arguments or their making up.

'The Blackbirds had returned to their nest again. I saw the female arrive with some moss in her mouth, attempting to reinforce some of the holes that had appeared during the winter. The male perched on a branch nearby and sang a musical accompaniment to her labours.

'How swiftly that winter had passed. Not having to think about rising early for work; leaving the house when it is still dark outside, and not getting home until the sun has gone down again. Not having to stand cold on the station platform and listen to the imaginative excuses of the railway announcer for that day's train delays - leaves, rain, snow, illness. Colds and 'flu, bugs and germs - inside number five I was cocooned against infection, immune to the world outside. My brother provided a protective barrier behind which I continued to hide. The hours of daylight being shorter, my brother was home much earlier during those months, and spent longer in my room with me, discussing his day and the sightings he had observed. He used to go to the woods a lot, even though they were quite a long walk from where we lived. The reservoir was even further, but he'd often return with stories of a day spent by the water-side. Every other Tuesday he had to sign on and on those days he left his rucksack behind and would wear his suit and tie. Most days he worn jeans and a pair of dark brown walking boots, worn and battered and permanently encased in a layer of dried mud, which used to leave grubby deposits on the carpet in the perfect mould of the tread of their soles. He never seemed to notice, but it was his house, so who was I to complain, and in most other respects everything was kept clean and tidy. And this little thanks to me.

'We had a rota of sorts. We each looked after our own rooms. My brother cleaned the kitchen, washed the dishes - although I did my own breakfast bits - cleaned the cooker, defrosted the fridge and scrubbed the floor. He did all the laundry too, which either meant washing everything by hand or taking a load down to the launderette around the corner. He seemed to quite enjoy going to the launderette because he would sometimes disappear during the evening and go out with a large bag more than once a week. He used to get his clothes very dirty though down in the woods. My brother kept the landing tidy, and the stairs too, I guess. And I would also occasionally see him cutting things back in the garden. Rather halfheartedly though: I don't think he had much love for horticulture. I was responsible for the bathroom and toilet, but neither needed much more than a damp cloth once a week, and certainly neither received any. The Jeffries - old Mrs Jeffries and her filthy son Robert - only ever looked in briefly once a month to collect their rent, which my brother always had ready to hand over to them while they waited on the doorstep, and only ever twice to my knowledge did they step inside the flat, once when they noticed the chipped basin, and once because Robert needed to use the toilet. That day I cleaned more thoroughly.

'I heard Detective Inspector David Sutton talking on the radio again one morning. He was appealing to the public for help in the murder enquiry. Had anyone been in the vicinity? Had anyone noticed anything suspicious? Any information given will be treated in the strictest confidence. Apparently the victim had been Japanese.

'The Shags were arguing again that night.

'"Will you keep your voice down?"

'"No, I will not."

'"You heard what he said."

'"Who?"

'"The bloke from next door."

'"Him. You think I can't do what I want in my own house because some jerk from next door comes round complaining? He wants something to complain about let him complain about THIS."

'"Will you shut up?"

'"NO."

'"Just shut the fuck up. I can't stand this any longer."

'"You seemed to stand it long enough last night."

'"Really?"

"'Yes, really."
"'Really?"
"'Yes, really."
"'Mmm. R-rrr-eally?''

Chapter Twelve

'The Blackbirds were visiting the nest more regularly now. They were taking it in turns to bring new twigs and leaves, and mud to bind the whole structure together. It was a miracle that it had survived at all from one year to the next, since it had still looked so precariously balanced, and I was sure that one strong gust of wind would bring the whole thing down. Perhaps this has worked in their favour though, and had been what has deterred unscrupulous bird pirates from taking it over. I was able to observe the male through my binoculars for several minutes one day as he sat absolutely still on the Grouses' fence. He really was a fine-looking individual. So jet black, his feathers appearing to glisten as if wet, and his beak in contrast, brilliant orange. So too was the ring around his eye - I'd never really had the opportunity to properly look at that before. A perfect orange circle around a bold black eye. One hop and he had vanished from the sight of my binoculars, but I was able to pick him up again very quickly and refocus the lens. Strong, dark legs, and crabby hooked feet, grasping securely on either side of the wooden fencing. His beak opened slightly and a few notes escaped: "See me fly".

'The man with the greased-black hair and neatly clipped moustache had just parked his shiny pale blue Escort in the same spot, behind the motorbike. He had a new briefcase, a rigid black rectangle. The briefcase of an executive. Perhaps he had had a promotion? Or a birthday? Six steps away. Six steps back. Recheck the lock. Everything was OK.

'There were three letters on the kitchen table. My brother must have not had time to open them before he went out. Strange though, because the postman didn't normally deliver until later. I always used to love the post arriving when I was at work. First there was my post at home - sometimes it would arrive before I left for work in the morning; sometimes it would be something to look forward to on the journey home at night. And the post at work. Three times a day, Harry with his mail-trolley would look in. First thing in the morning with the main post of the day; at lunchtime - normally internal memos and a small second post; and at 16.30 to see if there was anything to go out. Harry had worked in the merchant navy for thirty years and had taken an early pension. He would show me his holiday snaps and talk about his "girlfriend" which used to make me chuckle to myself until one day I saw a photo of Harry's twenty-something blonde companion and realised it was not an inaccurate description. He used to drink in the Two Dukes pub at lunchtime and always smelt of a combination of stale smoke, sweat and beer on his afternoon rounds. If I had anything important to post out I would always take it along to the mail-room personally.

'The top letter caught my attention because it had my name on it. And my old address on it, even though I hadn't been back there for almost a year. And so did the one underneath. And the one underneath that. I picked them up and was about to take them back to my room when I thought perhaps I should wait for my brother to come back? How had they been delivered here? My brother would know. I turned them over and looked at the envelopes. One was from the Electricity Board. I held it up to the light and tried to see if I could read anything through the window at the front of the letter, but only my name and address were visible. Another looked as though it were from my credit card company, I remembered their style of envelopes and the postmark was familiar. The third was personal. The stamps were Australia Mail and I recognised my friend's neat, angular handwriting. It was date-stamped one week previous. The envelope was covered in colourful sticky transfers of fish and seahorses and shells, and on the reverse was a return to sender address and in bold print three words "Where are you?".

'I took the letter back to my bedroom and laid it down on the desk. I busied myself sorting through my bird books, taking them all out of the bookcase and putting them back again in alphabetical order of author. I had done this twice before and each time had concluded it was no good, because the shelves at the top were smaller than the shelves at the bottom, and almost all the books at the beginning of the alphabet were too large to stand up straight. I went back to the letter on the desk and picked it up. Did I really want to open it? I remember thinking, it was a lifeline back to a world that I wasn't sure I wanted to return to. Perhaps if they had been sorted in alphabetical order of title they would have fitted better?'

'My brother said the postman had brought them. That he had spoken to the post office and arranged for mail to be forwarded. I wasn't sure I believed him, but I wasn't very interested, so let it go. I threw the two official letters in the bin unopened, but kept the other letter in my room, sandwiched between the *New Naturalist Book of Waders* and *Garden Birds*.

'The postman was talking to Polly Plover again the next morning. We had no mail that day.'

Chapter Thirteen

'The male Blackbird had taken to perching on the Grouses' TV aerial. Every afternoon he was there, singing long and loud. We didn't have a TV. My brother said that daytime TV is all crap: sofas, dysfunctional families and kid's cartoons. I did sometimes wonder if Mr Benn was still on, though. That is my memory of daytime TV. Perhaps it has never been off?

'I was never interested in Mr Benn's amazing cartoon adventures. Zoo-keeper, pirate, cave-dweller, cook: I had been them all myself. In my youthful imagination I had visited the shopkeepers' costumiers every morning to appear "as if by magic" in some new 'guise; with some new persona. Knight of the Round Table, astronaut, deep-sea diver, clown: I had been them all. I was far more interested in where Mr Benn lived. Festive Road. Number fifty-two. A street like any other. Where bowler-hatted men walked to work. And mothers pushed their prams along the pavement. Where dogs sniffed at trees. And children played ball in the street. And where Mr Benn would walk day after day, to the costume shop. Day after day, greet the shopkeeper. Day after day, choose a costume. Day after day, go into the changing rooms. And day after day dream he was somewhere else and someone else. Day after day. Plus repeats.

'Hello children; prepare for life.'

'Scarlet Ibis had stopped Polly Plover in the street. She was holding out a small solitary woollen bootie and pointing at Polly's baby in her padded wheel-along buggy. Polly was shaking her head and shrugging her shoulders. Not one of mine. Blue is not my child's colour. Perhaps it belongs to her down at number thirty two, her who's just had twins. Scarlet Ibis put the little lost item back on top of their low front wall and shrugged too. Perhaps she'll be along and see it. Scarlet Ibis's daughter joined them in the street. Scarlet Ibis rested a protective hand upon her head and made her face forward, rather than stare vacantly down at the car hubs in the gutter. Polly's conversation alternated between daughter and mother. I like your hair scrunchy, is it new? She's getting big, isn't she? How are you getting on at school? Before you

know it mine'll be that age too. Have you got a boyfriend?
'As if innocence isn't lost sooner enough.'

Chapter Fourteen

'"Are you going to call for her?"

'"Who?"

'"Letty, of course."

'"No. How many more times do I have to tell you. She can't make it this morning. She is visiting her sister in Greenford."

'"Greenford? I thought you said Catford."

'"No, Greenford. She went yesterday and is staying until Thursday."

'"So she won't be around for Tuesday either?"

'"No."

'"Not like her."

'"What isn't?"

'"To miss a service."

'"No."

'"And to miss a Tuesday."

'"No, not like her at all."

'Sunday morning and the Grouses were off to church.

'There was St Aloyious on the corner. I imagined that they went there. Very formal, very proper. Sometimes they had bells. Particularly in the summer when they must do more weddings. Mrs Grouse would sit in the third pew and would not remove her hat and Mr Grouse would sing in an out-of-key falsetto that would cause all the choirboys to exchange glances and smirk. The congregation would stand and sit and stand again, and when invited, form an orderly queue to take communion, when Mr Grouse, cross-legged, would rather be queuing for the toilet instead. A heady combination of incense, guilt and relief would hang heavy in the air as Amen would sound the end of proceedings and signal for thoughts to turn to roast beef, gardening and Sunday afternoon naps. Mrs Grouse would look around to see who has not turned up today and Mr Grouse would put a ten pence piece in the collection bowl and shuffle it around as though it were a pound. Both would shake the vicar by the hand and thank him for his sermon. "Same time next week" and "Sorry, would have loved to come to Tuesday service, but it's Bingo don't you know."

'Sundays for me have always meant farewells. Kissed

departures on railway platforms. Friends returning to their distant houses. Loved ones arranging "when shall we meet again." Sundays herald the return to routine. Goodbye weekend, hello Monday.

'The jolly-faced young estate agent was working overtime again. The red and white Citroen 2CV was parked outside of number three, facing out into the middle of the road as though he was expecting to have to make a fast getaway. He wasn't wearing his usual shiny blue suit that day, although he still had on the same white socks and training shoes. He wore a thick V-necked cricket jumper over a dark T-shirt and soft baggy jogging bottoms, which tied up at the waist with a draw-string and hung down loosely between his legs like the flesh on an old woman's neck. He glanced at his watch as he stood on the pavement, looked up and down the street, and then rummaging in his roomy trouser pocket for the front door keys, opened the gate to number three and walked up the front path and straight into the house. No trying to resurrect the For Sale sign today.

'The jogger arrived ten minutes later. A tall man, quite athletic; the hard lines of his muscular torso revealed beneath his sweat-stained running-vest. He was wearing jogging bottoms too, but patterned ones, bold swirls of blues and purples and blacks, like those advertised in mail-order catalogues. Like those I disliked so much. He paused outside number five, still running gently on the spot while at the same time looking up at the house, trying to make out the number, before suddenly his attention was taken by a call from next door and with a wave of recognition he jogged on a dozen paces, took the low wooden gate at a vault, and disappeared from view beneath the porch of number three.

'As a potential future next-door neighbour I thought Roadrunner no more likely than the House Martins, despite his visit lasting fully two hours and the parting hand-shake and embrace on the pavement between him and the jolly-faced young estate agent being rather more than just cordial.

'I wondered who had lived there previously. I had grown used to next-door standing empty; to the overgrown front garden and the broken fence; to the ever-growing scattering of crisp packets and plastic carrier bags in the bushes, and beer cans and fast-food containers in the long uncared for borders. I had got accustomed to the Grouses walking past and tutting, "what a state", and the postman passing by without a glance. And I enjoyed watching the male Blackbird singing of the joys of fatherhood with a sense of proprietorship from the top of the post of the broken For Sale board. It was hard to imagine that it could once have been a happy place, with a neat trimmed lawn and flowers in precise rows; with a regular family that went to work and went to school and went shopping and had two holidays each year, and were proud to return each time to this place that they called home.

'Detective Inspector David Sutton was talking on the radio again that night. It was unusual for me to have the radio on in the evening but it was also unusual for my brother not to be here to talk to me instead. He had said that the police were no nearer catching the killer of the Japanese woman. He had thought it unlikely that they ever would. I had been pleased to hear that Detective Inspector Sutton sounded rather more confident. He had said that the police were following up fresh evidence and had come up with several new leads in the "course of their enquiries".'

Chapter Fifteen

'It was raining. It started with a faint brush of wind and a smattering of fine spray on the window. Then larger drops began to fall, heavy, straighter and more determined, bouncing back into the air off the white wooden window sill. Clear individual drops, more secure in their separate identities, that would sparkle with vitality and life. Until the drops became hard black lines and the sound of distinct splashes was replaced by the constant background rush of the anonymous whole.

'Puddles in the road became rivers and the gurgling protests from the struggling drain covers were drowned and swept away. The bushes in the cemetery that had first shone, bright green, invigorated and fresh, they too were battered into submission and hung limp in leaf and branch and spirit.

'And momentarily it fell harder still. A sudden increase of noise and tempo that you knew could not be sustained for long. A more frantic, frenzied pummelling; a desperate bid to break all lingering resistance. The window was water, a blurry sheet blocking out the drowning world beyond; obscuring like a foggy mirror in a bathroom, which once had shown the truth so clearly and which you thought could never ever lie. I could not see the sky to see if there were further black clouds in the air. I could not see the Grouses' house, nor look into Craig Cuckoo's bedroom. And I could not see the birch tree to tell if the Blackbirds were safe in their nest. My world was suddenly reduced to four walls, a mattress, and a cupboard. Much as it is again now.'

'It cleared, of course. By the afternoon the sun was shining and the only sign of the storm were the last few remaining puddles in the middle of the road, lying in the holes that the workmen had left when they had laid the cable lines.

'I was watching the Blackbird's nest almost continuously now. The female sat on her downy cup of sticks and moss with the pride of possession and the stillness of contentment. It must be almost two weeks since I had first seen her settle to her noble task of incubation. Her companion visited her regularly: bright berries and tempting worms hanging invitingly from his bill a sign of his devotion.

His visits were brief though, his not wanting to draw any unwelcome attention to the scene of the eventual rise of his succession. He was a performer too: not for him the Stoic silence and uncomplaining patience of his mate, he had something to sing about and he wanted everyone to know. His loud warbling song and hopping black presence were as familiar a part of King Street routine as the activities of any of its human inhabitants.

'The female bird shifted slightly on the nest and raised herself to change position. She was a rather drab individual beside the effervescent male; the epitome of the down-at-heel housewife and without even the opportunity to rebuke his behaviour when he arrived back late after a day on the fence. Dark brown head, back and wing feathers with a lighter mottled breast, she looked rather like a washed-out thrush. Even her beak had none of the golden glow of her companions', and was instead tarnished and patchy, like old yellow nail varnish left on too long and allowed to chip away. Her eyes though shone with a deep vitality. Bright and beady. Dark and watchful. Unfathomably knowledgeable, a glassy observant circle looking straight back at me up the lens of my binoculars. She cocked her head to one side, and as I readjusted and refocussed, fixed me with a gaze as if to say "you lookin' at me?"

'It was while looking up details of the typical length of a Blackbird's incubation period in my copy of *Garden Birds* that I remembered the letter. It fell out as I pulled the book out from the shelf. "Where are you?" The words stared out at me. My brother was out but I still looked guiltily around at the door worried that I may be being observed. Why I should have been worried, I do not know. You must remember that I still wasn't quite myself. I picked one corner of the envelope so that I could get my finger inside and ran it along the length of the fold to make a torn and ragged opening. The letter was handwritten, quite brief, on rather thin, blue-lined paper. It was written on both sides of the page and the ink showed through making it difficult to read. I saw my name at the top and then skimmed through it picking out odd passages here and there to stop and read properly. "... been worried, no reply to my phone calls or emails to work." and "... let me know you're OK. I can't pretend that I understand if you don't want to keep in touch any longer, but just let me know that you're OK. Just a few words, to tell me why." I could do that. No, I wanted to do that. I hadn't meant for my friends to be worried for me. A brief note. I could ask my brother to post it for me.

'I tore out a blank sheet from the back of the notebook in which I record my bird sightings, and sat down at the desk. What to say? I wanted to explain that I was no longer living at my flat, that I wouldn't be going back there, nor to work, and that I couldn't be contacted on the email or by phone. That I was living with my brother and how good he had been to me and that I wanted to keep in touch and to write to me at number five, King Street. I wanted to say how much I valued our friendship and to say that I was sorry I had not been in contact earlier but that circumstances had been difficult this year and I had had a lot of readjusting to do. I wanted to write about how things had changed - how my priorities had changed - and about what was important in my life now. Yes, that more than anything. What was important in my life?

'I wrote: "The Blackbirds have three eggs. They should hatch any day now".'

'The light was on in Craig Cuckoo's bedroom very late that night. I know because I slept badly and kept on getting out of bed and standing at the window. I could hear the faint rhythmic sound of my brother's snoring in the room next door and the gentle patter of rain on leaves as the next wave of showers passed over. I thought it was a cat, the movement along the street, underneath the street lamp, but as it approached nearer and drew out from beneath the shadows of the cemetery wall I could see that it was a fox, old and mangy, and limping slightly on a back leg. My movement at the window must have caught its attention because it stood still in the middle of the road and looked up at me in the moonlight, before, unimpressed, walking on. I looked across to Craig Cuckoo's window and there, looking out, illuminated from behind by the glow from the large white lampshade he had hanging from the ceiling, a young Oriental woman with a small round face and long, lustrous black hair. She watched the progress of the fox down the street until it was finally out of sight and then turning away from the scene, switched off the light.

Chapter Sixteen

'May 17th was not a good day.

'The jolly-faced young estate agent must have arrived very early because his red and white Citroen 2CV was already badly parked outside of number three, facing out into the middle of the road as though he were expecting to have to make a fast getaway, by the time I woke and drew back the curtains and heard the pigeon. Right outside the window I could hear it coo-ing, signalling the start of a new day.

'The Grouses were just leaving their house: the transition from ghastly tea-cosy to large misshapen piece of green fabric indicating, in Mrs Grouses' mind at any rate,, that summer had arrived.

'"Have you got your brolly with you, just in case?"

'"The forecast said it wouldn't rain today."

'"And when have they ever been right?"

'"They were right yesterday."

'"What did they say then?"

'"That it'd be fine."

'"Huh. Not likely to have two fine days running."

'"Look for yourself, there's not a cloud in the sky."

'"Perhaps."

'"On the other hand ..."

'"What?"

'"Hold on there a minute. I think I may just pop in and get my brolly."

'Scarlet Ibis was standing on the front steps of number ten, checking that her daughter had packed everything in her school bag. Pencil case. Swimming kit. Towel. Dinner money? Dinner money! Hang on. I've got something upstairs. She reappeared and counted out several coins, before a hug and a kiss and a wave. Have a good day. See you later.

'Mrs Peacock was in the middle of the street directing traffic and Craig Cuckoo was standing at his open window, bare-chested, smoking on a home-made cigarette and flicking the ash down to land outside Mr Nightjar's basement dwelling.

'The postman was walking past the cemetery wall, head down, sorting through the letters in his hand to see if there were any for number eight. Polly Plover was walking in the opposite direction, on the other side of the road, pushing her baby in its buggy. She waved to me and smiled, and called out to the postman, "Good morning. Anything for me?"

'It all happened so fast. The man with the greased-black hair and neatly clipped moustache was driving his shiny pale blue Escort and had no time to stop. It was only his quick instincts that prevented a tragedy. He pulled the steering wheel hard right and then was almost able to correct himself, but couldn't quite avoid clipping the side of the jolly-faced young estate agent's red and white Citroen 2CV which was so badly parked, facing out into the middle of the road.

'It was Polly Plover's fault. She admitted it. She had seen the postman on the other side and stepped out into the road without looking. She had seen the pale blue Escort at the last moment and with a cry of panic pushed her baby's buggy with all her force across the road and out of harm's way, just managing to step backwards herself to avoid a fatal impact.

'Everyone was in the street now. The jolly-faced young estate agent was examining the damaged side of his red and white Citroen 2CV, his face now less than jolly. The man with the greased-black hair and neatly clipped moustache was standing in the middle of the road, arms spread wide, saying, "What else could I do? She came from nowhere. What else could I do?" The residents of number ten - Craig Cuckoo, Scarlet Ibis, even Mr Nightjar - were all standing in their front garden, discussing what they'd seen. Mrs Peacock had a comforting arm around Polly Plover, who in turn was holding her crying infant, rocking her back and forwards, and making sure she was OK. The postman was on his hands and knees examining the baby's buggy which had careered into the bottom of the birch tree and struck it with a jarring impact. "Young one's lucky to have got out of this." was his conclusion, "I'm afraid the wheels have buckled right under. It's had it."

'All this time my eyes had been on the Blackbirds. The male was on the Grouses' fence, running back and forth in agitation and chattering in a wild, excited fashion. The female was no longer on the nest and was nowhere to be seen. The nest was tilted, more precarious than ever, shaken over on one side by the force of the buggy's impact, revealing one small, scrawny black infant, and two pale blue unopened eggs. Teetering over a deadly precipice, the tiny new hatchling struggled to right itself, first shuffling one way, then back the other, before, in its clumsy manoeuvrings, over-balancing, agonisingly bringing itself, the nest and its two unborn siblings plummeting earthward. I watched through my binoculars as if in slow-motion. The reptilian-like bag-of-bones, plunged blind-eyed ever down, its useless half-formed wings beating in a mockery of flight. I watched its descent through the high canopy of green leaves, none able to provide a soft bed to break its fall; onto the thicker branches, where it struck its head awkwardly and was thrown sideways, its feeble neck unable to hold itself proud to the last; and then straight down, faster and faster, past the vertical white trunk, counting off each passing black knot on the bark - one, two, three, four - until the final impact, as the pavement rushed up with an unshakeable inevitability. The two eggs landed a second later; so perfect, so spherical in shape that I expected them to bounce, once, twice, and settle safely. Hard earth is not so forgiving though. Splat. Splat. And finally the nest, broken and battered in its descent, bounced once and came to rest, unnoticed, alongside the wheel of a parked car.

'The jolly-faced young estate agent and the man with the greased-black hair and neatly clipped moustache exchanged insurance details, shrugged shoulders and parted on a joke. Mrs Peacock scooped up the trailing hem of her sari, climbed aboard her husband's car and drove away. Craig Cuckoo returned inside to his second floor flat; Scarlet Ibis to her first floor flat; and Mr Nightjar to the basement. The Grouses reemerged from their house, still in three piece suit and misshapen green fabric, but now both carrying umbrellas.

    '"Always something with that family."

    '"Yes, she's not been very lucky has she?"

    '"Burgled, last time wasn't it?"

    '"I remember."

    '"Last year, do you remember?"

    '"Yes."

    '"All those police around, do you remember?"

'"Yes."

'"Do you remember?"

'The postman delivered one letter to number eight, three to number ten and carried on his round. And Polly Plover carried her now quiet daughter in her arms back inside her house, trailing the wreck of the broken and useless buggy behind her.

'Everything was all right again in King Street.'

Chapter Seventeen

'I don't know how I first heard that Polly Plover's baby was dead. It wasn't from the radio, although I heard it there later. Nor was it from the policeman who called. I knew about it before then. I think it was from the single scream of anguish that rent the morning calm and its memory which hung over King Street like the echo of lost lives once the avalanche has passed.

'Of course, Polly Plover was not her real name. You know that. It was Susan Croft. Mrs Susan Croft, wife of Richard Croft, parents of Hannah Croft. The radio told me that much. Actually I found out a lot about my neighbours that day. It is amazing how much you take for granted and how appearances can be so deceptive.

'Take the Grouses. I mean the Summers. Man and wife. Happily married for thirty three years. They run a community counselling service affiliated to a happy clappy church in the neighbouring town. Apparently they proved to be a great comfort to the Crofts in their time of bereavement.

'And Craig Cuckoo. The policeman told me that he was an aromatherapist working from home, when I voiced my suspicions about the many - and varied - visitors he had been entertaining. Geoff is his name. I can't remember what the policeman said his surname is, but it wasn't Cuckoo. Apparently he advertised in the *Yellow Pages*, so I could have found out.

'I even saw Mr Nightjar emerge from his daytime bunker to lay a single flower of condolence at the Croft's door. Actually, the only people to have emerged from the episode with discredit were to be the Peacocks: there was a rather nasty scene in their front garden when the police called around on routine questioning and ended up reprimanding Mr Peacock for a minor motoring offence.

'I didn't know all the details then. The policeman that called was naturally very cagey and didn't say much, other than to ask if we - my brother and I - had noticed anything unusual, or had seen anyone we didn't recognise in the Street in the last few days. We told him about the car accident the previous Friday but he already knew all about that. Someone must have told him that I spend a lot of time sitting at the window because he was most persistent about asking me if I had seen anything. Anything at all. Even the smallest details may be useful. My brother asked if there was reason to believe the baby's death had been anything other than natural causes. And the policeman said that they were treating the investigation as a case of murder.

'The radio confirmed this later too. In horrified and more sensationalistic terms. Dead in her cot. A young baby girl, only just turned one year old, was killed in her own home sometime during the early hours of yesterday morning. She was discovered by her mother earlier today. The baby - name at this time withheld - had died from multiple injuries, the result of a severe and systematic beating. Signs indicate that the back door of the victim's house had been forced open but that robbery does not appear to be the motive. Evidence left at the scene of the crime suggests that this death may be linked to the earlier murder of a Japanese student in Kent. No other details are forthcoming. Police are treating this as a case of murder by person or persons unknown.'

'I buried the baby Blackbird that evening in the back garden. It was my first time outside of the house in over thirteen months. My brother had only just been able to retrieve the little body in time, because a magpie had already spotted it and had taken a few tentative pecks, and looked all set to take to the air with its bloody bounty. It took me several days to pluck up the courage to step outside, but once there I felt quite relaxed. I thought, perhaps this was to be another new beginning for me.

'I placed the tiny shrivelled carcass in an empty margarine tub to keep it protected and buried it in several inches of soil beneath a rose bush. On the fence, beside me, its father sang a twittering requiem. No other mourners were present.'

Part Four

Lundy

Chapter One

'It's finished. What do you think?'

'I'm sure it's very good, darling.'

'You will read it, won't you?'

'Yes, of course. When I've finished this one.'

'What's that?'

Diana turned the novel over in her hand so that her husband could see. 'Anna Karenina.'

'How far are you through it?'

She flipped the book back again. 'Page thirty-two.'

David pushed back the bed covers, swung his legs over the side of the bed and stood up. He crossed the room and picked up a bulging folder of papers that had been lying on the dressing table. He slotted the last two sheets of A4 paper that he had been carrying in at the end of the file and brought the whole bundle back to the bed.

'Perhaps you could just read this first. It won't take long. Look there's not too much here. I'd really appreciate your opinion.'

'Really? That would be a first.'

'No, really. I must admit it was harder than I thought.'

'What was?'

'Writing a crime story. I can see why those other authors get it wrong. The characters, the plot. It's all quite difficult. Have a read and see if you can guess who done it.'

'But I know who done it.'

'How do you mean?'

'Well, I thought you were writing about the Twitcher case, weren't you? I know who done it. I've had to listen to you often enough these past few months explaining who done it every night. It's been on every news programme. It's the headline of every newspaper. How could I fail to know who done it?'

'So, pretend you don't. Please, have a read, Diana. I think you'll enjoy it. I quite like a bit I wrote about ...' David shuffles through the mass of papers looking for the particular passage, 'Yes, here. It's just after the mother has ...'

'For God's sake don't tell me. I know enough about it

already without you explaining individual sentences. Yes, yes, I'll read it. OK?' Diana lays down *Anna Karenina* on her bedside table. 'Hand it over then.'

David hesitates, 'There's just one thing I wanted to explain.'

'Yes?'

'It's about ... well, it's about the sex scenes. I just wanted you to know that it's not you.'

'What do you mean "not me"?'

'That it wasn't you I was describing.'

'Well, who was it then?'

'No. I mean, it wasn't anyone. You know, it was just imaginary. I didn't want you to think I would write about ... well, you know ... us.'

'So you're telling me that you've been thinking about imaginary sex while you've been laying next to me here, scribbling away on your pad these last few weeks?'

'It wasn't easy.'

'No, I bet it wasn't.'

'You'll still read it?'

'Yes, of course. I want to know what you imagine.'

Chapter Two

Detective Inspector Daniel Seaton clasped the collar of his anorak more tightly around his throat to keep out the biting cold sea wind and stared forward. Fixedly forward.

Eyes on the horizon. Just keep your eyes on the horizon. Not much further to go now. Just hang on a little bit longer. Up and down. And up and down. No. Keeping looking straight. Concentrate on looking straight ahead.

'You OK, old chap? Looking a bit green.'

Daniel tried to turn his head to see who was addressing him, but finding the voluminous hood of his coat not turning with him, ended up answering in muffled tones from within the sodden folds of material.

''m sorry. Was'at?'

'I said you're looking a bit green. Not a good sailor?'

Daniel extricated himself from his rain hood to see an elderly - although sickeningly perky-looking - gentleman in a white and blue polyester anorak and vaguely nautical cap standing over him.

'Not too good, no. It's a bit rougher than I expected.'

The old chap, taking this as an invitation, seated himself on the hard wooden planking that passed for a bench next to Daniel. 'Rough? I can tell you about rough.' He took off his cap - significantly - and held it in his hands on his lap. 'Antigua. Now that was rough.'

'Really?'

'The waves there make these look like ripples on a pond. Six weeks sailing in the Caribbean. Big as houses some of those waves out there, I can tell you.'

Straight ahead. Keep your eyes on the horizon.

'Threw our little tub around like a feather in a whirlwind. The wife'd tell you. Deidre. Deidre? Oh, looks like she's disappeared for the moment. But she'd tell you. Like a feather in a whirlwind.'

Not far to go. Just concentrate on looking straight ahead.

'And do you know what? Sick? Not me, not once. I've got a constitution like an ox. Poor Deidre though. No stomach on her. That's what I always say, no stomach on her at all. You've never seen someone so ill. You have to laugh. She'd tell you.'

Horizon. Straight. Concentrate.

'It's just what it reminded me of when I saw you sitting there. My Deidre. She goes just the same. Green around the gills, I say. And all hot and sweaty too, she does. Just before she's about to be sick that is. You looking a bit sweaty, old chap? Oh, I say, here comes a big one. Whooooa-eeh, that was a big wave. They'll have to watch themselves those people standing up front. Absolutely drenched in spray. Here, hold on. Let me see what I've got in my bag here for you. Yes, here we are. Do you fancy an egg sandwich?'

Daniel had already got the empty carrier bag in readiness for such an eventuality, and as discretely as the circumstances would allow in the cramped conditions on deck, opened it wide, bent his head so that it almost disappeared within the opening of suffocating plastic, and heaved copiously, once and then more violently, so that he felt his whole body shake from the depths of his stomach up to his shoulders, once again. He sat motionless, his face still buried within the anonymity of the bag, doubled over, so that the puke-filled carrier hung heavily between his legs. He wished that when he emerged from this stenching pit of shame, everything would be different. That he will be on dry land, not the endless rolling torment of the Bristol Channel. That everyone will have disappeared from the deck of the boat to allow him a private moment to clean himself up and rediscover something akin to respectability. That the rain will have stopped, the clouds dispersed, and the sun will be shining. And that the annoying old man with the annoying sailor's cap will be gone. Preferably overboard.

He looked up, his eyes still shut, and did feel slightly better. The sensation of sickness had passed. So too had the clammy flush of nausea, and the feeling of lightheadedness. It even felt warmer. There was a heat shining on his face and through the darkness of his closed lids he could see a slowly spreading wave of red. He opened his eyes and looked upon a window of blue sky and a brightly glowing sun. Life, that only seconds before had seemed intolerable, suddenly seemed to begin anew. It was then that Daniel remembered his final tormentor. The old man? Moved on. Now chatting to a couple of elderly women standing by the right-side guard-rail.

Daniel tied the handles of the carrier bag in a secure knot to prevent any unpleasant seepages and then fished around beneath his anorak and in his trouser pocket, in the hope of finding a tissue with which to wipe his mouth and make himself presentable to the world again. He was stopped in his search by a large white piece of material being fluttered in front of his face, blowing in the strong winds like the ensign on the rear mast.

'Here, use this.'

He looked up to see an attractive young woman offering him a cotton handkerchief.

'Thank you.'

Daniel rubbed the soft linen across his lips, moistening the fabric slightly, and then wiped it vigorously across his cheeks and over his chin. He smiled as the woman wordlessly pointed to the bottom of his nose, and he reapplied the handkerchief to remove the offending chunk of vomit.

'Thank you.' He began to hand the material back, before noticing how stained the spotless white square had become, 'I'm sorry, I've made it very dirty.'

The young woman held out a hand to take the handkerchief back but was stopped by a call from one of the two men in the group to which she belonged.

'That's OK. You hang on to it. Never know if you might need it again.' he joked.

'Thank you.' Daniel pocketed the grubby cloth and watched the small figure return to her two companions, who were smoking and laughing together at the very rear of the boat. Very attractive. Although why did he think rather sad? The eyes. It must have been the eyes. Big brown holes that seemed to support no life. Just a staring concentration. And no expression. Perhaps she was rather simple. Shame. Very attractive, though.

- - - - - - - - - -

'Daniel Seaton? He wouldn't be based on anyone I know, would he?'

'You can excuse me some small vanity, can't you? What do you think though?'

'I don't know yet. I've only read one chapter. All you've done is chuck up and ogle some young floosie. What do you want me to say? Come on, turn out the light now, David. I'm tired. I'll read the rest tomorrow, when I am thinking a bit straighter.'

'But what do you think of it as a start?'

'Tomorrow. I'll tell you tomorrow.'

Chapter Three

Land ahoy! The hum of engines slowed and stopped and was replaced by the rattle of metal on metal, as rung after orange-rusty rung of iron chain was played out overboard, and the bulky anchor was lowered into the now brilliant blue depths of the bay. It was hard to imagine a sea that had only moments before seemed gripped by a permanent granite grey, now looking so clear and inviting. The *MS Oldenburg* came to a gentle rest, bobbing slightly from side to side on a modest swell of expectation.

The island of Lundy presents a formidable face to seaborne arrivals and landing is no easy matter. Its cliffs rise four hundred feet, seemingly without interruption along the island's three-mile length, and jagged outcrops of rock jut from the sea, making the waters dance white with agitation. It is not surprising that over the years this natural fortress has been able to repel invaders as diverse as the Knights Templar in the 12th Century to the Inland Revenue in the 1920s. Millcombe Bay, lying to the south of the slightly more sheltered eastern side of the island, provides the only safe anchorage for the regular vessel that brings passengers over on the eleven mile crossing from the north Devon coastal towns of Bideford and Ilfracombe, and from here a zig-zag track, still barely discernible from the boat, meanders up the crumbling rockface, like a running scar, to arrive at the tiny collection of stone buildings that comprise the main settlement on the island.

Talk of building a jetty so that visitors can make a dry-landing, has been just that for years - talk. Instead each intrepid island explorer has to transfer from the *MS Oldenburg* into one of the small motorised launches that runs between the boat and shore and land in the time-honoured tradition - scared and wet.

Lundy has a varied and interesting history. From the archaeological discoveries of tiny worked flints on the island it is apparent that Stone Age man had settled here as far back as 7000BC and there is evidence that the land was used for agricultural purposes throughout much of the Bronze and Iron Ages; a significant population existing around 600BC.

Christianity came to Lundy in the fifth century AD and four inscribed memorial stones dating from this period are still visible in the cemetery grounds, close to the Old Lighthouse.

The first actual historically recorded owner of the island was a Norman knight, Henry de Newmarch, but it was a family of French brigands, the Mariscos that first put Lundy on the map. William de Marisco was responsible for a long campaign of piracy and lawlessness against the English mainland, culminating in an assassination attempt on King Henry III, a treason for which he was hung, drawn and quartered in 1242. It was at this time too that Lundy's castle was built.

After the end of the Mariscos' ownership the island passed to the Crown and had a succession of temporary tenants before once again passing into private ownership in the sixteenth century when it was acquired by the famous Elizabethan seafarer Sir Richard Grenville. Sir Richard had little enough time to enjoy his island bolt-hole though, perishing aboard the warship *Revenge* when it took on the might of the combined Spanish fleet. Sir Richard's death saw a return to lawlessness to this remote corner of the Bristol Channel.

In 1748 Thomas Benson was given the task by the government of the day of transporting British convicts to colonies overseas. Taking this at its most literal, Benson decided a quick and cheap solution would be to off-load the felons on Lundy. Using the prisoners as slave-labour Benson and his conscripted work-force were responsible for the construction of many of the walls and buildings that still exist on Lundy to this day. A number of convicts managed to escape to the mainland though and Benson's crimes were discovered and so Lundy was to once again be sold, first to the M.P., Sir John Warren, then to a local landowner John Cleveland, before the island was bought at an auction by Sir Vere Hunt, only for it to be lost again by his son in a game of dice. Lundy was not to have a landowner again that rightly deserved such a title until 1834, when William Hudson Heaven bought the granite isle with the unsavoury reputation, for a reputed nine thousand guineas.

The 'Kingdom of Heaven' as it became known lasted from 1834 to 1918. Heaven had always dreamed of owning

Lundy and two years after actually purchasing the island built a magnificent residence - Millcombe House - on the eastern slopes as a home for himself and his family. Lundy prospered during Heaven's life - new properties were built, as was the essential track from the Landing Bay beach to the cliff summit. Upon his death in 1883 his son, the Reverend Hudson Grosett Heaven continued his father's dream. He was responsible for the building of the Victorian gothic-style church which now stands at the southern end of the village.

Perhaps the last chapter in Lundy's eccentric history of ownership occurred in 1925 when the island was sold to Martin Coles Harman. Harman was a keen amateur naturalist and went on to establish the Lundy Field Society, devoted to the cataloguing and preservation of the island's distinct flora and fauna. Harman introduced many new breeds of animals to his animal home, meeting with mixed results. Sika deer were successfully introduced, and a small herd of these beautiful animals continue to live on Lundy's protected east side. Red deer proved more troublesome though and after several attacks on visitors they were removed in the 1960s. Wallabies were an even greater disaster, most notably when two specimens plummeted to a watery end in one of Lundy's many wells. And a pair of mute swans let loose on Pondsbury Lake must have felt one blast of the island's ferocious winds, before taking flight, never to be seen again.

During his thirty year ownership, Harman impressed upon the island a distinct identity which persists today. He dispensed with the services of the G.P.O. in 1928 and introduced his own postage stamps. During this period also, the island pub was not licensed premises and the residents were not subjected to mainland taxes or included on the electoral register. Harman even minted his own coins, Puffinage, but this act of independence went a step too far for the British government and he was charged under the 1870 Coinage Act.

In recent years Lundy has become the property of the National Trust and is maintained day-to-day by the Landmark Trust, who rent out a number of the island's characterful properties to holidaymakers.

It was only the thought of an imminent transfer to his own characterful property that got Daniel into the launch at all. After his perilous voyage in a big boat the last thing he wished to do was to get into a smaller boat, but there seemed no alternative other than to return directly to the mainland. The transfer actually proved far less precarious than it had at first looked, and with storm clouds once again brewing, Daniel began to wish that he had taken his opportunity to go across on one of the first launches rather than delay his watery nemesis. Back on dry land for the first time in four hours, Daniel began to appreciate why the Pope always kissed the ground on arrival.[1]

- - - - - - - - - -

'Blatant plagiarism.'
    'What is?'
    'Absolutely shameless.'
    'What is?'
    'That bit about Lundy and the Inland Revenue. All the facts and figures and stuff. How did you know about that?'
    'Just information I picked up, I suppose.'
    'Oh, no. I don't think so. It was from that old copy of *Wanderlust* magazine. I wondered what it was doing back on the top of the pile the other day. I read the article again myself. Puffin Island they called it. You've copied it from there, almost word for word. I only hope you've given the poor author some credit.'
    'I was planning to do a bibliography. Give me a chance. Anyway you can't alter the facts.'
    'Really? I would have thought you, of all people, would know that the truth's rarely that black and white.'

[1] Construction of a permanent concrete jetty was completed on Lundy during the summer of 1999. This now means that passengers can land directly from the *MS Oldenburg* on to the shore; greatly reducing the time for disembarkation and meaning that sailings can take place at times when weather conditions would have previously made it impossible.

Chapter Four

The path from the landing bay up to the village was quite steep and a hard pull on legs still not entirely adjusted to being back on terra-firma.

Teresa, James and Martin had been among the speediest passengers to alight from the first dinghy that had come ashore and now had a good head-start up the cliff. James looked back to the straggle of humanity gradually making its winding progress along the path below them.

'Do you think those two will make it?' He pointed to a couple of elderly women some considerable distance behind: one short and stout and wearing a rather masculine green-checked blazer, the other taller and more poised but now leaning for support on the top of a delicately carved walking stick.

'Probably find they could walk the hind legs off any of us,' replied Martin. 'They look the country types. Jolly hockey sticks and bugger three badgers before sunrise.'

'Let's hope they're not staying anywhere near us.'

'Why? Have you spotted someone else you fancy shacking up with?' asked Martin.

'No, hardly. I just don't want neighbours that are going to be popping in and out all day long, because they can't get their oven to light, or when they've found a spider in the bath.'

'Or when they want a hip popping back into place.'

'Or a colostomy bag changed. No really, I didn't see anyone on the crossing that looked very interesting.'

'I thought the man who was sick looked nice.' It was Teresa who spoke for the first time.

'Really? I thought he just looked sick.'

'I hope that school party are not going to be staying the whole week.' said James. He unconsciously sleaked his hand back over the side of his head, pushing his fair hair back from where the wind had made it fall haphazardly over his ears. His hair was cut short in front and long behind, in a style that Proust would have described as *Bressant*, but which was nowadays known, rather less flatteringly, as a mullet.

'You can't have the island all to yourself, mate.

Although it will seem it often enough, like I've said.' Martin looked slightly anxiously up towards the clouds, that were once again gathering to form a despondent crowd. 'Come on, get a move on you two. We've been lucky to get off the launch in the sunshine, but it looks as though it's going to pour down again any second.'

They felt the first drops of rain fall no sooner had the words left Martin's mouth and the threesome broke into a brisk walk and were able to rapidly cover the remaining open ground between the bay and the first shelter offered by the village before the worst of the deluge was upon them. Further back down the track Detective Inspector Seaton was not so fortunate.

Having hung around on the beach to confirm that he didn't have to wait for his luggage and that it would be transported to his accommodation for him, Daniel was still at the foot of the cliffs when the rains returned with a vengeance. Today was providing a rapid and highly illustrative lesson into the vagaries of the Lundy weather.

The only immediate shelter that offered itself to Daniel was a small man-made cave at the base of the wall of sheer rock. The opening was piled high with rubble and leaning against the stone walls were a variety of builder's tools, indicating that it was used as a temporary store for the workers engaged in the construction of the new cliff road and landing stage. Daniel squeezed past a toppled Road Closed sign, still adorned with streamers of red and white tape, and stood in the dingy but dry hollow, looking out onto the bay, where crew members were still unloading supplies and luggage from the stationary *MS Oldenburg* regardless of the miserable conditions. A rather fine ship, he thought, now that he was able to assess her with a logical brain rather than a heaving stomach.

'Nice vessel, isn't she?' The voice belonged to a bald-headed elderly gentleman who appeared from around the side of the cave entrance and joined Daniel taking shelter. 'Built in 1958 in Germany. Did you see all the original panelling and brass fittings in the saloon on the journey over?'

'I'm afraid I didn't. I was rather ... distracted.'

The newcomer continued, 'Lovely sight they are. She

came here to Lundy in 1986 and has been ferrying passengers back and forth ever since.'

'You seem to know a lot about her.' Daniel commented. 'Have you been here before?'

'Many times. Donald Trigg's my name. I'm sure I'll be seeing you around, if you're staying.'

'Yes. Yes, I am. I've rented Old Light Cottage.'

'Here for the birds?' enquired the old man.

'Excuse me?'

'An ornithologist, are you? That's what most of them are that come here.'

No, quite the opposite, Daniel thought. He would be only too glad to get away from them. But he said, 'No. Just for some peace and quiet. It's been a stressful few months at work and I am in need of a break. Recharge the batteries, you know.'

'What's it you do?'

Always the big dilemma. Can an off-duty policeman ever really be off-duty once people know what he does. To tell or lie? Daniel hedged with vague. 'I'm a civil servant.'

'What a copper?'

'Why do you say that?'

'No one has a stressful few months being a civil servant.'

'Yes, a copper.'

Donald smiled, 'Don't worry, lad. I won't tell anyone.'

They stood in silence for some moments watching the rain form increasingly larger puddles in the half-made up road. Daniel stuck his hand out from its dry enclave and felt each cold patter of water strike his skin with a shiver. 'Is it always like this here?'

'No,' answered the island sage, 'sometimes the weather can be quite bad.'

- - - - - - - - - -

Diana flicked through the remaining pages of the manuscript impatiently. 'So when does the murder happen?'

'Hold on, can't you? I've got to set the scene a bit first.'

'But I know all this.'

David snatched the bundle of papers out of his wife's hand. 'Maybe you're not the best person to read this after all.'

'No. No, come on. Hand it back. I'm teasing. I am interested, really. Besides ...'

'What?'

'I haven't reached the juicy bit yet, have I?'

Chapter Five

The Marisco Tavern was packed. It was lunchtime and a gang of itinerant sheep-shearers, over from the mainland for a couple of days to shear the island's flock, had taken over the establishment for their mid-day fare. The poor weather didn't help either and the day-trippers who would all normally by now have dispersed themselves far and wide, in the hope of covering every square inch of the island in the precious few hours they had been allotted ashore, were also taking shelter in the warm sanctuary of Lundy's sole public house. Daniel sat, half-on, half-off a small corner of wooden bench - the last available seating he could find - his back to the noisy group of farming-types with whom he shared the table, and sipped a double whisky.

'Take a holiday.' His boss had told him. 'It's become too personal. You can't see anything beyond your own wrath. I'm reassigning Peters to take over the investigation.'

He'd argued although he knew it was true. The case had got the better of him. And yet it had all started out so simply. A death, or rather a murder. Nothing new there, he'd seen plenty of them before. And clues. So many clues, it seemed only a matter of time before following up one of the leads would lead to the jackpot. But then there had been another killing. The kid - I mean, just a baby. That had been the final straw. He should have been able to be detached. He knew he could best serve the poor child's parents by remaining professional; by sifting through the evidence and doing his job by bringing the killer to justice, but emotion had got the better of him. And if he was being true to himself, the emotions he had experienced were not sadness and sympathy for the death of a girl not yet old enough to have said her first word, it was anger at being frustrated by the killer - this so called 'Twitcher' - once again. And so he had argued, but he knew that what his boss had said was true: he had become blinded by his own rage and was no longer fit to lead the investigation. He had heard the radio announcement of his replacement on the case as he was packing his luggage for the journey. One reason for his choosing Lundy. Total isolation would prevent him being even tempted to meddle in the continuing hunt for the murderer. Peters is a good man. It's his responsibility now.

Another reason for choosing Lundy was Mickey Wragg. Mickey was an old school friend who had been living on Lundy for several months now, having picked up some labouring work, helping with the construction of the new cliff road. Daniel had received a letter from Mickey only a couple of weeks back, saying that he ought to 'come visit' since the island was 'good crack'. The thought of catching up with his good-hearted old friend had seemed a cheery prospect after the previous desperate months. It was only now, after enquiring at the bar, that Daniel discovered that Mickey had been airlifted off the previous week having broken his leg 'fooling around in the Landrover.' Two weeks of his own company to dwell on recent past events now seemed far less inviting.

He looked at the map of the island. Three and a half miles long by half a mile wide. To the south, the tiny village comprising one shop, one pub, one church and a small collection of cottages and farm buildings, and the rest just wide open spaces of grassland, cliff and moor. Daniel took a final swig of his drink, looked outside at the endless rain, and dreamed of suburbia. There would probably be cricket on Sky at the moment, or at least the highlights of one of yesterday's games. He had been released from the case, he didn't have to go in to work, he could be sitting comfortably in his lounge now, in the comfy chair by the window that Denise always sat in if they were both home together in the evenings, feet up on the pouffe, a four-pack of cold beers in the fridge, a ready-meal in the oven, and vegetate. Get up late. Watch the sport. Read the newspapers. The same newspapers that tracked his every move on the investigation. That demanded instant results, where his boss and even the public recognised the virtue of patience. That ultimately clamoured for his resignation. And would now be crowing.

'You've got to pity the campers, haven't you?'

Daniel was waken from his reverie by a voice at hand. It was apparently a day for uninvited introductions.

'Pardon?'

The woman's voice continued, 'On a day like this. You've got to pity the campers.' And then suddenly realising that she may have made a faux pas. 'Oh, I'm awfully sorry. You're not a camper yourself are you?'

Daniel smiled to see the worried expression. 'No, don't worry. I'm renting Old Light Cottage. Actually, I've only just arrived and have still to discover exactly where it is. What with this terrible weather I decided I was more in need of a stiff drink than to find out where I will be staying for the night.'

'You'll like Old Light.' The young woman seated herself opposite Daniel on a bench just vacated by two burly shearers. 'Do you mind if I join you for a few minutes?' She extended a friendly hand, 'My name is Lex.'

'Daniel.'

She had a firm, rapid shake: squeeze once, down, release. Daniel put her in her early-thirties. Dark shoulder-length curly hair and a rather serious face, with a solid square jaw and chin. Not unattractive, but nothing special. She studied Daniel with intelligent and deep-set eyes and with such fixed concentration that Daniel felt compelled to break the silence first. 'Are you staying here yourself?'

'Yes, we're in the Blue Bung. I mean the Old School House. That's just what they call it around here. You probably passed it, just below the village looking out towards the sea.'

'Yes, I think I saw it on the path coming up. We?'

'Oh, I'm here with my friend Sonya. She's around here somewhere.'

'Tell me about the Old Light then.' Daniel enquired. 'I really should find where it is I'm staying. Which direction should I head for?'

'You can't miss it. Ahead and to your left as you leave here. You'll see the top of the lighthouse above the village buildings. I would have stayed there myself but it's only a one person property and coming with Sonya made it impossible.'

Daniel was beginning to find the young woman's unblinking stare rather disconcerting. His years of experience in the interrogation room had trained him in techniques of intimidation, but he felt his companion could have taught him several further lessons. He made his excuses to leave. 'Well, the rain seems to be lessening slightly. I think I had better be off and find my accommodation. Goodbye then.'

'Goodbye. I'm sure I'll be seeing you around.'

Daniel began to wonder if this wasn't some kind of special Lundy threat.

- - - - - - - - - -

'You can have that chair if you want to.'

'Pardon?'

'The chair by the window. You only needed to have said. I didn't realise that you ever wanted it.'

David look more bemused. 'Which chair?'

'The comfy chair by the window in the lounge. If you'd said you wanted to sit in it I would have moved. I'm not bothered, which chair I sit in. I always thought that you liked the green one by the door.'

'I do.'

'Then why sit in the other one when you've got the place to yourself?' his wife enquired.

'It's in the novel, darling. It's just in the novel.'

'You're sure?'

'Yes.'

Diana puffed up her pillows so that she could sit up straighter again and pulled the bedclothes back around her, before once again returning to the loose pages of her husband's manuscript. She was about to resume reading when another thought struck her.

'You're not putting your feet up on the pouffe though.'

Chapter Six

It was a lie. The rain was heavier than ever and the glass topped beacon of the lighthouse was barely visible through the encroaching mist. There was not a single other person out of doors in the village, and warm and secure inside, looking out of a cottage's window, a large black cat watched Daniel's soggy progress with an expression of self-contented amusement. From his tent, Oliver was watching also.

'Looks like the *Oldenburg*'s arrived.' he commented to someone concealed within the tent's depths. 'It's brought some new blood.'

His companion rolled over from where he had been lying face down on top of his sleeping bag reading a book, and sat himself up, leaning against the tent's end pole. 'Just as long as they don't interfere with the birding, I don't care.'

Oliver laughed. 'Leo. I think you may be even more obsessed than I am.'

'Not obsessed. Just serious. You said yourself, it's not a hobby to take lightly. We came all this way to see birds. I just want to make sure that now we're here we see as many as possible.'

'Yes, OK. I agree. By the way did you hear the shearwaters last night?'

'What! No. Where? When?'

Oliver laughed again. 'Your face. You're too easy. It's not even any fun winding you up.'

Leo was serious again. 'I'm determined to hear them before we leave. If the rain stops later I may have a root around that patch of moor beyond the Old Light and see if I can spot any signs of their burrows.'

'If the rain stops later.'

Daniel was cursing he had ever heard of Lundy, along with pretty much everything else in life too. His hair was wet. His coat was wet. His holdall was wet. His feet were soaked.

'Fuck, fuck, fuck.'

He had already followed one path which seemed to lead most enticingly in the direction he needed to go, only to find it stop abruptly at a large iron gate and a field of sheep beyond. Uncertain if he was allowed to cross the field or might instead provoke the wrath of an island farmer, Daniel had veered on the side of caution and had back-tracked to the village and crossed the camp-site, going through the gate and over the stile to the field beyond as he had been originally instructed to by the barmaid at the pub.

'Fuck, fuck, fuck.'

His hair hung in damp clumps across his forehead and water trickled down his back and into his eyes making it hard to see. Ahead though, his goal at last seemed attainable. The off-white stone column of the Old Light stuck out prominent from behind the wall of a small enclosure, containing the lighthouse itself, a large adjoining dwelling comprising - Daniel had done his homework - Old Light Trinity and Old Light Venturer, and two tiny out-houses, one of which Daniel presumed was the holy grail, Old Light Cottage.

He peered through a small, dirt-engrained window in the first building and seeing nothing inside beyond a pile of bulging agricultural sacks and assorted farm tools, hurriedly crossed the expanse of ankle-length wet grass to the other cottage, and with relief at seeing a key waiting invitingly in the door that positively sang 'open me, open me', stepped inside and out of the rain.

The Old Light was constructed by Trinity House in 1819 on Beacon Hill, the highest point on the island. Before this time Lundy had been unmarked and had stood as a hazardous obstacle in the middle of one of the country's busiest shipping lanes, accounting for over two hundred wrecks in its waters. One hundred feet tall and built of local granite it is a landmark that can be seen from almost every point on the island. Unfortunately it never proved so visible to the shipping it was meant to be aiding: due to the vagaries of Lundy's weather the island is often mist enshrouded and the guiding light from the summit of the tower was frequently obscured to offshore vessels. A system of firing warning cannons was introduced to supplement the light as a means of notifying ships that they were approaching dangerous waters, until in 1896 work commenced on building two additional lighthouses at either extreme of the island, and the Old Light fell into disuse.

The Atlantic-facing west coast of Lundy is the island at its most wild and rugged, with sea winds having had four thousand miles of unbroken ocean to travel across before tearing down on this, the first land encountered. Inside Old Light Cottage Daniel had removed his dripping anorak and deposited it in a soggy pile on the floor along with his bag, shoes, shirt, trousers and socks, and was now standing in just his underpants, listening to the sound of the wind whistling and howling around on every side. Against the window above the kitchen sink the wind was bellowing, blowing directly in, lashing the rain in a frenzy against the glass pane; wave after wave of pent up furious emotion. Through the window opposite, each gust was visible by the motion of the long grass, bent over and subdued by the barrage of the elements; standing upright only long enough to be beaten down once again. The view north through the end window, looked the most peaceful: a sight of boundless gently sloping moor, short springy grassland and sea and sky beyond, but that direction led away from the village, away from the landing bay and the *Oldenburg*, and away from any comforts of civilisation, and in these conditions it was not a place to be.

Daniel pulled back the bed-covers and sank back onto the firm mattress, grateful to accept the reassuring embrace of the warm blankets, his wet hair leaving damp traces across the pillow, and, pulling the sheets right back over him, blocked out the light, the rain, the wind; blocked out all thoughts.

- - - - - - - - -

'So, what do you think?' David persisted.

'Does it never stop raining in this book?'

'Tomorrow. Briefly.'

David noticed the expression of doubt still clouding his wife's features, and continued, 'What? What else?'

'Don't get me wrong,' Diana answered, her train of thought advancing slightly trepidatory, 'but, you appear slightly younger in your writing than you do in real life. Of course, I'm not trying to suggest that you are old at all. It's just that in this,' she waved the loose sheets, 'you do seem, well, rather young.'

David was not as outraged as she had anticipated. 'What do you expect.' he answered, continuing tongue-in-cheek, 'Here I am with a chance to give myself a place in literary immortality. I'm bound to try to shave a few years off, aren't I? Rather be remembered for the youth you were, than the old man you will become.'

Diana looked at her husband, serious now, 'Do you ever wish you could turn back the clock?'

'Somehow I don't think the dial would turn back far enough.'

Chapter Seven

'I think this bit's out of bounds.'

'No such thing, as far as I'm concerned.' countered Mark with bravado, at the same time swinging one leg into mid-space and easing himself over the side of the cliff edge.

Brad continued to sound cautious. 'Don't be a prat, mate. You know it is. We're not allowed to climb here during the seabird breeding season.'

The answering voice floated up to Brad from some distance below, where his fellow climber had already made the beginnings of a rapid descent down the wall of rock. 'And just when would that be exactly?'

'I don't know *exactly*. I just know that it is now.' Silence from below made Brad continue, 'Are you coming back up, or what?' A further silence brought Brad to the very edge of the vertical precipice to see what had become of his wilful friend. The cliff face sheered away steeply and then cut back in on itself forming a perilous-looking overhang, below which the sea looked steely and wild, frothing in the anticipation of luring a careless climber plummeting into its watery depths. Mark was nowhere in sight, but the rope that anchored him with some degree of safety to the cliff top ran flush across the flat vertical expanse of rock before disappearing somewhere beneath the overhang, indicating that Mark had decided to ignore his companion's warnings and had continued on his descent. Brad was in a quandary. The climb did look exciting, and it would be interesting to see if it was possible to get right down to sea level once the awkward overhang of rock had been surpassed. On the other hand, they had both had quite strict and very specific instructions from the island's conservation warden when they had first arrived as to just where they were allowed to climb and where they were not. The seabird breeding season runs from 1st April to 31st July and during this period many of Lundy's rock faces are off limits to climbers.

'If in doubt, don't.' It was an old maxim that Brad had rigidly stuck to with regard to his climbing - with regard to the rest of his life too, so Mark constantly told him - and he decided today was not a day to disregard his better sense. He sat down on the short grass at the cliff top, crossed his legs, and drew out a bottle of Lucozade from his rucksack. He'd wait for Mark here, where he'd no doubt return with stories of his daring exploits on the rock below and tell of how fantastic it had all been and want to know why hadn't Brad come along. Two days of climbing wasted now. Yesterday because of the non-stop rain, and now today because Mark had gone off on a glory trip of his own.

The sky that yesterday had been full of clouds was today clear and blue and bright, and Brad sipped on his drink and watched the raucous mass of sea-birds, some circling high in the air above him, most battling and squabbling for space on the narrow ledges and crevices of the rock face below. He recognised Guillemots, black-coated and looking like cliff-dwelling penguins, huddled together beneath one great gash in the craggy slopes and, solitary atop the highest point, a Great Black-backed Gull, far larger than the other birds, emitting an occasional throaty cry. The rest were just seagulls to him: Fulmar indistinguishable from Herring Gull; Kittiwake from Arctic Tern. Caught up in his observations, Brad's attention was suddenly taken by a larger movement below, and he was surprised to see first the head and shoulders and then the bright blue of his friend's jacket appear from below the overhang, hands reaching upwards for a secure grip, muscles flexed in order to lever the rest of his body over the dangerous drop and on to the firm rock above. Within seconds he was standing beside Brad on the summit, bent double, panting from his exertions.

'Why back so soon?' enquired Brad, 'Is it not possible to get down all the way?'

Mark ignored the question, took a further couple of seconds to catch his breath and then sat on a tuft next to Brad. He unhitched the small rucksack he was carrying from his shoulders and undoing the drawstrings brought out a torn and dirty red rain-hood.

'Look at this.'

Brad took the object. It was made of a waterproof polyester and looked typical of the kind that would have been zipped on to the top of a kagoul. 'So? What about it?'

'I found it down there.' Mark explained.

His voice was rather high-pitched and shaky and unlike his normal arrogant self-confidence and Brad didn't think this was purely as a result of the strenuous climb. 'What's wrong?'

'It was stuffed in a small hollow. I put my hand in to get a grip on the rock and pulled it out. I thought it was rather strange because it wasn't as though it had just blown off or fallen there accidentally, it had been stuffed in quite deep, as though it had been deliberately hidden. There was this too.'

Mark was searching in his bag again and pulled out the chunky grey metal handle of a Stanley knife. The blade had split off close to the handle and formed a vicious-looking serrated edge. 'It was wrapped inside the hood. There's blood on the handle too.'

'How do you know?'

Mark displayed the brown stains. 'It's what it looks like to me anyway.'

Brad still looked slightly puzzled by his friend's state of anxiety. 'So what's the big deal? It's the kind of thing any climber could have used. If he busted the knife and cut himself he might just have left it there.'

'It's not these things I've brought up that are bothering me. It's what I've left behind down there that we've got problems with.'

Mark told the full story. First to Brad, there and then on the cliff top. Then again to Brad back in their lodgings in the Castle, while they deliberated whether they couldn't perhaps forget the whole thing, or whether they were obliged to report their discovery, and so reveal that they had been breaking island rules by climbing in a restricted zone, and then finally to the island warden, Julie Dee, in her office in the village.

'I'm not absolutely sure.' Mark explained, 'I didn't actually go down to the ledge itself. But it looked like a body to me. Or rather a skeleton.'

'Tell me again, exactly where.' Julie asked.

'It was the south side of Jenny's Cove. You know where there is that large slab of granite jutting out after the short slope, it was down below there, about one hundred feet above sea level, perhaps a bit more. It's quite concealed by other rocks, and not really visible until you are directly above it.'

'And you said on a ledge?'

'Yes. Although it looks as though there may be a cave, or at least a small opening in the rock there too, because I could only just make out a few bones, and if it is a body the rest must be laying inside the entrance.'

'And you are quite sure what you saw? If it is a body, you understand, we'll have to go down and investigate and I don't want to risk anyone on those cliffs unnecessarily. Sheep sometimes fall. It couldn't have been the bones of a sheep you saw?'

'No. It was an arm. The bones of an arm and a hand. I'm pretty convinced. I would have tried to go down myself but for all the birds flapping about. The bloody things were everywhere. Quite a few are nesting on that ledge and they seemed pretty upset about me getting even as close as I did.'

'I think I had better go and have a look myself before I decide if we are going to need to bring in anyone from the mainland. Would you be prepared to climb down again and pinpoint this ledge for me? If it's as concealed as you say it might take me a while to find it on my own.' Julie asked.

Self-confidence now fully restored, Mark was only too happy to lend a masculine helping hand. 'Sure. It's quite a climb down though. Have you much experience?' He could scarcely keep the tone of underlying innuendo from his voice.

Julie looked him squarely in the eye, unsmiling, 'I'll meet you at Jenny's Cove at nine o'clock tomorrow morning, sharp. If you hadn't wasted so much time and had come to me immediately upon discovering this, we could have done something today. But by the time I've got my gear together it will be too late now. Nine o'clock tomorrow.'

Always one for the last word, Mark countered, 'Sharp.'

- - - - - - - - - -

'I don't remember many of these names from the actual case.'

'No, I've changed them to protect the innocent.'

'And the guilty?'

David didn't answer for a moment. Guilt. Was one

really only guilty when the verdict of the 'twelve souls good and true' was announced, or like truth, was it something inseperably tied up with the act of crime itself? Perhaps it depended on the judge. Who do any of us ultimately answer to? God? The man in the white wig with the gavel, who carries the weight of institutional judgement upon his shoulders? Ourselves? Surely then we would all be considered guilty. No, perhaps guilt should remain a hidden thing, an agnostic emotion, which like the rainbow only exists when it is revealed to us. Finally he replied to his wife, 'No, not the guilty.'

Chapter Eight

'It's better than sex for you, isn't it?'

'What is?'

'All this.' The young woman was sitting on the edge of a chaste-narrow single bed. She held up a small book in her left hand.

Her school-teacher colleague looked up from where he sat cross-legged on the floor, where he had been fruitlessly occupied, trying to stuff some bulky woollen clothing into an all-too-small, light-weight back-pack, accompanying his labour with a continual monologue of whispered curses. He finally threw down the thick jumper in annoyance. 'What?' he asked, angrily.

'This.' She begun to flick through the pages of the book. 'This really turns you on doesn't it?' She started calling out names at random from the pages before her. 'Goldcrest. Chiffchaff. Wheatear.'

Her colleague had caught on by now to the teasing and, his humour restored, was simulating sighs and groans of mounting ecstasy at each fresh announcement on the roll-call of bird names.

'Blackcap.' Her tongue rolled sensually around the different syllables, prolonging the enjoyment.

'Ummm.'

Great Spotted Wood - pecker.'

'Yes.'

'Little Bunting.'

'Not Little Bunting. Oh, yes. That's good.'

'Redstart.'

'Ummm.'

'Deep throat.'

'Eh?'

'Oh, sorry. Whitethroat. Rather different I suppose.'

'Just a bit. What about a goose? Can't you give me a goose?'

'Will a tit do instead? I can give you a tit'

'Great or Blue?.'

'Both, it's so cold in this hut. I could give you Thrush too.'

'I think I might be better off without that.'
'Let's settle for a Shag then.'
'Sounds good.'
'How about a Woodcock?'
'Ummm.'
'Diver.'
'Ahhh.'
'Wagtail.'
'Ungh.'
'Swallow.'
'Yes.'
'Nutcracker.'
'Painful.'
'Booby'
'Ummm'
'Horn - bill.'
'Enough, enough.'
'Was that good for you?'
'Let me tell you something. Seriously. Imagine the best sex you ever had in your life, multiple it by a thousand times, and that is a Little Auk.'

The young woman laughed and then shuddered exaggeratedly, 'Ugh. Too much information. You're disgusting. I've had enough of your pornographic reading material.' She threw the book back down on top of the bed-clothes. Only then did she seem to understand the implication of the back-pack lying on the floor. 'What are you doing anyway, packing up? Where do you think you're going at this time of night?'

'Night? Listen to yourself, it's not even dark out yet. You'd think you'd been on the island a month to hear you, rather than just one day.'

'So where are you going?'

'Out. Just, out.'

'And what about me?' she asked rather pitifully.

Her colleague shrugged, 'What about you. Someone's got to stay in and keep an eye on all those brats.'

'Coming down the pub?'

'You ask as though there were another option.' James

sat moodily on his bed.

Martin groaned inwardly at his friend's negative response, but tried to keep his own feelings from showing in his voice. 'Come on, mate.' he continued enthusiastically, 'It'll be a laugh.'

'Oh, yes. For who?'

Martin sat down on the bed next to James. He adopted his most sympathetic doctor-patient tones, 'Hey, it's early days. You ...'

'Early days!' James exploded. 'It's been almost a year.'

'No.' Martin jumped in again, trying to correct the misunderstanding, 'I mean since we arrived on the island. Give it a bit longer. The change will do you good. Take your mind of things.'

James was not to be persuaded so easily, 'Huh.' he grunted, unconvinced.

'No, really. The fresh air. The beautiful scenery. Come on, you've got to admit it's better than being back in the 'burbs.'

'Wouldn't be difficult.'

Martin changed tack. 'Teresa seems to be enjoying herself.'

James looked slightly more interested, 'Yes, what has she been doing today? I haven't seen her since first thing.'

'Me neither. I told her to meet up with us in the Marisco later though. She'll probably be in there now.' He tried again, 'Come on, I'll buy you a beer.'

'You know I don't drink.'

'Well, an orange juice then.' Martin couldn't help the frustration creeping through. He unwisely added some homespun words of advise, 'You've got to put all this behind you, you know. You said yourself, it's been a year now. That's too long to still be lost in this depression of self-pity. It's time you faced facts ...'

'Facts! I don't even know the facts. That's what's so depressing.' James turned away and theatrically threw himself down on to the bedclothes, hiding his head in his hands, trying to block out the world, like an ostrich burying its head in the sand. Martin remained motionless beside him; his silence half full of anger, half full of helplessness. Eventually James emerged from his melodramatics, and looking up, embarrassed that his friend had witnessed his outburst, said in conciliatory tones, 'You go on ahead. I just want to potter around the room for a while. Tidy up. You know what I'm like. I'll see you down the Marisco later.'

Martin looked uneasily at his friend, trying to judge his mood, but then decided the sensible course of action was to go along with his wishes. 'OK.' he said, 'But don't be too long. The offer of a drink doesn't stand all night.'

The first stars were just beginning to show bright against the darkening sky. Donald remembered as a kid how he would lay outside and try to count them, restarting time and time again, as the sky turned blacker and more and more twinkling lights appeared where previously there had been none. He had thought back then that the night-time was the window on to the universe, when the most distant galaxies became visible, when the stars revealed their secrets, and when truth itself emerged from behind the day-time lies that so often sought to conceal it. Now as an old man, he was glad to be no longer troubled by such romantic fallacies. That didn't stop him from still loving the night-time though. Perhaps his thoughts might still be considered romantic but they were now grounded in the more practical aspects of the hours of darkness. He enjoyed the peace. The black cloak that he had once thought was drawn back in revelation, he now enjoyed for exactly the opposite reason - it's power to hide and conceal. It enveloped the immediate so entirely, so conscientiously, not letting any light escape its embrace. It wrapped around the ugliness of reality, replacing it with an imaginary perfection. Most of all, it wrapped around him, making him invisible to walk around his perfect imaginary world, protecting him from the harsh memories of a day-time world, memories which had once been childhood dreams, turned to adult regrets. Darkness might now be a cure. Wasted time was the disease.

He enjoyed the quiet. This quiet particularly. The roll of the distant waves, their moonlit white crests often the only movement visible against the great black backdrop of the sea. The hushed dormitory sound of sheep conversations, as a fearful bleat is answered by an invisible, reassuring baa. The silence of the sky, almost oppressive in its stubborn resistance to make a sound. He enjoyed the secrecy too. Perhaps this was a throwback to youth, but the night still had the power to thrill him; to fill him full of guilty thoughts; to make him tingle at the potential for unobserved actions. The daytime elderly Stoic would not have recognised its lunar-phase counterpart, when like a geriatric super-hero, the physical shackles of advancing age could be mentally cast aside, and the imagination of youth was allowed free reign once again.

One shadow was not imagination though. Instinctively Donald knew it was a person. From his position atop the Old Light tower he was looking down on someone standing motionless in the deepening shadows beside the wall of the enclosure below. Life must emit its own unique signal, distinct and recognisable even on occasion when the five senses might suggest otherwise. Donald remembered a recent visit he had made to London: it had been late at night and he had been walking on the pavement alongside Coram's Fields, separated from that small inner city farm by a line of high, pointed railings, and beyond, a flat-roofed stable-block. He had thought it was a black bin bag full of leaves at first, peculiarly positioned though, half-straddled over one corner of the low flat roof. Despite the surrounding illumination of street-lamps and lights from the windows of students burning the midnight oil in their square-block university accommodation opposite, the particular object that caught Donald's eye had been surrounded by almost impenetrable blackness. And yet he knew somehow that it was alive. It wasn't a bag of leaves, there was a presence about it, an aura that kept him looking; a fascination to decipher the lines and contours of the shapeless mass and give them form and name. It shuddered: not at the mercy of the wind, but by its own volition, and Donald knew that he was not mistaken, but it was not until the peacock, its own sixth sense no doubt stirred by the presence of another life-form, moved and raised its tiny, crowned head, that Donald was properly able to identify the trailing plume of feathers for what it actually was.

He looked back to the shadow on the wall below him, but it had gone.

- - - - - - - - - -

'So was that the sex scene? You build up all this hype, for what? A few birds' names told in a sexy voice.'

David tried to interrupt, 'No ...'

'False pretences, that was it is. You get me to leave *Anna Karenina* for the promise of some titillation. And what do I get?'

'No ...'

'A damp squib.'

David ceased trying to explain. He mumbled under his breath, 'Yes, darling. I went for an accurate depiction.'

Chapter Nine

Mark let the rope run smoothly between his gloved hands and lowered himself downwards. On the comparatively gentle incline of the higher slopes he was able to keep his feet pressed firmly against the rock wall and, arching his back to take the strain of his weight on the rope, walk backwards down the cliff face. He knew now, from his first experience on this descent, that he wouldn't have to resort to scrambling around for hand and foot holds until he came to the difficult overhang, still quite some feet below him. He tried to clear his mind of the argument he had had with Brad earlier that evening, after they had left Julie's office, and when Mark had told him that he intended to ignore the warden's advice and embark on another descent of the cliff face that evening.

'She may not be ready until later, but I've still got all my gear set from before. I'd be down and back before dusk. Are you coming?'

Brad, already exasperated by his friend's cavalier attitude earlier that day, snapped back, 'You must be fucking joking? You heard what she said in there. This is a serious business. What do you think you can do if you do go down anyway? Use your brains.'

'I can make absolutely sure it was a body I saw.'

'You already said you were sure.'

'I am.' said Mark. 'But she isn't. You heard what she said, silly cow. "I don't want to risk anyone unnecessarily". Herself included, by the sounds of it. Well if I go down again and bring her some evidence she won't have to worry.'

'Leave it. We've wasted enough time as far as I'm concerned today.' Brad continued more soothingly, trying to extend a hand of peace which his friend could accept and still be able to back down with honour in place. 'Come on, let's go to the Tavern, and I'll buy you a beer. Set you up for tomorrow morning. Nine o'clock. Sharp.' he joked.

Mark's mind was already made up though. 'You go to the pub if you want to. I'm making that climb tonight with or without you.'

Brad's farewell remark of 'Fuck off then' were the words that still sounded in Mark's head as he played more rope through his grasp and descended lower. That and the snooty warden's tone of voice: who did she think she was, treating him as though he were just a schoolboy.

A shower of loose scree and small pebbles dislodged from somewhere above him and a tiny, but sharp, stone struck him painfully in the face. Mark wound the anchoring rope, once, twice around his right arm, leaned further backwards so that his feet were flat to the cliff, and pulled it taunt with one hand. One arm now free he pulled off his glove using his teeth and ran a finger across his cheek. Examining it he saw a trace of red blood that had been drawn from the cut. He cursed, sucked the blood off his finger and was preparing to put his glove back on, when a movement from the cliff top caught his eye. It was already beginning to get slightly dark but Mark was sure it had been the head and shoulders of a person peering over the precipice, only to jerk back out of sight again as he looked up.

'Brad is that you?' he called. 'Brad.'

Silence from above, except for another small spray of soil and stones. Mark though was still not convinced that there wasn't someone above. He called again.

'Careful up there, will you. You're dislodging all kinds of stuff. Hey! Hey, what are you doing?'

The rope that Mark had wrapped around his arm was suddenly wrenched violently upwards, causing him to lose his footing on the vertical rock face and crash into it face first with a sickening impact. He dangled momentarily on the life-saving rope which was still secured at the summit, hanging limp like a puppet that has had its strings cut, before his head cleared slightly and he instinctively started searching around for crevices in which to secure a grip for his hands and feet. His nose had struck the hard rock wall first, before he had had a chance to put out a hand to prevent the collision, and the whole of one side of his face throbbed from where it had struck the rough surface, and was feeling grazed and stinging. He could sense that blood was pouring from his nose and down into his mouth and over his chin; it tasted thick and salty seeping over his lips and on his tongue.

Mark managed to regain some kind of balance again, both feet stuck firmly into fissures in the cliff's pitted surface, one hand grasping securely a pommel-like knobbly outcrop, and shook his head, trying to clear some of the sense of dizziness. He looked up and now clearly saw a figure standing silhouetted on the top of the craggy incline.

'You fucking idiot. What do you think you're playing at?' Mark shouted. 'You could have killed me.' He saw the figure on the summit was still holding on to the anchoring end of his climbing rope and continued, 'Give me a hand. I may need a pull to get me back up again.' And not receiving any reply from above, continued, 'Are you going to help me, or what?'

His answer came in the sound of a rushing noise, as, too late, Mark realised that the person on the cliff top, far from intending to help him, had actually detached his mooring rope and had now let it drop over the edge, so that coil by fatal coil it was falling past him and plummeting into the void beneath the deadly overhang of granite. There was no time for him to unclip the rope from where it was joined to his belt, and Mark knew that it was only a matter of seconds before himself, and the tenuous grip he had on the rock wall, would be the only things that were preventing the heavy weight of rope from completing the descent to which gravity compelled it. The very thing that only moments before had been his lifesaver, now looked likely to be the instrument of his death. He braced himself as best he could to try and absorb some of the impending impact and began to count.

'One.'   Ten feet of rope.
'Two.'   Twenty feet of rope.
'Three.'   Thirty feet of rope.
'Four ...'

'... and out.'   Daniel placed down on the table-top three Jacks, a straight of six, seven and eight of Clubs, and laid his final four of Diamonds on one of his playing companion's runs.

'You're too good for me.'
'Luck.' said Daniel. 'Just luck.'
'I've been left with two Queens.'
The third player at the table laughed and said in a theatrically camp voice, 'What could be more appropriate for you, Raoul?'

Daniel smiled weakly. He had suffered three quarters of an hour of the two men's back and forth banter, and was beginning to feel like the straight man caught between two comedians who were fine-tuning their routines. The straight man caught between something anyway.

Raoul's colleague in mirth rose to his feet. 'Can I get anyone something else to drink?' He pointed to Daniel's glass and laughed. 'Looks like you could do with filling up.'

Daniel put his hands up in mock defence. 'No. No, really, Eric. This round's on me. What are you both having?'

'Oh well, if you insist. I'll have a short one.'

Daniel jumped in before Raoul had a chance to say a word, 'And the same again for you Raoul? A pint?'

The Marisco Tavern was getting busier. Daniel had arrived at seven that evening and had been able to enjoy a refreshing pint of Old Light Bitter and the last helping of skate wings in mushroom sauce in relative peace, sitting up, on his own, at one of the tables on the balcony that overlooked the main room of the pub. He had been cornered by Eric and Raoul as he had come downstairs to get himself another drink, and despite initially welcoming the chance of conversation and the friendly offer to join them in a game of rummy, he was now glad of a brief respite. He recognised several faces in the bar from his day around the island, and he smiled and gave a nod of acknowledgement to the attractive young woman who had lent him her handkerchief on the boat, and who was now sitting on her own in a dark corner of the room, a glass of orange juice and a half-consumed pint of beer sitting on the table in front of her.

A local man - one of the construction workers by the look of his clothes - made space for him at the small counter that passed as the bar, and Daniel gave his order.

'Two pints please. And a whisky.'

'Famous Grouse?' queried the barmaid.

'Yes, I'm sure that's fine.' Daniel half-turned to see if Eric was likely to have any opinion as to which brand he preferred, but the tall man was so enthusiastically recounting a story to his friend that Daniel decided not to interrupt him. 'Yes, Grouse please.'

A voice at his shoulder broke in, 'Can you get me a

half while you're at it too?'

Daniel recognised Lex from the previous day, although this evening she had her hair secured up with a silky green scarf, tied bandana-style above her head, and she was wearing dark eye-shadow and thick mascara which served to only further accentuate her piercing eyes. She smiled as he turned to her and handed him a pile of loose change, 'I think that's the right amount.'

Daniel waved the money away, 'That's all right. Let me. Is your friend with you? Can I get her anything too?'

Lex looked about vaguely and waved a dismissive hand, saying, 'No, don't worry about Sonya. She's around here somewhere, but she's not much of a drinker. Have you had a good day?'

'Yes, fine, thanks. It makes all the difference when the sun shines doesn't it?'

'Doesn't it just. Have you been exploring?'

'Yes,' said Daniel, 'I got up quite early and walked along the west coast as far as the Old Battery.'

'That's not very far.'

'No. But I kept on getting diverted by things and it seemed to take quite a while. There is a little brook, just running over the short grass and down and over the cliff edge, quite close to where I'm staying, and I stopped and watched a bird hopping around on a rock beside that for ages. It looked a bit like a Blackbird but it had a broad white band across its chest. I don't know what it was.'

'Ring Ouzel.'

Daniel and Lex both looked around at the interruption.

'Sorry, didn't mean to listen in. But it was probably a Ring Ouzel.'

The newcomer was a middle-aged man, short and rather stocky, standing with his feet placed wide apart and his hands plunged deep inside his trouser pockets. He rocked back and forwards slightly on his heels and his fingers fidgeted around in a nervous fashion making the fabric of his trousers agitate. He continued, 'Not uncommon, I'm afraid.' And then apologised in a good-hearted fashion, 'Sorry, I'm sounding like a bore. And that's just what I'm trying to escape from.' He gave a nod of his head to a table by the window, on which sat two women, and an elderly man, who Daniel instantly recognised as his tormentor from the boat crossing.

Daniel asked, 'Is one of those two Deidre?'

The man looked across, 'Yes, the one on the left, with her ears pinned back. The chap doing all the talking is her husband Timothy.' He turned back to Daniel and Lex, 'Sorry, I've not introduced myself.' He pulled one hand out from the cavernous depths of his pocket and shook both of theirs, 'Reg.'

While Daniel took the drinks over to Raoul and Eric who were still engaged in such an animated discussion that they barely registered his approach, let alone his hasty departure again, Lex asked Reg about his party.

'Is the other lady your wife?'

'Yes, Margaret. We're staying in Bramble Villas.'

'What, that big colonial style building down by the cliff path?'

'That's right.'

'The views must be wonderful from there.' said Lex.

'Unfortunately, Timothy and Deidre bagged Bramble Villa East before us, and that has the nicest views out over the sea. We're in the west one. It is still lovely, though, yes, and the veranda out the front is really nice. I've been sitting out there all day long today.'

Daniel joined them again. 'It has been a marvellous day, hasn't it. So different from yesterday. I really just wanted to turn the boat around and head straight back to the mainland what with all that rain coming down.'

'Is it your first time on the island?' Reg asked.

'Yes. How about you?'

'My first. But Timothy and Deidre have been here before. Timothy is an amateur insectologist. I think that's the word for it. Anyhow he studies all kinds of creeping crawling things. Apparently there are some peculiar little bugs on Lundy which don't turn up anywhere else on the planet. He gets quite excited about them. God knows why. I've seen some of the little beasties trapped in one of his specimen jars and they just look like ordinary fleas to me. He doesn't stop talking about them, though. That's why I hope you don't mind me coming over here to escape. Look at him now.'

They all watched the seated figure: mouth constantly moving, finger wagging, arms waving to empathise a point, completely oblivious to the stifled yawns and glazed expressions of his trapped audience of two.

Lex turned to Reg sympathetically, 'You poor man. Stay as long as you like.' And then changing the subject. 'So how did you recognise the Ring Ouzel? Are you an ornithologist?'

'An amateur one.' Reg then hastened to reassure his two new friends, 'Not like him, I promise you. I won't bang on and on about birds. I just find it interesting to be able to identify what it is I'm seeing, and here on Lundy there are so many unusual species. It's the only reason I agreed to come.'

'Any good sightings today?'

'Yes, the most satisfying was Timothy slipping on some damp grass outside the village shop and landing on his arse.'

- - - - - - - - - - - -

'Did most of your investigating in the pub, did you?' asked Diana scornfully.

'A good detective must follows his leads wherever they will take him.' answered her husband with a sly smile.

'Really?'

Chapter Ten

Brad was getting drunk - quickly and successfully. He was returning to his seat, carrying his sixth pint of Woodpecker cider of the evening, when he almost stumbled into Martin and James who had just entered the Tavern and were standing by the bar trying to locate Teresa among the ever expanding gathering of drinkers.

'Watch out, can't you.' said James, taking a step backwards to avoid the other man's lumbering passage.

Brad looked up, his eyes already unfocussed and fogged, his brow slightly furrowed with surprise at the encounter. 'I'm sorry?' It was spoken half as apology, half as questioning challenge, and James looked all set to rise to the bait, before Martin took him by the elbow and directed him towards where Teresa was sitting.

'There she is.'

Teresa was still sipping from her glass of orange juice, tucked back almost out of sight in a corner of the room made gloomy by the overhang of the first floor balcony above. On one side of her were the stairs leading up and next to them a long thin table on which people had casually thrown their rucksacks and jackets upon entering; on her other side was a fireplace, cold, blackened, and unused during the supposed summer heat. She sat at a tiny circular wooden table, around which hers was the only chair.

'What are you doing here?' James asked.

Large, slightly vacant eyes turned to him, 'Pardon?'

James continued, 'It's not the most inviting corner, is it? You could have saved us a couple of chairs too.'

'I'm sorry. I didn't think.'

While Martin deposited his rucksack underneath the table, James pounced on a wooden stool and a bulky leather-backed chair that had just been vacated by two local villagers, and with a cursory 'Don't mind if I take these?' dragged them across to the small table in the corner.

'Here we go.' said James, selfishly settling back into the comfort of the large armchair, and then to Martin, 'Right, I've got the chairs, your turn for the drinks. I'll have a tomato juice and it looks as though Terri is still OK with her orange. Whose pint is this?' he enquired holding the glass up for inspection as though it were an unsavoury medical specimen.

Martin answered, 'It was mine from earlier. I popped in briefly. It looks a bit flat now.'

'Do they have crisps?' the young woman enquired of James.

The still standing Martin addressed her, 'I expect so, I'll find out.' and turned and went to the bar.

'Are you having a good day?' James asked his sister.

Terri took another sip from her glass before replying, 'Yes, I like it here.'

'And you're OK about sleeping in the lounge? We didn't disturb you going out this morning? It's just that it's awkward otherwise. I mean you couldn't very well share with Martin, and although I'm sure Martin wouldn't mind having that bed and you and me sharing, it seems more convenient this way round.'

'No, it's fine.' Teresa answered. 'I rather like it. I woke up this morning and was able to look straight out to the sea, it was lovely. What time did you get up?'

'Early.'

'Very early,' emphasised Martin who had just returned holding two drinks, and clasping two packets of crisps clenched between his arm and his side. 'Hope salt and vinegar is OK. They haven't got very much choice.'

'Terri's just been telling me about her day.' James explained to his friend. 'She's...' He broke off to turn around and look as a loud clatter of chairs from the other side of the room took his attention. 'It's that clumsy prat again.'

Brad had joined Raoul and Eric and had unwittingly taken on the role of stooge so recently vacated by Daniel. The three men were holding forth in loud and - in Brad's case - drunken voices, and it was in trying to further emphasise a particular point that Brad had stood up and overturned his chair, setting all three of them off again in gales of uproarious laughter.

'Can't hold your drink?' jeered Eric good-humouredly.

'I could give you something to hold.' said Raoul bawdily, setting off another fit of merriment.

Brad righted his seat and now sitting astride it, his head resting on his folded arms across the chair back, tried to regain his composure and resume the conversation they had been having. 'What was it you were saying about the lad?' he asked, his alcohol-blurred mind struggling to remember just exactly what they had been talking about.

'Mollycoddled.' said Raoul.

'How so?' asked Brad.

It was Eric that took up the story, 'It's that mother of his. I feel sorry for the little chap. All this lovely open countryside to run around and play in, and she doesn't let him out of her sight. I saw them today watching the seals by the North Light. Poor little chap. He looked so miserable. She's never an inch from his side. Clucking around him like a mother hen.'

'What's his name?'

'Graham. I've heard her calling him in the morning. And she is Liz. She did say hello and introduce herself I'll give her that. Their tent is quite close to ours.' said Eric.

'Are you in that field by the Quarters?' asked Brad.

'Yes, we're campers, don't you know.' said Raoul, and laughed at the joke that he had recounted so often now it had become something of a catch-phrase for him.

Brad smiled broadly, if rather bemusedly, at the other man's humour and glanced from one to the other of his adopted drinking companions, before saying, 'I think I must have passed your tents this morning as I was going to Jenny's Cove. There are three tents aren't there?'

'Yes,' said Eric. 'A peculiar couple of chaps in the other one.'

'Not funny peculiar.' said Raoul.

'Oh, no, not funny peculiar.' continued Eric, 'Very surly they are. Ornithological types. Up with the lark, every morning and off out with their binoculars.'

'Well you know what they say about the early bird ...' Raoul was not allowed to continue with his pun.

'Do you know I bumped into one of them in the shower block this evening. "Spotted anything good." I asked. Not a word of response. Didn't even look me in the face. Eyes to the ground. Very surly. Wouldn't let me borrow any shampoo either.'

'We're not bothering with them anymore, are we Eric?' said Raoul.

'No, take as you find, I say.'

'I don't think I've seen them around,' said Brad. 'They're not in here tonight?'

'Oh, no.' Raoul sucked in air between his teeth with an exaggerated gasp, 'I'm sure they'll already have their heads down.'

'Early to bed, early to rise.'

'I'll give you something to rise.' laughed Raoul, looking around his audience for signs of appreciation, and striking his hand on the tabletop to indicate his amusement; every inch a parody of the music-hall performer slapping his thigh.

Trying to reclaim centre-stage, Eric, lowering his voice, continued recounting his own brand of island gossip. 'Have you heard what they're saying about the chap up at ... what's-it-called. That place way up top.'

'Admiralty Lookout,' supplied Brad.

'That's it. Killed his wife so they say.'

'No.' For once Raoul was all attention.

'Arrived together a week ago. And she's not been seen since.'

'So?' Raoul sounded disappointed that there wasn't more conclusive evidence to support the previous claim. 'That doesn't prove anything.'

Eric continued, 'I'm not saying it does. I'm just saying what they're saying.'

Raoul made an expressive gesture to show what he thought of the story, and a dismissive Mediterranean 'Pfff. A canard.' Adding, with instantly restored good humour, 'My little duckie, Eric.'

'Having a good time?' The new voice was female and belonged to the Warden, Julie, who had just entered the bar, and had now put a friendly - if bestilling - arm around the shoulders of the seated Raoul. 'It's not often the visitors are more rowdy than the locals.' she joked.

Raoul looked up, his face still flushed with high spirits, 'Julie. Julie, my love. What larks! Won't you join us in a drink?'

'Thank you, another time perhaps.' She took a couple of steps back. 'I'm actually looking for Tom. Has he been in tonight?'

'Tom?' questioned Eric.

'I thought I saw you chatting to him yesterday. Isla's husband. From the shop.'

'Oh, Tom. I didn't realise that was his name. Yes.' Eric turned to Raoul to ask, 'Have you seen Tom today? I'm pretty sure he's not been in the Marisco this evening. Not with us anyhow.'

'No matter,' said Julie, 'I just needed to borrow something off him. I'm sure I can catch him in the morning.'

Eric continued, 'Not anything we can help with?'

'Not unless you've got several hundred feet of rope stored away in that little tent of yours,' smiled Julie, and then seeing the looks of incomprehension of the faces of the three men, thought she had better explain by saying, 'Just a climb I've got to make tomorrow. Make sure that mate of yours is up good and early.' she finished by addressing Brad alone.

'You be careful.' said Eric fatherly, as the woman made to leave.

Julie laughed again, 'I could say the same about you three. Don't drink too much. Goodnight.'

With Julie's departure the group fell quiet, until Raoul suspecting that the earlier atmosphere of easy merriment would not be recaptured that evening, pushed back his seat and got up, saying, 'I reckon I'm all done. You coming, Eric?'

The older man rose too, slapping Brad across the back as the pair prepared to go, 'Hear what the good woman said, Brad my lad. Don't drink too much. See you tomorrow.'

Brad watched the couple walk across to the door. Eric had his arm around the shoulders of his younger friend, who was once again animated and chattering away freely, his hands moving expansively. Raoul made a gesture, mimicking the movement of a pint glass being lifted to the mouth, they both laughed loudly and looked back briefly in Brad's direction, before the door closed behind them and both men were lost to the night.

Daniel was observing their departure also, 'Phew, looks

like I'm safe. I was dreading them collaring me again. I can only take that pair's humour in small doses.'

The numbers in the pub had thinned out quite noticeably and certainly the noise level had decreased significantly with the departure of the two comedians. Daniel was still talking to Lex and Reg and they had managed to secure for themselves a table by the window, upon the departure of the group comprising Reg's two travelling companions and wife. 'See you a bit later, love,' had been Reg's rather too obviously gleeful send-off.

'So, tell me,' asked Lex, 'What is the great attraction of bird-watching?'

Reg smiled. 'I think perhaps it is rather obsessional. My wife would say so, I know.'

'I've heard of a golf widow, or an angling widow, but is there a birding variety too?' asked Daniel.

'Oh, yes,' continued Reg jokingly, 'And I can scarcely believe that you would lump the noble craft of ornithology with those other two base activities. I mean golf.' He spat out the final word, as though it were a lemon, 'It's just an excuse to don tweed trousers, tasselled shoes and white gloves, and cut great swathes through the countryside in the name of sport. You show me a golfer, and I will show you a sartorially challenged eco-vandal.' Reg continued talking, ever more confidently, seeing the amused appreciation of his two new friends to this impassioned oratory. 'They even have the affrontory to crib birding terms for their peculiar practices. One under par. What do they call it?' He glanced from Daniel to Lex, but then answered his own question before either of them had a chance to respond, 'A birdie. Ridiculous. Two under? An eagle. And most ludicrous, but perhaps thankfully less common, three under par? An albatross. An outrageous liberty with language. And then fishing. What's that all about? Rain or shine. Row upon row of them in their multi-pocketed macs, lined up by the grubbiest sewer of a canal-side, choked full of shopping trolleys and old tyres, waiting. For what? Their rods held out lifeless. Their lines drifting aimless and uncontrolled. Tin of maggots and a box of fancy hooks and bits. Thermos of tea and something nondescript wrapped in kitchen foil. Just waiting. Now that's obsessional.'

'And bird-watching?' Lex prompted again.

Reg looked skywards, putting on the far-away, dreamy expression of the devoted, 'A sport of kings.'

'How so?'

'Did you know that birds can trace their ancestry back to the dinosaurs? Modern day descendants of the most magnificent creatures that ever walked this planet. That's how so. They can tell by the bones. Amazing really. Hollow bones, that's the key. Such a proud and historic lineage. To think, that seemingly insignificant sparrow that you see, nervously pecking at the grass in your back garden every morning, can trace it's ancestry back to the Brontosaurus. Or the Tyrannosaurus Rex. A king. There's royalty for you. How many people could claim such nobility? Not you, I'd guess. Nor me. Nor my Margaret, that's for sure.'

The thought of his wife made Reg break off in mid-speech. He had a sudden pang of guilt about having deserted her so precipitously earlier to a continued evening of boredom at the hands of the verbose Timothy.

'I'm sorry, I get carried away. I think that it is time that I left you two good people, and found out what has become of my wife.' said Reg, standing. 'You've suffered plenty long enough from my ear-bashing. Perhaps I'll see you both in here tomorrow tonight?'

'Yes, that'd be nice,' answered Lex. 'I think I owe you a drink, as well. What plans have you got for tomorrow?'

'I think that will rather depend on the weather. I suppose no one's heard the forecast?'

Daniel replied, 'I was stupid and didn't bring my radio with me, but I saw someone looking at the barometer earlier this evening and they looked quite happy, so I guess it may be fine again.'

'Sounds promising.'

There was another sudden loud crash, which caused the three of them to look around to discover that Brad was once again the cause, as he had slumped sideways off his chair and was now struggling, rather unceremoniously, to get back to his feet. Reg decided to play Good Samaritan, saying to Daniel and Lex as a parting shot. 'I think I had better take this lad in hand. Make sure he finds his way back to wherever he's staying tonight. It's pretty dark outside now and I can just imagine him stumbling off through the farmyard at night and leaving all the gates open, or worse taking a wrong turn over a one-way cliff. Sleep well you two.'

Reg offered Brad a steadying hand and Daniel and Lex watched the stubby little man and the drunken giant wend a precarious, wavering route around the obstacle course of stools, chairs and tables, and then followed their progress as best they could for some minutes, as they passed across the grass outside the window and down the incline, before the darkness finally swallowed them up.

Lex was the first to speak, 'He was very nice. I think that he thought that we were a couple.'

'Really? What makes you say that?'

Lex continued, 'I don't know. I suppose it would be natural to assume it though, wouldn't it?' She cocked her head to one side, looking at Daniel in the same way that a thrush does, when it is contemplating its first worm of the day, 'After all, we have been sitting quite close together all evening. Don't you think we make a good couple?'

'I hadn't really thought about it.'

They sat in silence for some moments, before Daniel asked, 'Whatever became of your friend?'

'Sonya?' Lex turned away from the scene of the now empty pub to face Daniel squarely, pursing her lips and moistening the top one unconsciously with the very tip of her pink tongue. Her eyes held him with a basilisk-like intensity and the corners of her mouth turned up in a mischievous smile, 'I don't know. She's around here somewhere.'

- - - - - - - - -

'Is there anything you haven't told me about your trip to Lundy?' enquired Diana, suspiciously.

'Such as?' hedged David.

'Such as a young woman called Lex?'

'Pure fantasy, I promise.' her husband tried to reassure her, 'I couldn't have a story without a love interest, could I?'

'Did you have to take the part of the romantic lead,

though?'
      'There was no one else fit for the role.'
      'Hmmm.'

Chapter Eleven

'I've got seven Razorbills on the short ledge, just above and a little to the left of the rock shaped like a flat iron.'

'Eight, I think.'

'Yes, eight.'

'And a nesting Fulmar a little further along to the left.'

'Where?' Oliver scanned across the expanse of bare rock with his powerful binoculars, constantly twiddling with the central adjustment dial to maintain the focus and keep the picture he was seeing sharp.

'Tucked quite far back in that dark crevice where the big slab juts out.' described Leo, not moving his eyes from the sight.

'No, I've still not got it. How far along from the Razorbills?'

Leo took his fellow-spotter through an inch by inch description, panning along with his own binoculars as he called out, 'OK, have you got the Razorbill at the far left hand end, the one that's slightly separate from the main group?'

'Yup, got him.'

'OK, go up, just a fraction. You see where there's that little patch of green on the rock.'

'Yes, got that.'

'Left about twenty feet from there you've got a huge great flat slab of granite.'

'Which one?'

'The one that's splashed white from the gulls above. No, you've gone too far. Come back towards the Razorbills a bit.'

'Oh yes, got it.'

'Just below ...'

'Yes. Yes, I've got it. It is hidden a long way back. I don't know how you managed to spot it. Can you see any chicks?'

'No, not so far, ' said Leo. 'Although it's hard to tell if she might not have any underneath her.'

'Unusual looking bird, aren't they. Quite different from the other gulls.' Oliver looked up from his binoculars and continued 'Did I ever tell you about their projectile vomit?'

Leo groaned loudly, but lowered his binoculars also and turned to his companion with an expression of good-humoured weariness, 'Only one million times. But tell me again.'

'The female Fulmars are very protective of their nests and chicks, and it is how they fend off potential aggressors. Anything coming within six feet of their nests gets showered in foul-stenching projectile vomit. Very effective. I knew of a rock-climber once who disturbed a Fulmar's nest during the breeding season who...'

'I know. I know,' complained Leo, 'You've told me before. He couldn't get rid of the smell from his clothing for months and in the end had to burn them.'

'Well, throw them away. I don't know about burning.' corrected Oliver. 'Hang on, what's happening there?'

It was still early morning, but true to Eric's observation of the night before, the two avid bird-watchers had risen 'with the lark' and had set off early with their binoculars, notebooks, and a flask of hot coffee, to take up a position overlooking the nesting cliffs of Jenny's Cove on the west side of the island.

It had been cold first thing, although the clear skies carried the promise of a fine day ahead. The grass in the camping field was long and uncut and wet from the early morning dew, and the bottom of both men's jeans were quickly stained dark with the cold dampness as they brushed through the verdant tangle. The west field was now full of sheep, all freshly-shorn: some noisily munching on the rich feast of untouched grass, looking up only long enough to reassure themselves that these strange intruders meant no harm, before head down once again, returning to their repast; others, more wary, standing their ground only so long, ever watchful of the strangers' determined approach, before discretion getting the better of valour, puts them to a panicky, splay-footed flight; others still, slept on, dreaming sheep-dreams, oblivious to the two men's passage. Once over the stile, the pair took a wide circuit away from the Old Light enclosure, where four horses stood, nodding their heads up and down as though in universal agreement, white air spiralling upwards from their nostrils in noisy blasts, and instead followed the path that ran along the very top of the west cliff, following it around past the slightly crumbled stones of the Quarter Wall, momentarily cutting back inland at the point of the old earthquake, down the grassy slope and over the muddy stepping stones that ford the stream at Punchbowl Valley, before once again emerging at the cliffs and their objective, Jenny's Cove.

Both young men climbed over the rather more solid obstacle of the Halfway Wall and settled down on a gentle grassy incline, in the shelter of two huge granite boulders, with an unobstructed view across to the severe-looking rock faces on the south side of the cove, which provide safe home to a large number of the island's seabird colonies.

Leo sat with his long legs stretched out in front of him, leaning his back against the hard rock of one of the boulders, his elbows dug tight into his sides to provide support as he held his large binoculars unshakably firm up to his eyes. Oliver favoured lying on his stomach, right up at the cliff edge, his elbows forming the lower points of a triangle, of which the lightweight binoculars he held clasped to his face were the pinnacle. It was in this position that he first noticed Julie.

'Isn't that the conservation warden?' he asked Leo.

They both watched as Julie slung the large rucksack she was carrying off from her shoulders and began to unpack an array of climbing equipment. She kept glancing at her watch as she first made fast her ropes to the cliff top, then checked and rechecked her metal clips and fastenings, and finally stripped off her bulky woollen jumper to replace it with a lightweight showerproof jacket, which billowed out like a balloon in the morning breeze, before Julie zipped it up tight to her neck. She looked at her watch once again, then stood with her hands on her hips, facing away from the sea and looking back in the direction of the village.

'Must be waiting for someone.' said Oliver. 'What do you think?'

Receiving no reply he looked over his shoulder, to discover that Leo's attention was no longer focussed on the slender figure on the opposite cliff summit, but instead he had his binoculars back up to his face, pressed hard up against his eyes, and was staring directly out to sea. After several moments and suddenly becoming subconsciously aware of Oliver's eyes on his, Leo looked up from his bulky lenses, and said to his companion, quizzically, 'Sorry? Were you saying something? Did you see the big Gannet out there?'

Daniel had woken with a slight hangover. Not a headache as such, just a niggly feeling at the top of the skull that he recognised as one beer too many and regret, mixed in fairly equal quantities. He had forgotten to spark up the gas heater in his cottage before he had gone to sleep, and a restless night that had succeeded in depositing most of his bed-clothes on the floor, combined with a chill early morning wind blowing in from the west that rattled the window in the kitchen incessantly, made him feel cold and lonely.

He scooped up a sweater from an untidy pile of 'already worn' clothes on the floor, and pulled it on, and dug out the pair of thick '1000 mile' socks from the depths of his walking boots into which he had stuffed them the previous afternoon, and sat on the edge of the bed to haul them up and over the end of his pyjama bottoms. Coffee. That was what he needed. Coffee, coffee, coffee. And quickly.

The box of matches he had brought with him had been one of the worst casualties of his initial drenching on arriving at the island, but he was at last able to fire one into incendiary action and ignite the gas on the stove's front hob. He filled the kettle with water from the kitchen sink and placed it above the heat, where it began to whistle away encouragingly. Strange to be going back to using an old style kettle, Daniel had long since got accustomed to the plug-in electric variety. Or more often than not, having his coffee made for him.

Out of the window, the Old Light stood tall and bright against the clear blue sky. Despite the wind, it looked like it was going to be a fine day again. On the open-air balcony, just below the glass beacon of the lighthouse, Daniel watched a figure walking around the whole circumference anti-clockwise, disappearing out of sight momentarily, only to reappear again and stop and lean over the white-painted iron balustrade, facing north. It was Donald Trigg. He hadn't seen the old man since his initial encounter when sheltering from the rain. Daniel felt slightly aggrieved. The day before he had mentally planned to make a visit to the top of the Old Light his first excursion of the day, and now someone else had laid claim to it. Living in Old Light Cottage Daniel felt a sense of proprietorship to the lighthouse and all its grounds. How dare someone else make use of *his* lighthouse. Aware of a suddenly more furious note from the kettle steaming at his side, Daniel diverted his attention from his observation and attended to the more pressing matter of the moment. Coffee. And a change of plan.

Three quarters of an hour later was to find him, good spirits returned, marching briskly up the central track, which runs like a backbone north-south along the length of the flat inland plateau of the island. He had stopped off briefly at the village shop to buy a couple of cans of soft drink, some rolls and cheese to make a mid-day snack, a packet of Penguin biscuits, and a slab of chocolate covered flapjack that he hadn't been able to resist - hadn't been meant to be able to resist.

Although the sun was still only shining weakly, the wind was noticeably lessened, away from the exposed west-side slopes, and Daniel had felt confident enough of the conditions to stride out wearing just his replica football club team-shirt and a pair of sports shorts, which were rather more skimpy than he had remembered them being. Combined with his heavy dark walking boots, and woolly socks which were pulled up almost to the knee, Daniel thought that he probably looked a bit of a prat, but considering the only encounters he was likely to have would either be with similarly attired walkers or with critically-indifferent sheep, he had decided that he didn't really care. After all, part of being on holiday was the opportunity to look a prat without fear.

Once away from the village, the gravel track followed a course running alongside a low stone wall for some distance, keeping one field of sheep separate from another. The turf at the side of the path was muddy and cut up and showed the deep tyre impressions of a heavy landrover or tractor. Rain water still lay in some of the deeper track marks and formed in puddles where the gravel sloped off towards the wall. Soon though the cultivated pastures gave way to open heath and the only signs of human intervention on the unfolding landscape became the landmark Quarter walls which cross the island from east to west, the occasional stone ruin of a long since abandoned cottage, and the intermittent marker stones which define the path along the wilder course of its route.

On either side now the ground was covered in thick, coarse tufted grass, out of which bright wild flowers strove to rise their tiny colourful heads. Birdsfoot Trefoil, red and yellow. Livingstone Daisy and blue Ajuga. Campion and Valerian each trying to compete with each other to be the brightest red, and everywhere the subtle pink of Thrift. Overhead, larks and warblers sang sweet songs, each trying to outdo the other in the competition for a mate. Presentation. Artistic merit. Interpretation. Every one a ten out of perfect ten. And ahead Pondsbury, the largest expanse of fresh water on the island, in reality little more than a reedy, boggy pond, and beyond this the gentle rise of Tibbetts Hill in the far distance.

Daniel was thinking about the previous evening and Lex. He had been rather drunk. Perhaps he had misinterpreted the signs? She had been rather drunk. Perhaps she was regretting the whole incident this morning? Or had there even been an incident? He wasn't sure. The last thing he remembered was being in the pub and noticing a dangerous look in her eyes which had said to him 'flee now', and then of him making a rather hurried and feeble excuse about having to be up early next morning, and saying goodnight. Perhaps it was just him being silly. It meant nothing. It was nothing. He was under no delusions that he was no spring chicken any longer. He was flattering himself that this younger woman could be interested in him. How did he feel about that, though? That was the real problem. He didn't know.

The sun was just beginning to shine with real warmth to it and Daniel felt the first burning pricks of heat on his forehead and on the exposed flesh of his forearms, which were showing pink and blotchy. The only clouds in the sky were long thin wisps, ethereal, and transient as the vapour trails from a passing formation of jet aircraft. It was too nice a day to spend worrying over the difficulties of half-imagined romantic intrigues.

A large herd of Soay sheep were grazing on the thinner

grass of the Middle Park: dark-coated, shaggy individuals, they looked more like goats than their white-fleeced domestic cousins. A large male, his fur hanging off him in moulting folds, head held high to show off his proud curling horns, watched Daniel's approach warily, before, with a barely discernible sign, indicating to his flock it was time to leave, and one by one the group formed line, and unhurriedly moved off out of sight, beyond the next hillock.

Ahead and standing on a cleared expanse of high ground in a circular stone enclosure was the solid grey-stone structure of the Admiralty Lookout. Outside, a very tall, bearded man was battling with the vagaries of the wind at this most exposed of summits, trying to steady a washing line that had been make-shiftly strung from a window in the building and anchored by a stone atop the surrounding wall. His bulk made him look slightly comical hanging onto the line, whilst holding a moth-like fluttering black brassiere in one hefty hand, and trying to grapple with a bag that contained clothes pegs in the other. Spotting Daniel did nothing to ease his frustration and only added to his obvious embarrassment.

'Need a hand?' Daniel called as he approached nearer.

'No. I can manage, thanks. It's just this blasted wind. Starts up again when you least expect it.'

He was a young man, Daniel could see now that he was closer. Wearing tight black jeans, a black T-shirt and a leather jacket over the top. His hair - also dyed jet black - was long, although thinning, and blew in wispy strands around his face and constantly into his eyes and mouth, from which he had to spit and pluck them out. His face seemed unnaturally pale, but whether from an application of regulation Goth-style face powder, or just too little exposure to the sunlight, Daniel could not decide. Level now with the building, Daniel continued, 'Lonely spot you've chosen for yourself out here. Are you on your own?'

The man glanced from the bra he still held, back to Daniel before answering, 'No. She's inside. She's not too well today.' and then collecting up the remaining pile of washing that was laying on the ground, ended the conversation by saying, 'I think I'll finish this later. Goodbye.' and went inside.

The wind dropped again as did the contours of the land and Daniel found his pace increasing. Surmounting the Threequarter Wall, the scene ahead was of a hummocky landscape of dark purple heather, spiky yellow-flowering gorse and green fern-like bracken, and with each successive north-bound footstep across this carpet of vegetation, the sky seemed to ever grow in size, as the land about diminished, surrendering all pretence of being infinite as it slowly receded on all sides, like a platform of soap bubbles evaporating one by one in a bath, giving way to sheer cliffs and sea below, and leaving just a thin peninsula of white-rock pavement as a last gang-plank of terra firma.

A zig-zag path trailed languidly downwards, snaking back and forth across the cliff face in easy meanders, before being suddenly replaced by rapidly-descending, steep stone steps, only made scalable by the reassuring presence of a rusting iron handrail. On the headland was the sparkling white building of the North Light, and below that the sea, caressing the rocks with gently lapping seduction before revealing the deception of its touch, by exploding in a passion of noise and seething white froth.

Daniel sat on the lowest step he could which still remained dry even at the peak of the sea's most tempestuous outbursts. A short distance away from him a small head bobbed in the water, to be lost from sight momentarily beneath a larger than average wave, only to reappear again in the same position. Black eyes, deep and watchful, full of the knowledge of the oceans, curious of the ways of the land: Daniel watched the seal watching him and wondered who would get bored first.

- - - - - - - - - - -

'Did you like the reference to you in the last chapter?' David enquired of his silently reading wife.

Diana looked up from the manuscript. Laying beside her, her husband had the expression of an over excited Golden Retriever puppy, an expectant smile on his face, ready and waiting to be praised. She decided it was quickest to humour him. 'To me? I didn't notice anything, darling.'

David eagerly took the wad of papers from her. 'Yes, yes. It's here somewhere.' He mumbled to himself as his eyes skimmed over his hallowed words. '.. whistle encouragingly ... old style ... electric variety. Yes, here it is.' He pointed out one sentence, which Diana read aloud, pithily.

'Or more often than not, having his coffee made for him.'

Chapter Twelve

Free. Free! It was such a novel experience Graham scarcely knew what to do first. The choice was mind-boggling. If he had been old enough to have been interested in the film, visions of Julie Andrews, arms waving, skirt billowing, twirling around, running up the green hillsides in *The Sound of Music* would have sprung to mind. Being of more juvenile mind and more manly tendencies, instead he contented himself with a short sprint down one slope of the bank, leaped across the trickling brook at the bottom in a single bound, and then hared up the opposite bank as fast as he could, before sprawling himself flat on the short grass at the top, arms splayed out in front of him, skidding forward, in imitation of one of his footballing heroes scoring a goal. He laughed excitedly at his daring. Green open spaces all around him in every direction and he could go where he pleased, do what he pleased, shout as loud as he pleased. He experimented with this last notion forthwith. The whole island as playground: no fences to pen him in; no signs saying 'Keep Out' or 'Private'; no teachers giving him instructions; no boys to pick on him; best of all, no mother to tell him what was best for him - which shoes to wear, which books to pack, which sweets to buy. This must be what it is like to be an adult. Free. Free!

Even now though, freedom comes with a price attached. Graham looked down to his newly bought jeans and saw with sudden dismay the long, green grass-stain streak running the length of one leg, and the fresh tear in the knee. He knew his mother had worked an overtime shift especially to buy the particular brand-name jeans he had asked for - the same ones that all his mates were wearing - knew that they were a holiday treat; that the whole holiday was an expensive treat they hadn't really been able to afford. She hadn't said as much, but he remembered his mum's worried expression when those letters from the bank kept turning up. He'd seen the checklist she'd made in her diary, which she thought he didn't know about: council tax; mortgage; endowment; water; electricity; phone; TV stamps; credit card; Davis' Collection Services - he didn't know what that was, but it sounded like another worry. In fact he couldn't remember a time when his mum's expression hadn't looked worried. She'd be worried now. Wondering where he was. Come to think of it, just where was he? He'd come a lot further than he had intended. Perhaps he ought to be heading back? Although now, he wasn't even quite sure which way back was. And then there were his jeans. How could he explain what had happened to his jeans? An accident. Yes, it was believable enough. He had slipped and torn them. She couldn't tell him off for that. An accident. They happen. But even as he tried to convince himself, he realised that his mother's future words, be they reprimand or otherwise, could not be worse than his own sense of self-recrimination. He had let her down - her trust, her love - let himself down - his deceit, his weakness. Guilt and freedom inextricably linked from childhood to the grave. And money? It might be possible to buy yourself freedom, but no amount of money can ever pay off the guilt.

It just wasn't fair. John had understood. John had had an expression for it, which had made him laugh, even though he hadn't really understood what he had meant by it: 'Don't let the bastards grind you down.' That was it. Bastards. That was what had made him laugh. That was what they all were. That was what John had said. Graham shouted the word aloud, his doubts momentarily allayed as he remembered his earlier conversation.

He had been looking at the pig, in its compound behind the garden of the Marisco Tavern, snuffling away at the turnip tops and green carrot leaves that someone had thrown in the muddy patch near the gate for its breakfast. His mum had been in the shop, buying food and things, and he had said he would just have a walk around outside. She hadn't even wanted him to do that: 'Don't go far'. Far, huh! If she could see him now. Actually he hadn't intended to go anywhere at all, not until the man had said he could show him a horse with one ear missing. The man had come up behind him at the pig sty.

'Big one, isn't it?'

'Yes,' Graham had agreed.

'Like animals do you?'

'Yes,' Graham had said.

'Come on then. I'll show you something that will surprise you.'

And so he had gone.

The horse had not been as surprising as it had been billed to be, and far from having one ear missing, it had actually only had just a small corner lopped from the tip of one still very much in evidence flapping tuft. Graham hadn't been too disappointed though. His new friend was proving good entertainment, and Graham had found himself tagging along behind the big man. He had never met anyone quite like him before; the way he looked; the strange clothes he wore; the way he spoke - that most of all. He had talked to Graham like an equal, not patronising, not putting him down, not treating him like a kid. It was a new experience for Graham, one that had bolstered his confidence, and he had soon found his tongue running away with itself in his enthusiasm to continue this unexpected conversation.

'It's our first time here. We went to Wales when I was little, but I don't really remember that. Have you ever been to Wales?'

'Lampeter. I went to university there.'

'University, really? We have a university where I live. Mum says that I'll go there.

'Where's that?'

'Luton.'

'University of Luton? Yer, fucking right.'

Graham had tried the word experimentally around his mouth, silently playing with the two syllables, letting the sound slip secretly over his tongue, before he braved up the courage to imitate his hero, 'Yer, fucking right.'

He had been so enthralled that when John - as the stranger had introduced himself as - suddenly said, 'Right. Well I'll see you around then' and opened the door to his cottage, disappearing inside without a further look back, Graham had been left standing alone, in an unfamiliar part of the island, and with no clear idea of the way back again. He had looked at his watch and realised with some horror that he had been walking for over half an hour. His mum would be frantic. And furious. But then, what was it John had said, 'Fuck it. Live a little.'

And so it was that Graham found himself, alone on the grassy slopes, next to the cliffs above St Mark's Stone, torn between the conflicting emotions of excitement and anxiety. And so it was that Graham saw the man on the rock.

Graham knew that the man was up to no good, without being able to pinpoint just what it was about his behaviour that led him to believe this. He was to be confirmed in his suspicions by subsequent events. For the moment though, Graham, driven by an instinct which told him that the man would not approve of any witnesses to his actions, concealed himself by laying flat on the ground behind a patch of tall grass at the cliff edge, so that he could continue watching but without revealing his presence.

It's a drug. The high. The adrenalin rush. Call it what you like, there is nothing else like it.

It's not just that it is illegal either, although that is an extra buzz. No, it's the danger. Pushing yourself to the limits. Going in where others fear to tread. It combines so many disciplines too. And discipline itself. That of course is vital. Self-discipline. Mind and body. That is why it is important to exercise first. To stretch the physical, cleanse the spiritual, and concentrate the brain. To take away the fear. Because if you can take away the fear you can do anything.

Anything.

You might think it is a spur of the moment thing. Not so at all. No way, Jose. It takes days, sometimes weeks, of planning. Sometimes it feels like organising a military campaign. When the stakes are high you want to do everything you can to minimise unnecessary risks. That is the key. Planning. And organisation. It's like the Boy Scouts say, 'Be Prepared'. You have to keep in mind too, that it is a job. Be professional. Obviously, it is a pleasure as well - no point in doing it otherwise - but the bottom line is standards. There is no place for the *dilettante* in the world of egg collecting these days.

Egg collecting. It is far too passive a description. This is no longer the pursuit of Victorian gentlemen in tall hats and black tails. Ornitho-activist, or Extreme Birder. That's what the modern *parlez* is. *Comprendez?* And it is dangerous. Make no odds about that. You've got to give the birds their due, they're not out to make it easy for you. Tall trees. High rock ledges. They nest in places that would make your toes curl. But if you can't stand the heat don't go into the kitchen. Then there's the Law on your back. And the public too. No one these days loves an egg collector.

'Graham!.' It was a shrill female voice. 'Oh, thank God, you're all right. I've been so worried.'

Graham was walking along the main central track heading back into the village. His interest in the man on the rock having long since disappeared, he had taken stock of his bearings, and shoulders hunched, feet dragging and mouth turned down in a determinedly sullen expression, looking every inch the model of the dysfunctional Perry-teenager, he had given in to the inevitable and started on his homeward path. He now surrended himself to the reuniting embrace of his distraught mother.

Liz held him to her, tears of relief flowing down her face, repeating over and over again into the back of his head, 'I've been so worried. I've been so worried.' Her joy turned to anger though as speedily as her tears dried up in their tracks, as questions replaced delight and her logical, reasoning mind wrestled back control from her free-wheeling emotional lobe, and demanded explanations for the torment she had so recently been put through. She held Graham by both shoulders and looked directly into his face, her tone now far less loving, 'Just where on earth do you think you've been? How dare you go running off like that. What have you got to say for yourself? Answer me.'

Graham looked back into the face of his mother. The barrage of questions were a blur to him. All he could focus on was the small nervous tick which pulled at the corner of his mother's mouth as though a cruel puppeteer was tugging on an invisible string, and which became more pronounced whenever she was angry, or frightened. Twitch. Twitch. Twitch. It was mesmerising. He tried to tear his eyes away, but found that he could not. Twitch. Twitch. Twitch.

'Graham! What's wrong with you?' Liz was shaking him now in her frustration and from the explosive release of emotion. She saw as if for the first time the state of his clothes, 'Your trousers! What have you done to your new trousers?' She seemed to be building up for a renewed wave of hysteria when suddenly Graham was released from his transfixion and in one great, garbled outpouring silenced his mother by giving her an account of his adventures, culminating in watching the nest robber.

'He had his head covered by a balaclava and he was doing press-ups on top of a large rock right on top of the cliff edge. Then he stretched his legs and shook his arms around, like they do on the athletics on the tele when they're warming up. Then he climbed down in between a small crevice in the rock face and came out again much lower down on a grassy slope. He was frightening the birds too, because they were all flying up into the air, and circling around, and squawking and making so much noise. One big gull actually flew right at him several times and he waved his arms at it to make it fly away. He lay down on the slope and I saw him put his hand into a sort of hole in the bank, but he mustn't have been able to reach or something, because then he started stamping on the ground above, until he had made the burrows all cave in, and then he fished around again for a bit and put something into his bag, and then he climbed back again. I think he was stealing eggs. I've read about it. Should we report him?'

Graham's verbosity had allowed Liz's emotions to temporarily disperse, and she put an affectionate arm around his shoulder, guiding him back towards the cluster of buildings in the distance, 'I'll tell you what we are going to do. You are going to go back to the tent and change out of those clothes, and I am going to try and mend that hole in your knee.'

- - - - - - - -

'Couldn't resist a Luton jibe, I see.' Diana teased.

David shrugged, 'That wasn't a jibe. That was me being generous. You should have read my first draft.'

'I don't know why you can't just leave Luton alone.'

'Have you ever been to Luton?' David asked.

'No.'

'Leave it then.'

Chapter Thirteen

'Has anybody seen either of the guys who are staying up at the castle this morning?'

It was Julie who spoke.

The Marisco Tavern was by no means full - not yet swollen by the arrival of the day-trippers; still too early for any lunchtime imbibers - but nevertheless several heads turned in her direction, either eager to help , or eager to learn more.

One of the construction workers spoke up, 'What, the bloke who was crashing around in here early last night?'

'He was worse later on, after you left. Absolutely out of it.' replied his companion.

'Yes, he's one.' said Julie rather impatiently, 'Although it's his friend I really want to find. They are here for the climbing.'

'Have you checked in the book.' suggested the barmaid, helpfully, nodding towards an open register on a table by the door. 'If they've gone out for a climb this morning they may have jotted down in the log where they were planning to go. Some do, some don't.'

Julie shook her head, 'I didn't think of that. Stupid of me. Thanks, I'll check.'

The register was a record of the proposed day itineraries of Lundy's visitors. It's purpose was to give a guide to the whereabouts of the island's itinerant population in case of emergency, or, in the unlikely event of someone going missing, to help rescue teams narrow the field of search. Few visitors actually bothered to make use of the book, and most weren't even aware of its existence, but climbers were generally an exception - most realised that the perilous nature of that sport didn't have to be made even more hazardous by not taking a few elementary safety precautions, such as letting someone know which climb you intended to undertake before setting off.

Julie thumbed back from the blank sheet that the large book stood open upon, to the last neatly hand-written entry. 07.50 that morning, Mrs Pugh and Miss Tranter, *a walk to Rocket Pole Pond, e.t.a. 08.30*. There were no other records for the day. She ran her eye up the page to the previous day's log, and then to the one before that. Mrs Pugh and Miss Tranter appeared to be regular diarists: the same small controlled handwriting featured repeatedly. *09.10, east-side walk to the Quarry Beach, e.t.a. 11.00. 14.35, intend to watch for whale sharks from the cliffs of Lametry Bay, e.t.a. 15.30.* An additional note was added in a different coloured ink, *saw none*. And for the previous day: *08.55, long walk up central path to Tibbetts, e.t.a. 12.00.* This too had an appendix: *rain stopped play 09.45.* There was no sign in the book of either Brad or Mark having recorded their climb of the day before and so Julie was not surprised at not discovering their current movements from the tome of knowledge. She snapped the large volume shut with an audible thwack.

'No luck?' called out the barmaid.

'No, none. They both seem pretty irresponsible. I'm not surprised they haven't kept the log up to date.'

'Do you want me to tell them anything if I see them?' the barmaid asked.

Julie moved closer to the group drinking by the bar counter. 'No, it doesn't matter. I'm sure I'll catch up with them later.' She continued, 'I was meant to be meeting up with one of them to help me with a climb first thing this morning, but he didn't show. In fact, I think the pair of them have been leading me off on a wild goose chase for some reason best known to them. Bloody time-wasters. Perhaps I'll have a fruit juice now that I'm here, Tina.'

'Orange?'

'No, I've changed my mind. Make it a whisky. It might warm me up. It was blowing pretty cold on the cliff top this morning.'

One of the workmen who had been leaning on the bar, listening, joined in the conversation. 'Where was it you've been then?'

'On top of Jenny's Cove.'

'For climbing?'

'I know. It's off limits,' and Julie recounted the story of the day before, as told to her by Brad and Mark.

'Sounds like you'll be wanting that copper.' the man continued, after hearing Julie's account.

'What copper?'

'The one staying at Old Light Cottage. That's what the chaps have been saying he is at any rate. We were only just talking about him. Thought he might be able to solve the mystery of the missing woman.'

Tina cut in, 'Don't go winding the Warden up, Jim. You know it's just nonsense.' She carried on explaining since Julie clearly looked interested. 'It's the woman staying up at Admiralty Lookout. She's not been seen much. Some of the lads were joking she'd gone missing.'

'Killed's what I heard.' said Jim.

'Murdered.' piped up a voice from the back of the room.

Tina, the voice of reason, interjected, 'Stop it now. A joke's a joke.' She turned to Julie, 'You know what it's like up there. Anyone that rents the Old Lookout does it because they want peace and quiet and to be left undisturbed.'

'Undisturbed for what though?' continued Jim, anxious not to let the joke drop.

Julie had heard too much scandal-mongering in the Marisco over the years to treat the current conversation as anything other than what it was. Pure fiction. Instead she returned to a piece of news that might be based somewhere in fact. 'So there's a policeman on the island?'

'That's what I hear.'

'Really? I didn't know. He was in here last night as well, wasn't he?' Julie asked.

'Seemed to me like the whole island was in here last night,' Tina joked.

'Talking to one of them from the Blue Bung, he was.' confirmed the man.

'Well if my missing duo haven't reappeared by this evening I might take your advice, Jim. Although I can't imagine he could be a better detective than yourself. Not much seems to get by you in this place.' laughed Julie, the whisky fast restoring her even spirits.

'Can't help but pick up a bit of ...'

'Gossip?'

'News, was what I was going to say,' continued Jim. 'Not somewhere small as this.'

'Someone else you might try,' cut in Tina, 'Is the little chubby chap at the Brambles. I think that's where I heard he was staying. He was in here last night and I'm pretty sure I saw him helping the drunken guy you're looking for home last night. Although how far they got I don't know, the big bloke looked like he could barely stand up and the little one wouldn't have been strong enough to be able to lift him.'

'Do you know his name?' Julie asked.

'The little chap? No, 'fraid not. But I'm sure I heard him talking about Brambles.'

'OK, thanks,' said Julie. 'I'm sure I'll be able to find him.'

The seal had long since tired of Daniel's company and Daniel himself having become weary of staring out over a now lonely sea, had completed the climb back up the path to the cliff top and was now following an ill-defined track through the short grass, back along the west side of the island.

Halfway back to his cottage Daniel's attention was taken by something shining in the browny-green stubble ahead, as though the sun was reflecting off something metallic half-buried in the grass. Approaching nearer, he saw that it was actually a large beetle, it's shell a gleaming iridescent green, sparkling as brightly as newly polished silver. He lifted the creature up with a short stick and transferred it gently onto the palm of his hand. It seemed quite at home, and shuffled slowly back and forth, not attempting to discover any exit from the soft pink bowl into which it had been placed. Thin black legs stuck out: jointed and delicate. Its head, curious, like that of a tortoise slowly exploring beyond the limits of its shell, probing forward, taking in its surroundings with a sense of silent awe. Two scratches - scars of battle - evenly carved, one on either side of its body, showed up white against the brilliant colour of its casing like flaws in a precious stone. But otherwise it was perfect. A Lundy emerald. But where that jewel is cold and dead, this gem was magnificently more special by having been puffed so full with the breath of life, and so given the chance for infinite unpredictability and variation. Nature in microcosm, viewed through a critical jeweller's glass, has no time for fakes or imitations.

Daniel carefully returned the genuine article back into the camouflage of a thick tuft of coarse grass, and reflected how such fragile beauty is often stamped upon and destroyed, when at the same time, the harsh, indestructible lines of cool minerals are so revered and handled with the delicacy of queens. A slight noise made him look up from his crouched position in the grass and he saw, some distance ahead, standing, facing out to sea, high above the precipitous cliffs of Jenny's Cove, the young woman from the boat again. She appeared lost in contemplation of the scene before her, seemingly oblivious of her proximity to the lethal drop, a mere stride away. Daniel watched her for a few minutes unseen, before retracing his steps and skirting back along the route he had previously come along, until he came to a point where the path forked, and which enabled him to take a more inland route, passing by outside of her line of vision.

Fragile beauty or cool mineral? He wondered.

- - - - - - - - - - -

'I'm tired, David.' Diana laid the manuscript down on the bed covers beside her. 'I'll read some more in the morning.' She turned her back towards her husband, and murmured, 'Turn out the light will you.'

David took up the discarded papers and smoothing them down lovingly, knocked them into a neat bundle, and stowed them safely away on top of his bedside cabinet. He climbed out of bed and crossed the carpet, and with one hand mimicking the shape of a cocked revolver pointed at the oblivious form of his dozing spouse, he flicked the light switch, sending the room into darkness.

'Click.'

Chapter Fourteen

'Skylark!'

'Sure?'

'Sure.'

'Not another Willow Warbler?'

'No. It is altogether different.'

'OK. That's seventeen-fifteen to you.'

A brief silence before, 'Kittiwake!'

'Where?'

'There, circling at 5 o'clock. Oh, it's just disappeared beneath the edge.'

'Sure?'

'Sure. Come on eighteen-fifteen. Eighteen-fifteen.'

'Hang on. No, I don't think so. You've already had Kittiwake. Look, that was your number three.'

Reg handed over a sheet of paper to Oliver. On it was marked the two men's names at the top, and beneath each, two columns of bird's names.

'Kittiwake. Seen it. Done it. You can't count it twice.'

'OK,' conceded Oliver, grudgingly.

'I, on the other hand,' continued Reg, 'Haven't already got it marked down on my column, so I think that makes it seventeen-sixteen.'

'You can't have that,' complained the younger man. 'You didn't even see it, you were still too busy scribbling down the last sighting.'

'Lesser Black-backed Gull! Seventeen all.' shouted Reg pointing skywards.

'I think that was a juvenile Great Black-backed Gull.' The interruption came from Julie, who had appeared over the top of the rise with the intention of descending into Millcombe Valley, when she had caught sight of the two men's amicable squabbling.

'Still seventeen-sixteen then.' said Oliver.

'What's the competition?' enquired Julie.

'Oh, nothing very serious,' explained Reg, 'We're just trying to see who can 'spot' the fastest.'

'Nothing very serious! Don't let my friend, Leo, hear

you say such blasphemies. Bird watching is deadly serious to Leo.'

'It's not the best side of the island for bird watching,' said Julie.

'That's half the fun,' replied Reg. 'It's more of a challenge. Besides, I am having difficulty enough to keep up with writing down each sighting as it is, while still keeping one eagle-eye out for the next one. You're the conservation warden, aren't you? I think I saw you come into the Marisco Tavern last night.'

'Yes, that's right.' Julie introduced herself. 'You wouldn't be staying at Brambles, would you?' she continued, her mind returning to the purpose of her walk, and regarding with interest the bird-watcher's squat and portly frame.

'Quite so.' confirmed Reg.

'Then you may be able to save me a walk. I was hoping to have a word with you.'

Oliver motioned that he would leave the two of them to their discussion, but Julie asked him to stay, 'Don't worry, it's nothing very secret. In fact you may be able to help too. I suppose you weren't in the pub as well last night, were you?'

'No, can't help there,' Oliver replied. 'We - me and Leo that is - had an early start this morning, and we - Leo that is - decided we didn't want to be suffering with hangovers. We were up at Jenny's Cove first thing. Saw you there, in fact.'

'Maybe you can help then,' said Julie.

'Just tell me how.'

'Do you know the two blokes who are here for the climbing? Big blokes, both of them. They are staying at the Castle.'

'Tell me about it,' chipped in Reg, 'I had to help one of them back there last night. Absolutely plastered he was, and weighed a ton.'

'It's only that, I was meant to be meeting his friend at Jenny's Cove this morning to help me clear up a little mystery, but he didn't turn up. That must have been when you saw me.' Julie addressed Oliver.

Reg continued, 'If he was in anything like the same state as his mate was, they're probably both still holed up at the Castle, nursing sore heads.'

Julie shook her head. 'No, I tried there straight away, when he didn't show, but no sign of them. You didn't see either of them on the cliffs this morning before I turned up?' she questioned Oliver. 'Or any sign of his mate, when you went to the Castle last night?' looking at Reg.

Both responded in the negative. 'No,' said Reg, 'In fact, I didn't quite get him - Brad is his name by the way - back to the Castle.'

'Oh, what happened?'

'Well, as I say, he was in no state to be heading off in the dark on his own, so I felt obliged to try and guide him home. He said his name was Brad, repeatedly in actual fact, and I discovered he was staying at one of the properties in the Castle, so we set off. It took ages. He was an absolute dead weight and although he was able to walk a bit, he needed my support most of the time. We were weaving all over the place. As you can see, I'm not the biggest of fellows, and it was difficult to keep him on track. I got the impression he had had an argument with his friend, because he kept cursing someone ... Mark?'

'Yes, that would be right,' said Julie.

'Saying what an idiot he was. I agreed with him, although I don't know what it was all about. Well, we eventually got to the beginning of the long straight track that leads directly to the Castle, and there was a light on ahead to guide him, so I left him at that point, because he assured me he was all right to make the last stretch on his own. I must admit, I was anxious to get back too. I had said to my wife I would be along shortly, and I knew she would have been getting worried.'

'So you didn't actually see him to his door?' asked Julie.

'No, as good as, though. He only had a hundred yards or so to go, and he couldn't have strayed off the path. The banks on each side of the track are quite steep, and I couldn't see him clambering up over them in his condition. Why the concern?'

The conversation was momentarily interrupted by Oliver, 'Chaffinch! Sorry, force of habit. I couldn't help myself. You said about a mystery earlier?'

Julie was beginning to tire repeating a story which she was increasingly of the opinion was just a practical joke played by the two climbers at her expense, and tried to bring a veil across her investigations by saying, 'I'm sure it's nothing. I just don't like to have my time wasted. I'll take it up with the pair of them when they finally appear. Thanks and good luck with the competition.' She turned and was about to retrace her steps to the village, but couldn't resist one parting shot, 'Raven!'

The view from the top of the Old Light was fast fading with the diminishing daylight. Donald turned down the top corner of the page, and put a firm crease in it to form a neat rectangle of paper, to mark the point of the book he had reached. He stood up, stretched his arms high above his head, and then placed the large hardback volume on the sagging, red-and-white striped fabric seat of the deckchair he had just vacated. The chair commanded an enviable position, high up in the lamp-room, on the metal platform which would have originally housed the mechanism for the lighthouse's shining beacon. The site was protected from the elements by a glass-panelled turret, which outside was topped by a large, golden globe and an arrow-pointing weather vane. The three hundred and sixty degree view through the windows was magnificent: north, the island stretched to the horizon, as a never-ending land; east, the bright white-washed walls of Stoneycroft, and a crisscrossing network of angular grey stone walls and green enclosures; and beyond and to the south, the high tower of the church, marking one end of the village, and the long, low line of the rooftops of the farm; to the west was sea, only sea. Looking closer, Donald, saw two horses grazing on the heights above Pilot's Quay; sheep in the furthest field, tiny and white as snowdrops in the grass; the proud crosses and toppled stones in the graveyard below; and the determined approach of a lone figure from the north, who surmounted the rise above the Old Battery, disappeared momentarily behind the gentle contours of a low slope, only to reappear, following the faintly defined path across the west of Ackland's Moor to the base of the Old Light itself. Donald stepped across from the metal platform, down a very short flight of steps, and opened the short, but heavy, iron door which gave access to the open-air balcony which skirted the complete circumference of the lighthouse tower, to hail a greeting to the newcomer.

'Hello there,' he called, exaggeratedly cupping his hands over his mouth as though to amplify his voice. 'Are you coming up?'

Daniel lifted his head and waved to the figure high above him. 'I'll be right with you.'

Daniel wondered if the old man had been up the tower all day long. Did he eat up there? Where did he go to the toilet? Best not to think about it. Having felt territorial and reticent about meeting Donald this morning, this evening, and after a long day's walking around the island without having spoken to another person, Daniel was actually quite pleased to chance upon a friendly encounter. He walked around the large, two-storey property, which adjoined the lighthouse tower, until he came to a door, which stood half open, leading inside to a bare, stone anti-chamber. Hard, drab-grey slabs of granite spiralled upwards from the room, as, hemmed in by a black iron balustrade, they formed a gloomy staircase, circling skywards into near darkness high above. Once the door to the outside was shut, the only light into the body of the tower came from two small windows set much higher up in the construction. Daniel put his boot squarely on the widest part of the first step close to the wall, his hand on the rough guard-rail, his eyes kept firmly looking downwards, all the time concentrating on his next footfall, and started his ascent. The steps narrowed as he climbed higher, tapering ever upwards, and the camber of the walls above him became oppressive, closing in, causing him to over-compensate and stoop unnaturally. The stones around him looked damp and clammy: on the steps, on the walls, on the ceiling still high above him; and, despite the cavernous emptiness of the chimney on one side of him, he was seized by a sensation of claustrophobia: the floor rushing up to meet him as he hurtled earthward; the ceiling pressing him down to form the lid of a stone coffin. Daniel stopped, tore off his day-pack and threw it down on the step above him, and sat, sucking in big mouthfuls of air, his head flung back, his eyes closed. Get a grip. Deep breath. Daniel opened his eyes, looked down and saw the spiral of steps corkscrewing into the void; suspended; not anchored to anything above, not leading to anywhere below. Endlessly down into oblivion. He was on the edge of the step now, overbalancing. Teetering; his head swimming; unable to drag himself back to safety. On the very edge, rocking back and forth. And back and forth. And back. And forth. And now he was rolling, head-over-heels; a non-stop, rollercoaster plummet; picking up momentum, down and down, faster and faster, round and round, quicker and ...

'You're taking your time. Are you coming up?' It was Donald.

Daniel sucked in another gasp of breath through his clenched teeth. The ceiling above him was spinning but he was just able to focus on the concerned visage of the elderly man; his face appearing - seemingly disembodied like the Cheshire Cat - through an opening not far overhead. Beyond Daniel could see the sky and the last weak rays of evening sunlight. He gathered up his rucksack and got to his feet.

'Give me a second or two. I'm just coming.'

It would be nice to say the view made the climb worthwhile, but by the time Daniel finally reached the summit of the tower and was standing next to Donald on the uppermost gallery, darkness was fast encroaching and only the nearest landmarks were still visible. Donald pointed to a thick bank of cloud amassing on the horizon.

'Looks like the weather's changing for the worse again. I won't be out late tonight.'

'Are you often?' asked Daniel.

'Some nights. I like it up here. It's peaceful. Away from everything. I often stand up here at nights and watch the lights of the ships in the Channel. On a clear night you can see the lights shining all along the Welsh coast.'

'Last night?'

'Yes,' said Donald, 'I was up here, last night. Ideal conditions for collecting one's thoughts. Very calm. At least at sea it was.'

'What do you mean?'

'They say the sea is a dangerous mistress, but I think there were far more deceitful ones at work on land last night.'

'Say on.'

'I think I have already said too much. Another saying for you: silence - like tomorrow's sunrise - is golden.'

- - - - - - - - -

'That bit was accurate at any rate.'

'Which bit?' asked David.

'About you not liking heights.'

'Yes.'

'Or confined spaces.'

'Yes.'

'Or ...'

'OK, OK. That's enough.' David interrupted.

'... criticism.' Diana finished, to herself.

Chapter Fifteen

The door swung over like a gaping yawn and with the noise of renting timber. It had taken four swings of the heavy hammer to break the surround of the lock, followed by a determined shoulder-barge on the wooden panels to force an entry. It had been possible to muffle the sound of the hammer blows with a piece of towel, but the final shuddering impact had echoed loud in the peace of the evening air. A pause outside to listen, but everything still seemed quiet: the distant bleated conversation of sheep in a far field; a sudden rush of wind like a jet engine, only to fall silent again; the faint background hum of night insects. Everything was as it should be. Was it worth risking a look around the corner of the cottage, up to the platform of the Old Light? He would be up there now. Could he have heard anything? The wind was blowing in the opposite direction. It should be OK. The door of the cottage was out of sight of anyone at the top of the tower. Why take the risk of being spotted? He'd entered the door at the bottom of the lighthouse several minutes ago. And he'd be up there, how long? Five minutes? At least. Five minutes, though. It wasn't long. Now was the time for action, not worry.

The light inside the cottage was dim, but it would not be possible to turn on a switch for fear of being observed. A torch would have been useful. An oversight. It was a surprise that it had started getting dark so early tonight. Yesterday had been different.

Where to look? The open closet by the door held household items: an ironing board hanging on a hook, a bright red plastic mop and bucket, and a pair of wet training shoes, thick with mud, standing on a piece of newspaper.

There was a small entrance hall, which was clearly empty, and then the remainder of the cottage comprised one room, which served as bedroom, sitting room, and kitchen combined. From a window above the kitchen sink it was possible to see the lighthouse, looming tall, immediately overhead. There was one man on the outside veranda. An old man. Did that mean he was still on his way up, or now on his way down? No time to speculate. Five minutes was the gamble. And one minute had already passed.

Draped over the back of a chair, which was tucked underneath a large wooden table, was a dark-coloured anorak. A small pool of water on the wooden boards beneath the chair revealed where the wet coat had been dripping all day long. It still felt damp and clammy to the touch. Had it been the one he'd been wearing? There was nothing in the big zip-up front pocket, except a folded sheet of publicity information about the island, which was now so sodden, and where the ink having run, resembled a poor attempt at marbled papier-mache. An inside pocket was also empty and it had already been pulled inside out to help it dry.

There was a huge mound of clothes haphazardly piled on the floor, as if the contents of a suitcase had just been turned upside down and left, and a few more unfolded items scattered over the unmade bed. If it hadn't been for the evidence of the smashed door, would this man even notice he had had an intruder?

Another quick look out of the window. Still only the old man visible. Where was he? Had he rushed straight up, not fancied hanging around when he saw the old man, and come straight back down again. If so, he could be back at the cottage at any moment. Perhaps just turning the corner now, and about to see the door. Keep calm. Look at the watch. Three minutes.

Pyjamas. Not likely to be there. Shirts. Underwear. Socks. None had been worn. A pair of fawn safari trousers. Laughable. What had he been wearing? There was a pair of light blue jeans straddled along the length of the heater. A paper tissue, two small coins, a crushed and empty packet of cigarettes, and a packet of mints. Nothing else in the pockets. Would he have put it in a cupboard? Unlikely, but ...

The unit underneath the sink was full of crockery: cups, saucers, pots and pans. Each, carefully inventoried on the list hanging next to the stove. In the cupboard next door were cleaning utensils. And the drawer above: knives and forks, a pair of scissors, a box of Swan matches. Where else? Nothing but books on the shelves and a pack of cards and a boxed game above. The bedside cabinet? Empty. A small alarm clock on top. And the cottage's log-book, open at an entry from the previous year. There were various papers on the table top and an old Penguin Classic edition of *The Red Badge of Courage*, splayed and coffee-stained, but nothing else. One minute.

Now the old man was missing too. No, there he was. He had just been around the other side of the tower, out of sight. Could he be talking to somebody? It was too far away to see if his lips were moving. Too dark to see anything anywhere. Enough. It had been a chance worth taking and it had failed. If it was here, it wasn't going to be found tonight. Not in this light. No point in delaying any longer and risk the disaster of being caught. Just slip away into the darkness. And no one need ever know.

The shearwaters were still at sea. Leo sat on the damp grass, his back leaning against the hard, uneven surface of the enclosure wall, and looked out across the darkening shadows of the moor. Their burrows were here somewhere, he knew it. But where? It was just a question of waiting and watching.

Leo unscrewed the top from his thermos flask, and watched the hot vapours of liquid spiral up into the cool night air. He poured himself a cup of warming tea and settled down to his lonely vigil, his thoughts on the day that had been. Shame Oliver had gone off in that huff earlier. Typical of him, though. He hadn't really got the patience that was required to be a dedicated ornithologist. It had been a Puffin too. No doubt about it. It was just his bad luck that he hadn't seen it before it had flown away. What did he expect - for me to lose sight of the bird just to show him where to see it? He'll be furious about the shearwaters too. Still, his loss.

The broad, flat expanse of moorland was in virtual darkness now. Faint, distant lights from the village provided an eerie false moonlight, and as Leo's eyes accustomed themselves to the low intensity, he was able to distinguish slight graduations of colour in the scene before him: lighter areas of brown on the summit of the slight, hummocky rises; darker browns and greys on the slopes and in the hollows; and impenetrable black, revealing the thickest vegetation and clumps of grass and gorse. A movement. A rapid shadow passing across a patch of illumination. Perhaps a rabbit returning from an evening liaison. Leo knew the shearwaters would still be at sea for possibly several more hours. There was no way of knowing just when they would decide to return home. Right now, there would be a large flotilla of them, floating somewhere just offshore, congregating in the darkness, assembling at some pre-decided point on the ocean, waiting. For what? Until the last of their number reappeared from whichever far-flung destination they had reached that day? Or, until the night was at its blackest, and they considered it safe to venture back to land? Or, perhaps until the seabird equivalent of 'last orders' was called, and the whole staggering, caterwauling band of stop-outs returned home to their critical, accusing spouses? Would that be where Oliver was now - in the Marisco Tavern, carousing with all the other drunkards?

Leo's thoughts were interrupted by a sudden noise. Not the banshee-like wail of the returning flock that he was anticipating, but a soft, furtive sound, of something trying to move silently close at hand. He slowly put down the cup he still held, and listened. There it was again. The sound of a footstep, too precisely placed to be that of a person walking naturally. It sounded as though it was coming from immediately behind the wall where Leo sat, but with the wind still swirling around in weird eddys and sudden noisy gusts, it was difficult to pinpoint exactly. Could it be Oliver had decided to join him after all? Or more likely playing the fool and trying to surprise him.

There was a prolonged silence, as Leo listened even more intently, trying to determine where and what his friend was doing. He wasn't in any mood to be scared witless by a drunken Oliver suddenly leaping out upon him, thinking it some hilarious prank. The silence continued: the only sound Leo could hear was the thump, thump, pulsing of blood coursing through his brain. He realised he had been holding his breath. Stupid. Relax.

The first noise happened too quickly for Leo to turn, before he heard the second on top of the wall. There was the sound of a shower of small loose stones being dislodged about thirty feet away, and then a dark shadow appeared, momentarily silhouetted, crouched on the wall's narrow vertex, before stealthfully sliding down the stonework like a dark stain. Leo was reminded of descriptions of nineteenth century *phansigar* assassins, who practised the art of *thuggee*, and who seemed to have the ability to approach their victims unseen and then melt away into their surroundings. He gave an involuntary sharp intake of breath, and thought he heard a similarly surprised note from the new night arrival, before a louder and less clandestine clamour took his attention. It was the shearwaters. Dark aerial rockets: torpedo-like in shape, with long narrow wings. Flying low. Wave after wave of them, just above the rise of the wall, swooping down into invisible burrows deep in the obscurity of the moor.

Leo stood up in jubilation and pointed to the sky, 'The shearwaters! Oliver. The shearwaters.'

- - - - - - - - - - -

'And I suppose the cigarettes were Condor brand?'
'What do you mean?' asked David.
'Woodpecker cider. Swan matches. Penguin books. I hope you are lining up some lucrative sponsorship deals if this book of yours is ever published.'
'I believe that there are very strict laws concerning product placement.'
'Not your area of expertise, obviously.'
'Nor cigarettes yours,' retaliated David.
'Oh?'
'Condors are cigars.'

Chapter Sixteen

It was by no means the first time that Daniel had encountered evidence of a break-in, but to his memory, it was the first time the crime had been perpetrated against himself.

The front door to Old Light Cottage was a mess. One timber panel was split right through from floor to ceiling, and the wood around the lock was splintered: the metal fitting itself, all but totally dislodged. Daniel cautiously felt around the corner of the door frame until his hand reached the electric light switch, and then throwing illumination on the scene, was instantly able to see that he was alone in the property. He crossed to the bed, and sat down with a sigh of relief. He didn't know what had been worse: the discovery of his castle invaded, or the dark descent down the lighthouse stairs with Donald Trigg's well-meaning encouragement following him at every step.

His hands were shaking slightly, and remembering the small hip flask of whisky he had carried on the walk with him and had not drunk, he searched around in his day-sack until he found where the small metal container had sunk to the deepest corner of that bag. He took a long quaff and felt instantly better. Daniel's holdall was half buried underneath the fast-spreading heap of clothing on the floor, and checking inside it, Daniel was able to ascertain that his wallet was still there, and from a rapid check, that none of his credit cards and no cash had been taken. If this had been the mainland Daniel would have presumed the break-in to be the work of vandals. Bored kids out for a few minutes mindless destruction of property. But here on Lundy the only kids he had seen were the party of school children who were staying on the island for a nature field trip, and who appeared to be regimentally confined to their quarters by two disciplinarian teachers, when they weren't actively engaged in their studies. Not obvious suspects. If it wasn't a random attack then, had he been targeted for a reason? Daniel couldn't think why. Again, perhaps on the mainland there might well be people who held a personal grudge against him, but here on Lundy? It made little sense.

Daniel was about to begin a more thorough

examination of the cottage to see if he could discover any clues as to the identity of his mystery visitor, or at least determine if anything had been taken, when he heard the faint sound of running footsteps across the grass outside. The footsteps stopped outside his door and there was the bat-flapping sound of a raincoat being shaken vigorously and a female voice registering a discomforted grunt of 'Urgh!', quickly followed by a more surprised exclamation, 'Oh!'. Daniel called out, 'Come in Lex. The door is open, as you can see.'

The figure that entered was swathed in a long, dark-blue, plastic cape; the head completed enveloped in a matching hood. The distinctive eyes that pierced through this rubberised ensemble were unmistakable though.

'Give me a hand with this, can't you.' Lex indicated the ties that fastened her hood close around her neck, 'The rain has made the knots wet and I can't get them undone.'

Daniel smiled at the woman's discomfort, but rose and was soon able to loosen the constricting strings. Lex pushed the hood back and shook her hair free, causing a shower of water to spray in an ark above her. 'Urgh. It's ghastly out there.'

'I hadn't realised it had started to rain.' Daniel said.

'It's only just started,' Lex replied. 'I thought I would make it before it came on, but it got dark so quickly too and I rather lost my way. Whatever has happened to your door?' she asked, suddenly remembering the sight of the broken panels as she had raised her hand to knock.

'I don't know,' replied Daniel. 'I've only just got back here myself and discovered it like that.'

'Was it a burglar, or an accident?' Before Daniel could answer, Lex had caught sight of the jumble of his possessions, haphazardly strewn around the cottage, and she continued with a gasp, 'Oh my God! Burglars! What a dreadful mess they've made.'

Slightly bashfully, Daniel replied, 'No, actually, it looked like this beforehand. I expect it was just vandals. Someone out to make mischief. They don't appear to have taken anything.'

Lex looked around the debris with mock disbelief,

before fixing Daniel with the now familiar stare and sideways grin. 'And how would you ever know?'

They tidied up together: Lex had insisted, and Daniel had given acquiescence, mainly because there wasn't a free surface on which to sit down.

'What the fuck is this?' Lex picked up an item of clothing of nondescript appearance, heavily caked with mud, and held it at arms distance, her nose wrinkled with disdain. 'I'm sorry, but this is only fit for the bin.' She continued, 'How could you have got this place in such a mess. You've only been here a couple of days.'

'I guess I'm not used to tidying up. I'm not at home very much.'

'Or have a wife to do it for you, perhaps?'

'Something like that.'

The room had regained some sort of dignified order and, weary after the events of the evening, Daniel sat down on the edge of the bed and regarded his visitor, 'What brings you out this way this evening?'

Lex completely ignored the unspoken invitation of the chair and joined Daniel on the bed. She kicked off the trainers she was wearing, raised her arms above her head, and allowed herself to fall backwards, full-length onto the hard mattress. Daniel turned to face her, 'That's not an answer.'

Lex lifted herself up onto one elbow and, with the same unconscious action as she had displayed the previous evening in the pub, ran her tongue moistly along the length of her top lip. She held Daniel with a defiant gaze. 'No?'

She pulled the jumper up and over her head in one fluid movement and lay back, her hands behind her head, waiting. Anticipating. The bed was narrow - barely wide enough for one - but that didn't matter because she didn't intend for him to be lying *next* to her for too long. She could feel a mattress spring pressing uncomfortably into her shoulder blade, and she altered her position slightly, but so that she could still watch him.

He stood at the foot of the bed, motionless but watchful, like a heron at the water's edge, waiting for the moment to strike. Absolutely unmoving. Except those eyes, which moved painstakingly, inspecting every inch of her body. From her toes, which waggled expectantly; each nail a flare, tipped with shocking red polish. Up her shins: smooth, shining and hairless. To the slightly pudgy mounds of her knees. Slowly over her thighs, dwelling on the gently disappearing curve where her legs pressed together, and on the border of her white knickers, from which a faint shadow of fine hairs was visible. Over the swell of the white cotton and the indentation at the cleft of her pudenda, and up past the elasticated waist band, which caused the skin of her abdomen to pucker. Ever higher, rising up her flat, sucked-in stomach. Pausing on the perfect belly-button. Not sticking out. Not corkscrewing in. But a perfect hollow straight to the soul. Onward, to her rib-cage, where her bones stuck out like chicken-wings, and up over the rise of her breasts, artificially bolstered and pushed together by a matching white cotton bra, through which the impression of her nipples were clearly defined dark peaks. Along the valley of her cleavage, until the hollow at the base of her neck, which shimmered wet; collecting sweat like a reservoir. Past the graceful lines of her neck and the rise of her chin, to rest on her lips: full and moist and red, like her toes. Burning beacons marking her extremities, like landing lights showing a pilot those areas that are safe. And those that are dangerous. Until finally their eyes met. And yet still he remained motionless. What was it she saw in his expression. Criticism? Contempt?

Slowly, he knelt, disappearing from her view. And nothing. Silence. Except the sound of her breathing. And then not even that, as the anticipation grew and she held her breath. Waiting. Waiting. The slightest touch on the bottom of her left foot. A gentle flicker, like a snake's tongue shooting out. The briefest sensation. And then repeated. And again. She felt his fingers making slow circles around the ball of her heel, and then the nails running delicately upwards over the ticklish flesh of her sole. His hand grasped her foot more securely now, to stop her wriggling against the teasing caresses, and she felt his tongue run along the base of her toes, searching into every hollow, forcing itself between each digit. He pushed her second toe apart a little from the next, and made room so that he could first kiss, and then completely envelope her big toe with his mouth. She could see his face again now. Concentrating. Serious. Moving back and forth, and up and down, as he sucked long and hard on her most extreme member. She felt a shiver run up and down her spine, but whether from fear or pleasure, she couldn't decide. Nor could she stop.

He held both of her feet now and pushed them slowly backwards so that her knees were forced to rise and her legs spread wide. She wondered how far he would go. How far she *could* go. His arms were stretched wide as her legs did the splits, and his head rested on the white triangle of cloth in her groin. She felt his tongue lick out again: hard and purposeful between her legs. She was aware of her heartbeat quickening, coming in fluttering, irregular pulses, and she tried to sit up, but couldn't move from her prone position. His tongue worked its way methodically around the perimeter of her knickers, half on the material, half on her naked white skin, and she felt the occasional painful tweak as he pulled on a stray pubic hair with his teeth. She wanted him to douse the rising heat in her groin with wet kisses, but still he worked slowly, teasing. Teasing.

The fine hairs all over her body were standing on end, receptive to every minute stimulation. He need not even touch her now: just the brush of air as his hand passed above her body was enough to cause the tingling thrill of excitement. She had to twist away from him; swivel so that she could release herself from his grip. She was panting louder now, less in control, and an involuntary gasp welled up from deep inside her. It was all happening too quick.

Lex sat on the chair in the room next door and listened to the sound of Sonya's mounting excitement. She was wet and she was angry and she was tired, but she couldn't go to bed when the room the two women shared was so clearly otherwise engaged. The memory of Daniel's polite but insistent rejection still made her redden with embarrassment, and she was annoyed with herself for having put herself in such a position of vulnerability. It wasn't even as though she had wanted *him*. She just didn't want to feel left out of ... what? This? The bump and grind and bouncing bed-springs? Sonya's dizzy conversations of 'he's so gorgeous' and 'it was marvellous'? Or perhaps just a 'normal' life that seemed to come so naturally to everyone else, and yet was for ever passing her by.

He'd be leaving soon - if the previous two nights were anything to go by - without an apology for any inconvenience caused, without even the slightest acknowledgment of her patient existence; the same self-satisfied expression of conquest on his face, the same arrogant smile as he put on his coat and left without a word.

- - - - - - - - - -

'Well, you were right.'
    'About what?'
    'That it wasn't us.'
    'What wasn't?'
'Your description of the lovemaking. I don't know where that all came from, but not from any experiences we've ever shared together, that's for sure.'
    'Like I said,' David repeated, tapped the side of his head with his finger, smiling, 'It's all from in here.'
    'Well just so long as it all stays in there.'

Chapter Seventeen

The rain fell unremittingly all night long, but by morning the dark clouds had moved on to fix their sights on different targets, and the island woke to a bright, clear dawn.

Daniel had spent a fitful night: partly alert to further malevolent visitors; partly alert to further benevolent ones. The rain had kept up a non-stop tympanic beat upon the window, and the swinging broken door had joined in with an occasional percussion accompaniment. After listening for several gruelling hours to nature's atmospheric jazz, Daniel had tried and failed to silence the persistent portal drummer with an elaborate system of strings and knots and, instead, had resorted to the cruder, but more effective method, of completely blocking the doorway with a heavy cabinet, which he dragged across from beside his bed. He eventually dropped off to sleep to the lulling sound of the wind's background snare-drum, fading gradually into silence.

Julie was standing with her hands on her hips, watching as Tom chipped out the last jagged pieces of broken glass in the window with a chisel. On the cobbled ground in front of the shore office, a small pile of the dangerous shards, were glistening in the early morning sunlight.

'I didn't know you were such a Jack-of-all-trades,' said Julie.

'Lucky for you that I am,' answered Tom, looking up from his work. 'There are some old sheets of glass stored up behind the barn. I'll see if I can cut one to size and fit it this afternoon, if that's OK. I'd better get back and give Isla a hand in the shop now.'

'I don't suppose you're any good at mending doors too, are you?' asked Daniel as he approached.

It was Julie who answered, 'Doors? Why, what's happened?'

'Looks like the same problem you've had. Sometime yesterday evening, someone managed to force the lock of my cottage and break a panel.'

'You're OK?' asked Julie, concerned.

'Yes, I'm fine,' replied Daniel. 'I was out at the time.

What's happened here?'

'I don't know. Jane came to open up the office first thing this morning and found the window smashed. It looked as though someone had thrown a brick through.' Julie turned to Tom who was hovering, waiting to leave, 'Thanks Tom, that's great. I'll see you later.'

Tom took his leave, adding to Daniel as he went, 'Come along to the shop after you've finished chatting, and tell me what needs doing with that door of yours. I'll see what I can fix up.'

Daniel asked Julie if she minded if he had a look inside the office.

'So it's true what they've been saying, is it?' she joked.

'What's that?'

'That you're a policeman.'

The broken glass inside the office had all been cleared away, and apart from the airy gap where the window should have been, the office looked much as it ever did: a small desk, efficiently tidied of paperwork; two metal filing cabinets; and a stack of maps and leaflets - most for sale at £1 each - detailing the varieties of island flora and fauna and where to discover them.

Daniel turned back to Julie, 'You said a brick. Have you still got it?'

Julie looked slightly puzzled, 'Well that's the strange thing. We didn't actually find anything.' She turned to a young woman who was standing behind the bench counter, which acted as a reception desk for visitors to the office, 'You didn't pick up anything before I arrived did you, Jane?'

'No, nothing. I didn't even clear up the glass until after you'd seen it.' she answered.

Daniel examined the window again. 'Have you checked to see if anything is missing?'

Julie appeared surprised, 'What, from the office? Do you know, it didn't even occur to me. Why, do you think it was a deliberate break-in? I had just put it down to someone from the pub having had too much to drink and getting rather carried away. The condition that Brad got himself in the other night, I could imagine him doing something stupid like this.'

Daniel agreed, 'It could be. I must admit, I thought the same about my cottage since nothing appears to have been taken, but it might be worth checking all the same.' He continued, 'I'd better go and find Tom about getting the door fixed now, but if you discover anything, perhaps you'd let me know later.'

'A policeman's work ...'

'... is not going to interfere with his holiday.'

Next to the pub, the village shop is the focal point for the island community. The small oblong room houses a surprisingly large range of groceries; fresh fruit and vegetables in plastic storage trays, tinned provisions in neat rows on the shelves, snacks, drinks and confectionery; household, toilet and medical items, to cope with any domestic emergency; books, guides and maps; and a selection of cheap souvenirs. It is also the island's post office and sells the unique Puffinage stamps, which traditionally are stuck on the top left hand corner on postcards and the bottom right on letters.

Both Isla and Tom were serving behind the counter when Daniel entered, and the shop was full of children from the school party, each either clutching a postcard, a Lundy souvenir pencil, or a bar of chocolate, and forming a largely disorderly queue to pay. The only other customer was the giant Goth that Daniel had met the previous day at the remote Admiralty Lookout, and who was now kneeling down, intently examining a small shelf of basic medical supplies.

'You've got a long walk for your shopping,' Daniel said breezily.

The young man swivelled round, looking slightly embarrassed, and with a less than friendly, 'Oh, it's you.' stood up and faced Daniel.

'How is your girlfriend today?' Daniel continued.

The concerned enquiry seemed to relax the other man and he replied far more amiably, 'Still not great. Thanks for asking. It's why I'm here, in fact. Normally we've got everything we need up at the Lookout.' He indicated the shelf he had been crouched by. 'They don't have a very large stock of medicines.'

'I'm afraid I can't help either. I didn't bring much in that line with me. Not unless it is something that can be cured with a Panadol?'

'No. It looks like a pretty bad bout of flu. It didn't help getting soaked in all that rain a couple of days ago and with no electricity up there, it's sometimes hard to keep all the rooms warm. She's been shivering non-stop.'

'It sounds pretty basic,' said Daniel.

'Yes, no electricity, only hand-pumped water, no bath or shower, even the loo's outside. It's a fabulous location, though. We've been coming back for the last five summers. You should read some of the entries in the log-book up there. They make for classic stories on a cold night.'

'Oh?'

Having discovered his voice, the Goth continued, 'There was one chap who just seemed to lurch from one disaster to another. He must have had a good sense of humour though because he made a record of it all. I can't remember all of the details, but he was staying there during a particularly harsh winter and the property was practically cut off from the rest of the island. It must have been bitterly cold and so he tried to make himself a fire in the hearth, but because all of the wood had got so damp he couldn't get the thing started. He remembered though, that there was some paraffin stored in the out-house by the toilet, and so he put on his heavy overcoat and traipsed out to fetch it, hoping that he could use it to ignite the fire. Well, of course, the expected happens, the paraffin ignites the fire only too well, and a great wall of flames shoots up, catching him by surprise and making him jump back. Worse though. While jumping back he knocks off and breaks his glasses, and then bending over to pick them up again he leans too close to the still raging fire and sets his coat alight.' The young man pauses briefly to rock with mirth at his recounting of the story, before continuing, rather lamely, 'I seem to remember he managed to set a chair on fire too, before getting it all back under control, but by then of course, his coat and everything were ruined and he didn't even have anything warm to wear to try and get to the village for help.'

'Well, I hope your problems don't escalate to make them worthy of a similar tale,' said Daniel.

'Problems?' The tone of voice had instantly switched

back to the defensive, before the storyteller realised what Daniel was talking about, 'Oh, you mean Sophie's illness. No, don't worry. Another day's rest and I'm sure she'll be fine.'

Daniel's curiosity had been aroused by the story in the log-book and so he returned to the subject, 'Do all of the cottages have these diaries?'

'Yes, I think so. Where are you staying? Have you not discovered your property's book?'

Daniel's thoughts went back to the contents of the orderly cottage when he had first arrived, and before he had wreaked his own form of havoc on it, 'Actually, I think I did notice a rather battered brown volume. I must have covered it up with something. I'll have a look when I get back. It sounds as though some of the accounts of past tenants will make for amusing reading.' Daniel noticed the young man's eye wandering while he had been talking, and turned to follow the other's gaze. Standing by the tiered rack of fresh produce was the young woman, Teresa.

It was the Goth who spoke to the newcomer, 'Hello. Don't I recognise you?'

Teresa looked up, taking in both Daniel and her questioner with the same wide-eyed vacant expression that Daniel remembered from the boat. 'No. I don't think so.' she answered.

'Yes,' the young man persisted, 'You were here last year. John. John and Sophie. We were staying up at the Admiralty Lookout. Don't you remember?'

If anything the owl-eyes widened further, before Teresa answered, 'I'm afraid you must be mistaken. This is my first time on Lundy.' and with a perfunctory 'Excuse me, I must be going' she turned and left the shop.

John turned back to Daniel, 'Strange. I could have sworn it was the same woman. Last April it would have been we were here, and there weren't many on the island then. I'm sure she was here with another couple. Staying up at the Castle, they were. Or was it just one guy, I can't remember.' He knelt down again, suddenly returning to the original purpose of his journey to the village, and effectively ended the conversation with Daniel by saying, 'Oh well, it doesn't matter. Perhaps I'll see you around again.' but in a tone that clearly stated, 'But it's no skin off my nose if I don't'.

Daniel did not seem to notice the slight. This time it was his gaze that followed the retreating figure of the private young woman through the shop window, as she followed the path beside the shore office and the Marisco Tavern, pulled and latched the iron gate to the field shut behind her, and crossed the rising expanse of green to the horizon, until she finally dipped beyond and out of sight.

- - - - - - - - -

'Did I spot a clue in that last chapter?' asked Diana.

'To what?'

'I have no idea. It's just that if it is supposed to be a detective story, shouldn't there be some clues thinly concealed in the text, so that the reader can try to guess whodunit?'

'Yes.' Her husband sounded rather dubious.

'Or are you of the school of detective fiction that introduces some previously unmentioned character in the final chapter and announces them the guilty party?'

'No.' David was still being evasive.

'Or did you just not think about it?'

'But I already know whodunit. It's obvious.' he tried to justify.

'Perhaps.' said Diana, turning over a page.

Chapter Eighteen

'What do you think, Aitch. Méséglise or Guermantes?'

Hermione Tranter crossed over to the window and inspected the sky with intense suspicion, clearly believing that the smallest and most innocuous juvenile cloud, secretly harboured a future delinquent deluge. She sniffed pointedly, before giving verdict. 'Guermantes, I think. It looks as though it may be fine.' Adding, with the experience of several days spent on the island, 'At the moment.'

Guermantes was the name the two elderly women had given to the route north out of their cottage. It was synonymous with a long walk, which required a fine day to complete. Méséglise meant a brisk stroll to the village and back, usually taking in a mid-morning pastry at the Marisco Tavern and occasionally, if the weather was particularly inclement, a nip of whisky. Méséglise was the route which both women professed to despise, groaning exasperatedly when they awoke to rain or when they could hear the wind howling outside, but it was the route which secretly both rather hoped for.

Gemma Pugh joined her friend in contemplation of the elements. Physically, as emotionally, they were very different characters: where Hermione was tall and willowy, Gemma was squat and rotund; where Hermione tended to be nervy and highly strung, Gemma was relaxed and generally cheerful by nature. Both were astute enough to realise that as a double act they were the stereotype of a particular variety of music-hall joke. Nevertheless they were good companions, united in their love for walking, wild flowers and the country life, and both had been looking forward to their trip to Lundy for several months. Gemma put a friendly arm around the waist of her travelling partner. 'Shall we take the hip-flask then?'

'OK, OK. So you're not a twitcher.' said Lex, adding *sotto voce*, 'Although, you could have fooled me.'

'Excuse me, young madam,' Reg continued their mock argument in assumed tones of deep aggrievement, 'I may be a few years older than you, but I am not deaf.' He flapped one of his ears with a finger. 'Trained in listening out for bird song at one hundred paces, these are.'

'All right,' continued Lex, 'if you're not a twitcher, then tell me who is.'

'I may be able to do better than that.' Reg took Lex's arm. 'I'll show you.'

They continued their conversation as they followed the line of the Quarter Wall across the width of the island, Lex hopping backwards and forwards, one minute treading on the fallen blocks of granite at the base of the wall, using them like stepping stones across the puddles of water, the next diverting off into the long grass, in an attempt to avoid the muddy patches of earth that depicted this pedestrian thoroughfare. Reg, oblivious to the vagaries of the terrain, kept to a straight course, his shoes steadily accumulating a muddy brown patina. He tried to explain to Lex the differences between himself and a twitcher as they walked, and why he considered the term an insult.

'Most people think of twitchers as just very keen bird-watchers. Enthusiasts. Fanatics even. It's not strictly true, though. They are a breed apart. I would call myself a keen bird-watcher, or perhaps better still a birder. I'm not averse to being described as an amateur ornithologist. But I am most certainly not a twitcher.'

Lex, now fallen several yards behind the *alfresco* orator, as she still maintained her tortuous zig-zag progress, and feeling rather like a schoolgirl protege out on an extracurricular nature study class, receiving the individual tuition of a benevolent master, called out, 'So what makes them so different? Twitchers.'

'Their language. Their look. Their motives most of all.'

'You don't sound like you like them very much.'

'I don't know, I suppose I should think "each to his own". Although after inadvertently getting caught up in a great gaggle of their number in Devon last year, I probably have reason enough not to feel very sympathetic to their pursuits.'

'Really? Tell me more.' Lex asked lightheartedly.

'Actually, it was rather an ugly spectacle.' Reg turned around briefly and looked directly at Lex, his expression untypically serious, 'No, I really mean it. Very ugly indeed.'

'What happened?'

They carried on walking side by side as Reg told his story.

'I was taking a short autumn break. Margaret had gone to stay with an elderly uncle who was unwell, and I was bored with my own company around the house. The weather was unusually nice too, and I fancied getting out into some countryside. We live in Coventry, you know. I mean it's OK, but it's not exactly the green fields and wide open spaces that I was longing for.'

'I can imagine.'

'So I plumped for Devon. I was rather congratulating myself, in fact. It wasn't a county I knew at all well. I'd driven through it plenty of times to go to Cornwall, and I'd stayed close to the borders before in Somerset, but Devon was somewhere I had always just missed out on. So, not having any definite destination in mind, I literally put a pin in the map at random and said I'd go wherever fate should decide.'

'And where did your pin take you?'

'The most beautiful little village. Lower Whatnot or some such name. Ideal countryside for walking. Fine weather. Good birding too. The autumn normally is a good time for stumbling across a few unusual migrants. I had three days of perfect peace and harmony. That was before they arrived.'

'They?'

'The twitchers. Over two hundred of them. Now I know it will sound selfish since the countryside is for everyone to enjoy, and you will think I sound rather obsessed myself, but on my walks I had discovered - me now, and no one else before me - this delightful little glade in the woods. Picture the scene. A clear, tinkling brook, its shallow waters running over a gentle cascade of smooth, oval boulders. A fine, dark wood, not large, but big enough to give the impression you were the only human for miles around. A pleasant slope to sit on. Even a conveniently placed tuft of grass to act as a soft cushion. A place so intimate that even the sunlight was only allowed to just peak in, its harsh beam diffracted into a thousand delicate rays by the canopy of leaves.'

'I didn't know you were a poet.'

'Hush. Just the noise of the water in the stream. The wind in the trees. And the birds. It was my place. I used to go there to read. And to listen. One day I even dropped off to sleep. Until the twitchers descended. The place was transformed overnight. Elbow to elbow they stretched the length of the brook, standing on my boulders, leaning on my bank, even sitting on my tuffet: binoculars focussed, telescopes poised, cameras whirring, tripods sticking into the ground. It was bedlam. They must have been tipped off about something being sighted locally. Something pretty rare too, for so many of them to turn up. I didn't even stick around to ask what it was, I was so annoyed. Of course by the next day they had all disappeared again, but the magic of the place had been lost by then.'

'Sounds awful.' agreed Lex.

'Yes, and all for a tick in a notebook. I don't see any real love for the bird involved. To me, it is more akin to a collecting mania. If it wasn't birds, it would be stamps, or foreign coins. Some of them would probably have been the oologists of a different generation.'

'Oologists?'

'Egg collectors. It's illegal now, thank goodness.'

'Surely it still goes on though, doesn't it? I'm sure I have occasionally read about cases in the newspapers.'

'Sadly, yes you're right. There's big money in it too. For some people just the fact that it is now illegal, adds to the excitement of gathering together a big collection. And if these people can't, for whatever reason, actually obtain the eggs themselves, they are unscrupulous enough to offer big bucks to others to do the physical collecting for them. I can't understand it at all.' Reg stopped his impassioned rhetoric and added in more conciliatory tones, 'Listen to me go on. I think I may have painted too black a picture of twitchers here. As a whole they're actually a very decent lot. I've even got one or two of them that I'd number amongst my friends. It's just that their love for this grand pursuit of ours is rather fanatical, and as with any fanaticism it only takes one or two bad pennies to turn it into something altogether more unhealthy.'

'You mentioned a different language before too?'

'Oh yes, they use all kinds of peculiar terms. "Dipping out".'

'What's that?'

'That means tears before bedtime. It's almost the worst thing that can happen to a twitcher. It means not seeing the bird you had hoped to see.'

'What could be worse?' asked Lex in exaggerated horror.

'Getting "gripped off".'

'Sounds painful.'

'Most twitchers would tell you that it is. Very. It means not only did you not see the bird that you had hoped to see, but worse, someone else did! Savvy?'

'Me comprendo.'

'And then there is "stringing".'

'Let me guess. Stringing someone along. Making out you've seen a bird when you haven't really.'

'Pretty much right. The birder's equivalent of "the one that got away".'

'What stops people from stringing all the time then? I mean bird-watching seems a pretty solitary hobby.' Lex didn't stop in her stream of thought even despite seeing Reg cringe involuntarily at the word "hobby". 'If all that a twitcher wants is to notch up the most ticks in his notebook, why doesn't he just stay at home and pretend he's seen lots of different birds?'

Reg looked at Lex, his expression full of pained patience, as of a teacher that had thought their prized pupil had grasped the complex subtleties of Relativity Theory only for them to fail to answer a rudimentary question on Ohm's Law. 'You haven't really understood any of this, have you?'

They walked on a short distance further, before Reg brought Lex to a halt beside one of the rough steps used for ascending the low blockade.

'Sorry, I must have been boring you with all this prattle.' He indicated a long section of flat stone atop the wall. 'Let's sit up here though and I think I'll be able to show you something that will amuse you.'

Lex cocked her head to one side and looked slightly dubiously, but then joined her stout companion, where he now sat on his cold rock perch, like a real-life Humpty Dumpty, his legs hanging in mid-air, kicking backwards and forwards with the childish excitement of anticipation. He might be rather patronising at times, but she had begun to find herself quite caught up in her companion's enthusiasm for his subject, and she was secretly intrigued as to what he had to show her.

'What are we waiting for?' asked Lex, after a minute's silence had elapsed.

In answer, Reg cupped a hand to his ear, and then pointed to the sky. In the direction he indicated a small speck was just visible, accompanied by the sound of a low distant drone. At first indistinguishable from the nearer flying dots that were gulls and terns, the size and shape of the small aeroplane gradually became apparent, as did its intended destination.

'It's not coming in here, is it?' asked Lex. 'Where can it land?' But even as she asked the question she noticed the narrow strip of moorland that had been cleared and cordoned off to form a short yet serviceable runway, and the white windsock that hung limply from its pole on the horizon. She looked questioningly at Reg, who silenced her with a bestilling hand and a 'wait and see.'

Closer, closer - the small propeller-powered craft seemed to momentarily disappear below the horizon of the edge of the island, and Lex feared that it must surely crash into the surrounding cliffs, and braced herself for the explosion, before it reappeared, seemingly now huge in the sky above her, with a renewed rush of turbulence and noise. It banked steeply once and then without more ado was gently idling across the hummocky security of terra firma.

The noise from the propellers had scarcely ceased and the blades themselves were still slowly rotating in their engines, before the rear door of the aircraft was violently thrown open and a large holdall, quickly followed by three strangely-attired figures, emerged. There was a brief animated discussion on the ground beside the plane, a rapid consultation of a large sheet of paper, and a succession of confused and varied hand signals and gestures, before a consensus of opinion seemed to be reached and the three figures started charging off across the moor directly towards where Reg and Lex sat.

'Twitchers?' asked Lex.

'Twitchers.' confirmed Reg.

If Lex hadn't known differently she could have been forgiven for thinking she was witnessing an army training manoeuvre. Each man - for men they all were - wore combat trousers, each of a different clashing camouflage shade: green and khaki, traditional; brown and fawn, desert warfare; and ... well, what field of combat were the final pair for? Pastel turquoise and bright blue. Tundra and swimming pool warfare? On top, one favoured a dark green roll-neck sweater, the second a leather jacket, the third - pastel cyan - was just wearing a thin T-shirt with a skull emblem and a heavy metal band logo emblazoned across the front. No anoraks - Lex was surprised. Each wore a hat, two woolly pull-ons, and the sartorially eccentric third a squashy, shapeless white affair, of a kind that Lex recognised a previous boyfriend of hers had worn to a cricket match she had accompanied him to, and whom she had remembered feeling embarrassed for then.

'I'm surprised they haven't asked the pilot to keep the engine running.' commented Reg. 'They'll be back and off again soon enough.' He continued with a descriptive running commentary of the three arrivals. 'Nice bins. Must have cost a packet. Don't recognise any of them. Fledglings, I'd say. Rich ones too. That plane charter wouldn't have been cheap. Nike trainers. They'll be unrecognisable before long. Heavy bag. Must be their tripods and gear. Not that they'll need much here. Hold on, here they come.'

Lex thought that the trio were going to pass by without a word, until one of them, perhaps recognising in Reg a semi-kindred spirit, grunted, 'Golden?'

Reg inclined his head in the direction they were already heading and they were gone without further exchange.

'Eagle?' queried Lex.

'Oriole.' corrected Reg. 'Not desperately rare. But rare enough to be worth a tick for a few newcomers.'

'How did they know?' Lex questioned, slightly bemused. 'You're not going to tell me telepathy, are you? My gullibility does have limits.'

'No.' Reg admitted, 'In fact, I think that I may be to blame. Pretty sure I am, actually. You see I reported it to *Birdline* first thing this morning. It's a sort of vast telephone database of current sightings.' he went on to explain.

'Why did you do that?' asked Lex. 'Particularly, after your experiences in Devon. I would have thought it was the last thing you would have encouraged.'

'It's a sort of point of honour, I suppose.' said Reg. 'Others might call it a generous spirit. Wanting other birders to be able to enjoy what one is enjoying oneself.' Reg opened his arms expressively, 'Sharing.'

Lex didn't fail to catch the wry smirk on his face though and was not fooled, 'And?'

'And I did have it all to myself all day yesterday.'

- - - - - - - - - -

Diana was laughing, 'And so when did you ever read Proust?'

'Before I met you, as it happens.'

'Really?'

'There are a lot of things you don't know about me, darling.' David smiled in a way that he hoped was enigmatic, 'A lot of things.'

Chapter Nineteen

'Graham!'

The melodramatically hushed tone of scandalised motherly outrage cut through the camp-site as loudly as if it had been bellowed through a tannoy system and piped into every tent. Raoul leaned over to where Eric was noisily rummaging through his rucksack and whispered, 'Shhh. Listen to next door. It sounds as though the worm has turned.'

'I won't fucking wear it.'

'Graham! I'm not going to tell you again.'

'Then don't,' came back the impeccably logical rejoinder, in a high boyish voice.

'And don't you ever use that language again.'

'I will if I want to,' came the defiant reply, reinforced in a slightly more self-conscious voice by, 'I will if I fucking want.'

'Graham! Where have you picked this up from? Is it those school children? What have they been saying to you? You know it's not nice to speak like that.'

Raoul was lying on his back, in the tent pitched alongside the one that currently resounded with the display of youthful rebellion, convulsed in silent glee. He kicked his legs in the air like a new-born baby, first liberated from the constrictions of its nappy. 'Oh dear. They grow up so quickly, don't they. Before she knows it he'll be snorting lines of coke, or bringing home some pregnant bimbo.'

'Or worse,' Eric slapped his partner's flailing feet, 'someone like you.'

The commotion at the village end of the camp-site hadn't gone unnoticed at Oliver and Leo's tent, even though it stood slightly apart from the other two pitches. Oliver was sitting on a small, foldable, canvas stool next to the open tent flap, picking dried mud out of the deep treads in his hiking boots with a grubby, flat-bladed knife. He was working diligently, his head bent industriously over his task, but it didn't stop him looking up at every fresh experimental expletive, a curl of a smile playing at the corners of his mouth.

Of the three sets of campers it was Oliver who saw

Daniel first. He saw him appear at the opening in the stone wall which connected the camping field to the main street in the village, and then, rather than follow the much muddied track, which designated the most direct route across the grass to the stile opposite, he watched him veer off to the left, stand momentarily outside the small tent occupied by the two rather noisy men, and then after a brief conversation, a sceptical glance and a cock of his head, crouch and disappear inside the canvas interior.

'It's rather squashed.' complained Daniel.

'Nonsense. Cosy.' replied Raoul.

Eric patted his hand on a cleared patch of ground-sheet in the furthest corner of the tent, close to where he still lay sprawled, 'You come and sit down here. Perhaps you can help me with my top.' he continued, as Daniel awkwardly tried to manoeuvre into the position he had been invited.

'Pardon?'

'My top.' Eric held out a glass container which appeared to contain dried fruit, sealed air-tight by a screw-top lid. 'I don't seem able to shift it and I know that Raoul has a very weak wrist.'

Daniel took the impenetrable receptacle and twisted it hard in his hands without anything budging. 'I think it needs a bit more torque. I can't get enough leverage while I'm sitting down. Perhaps if I ...'

'Don't stand,' both other men chorused in unison, as Daniel made moves to get to his feet.

'You've not been in a tent before, have you?' Eric asked, unnecessarily. 'The first rule is, don't stand up.'

'And the second is, don't fart in your sleeping bag,' said Raoul, throwing Eric an ugly grimace.

'And the third...' Eric was interrupted from continuing with a potentially interminable list, by more sounds of insurrection from next door.

'You can't stop me. I will if I fucking want.'

Raoul whispered confidentially to Daniel, 'I think we are witnessing puberty in all its glorious, multi-faceted action this morning.'

Daniel was relieved by the disturbance, to at last be able to raise the reason for his morning call, 'Actually, that may have something to do with what I wanted to ask you.'

'Oh?' said Eric.

'Well, kids at any rate.' He went on to explain about the spate of vandalism both at the shore office and at Old Light Cottage. He finished by saying, 'The camp-site is on the route between my place and the village. I just wondered if you had heard, or perhaps seen, anything unusual last night.'

Raoul gave Eric an impish smile but for once resisted the temptation of the innuendo, 'Unusual? Now let me think.'

Eric was more practical, 'About what time are you talking?'

'Just around dusk, as far as my cottage is concerned. I'd guess the office must have been much later, after everyone had left the pub.'

Raoul replied, 'Well, we were in the tavern until quite late last night and didn't notice anything untoward up to then.'

'When would that have been?' enquired Daniel.

Eric seemed unperturbed by the persistent questioning, 'What would you say, Raoul? Elevenish?'

'Maybe even a bit later. We were trying to delay having to come back to a damp tent in the rain. There were still a few folk left in the tavern, but most people seemed to have tucked up early.'

'And how about around the camp-site?' continued Daniel, 'Did you hear anything from the other tents?'

'No, all was quiet.' said Eric.

'Unlike this morning,' smiled Raoul, nodding his head towards the continued neighbouring debacle, from where the sudden increased volume of an exasperated mother's voice finally drowned out the sound of her son's spirited uprising and brought the family power struggle to a dramatic conclusion.

'You fucking little brat, you do whatever you fucking want then, but don't come fucking running to me when it all goes wrong.'

Daniel managed to squeeze himself out of the intimate confinement of Eric and Raoul's tent, and politely refusing the couple's invitation to join them for breakfast, strolled across to where Oliver was still sitting outside his alfresco accommodation. Daniel rubbed his hands up and down his legs as he walked, to restore circulation in legs cramped by the tent's lack of space, and he gave a mental nod of admiration towards the strength of constitution of individuals who chose to live in such close quarters in the name of fun. It was certainly no idea of a holiday to him.

Oliver greeted him with a smile, 'You survived the lion's den?'

'The lion's ...? Oh, yes,' said Daniel, catching on to the young man's allusion, 'Just about. It's a pretty lively crowd you've got staying around here.'

'All except me and Leo. We're fairly quiet.'

'Leo?'

'My friend.'

'Oh?'

Oliver felt he needed to clarify his description, 'I don't mean as in friend friend.' he said, glancing towards the other campers, 'We're both keen ornithologists and are here for the birds.'

'And have you found any?'

'Well Leo certainly appears to. He hasn't been back all night.'

- - - - - - - - -

'You seem to have written a lot about Graham?' said Diana. 'Was he based on anyone you know?'

David considered the question seriously before answering, 'Perhaps a bit of him is me at that age.'

'Is that how you felt? Who were you rebelling against at that age? Your mother would already have been ...'

'Dead. Yes. Perhaps the foster parents. I don't know. Perhaps the world at large. I seem to remember thinking it seemed a very unfair place at the time.'

'You've never really talked about this before.' Diana coaxed.

The tone of David's voice changed subtly: recognising the direction of his wife's inexperienced interrogation, he added 'Perhaps some of him is based upon the son I would have liked to have had too.'

It was an old conversation and one that Diana did not wish to return to.

Chapter Twenty

It hadn't really been the holiday he had envisaged. Strange how when you finally begin to believe you have laid a ghost to rest, that is when it chooses to pop out and come back to haunt you.

James had discovered the West Battery on his first day on the island and had made it his regular place of pilgrimage every following day since.

The Battery was constructed by Trinity House in 1863, and was intended to provide an alternative warning to shipping on occasion that the Old Light became mist enshrouded and ineffective. The Battery complex originally consisted of a stone gun platform half way up the west cliff, facing out towards the Atlantic, two eighteen pound cannon, a powder store, and several small cottages. The site remains largely intact to this day, although the cottages are now unoccupied and have since fallen into disrepair, their roofs collapsed in, and plants and multicoloured lichens increasingly over-run their once clean structures. Several small mounds of dried sheep dung within the ruinous stone walls and a trail of pea-shaped rabbit's droppings across the ground outside, reveal the various identities and decadent behaviour of the cottages' most recent inhabitants.

James sat on the flat platform, legs outstretched before him, his back resting up against the wall of the powder store. He had a fine view of the craggy coastline running away to his left, and an uninterrupted panorama of the sea ahead, although sight of where the one met the other, at the base of the cliffs below, was lost to him by the intervening continuation of the gun platform, which jutted proudly from the rock, like a prominent chin on the countenance of an immovable, stony-faced gentleman. He had been sitting on the very edge of this projecting feature earlier, gazing into the waters below, but whereas, on previous days, he had been contentedly occupied waiting and watching on the unlikely off-chance of spotting a surfacing seal or a big fish, today he felt restless and unable to lose himself in the pleasures of inactivity. He had moved back to the security of the stone wall in order to write, but even that had not been going well. Several sheets of paper had already been torn from his notepad and discarded: the tightly screwn, rejected pages lost now to the elements, the words and stories they told, to be read only by the sea and air. Normally, James would have abhorred such shameless littering, particularly in such an unspoilt spot as this, but overnight the island had lost its innocence for him, and in some small way he wanted to hit back and defile it. He re-read his latest attempt at penmanship, before consigning it to the same fate as its earlier discommunicated brethren, slowly and deliberately tearing it in half, then again in quarters, and then eighths, before finally allowing each piece of the literary jigsaw its freedom. A small gull swooped and pecked at one of the airborne pieces of paper, mistaking it for a potential meal, before agreeing with James' assessment of its merit, and allowing it to continue being blown seaward and to a soggy end.

James sucked on the end of his biro. One more attempt. It was important that he wrote this down. Come on now. Concentrate.

It was the sound of approaching voices that eventually ended a quarter of an hour of fruitful correspondence. James signed his name at the bottom of the page of script with a flourish he did not feel, and smote the last full stop with a force of finality. From where he sat he could not see the cliff path above and behind him, so he stood, circumvented the redundant cannon on the rock promontory, and peered around the corner of the powder store, anxious not to be seen himself, but interested to see who it was that presumed to invade upon his territory. Still some distance away, close to the top of the slope, he recognised the distinctive polar outlines of the two old women who had spoken to him the day before, when he had been quietly examining the mist nests and the elaborate Heligoland Trap that bird ringers had set up on the eastern terraces. He hadn't wanted to be disturbed then and he certainly didn't want to be now, but with the one path the only means of entrance or egress, and the Battery the apparent destination of the two walkers, a meeting and the inevitable exchange of polite conversation seemed unavoidable: 'Lovely day, isn't it?'; 'Doing some writing are you?'; 'Been to Lundy before?'; 'Lovely day, isn't it?'. No, the prospect was too horrible for words. Not now, not the way he was feeling, he just couldn't do it. There was no alternative: foolish though it made him feel, he would just have to hide and hope they didn't see him. He hurriedly folded the precious sheet of writing and slipped it into the inside pocket of his jacket, then scooped up the remainder of his belongings from the platform and put them in his day-sack, and then cast around his barren surroundings for some suitable cover.

'Lovely day, isn't it?'

'Yes,' agreed Gemma. "I'm so glad we decided on this route after all. Those early clouds all seem to have vanished now.'

Hermione drew up on her walking stick and came to a halt. 'Do you mind if we take a breather dear, before we carry on down?' She puffed out her cheeks, and took in a deep breath of air.

'No, not at all.' Her companion was only too keen to pause herself. 'Besides, the view from up here is magnificent. To think we spent all that money last year to go to the Canaries, when we can enjoy such beauty on our doorstep.'

'I wouldn't call a three-hour train journey and a two-hour boat crossing, on the doorstep exactly,' Hermione protested, although equally enraptured by the sight of sea and sky before her, continued more conciliatory, 'Although I know what you mean. It is very beautiful.'

'Doesn't it remind you somewhat of that bay in Turkey, what was it called ...?' Gemma reminisced, 'You know, those rough granite cliffs. And the sea! Do you remember me saying that I'd never seen such a shade of blue.'

'I do and it doesn't. It looks altogether different.'

Gemma persisted, 'But the water, just look at it. Who would have thought this was the Bristol Channel, you could imagine you were in the Mediterranean. Just look at the colour.'

Hermione tried - none to hard - to disguise a faint yawn. She knew what was coming and muttered under her breath, 'If only I had brought my paints along.'

'If only I had brought my paints along,' Gemma exclaimed.

'Yes, dear.'

They stared at the natural fusion of colour and form in companionable silence for some minutes: Gemma occasionally closing one eye and holding up a gauging finger, imagining the transformation of scene to canvas, of mixing the correct quantities of cyan and yellow to achieve that particular turquoise hue, visualising the breaking crests of the waves as white dabs on the end of her sabre-haired paint-brush; Hermione was wondering if it was too early for a quick snifter of Scotch. She was the first to break the silence.

'Who's that down there?' She held up her stick as a makeshift pointer, and then answering her own question, continued, 'It's that man from yesterday, isn't it? What on earth is the fellow doing?'

Gemma looked in the direction indicated and saw James, some distance below, ill-concealed, squatting down behind the brick rubble of one of the ruined walls of the nearest cottage. She laughed, 'Looks like he's been caught short, poor chap.' She pushed Hermione's still erect stick down, 'Put that thing away. I'm sure he doesn't want attention to be drawn to him.'

'Caught short, eh. That makes me think. Do you remember the time we almost went to Kythnos?'

Gemma groaned inwardly, as she recognised the start of an often told anecdote, and one which portrayed herself in a none too flattering fashion. Hermione was chuckling to herself as she continued, 'Do you remember, we were rushing to catch the ferry from Piraeus, and we were already late because the traffic was so bad. Do you remember?'

'Yes.'

'And you were bursting. Bursting, weren't you?'

'Yes.'

'And the traffic crawled along. And you were crossing your legs. And you didn't think you could hold on until we reached the port. And the traffic was going even slower. That's right, isn't it?'

'Yes.'

'And then suddenly you just hopped right out of the taxi, do you remember? Just opened the door and off you set. I wondered what in the name of heaven had come over you. And you sprinted across the road. I don't think I've ever seen you move so quickly. In and out of all those cars. And they were beeping their horns. What a noise! And where was it you found to go in the end?'

'In a bar.'

'A very seedy looking bar I seem to recall. And we never did catch our boat, do you remember?'

Gemma brought her friend's speech to a close. 'Are you ready to move on again now, dear?'

'Yes, I think so,' said Hermione.

'Onwards and downwards.'

Hermione stepped in to interrupt, 'Oh no. Let's go back. My leg is beginning to ache a little, and if we go down we shall be obliged to talk to that young man again, and I have absolutely no desire to renew his acquaintance. I've seldom met such a terrible bore.'

- - - - - - - - -

'I like those two. I hope they are going to turn up again.'

'That's almost the first complimentary thing you've said about the whole book.' said David with a hint of bitterness.

'Well I've not finished it yet.' explained Diana. 'One shouldn't judge a book until the last page.'

'I thought the expression was "by its cover".'

Diana palmed back the loose leaf sheets until the top one was uppermost again. It was a plain white sheet with the words Lundy and by David Sutton written across them in a hasty biro. 'Let's at least give it the benefit of the doubt.' Diana said, 'Last page.'

Chapter Twenty One

The glutinous purple blob, expanded and contracted, seething with a pent up latent anger. Or perhaps it was in the convulsive throws of a last desperate attempt to cling on to that fragile reality we call life. Whichever, Daniel was careful not to touch it.

There were several jellyfish stranded high, although far from dry, on the small expanse of beach. Lumpy little diaphanous mounds, gradually seeping into the sand like puddles. In the sea they swam proudly: a pulsating, air-filled, buoyant globe; a frilly skirt; and beneath its petticoats, waif-like tentacles trailing behind, slave to the water's currents as much as leaves blown in an autumn breeze. And each one carrying with it a stinging slap of rebuke to those foolhardy enough to ignore the latent sweet-shop message: look, but do not touch. Here on land though, with their dignity gone, they just became something squidgy to avoid stepping on, like a cow-pat in a field.

There were shells on the beach too: small pink periwinkles; long, dark razor-shells, with hairy beards protruding from beneath their rims; and delicate white spirals, all waiting to be ground down to form another grainy generation of sand.

A shrill scream reached Daniel's ears, followed quickly by another one, high-pitched and excited. It would be the school kids down on the rocks by the Landing Beach. He had passed them as he had followed the track down Millcombe Valley and walked across the concrete promenade, just above the cove. The *Oldenburg* had not yet arrived to drop of that day's contingent of trippers, and the waters of the Landing Bay were calm and still. The makeshift wooden pontoon, that was pushed out into the water to form a gentle transition between the sea and the shore, was left untended on the beach, looking like the devastated hulk of an unfortunate shipwreck, and the Landrover which would later ferry the visitor's luggage up to the village, was elsewhere. Even the construction workers who seemed to be constantly engaged raising clouds of white dust and filling the bay with the noisy sounds of their activity, appeared to have a day off. Daniel unshouldered his backpack, sat on the edge of the promenade wall, his legs hanging in mid-air below, his feet kicking backwards and forwards, and watched with amusement as two teachers, supervised by Julie, gave their chargelings a pep-talk about the ordeal that now confronted them.

'It may look cold, but once you're in you'll soon warm up.'

'Sir. It is cold. I put my foot in a pool over there and it was very cold.'

'Be careful near those rock-pools, the seaweed is very slippery. Now, who has been snorkelling before?'

One hand went up from the shivering, attentive cluster.

'Really, Jonathan? And where have you been snorkelling?' the young man continued, patronisingly.

'The Red Sea, Sir.'

'Really?'

'Yes, Sir. Twice. And the Cayman Islands. And ...'

'Yes, OK.'

'... the Great Barrier Reef.'

'OK. OK. I think we can take it that Jonathan knows how to snorkel. As for the rest of you, I want to show you some of the basics.'

'Will you be snorkelling too, Sir?'

'No, I will be watching from the shore this time. But the Warden and Miss Grant will be in the water with you all the time, won't you Miss Grant?'

'Will you Miss Grant?'

'Will you?'

'Will you?'

'Yes,' came the grudging reply, as the bespectacled, young woman shot a spiteful look towards her companion teacher, which was intended to convey 'you might have won the toss of the coin last night, but don't think that I'll be showing any leniency tonight when it is your turn to keep them entertained, while I'm off down the pub'.

'What do you do with your glasses, Miss?

'Do you wear your goggles over them?'

Sam Grant delved into the draw-string, rubberised bag, in which she had brought along the possessions she would be needing that day, and produced a vivid purple-coloured, customised face-mask and breathing tube.

'No,' she answered, 'I've got a special pair of prescription lenses in my face-mask.' She handed the apparatus to the nearest boy, 'Have a look through those, Tony.'

'It's all blurry. I can't see a thing.'

'No, but I will be able to underwater.' Miss Grant took the face-mask back. 'Listen up, everyone. I think Mr Dance wants to continue with his talk.'

'Thank you. Right. We'll be going in the water in the same groups of threes and fours that we divided into yesterday for the wild flower search. Now has everyone got their snorkelling equipment to hand. It's down there behind the rock, Alice.' He broke off to point out the missing tube and goggles. 'Now, test your face mask fits securely by pressing it against your face, breathing in, and if it still stays put when you take your hand away, it should be OK. Try and keep your hair out of the mask, Sharon. Tie it back if you need to. Everyone's OK? No, no, Peter. Keep breathing in. Better? Good. Now while I come around and make sure your breathing tubes are all fitted correctly, Miss Grant will tell you a few things you are likely to see underwater.'

'As you should already have read in your folders, the seas around Lundy are extremely unusual in the British Isles, and Lundy remains England's only statutory Marine Nature Reserve.'

'What's unusual about them, Miss?'

'Did you read your folder, Samuel?'

'Yes.'

'Well then, you should be able to tell me what's unusual about them. No? Anyone?'

One hand went up.

'Yes, Jonathan'

'The sea around Lundy is influenced by the Gulf Stream, making the waters unnaturally warm and clear. It also means that many kinds of marine life that would normally only live in the tropics can be found here, and nowhere else in Britain. Lundy is the only place where ...'

'Yes, thank you Jonathan.'

'... all five types of ...'

'Jonathan. Thank you. Yes, Jonathan is quite right about the Gulf Stream. Lundy is also the only place where all five types of British coral can be found. Now we don't normally associate coral with Britain, do we? Where else in the world might we find coral?'

'Red Sea.'

'Yes.'

'Cayman Islands.'

'Yes.'

'Great Barrier Reef.'

'Yes, very good.'

'Camden Market.'

'Yes,' Sam laughed, 'Perhaps there as well. So keep your eyes open for any underwater. I'm sure the Warden will point out any examples that she sees. Just make sure you don't touch.' Sam nodded towards Julie. 'Perhaps the Warden would be kind enough to tell us about any other local undersea denizens.'

'Denizens, Miss?'

'Critters to you, Alice.'

Julie had stepped forward from where she had been observing the group, sitting on a large seaweed bestraddled boulder. She was already stripped down to a bold-striped one-piece swimming costume, and looked toned and muscular to both Daniel and Drew Dance's appraising eyes. Her first sentence held the remainder of the band of daring divers equally spellbound.

'Of course the thing that everyone wants to see are the sharks.'

'Sharks!'

'Are there sharks, Miss?'

'Dangerous ones?'

'Like *Jaws*?'

'Or *Deep Blue Sea*?'

Julie laughed, 'No, not like *Jaws*. Although the sharks we have around Lundy are even bigger. They are Basking Sharks, but although they grow so big, they don't eat people, just tiny little organisms called plankton.'

'Like whales?'

'Yes, like whales.'

'And will we see a shark?'

'I'm afraid it's not very likely,' said Julie. 'Not underwater at any rate. I've only seen one once, and I've been snorkelling many times. If you really want to see one, you stand a much better chance if you go up on to the cliff tops and look down on them from above. Have a look in the church too, if you have time later. There is a big exhibit about Basking Sharks in the foyer, that you might all find interesting.'

Drew had by now completed his round of inspection and clapped his hands together for attention. 'OK everyone. Time to get into your costumes and into the water. Remember to rinse your face-masks in the sea before you put them on, it will help to defog them. Come along. Chop, chop.'

It was at this point that Daniel had decided to take his leave. He had no desire to expurgate painful memories of freezing swimming pools and icy school-day showers by watching a new generation undergo a similar torture. Experience 'makes a man of you' soon enough without sadistic teachers speeding up the process.

And so Daniel had followed the promenade around, out of sight of the snorkelling party, until it had given way to an irregular path of worn boulders and uneven grey stones, leading to a small, deserted patch of beach, in the shadow of the South Light, and squeezed between the rocky pinnacle of Rat Island and the crumbling, southern cliffs of Lundy itself. Looking on his map Daniel saw the area was called the Devil's Kitchen.

A bright red-billed oystercatcher watched him suspiciously from on top of a high barricade of fallen rocks. It was a surprisingly big bird, and seemed rather excited, running backwards and forwards along its wall of stones, trilling noisily, flapping its wings, and hopping up into the air, like a badly rehearsed ballet dancer whose opening night has come along too soon. Daniel didn't need the additional agitation. It had all started with Donald Trigg he realised now - if the old man had instantly clocked him as a police officer, what chance had he ever had of enjoying peaceful anonymity. The discovery of the damaged door the previous evening had only heightened his sense of mounting disquiet, and he now wondered if his island escape wasn't fast turning into his own Alcatraz.

Timothy was whistling a shrill but tuneful version of Gilbert and Sullivan's *Three Little Maids*. He was still wearing his trademark white nautical cap, but had now pulled on a navy, V-necked, monogrammed sweater over a white shirt, and sported a pair of cream-coloured trousers, immaculately pressed, with razor-sharp stand-up creases front and back. The thick, air-cushioned training shoes seemed a rather incongruous addition to his attire, but then so too did the fluorescent green fishing net, which he now suddenly started waving frantically around in the air above his head, reaching up to the full limit of the bamboo pole to which it was attached.

'Damn. Missed it.'

'What's that, darling?'

Deidre was sitting on a white moulded plastic chair on the wide veranda outside Bramble Villas. She had been gazing out over the short scrub and spiky bushes of the Millcombe Valley, and to the sea beyond, and daydreaming of past times: of the early morning sun rising over the Nilgiri Mountains, flooding the dark green woodland and rolling downs with brilliant light; of the orderly plantations of tea and coffee and tobacco beyond, and the bobbing heads of pickers and of wicker baskets filled with leaves, ever the scene of so much activity no matter how early she rose; and of a time when Ooty still was snooty, and before the tourists arrived and everything changed. It was the Villa of course that was making her feel nostalgic, she realised that. It was very much like the one her family had owned, built in the typical colonial style, high up on the hillside, overlooking the ramshackle tangle of houses in the town below and the reflected blue expanse of the lake. That was long before she met Timothy. She couldn't ever remember discussing her childhood with him. Or anything else, really.

'Red Admiral.'

'Is that good, darling?'

Timothy dropped his net on the ground, picked up a small, tightly-sealed jam jar, and came over to sit beside his

wife. He shook the jar slightly, and held it up for inspection.
'No, but these are. Just have a look at these little
beauties.'

Deidre peered through the glass, which was running wet
on the inside with lines of condensation. 'I can only see a few
leaves.'

'Lundy Cabbage leaves. And look,' he shook the
container again so that several tiny black dots attached
themselves to the beads of moisture on the surface of the jar,
'Lundy Cabbage aphids. They only live on this one plant and
no other in the whole world, and the Lundy Cabbage only
grows in this one small corner of this one small island in the
whole world. Incredible.'

'Incredible, dear.'

'And what's even more incredible, is that this one...'
He shook the jar again, 'No, this one here.' He pointed to a
speck indistinguishable from any of the others. 'Is a
completely new species. Several types of Lundy Cabbage
aphids have been previously identified and catalogued, but
none to my knowledge like this one. Can you see the slightly
elongated section between the second joint on the front legs,
and the more rounded mandibles? Quite unique. Who knows,
if it is a new species, perhaps they'll name it after me?'

'Would you fancy a cup of tea, darling?'

- - - - - - - -

'That Timothy was a dreadful bore. He really was just like the
way I've written him. Always banging on and on about those
awful insects. I got stuck talking to him one day after I just
arrived back from a long walk, and all I wanted to do was to
go back to the cottage for a cool shower and a freshen up, and
I must have had to suffer his non-stop monologue for the best
part of half an hour before I could find an excuse and drag
myself away. Absolutely incessant he was, and it wasn't even
as if he was chatting about something interesting. Just those
damn little bugs of his. I don't know how anyone could get
remotely excited about them. But all day long you'd see him
hunting around in the bushes and looking under leaves and
collecting the poor little critters in his specimen jars. It's his

wife I really pitied. I don't know how she put up with him.'
    'Would you fancy a cup of tea, darling?'

Chapter Twenty Two

Bang. Bang. Bang.

'Are you going to open up this door, or am I going to have to ...' Reality began to slowly seep back, forming a pathway of reason through the red mist that had clouded Liz's mind, '...have to ... have to go and get someone to break it down.'

Bang. Bang. Bang.

'I know you've got him in there.'

Oblivious to force or reason, the door of Admiralty Lookout remained stubbornly closed to the would-be boarder.

After their argument at the camp-site earlier that morning, Graham, far from running back to his mother to risk being spurned as she had already threatened, had taken Liz's words to mean that he was given free license to roam as he pleased, and had proceeded to do just that. His parting salvo had been, 'I'm going to stay with John. He understands me.' Since then Liz had waited, and she had waited, every moment expecting her errant son to return to the nest tearful and repentant for his foolish outburst and asking for her forgiveness, but when several hours had passed, when lunchtime had been and gone, and when there was still no sign of Graham, and no longer any prospect that he would be returning with his tail between his legs, she decided it was time to investigate herself. Her investigations had proved worrying. Yes, lots of the villagers seemed to know who John was. Yes, lots of the villagers seemed to know where John was staying. More worrying though were the descriptions of John as 'that strange, tall chap with the painted face' or 'the one that keeps himself to himself' and most alarming of all, the rumour she had now picked up from several different sources, 'the one they say's done away with his wife.' Whatever the truth or the lies, he did not sound the sort of person she wanted her Graham to be associating with.

It was a procession that had arrived at Admiralty Lookout. Like an Island Pied Piper, Liz had gathered followers as she had marched the length of the main track, her purpose, to rescue her son from evil incarnate. The purpose of her rag-tag band of disciples was in no way so honourable:

they had all realised that a show-down looked imminent, and it was a chance to revel in a bit of salacious pleasure and to confirm or otherwise if the week-long pub rumours had by any unlikely chance been true.

Bang. Bang. Bang.

The response when it came was from an unexpected direction. All eyes having been turned towards the small stone building, no one had noticed the approach of the white-faced Goth and the teenage lad from across the track to the east. 'Something I can do for you?' the tall figure called out, while the two newcomers were still some distance from the expectant gathering.

At the sound of the voice, Liz turned away from the wooden door, and, her face still contorted with anger, was about to transfer her fury towards the stranger who so clearly bore resemblance to the devil she had heard described. She was stopped in her tracks though by Graham, running towards her, his face lit up by a beaming childish smile, stripping away the years and once again transforming him into the idyllic near-babe-in-arms that she recognised, rather than the morning's incarnation of teenage-horror that she had shied away from with suspicion and fear.

'Come and see. Come and see.' He had caught up with where she was standing now, and was practically tugging at her clothes in his excitement to lead her.

'What is it?' Liz asked, instantly pacified by the unexpected turn of events.

'John's been showing me the Basking Sharks. There's three of them now, just off Tibbetts Point. They're fantastic. You can see them so clearly from the cliff top.' He was hopping now in his impatience to return to the spectacle. 'Come and see.'

The mention of John had once again raised Liz's suspicions but she was astute enough to realise that the chance of reconciliation with her son hung in the balance. 'Come on then,' she smiled, 'show me your sharks.'

John had almost joined the couple now at the enclosure surrounding his property. Graham ran up to him, 'Are you coming back too?'

'No. I must see how Sophie is. Remember I told you

she's not been well. She was going to take a sedative this afternoon, so she's probably still dead to the world.'

At the word 'dead' there was an audible gasp from the remaining spectators, who had hung around, hoping that the finale might hold more fireworks than the damp squib which had diffused Liz's spark.

John shook his head at the mentality of the gathering. He spoke to Liz, 'It's always the same. Wherever you go, just because you act a bit different, you always get these lot,' he threw a dismissive glance towards the bystanders, 'forever wanting to gawp and stir up trouble.' He turned back to Graham. 'Don't forget what I told you, "Don't let the ..."'

Graham jumped in with a cough, now embarrassed to have the profanity uttered in front of his mother, 'No. No, I won't.'

- - - - - - - - - -

'And so had he done away with his wife?' asked Diana.

'Girlfriend actually. No, of course not. But you know how these sort of rumours get started.'

'But did you actually see her?'

'No. She was ill.'

'Really?'

David rose to the bait, 'Now don't you start. She was ill. OK? Don't try to go making a mystery where there isn't one.'

'What? Doing your job for you, you mean?' asked Diana pithily, sinking back into the safety of the manuscript, before her husband could think of a reply.

Chapter Twenty Three

There was a large crowd in the Marisco Tavern that evening, but the atmosphere was strangely subdued.

It was Raoul who voiced the feelings of the whole, 'What's wrong with this place tonight? It's like being in the ballroom of the Titanic with everyone already knowing what happens at the final dance.'

Eric answered, 'I think the Warden's still worried about those two missing climbers. I heard her asking people again earlier if anyone had seen either of them.'

'I expect they just went back on the boat.' said Raoul.

'That's what I told her,' agreed Eric, 'But she seemed to think not. She said their bags were still up at the Castle.'

'Perhaps they're camping out for a few nights then. I know it's a small island, but there's plenty enough places to disappear if you wanted to live rough for a while.'

'Yes, perhaps. Our young friend from the camp-site looks none too happy either.'

The two men looked across to where Oliver was sitting at a table with Reg and Lex, all three of them not speaking, all staring desultorily into near-empty beer glasses. Finally Lex broke the silence.

'Come on then. I've told you why I'm so fed up. What's eating you two?'

They answered in unison.

'Leo.'

'Brad.'

Oliver continued, 'It's strange that he hasn't turned up yet. It's not unlike him to be out all night when he's trying to spot a particular bird. I remember him once rushing around to my place, first thing in the morning it was, absolutely soaked to the skin, just to tell me that he had seen a particular Barn Owl that he had been on the lookout for. He must have watched for it all night, in the pouring rain. He's like that. But it's unusual for him to be gone as long as this.'

'What was he hoping to see?' asked Reg.

'The shearwaters.' said Oliver.

'Oh yes, of course. Well I hope he managed to. It must be a magnificent experience.'

'That's what I mean. If he saw them, he would have been back straight away, wanting to brag about his sighting and make a note of all the details in his journal. He is very particular.'

Lex had listened slightly bemusedly to this description of fanaticism, and then asked Reg about Brad.

'Oh, it's silly of me.' said Reg. 'It's just that I feel a bit responsible for the lad. Apparently Julie's still not been able to track him down either, and I'm just worried that he might still be lying face down in a ditch somewhere, you know, if he took a tumble after that night he was in here last. I just wish now that I had seen him all the way to his front door. At least then I would feel I had done my duty.'

'We do make a sorry lot, don't we?' said Lex.

'I think the only two that aren't, are that couple over there.' indicated Reg.

Sam had kept to the promise she had made herself on the beach earlier, and had insisted that Andrew take the night watchman role that evening, to make sure their charges were not tempted to stray, or get up to any late-night antics back at the Quarters. She had seen the children safely into their bunks, and had left Andrew watching the tiny, portable black-and-white TV, that passed as the only form of entertainment in the communal area of their lodgings. 'Have a nice evening' drawled in a caustic, over-exaggerated American accent had been his parting barb to her, as she had taken her leave, intending to spend an evening of relaxed and *adult* conversation in the pub.

Her first glimpse of the interior of the Marisco Tavern had slightly depressed her, and she wondered if she hadn't yet again drawn the short straw, and that a livelier evening would have been in store watching a fuzzy-focussed repeat of Inspector Morse on the ten inch screen, interrupted by frequent calls from a nervous Alice Tovney wanting to be escorted out in the dark to use the toilet. The atmosphere in the bar was like a cold day in Siberia, and as all heads turned freezingly as one in her direction as she opened the door, she was reminded of the opening scene of *An American Werewolf in London*, and wondered which local was going to warn her not to go walking back across the moor on her own late at night. Take courage,

Sam. Nothing can be as intimidating as that first occasion as a student teacher, of walking into a class of marauding teenagers and having to restore order. Deep breath. Four strides to the bar. 'Whisky and ice, please.'

James was already seated when Sam asked if she could join him. Of all the faces in the room he had looked the most inoffensive. He had taken a little bit of thawing, and had rather stiffly refused her offer of a drink with a curt, 'I don't', but Sam was determined that she was going to make the most of her evening of freedom and had persevered, and the two of them were now engaged in easy conversation.

'So you didn't see anything?'

'Nothing at all, except for a few anemones and one crab. I had to spend almost of all my time fishing out the poor kids that were so cold they had practically lost the use of their limbs. It was a stupid idea of Drew's - he's my fellow teacher - in the first place. They needed wet-suits really.'

They were both laughing now. 'So what's on the agenda for tomorrow?' asked James.

'Bungy jumping from the North Light followed by falcon training on Tibbetts Hill.' joked Sam.

James was instantly interested, leaning forward over the table towards Sam, 'Falcon training? Are you interested in birds?'

Sam was surprised at her new friend's sudden alertness, 'No, it was a joke. I mean, I am quite interested in birds. But we are not going falcon training.' she tried to explain, thinking that James had not picked up on her jocular tone. 'I think we will be looking over the Old Light and the ancient burial ground tomorrow.' she continued, more seriously. 'Mix in a bit of history and archaeology as a variety to the nature studies.'

James had sunk back a little with a dismissive 'Oh' in reply and so, ever the attentive teacher, Sam tried to restimulate his interest by asking, 'Why? Are you interested in birds?'

'It's not my interest. It's my life.' he replied.

Daniel was feeling very suspicious. It didn't help that he was also acting very suspicious.

He had had an opportunity to do a lot of thinking, alone on the beach earlier, and he realised he could no longer allow himself to be a passive observer in the continuing drama that was developing around him; a drama that he had knowingly pursued from the mainland. He had originally thought that Lundy was going to provide nothing more than a bolt-hole - for him as well as others - whereas increasingly it looked as though it was going to provide a catalyst for more violence. He now wondered if it could provide an explanation too.

He had waited for darkness, and until he could hear the low hum of voices from the Marisco Tavern, indicating how most of the islanders would be passing the evening. He walked briskly along the road past the solid and silent hulk of the church, darkness following in his every footprint, not even the solitary glow of a lone devotional candle to brighten his path. Or lighten his task. The path forked: right, to follow alongside a low hedge across the southern extremity of the island - perhaps the way to go on the journey back - or left, along a well defined, straight track leading to the Castle. Daniel guessed from the description he had overheard, that this must have been the point that Reg and Brad had parted company a couple of evenings previous. There were no lights showing in the Castle tonight, and with the aurora of the village now well behind him, and the moon only showing weakly from behind the thick, night clouds, darkness was nearly complete. It was cold too: the gnawing cold of fear, and the clammy cold of dread.

Something scuttled across the path in front of Daniel, and he was just in time to see a large black rat pass like a shadow across the grey tarmac of the track and vanish into the dark obscurity of the vegetation on the verge. Daniel had read that Lundy had the dubious distinction of being one of the last havens in Britain for this larger cousin of the more common brown rat. He hoped that no other rats, common or human, were abroad tonight.

Lundy Castle was built by King Henry III in 1244, and the construction was reputedly paid for by the sale of rabbits, since the island was a Royal Warren at that time. The outer walls of the building have long since been reduced to little more than low lines of rubble by a combination of adverse weather and pillaging settlers, who used the stone to build their own dwellings, but the central keep, with its three-feet-thick walls of light-grey granite, still stands a defiant block against man and the elements. Three cottages were built inside the keep for the use of local fisherman, but these have since been turned into holiday accommodation, as has the rather incongruous granite structure built alongside the Castle by the Post Office in 1887, and which was originally used as a cable station.

Daniel climbed up the low bank to approach the Castle from the west side, stepped over the collapsed ruin of one of the outer walls, and entered the door that led into the central courtyard of the keep, surrounded by the white-washed stone walls of the three cottages on each side of him. The floor of the courtyard was made up of flat slabs of grey stone, and his footsteps seemed to echo unnaturally loud around the open-air amphitheatre. Windows looked down on him from every side and he wondered how many pair of unseen eyes could be watching: he felt like a gladiator entering the Colosseum, surrounded by a hushed and expectant audience, cloaked in the blackness of anonymity in their seats, just waiting for the house lights to go up and the action to begin.

He crossed to the most southerly end of the courtyard and cupping his hand around his eyes, peered into each window on the ground floor, before finally knocking tentatively on the wooden front door. There was no answer, as he had expected, and no lights had gone on in any of the other properties, and he began to feel more confident that he was indeed alone.

Disappointed to see the property was secured with a sturdy Chubb lock and recognising that it would defeat his own modest house-breaking abilities, Daniel turned to his cruder Plan B. The downstairs' window proved no match for the sharp, flat rock he had purloined earlier from the beach, and he was soon able to enlarge the hole in the broken pane until it was big enough for him to reach his arm in and unlock the window, without snaring himself on any of the shards of jagged glass. He tried to justify his actions by thinking that one more act of vandalism would go barely noticed after the spate of destruction the previous night.

Now inside the cottage, and with still no sound of human activity anywhere in the vicinity, Daniel decided his search would be made much more speedily and more effectively by throwing some light on the situation. He fumbled along the wall until he came to a small cabinet on which a table light carried with it the promise of illumination.

It was Mark and Brad's cottage. Daniel would have recognised as much, if he hadn't already known, by the jumble of bulky climbing apparatus that was piled up under the stair-well, close to the front door. Multi-coloured ropes, coiled and tied; metal clips and fastenings; and fearsome-looking boots, spiked and toe-capped. Daniel made a perfunctory search of the whole property, upstairs and down: two bedrooms on the first floor, one tidy, one bed unmade; large kitchen dining-room below with long pine table; small shower-room and separate WC; and a roomy, square lounge, with its sloping wooden ceiling, fireplace, and baggy loose-covered sofa and chairs. It was here that he found the book he had come for.

He turned to the last page of writing. It was dated three weeks previously and signed by a Mr and Mrs Arthur Pressman of Ripon, Yorkshire: *Smashing time, great weather and walks, we'll be back!* Brad and Mark had appeared to be as equally uncommunicative in their own property's log book as they had in the communal journal in the Marisco Tavern. No matter, it wasn't what he had really come for. He thumbed back through the pages, hoping that other visitors hadn't been so literary as to have filled the whole book with their musings, and that the previous years' accounts would still be recorded in this volume, and not in some dusty tome now consigned to archive heaven. April. April. That was what John had reckoned. Flicking back months and pages. February. December. Brave soul to have stayed here then. October. July. June. May. March. March? Daniel turned back again in the diary. No April. Nothing. No record of anyone having stayed. No account of the month ever having existed. Perhaps the tall Goth had been mistaken and it had been a different month. Daniel quickly skim-read the final entry for March and the first for May but both seemed innocent enough accounts of family holidays and happy, lazy island days, except ... the last entry for March seemed to end a bit abruptly, and wasn't signed in the usual fashion of Mr and Mrs Arthur Pressman of Ripon, Yorkshire, or Jim Tupp and Family of Atlanta, GA. Daniel examined the book more closely and noticed that deep in the fold of pages disappearing into the binding, there were several minute jags of paper, where a page, or perhaps two or three had been removed. Carefully removed, though, perhaps with a knife, because the extraction was certainly not apparent at a cursory glance. April, if not the cruelest month, was certainly becoming the most curious.

Daniel was disappointed though. He had come hoping for answers and he felt he was leaving with nothing but more questions. It was just as he was about to turn off the light, and with a final glance around to make sure that everything looked in order before he left, that he noticed the slight mark on the red tiled floor by the front door. Like the missing pages in the log-book, the blemish showed evidence of having been worked upon with care, and had been all but obliterated by thorough cleaning and scrubbing, but blood leaves its stain like a birthmark and is not so easily washed away.

The clouds that had been massing again all afternoon and evening, had formed themselves into a triumphant army in the short space of time that Daniel had been in the Castle, and now proceeded to throw down a barrage of artillery on the fortification below. Daniel considered waiting for the downpour to pass but, particularly after the discovery of the disguised blood patch, decided he didn't want to linger any longer than he had to in his present spot. He already felt defeated, another soaking would add little to his misery and discomfort.

What few stars had illuminated his journey to the Castle had now disappeared, and he blundered on blinded by the torrential rain, until he reached the comparative security of the main track. He dismissed his earlier idea of forking off around the southern edge of the island and returning to his lodgings via the cliff path, and instead retraced his steps, following the more direct route through the village, no longer caring if he bumped into anyone on the way. He passed the Old School and thought of Lex tucked up inside, warm and secure, and of her visit the night before. He hoped he hadn't been too rude with his rejection. And why had he refused? Love? Fear?

They were equally strong emotions. Except where love makes you lazy, fear can often make you bold.

The rain was cold and was making Daniel shiver, and he increased his pace through the familiar streets of the village, until he veered off to cross the camp-site and into the field beyond. He tripped over several sleeping sheep in his anxiety to return to the dry and warm of Old Light Cottage, and set the whole field off in a startled cacophony of annoyed bleats and disgruntled baas. He stumbled in the wet grass, falling headlong, his hands flailing out in front of him pitching into something moist and warm, which he was glad he could not see due to the darkness, but which he could smell all too well was none too nice. Back on his feet again, the vague outline of the impounding wall was upon him, and having lost his path and strayed from the direction of the gate, he followed the wall along until he reached the only exit. A fleeting hint of moonlight from behind the all-engulfing clouds, allowed him a brief glimpse of the old lighthouse tower not far away and to his right, and he was able to regain his bearings and hurry on with quickened pace across the springy turf and to the longed for sanctuary of Old Light Cottage.

He fumbled in his pocket for his key, momentarily thinking he had lost it in his fall and cursing Tom's efficiency at making the repairs to his front door, before his hand alighted on the missing object and he fell inside, blocking out nature's onslaught behind him with a determined bang. The difference between the noise and confusion outside and the quiet and calm inside was like achieving instant karma. Daniel fumbled around for the light-switch and was surprised when pressing it produced no results. He illuminated the dial on his wrist-watch. After midnight. He hadn't realised he had been out so long. The electricity in the village would have just been turned off. He had left a box of matches by the cooker, and remembering there were some candles provided with the property, Daniel was soon able to restore a romantic glow to his warm shelter. He stripped off his wet jacket and threw it down by the door next to his shoes, and then examined his mucky hands critically, sniffing each unsavoury finger suspiciously. He fished around in his trouser pocket for something to clean them with and drew out an off-white rag, already rather unpleasantly soiled as a result of his boat-crossing expulsions. He rubbed the soft material across his dirty palms, transferring more grime to the delicate linen. Daniel looked at the handkerchief with disdain. It was hardly worth washing; it was only fit to be thrown away now. He got up, about to discard the cloth in the rubbish bin, when his eyes suddenly alighted on a small monogram, meticulously stitched in a fine pink cotton diagonally across the bottom corner of the material. It was the initials H.C..

Happy Christmas? Habeas Corpus? Or Hannah Croft? Perhaps it hadn't been such a wasted night after all.

- - - - - - - - -

'Just as a point of style ...'

'Yes?' David asked, rather aggressively.

'Well,' Diana continued, 'It just seemed to me that your description of Lundy Castle, half way through the chapter, rather broke up the flow and suspense of that piece of description. I don't know if you'd agree with me?'

'And how would you suggest I put it?' her husband questioned, not expecting any further constructive criticism.

Diana was not finished though, 'I suppose I would probably have included it right back at the beginning of the book when you wrote that large chunk of blurb about Lundy generally. Or perhaps you could do it as a footnote.'

'Or leave it out altogether?' David asked sarcastically.

'Better still.'

Chapter Twenty Four

He would never forget walking into that nursery.

The walls were painted light pink up to the level of a waist-high decorative border of dancing unicorns and fantasy flowers, and then pure, virginal white above to the ceiling. Underfoot the carpet was so soft. The sound of each slow footfall swallowed up in a tender concertinaring of thick natural fibres and pastel shade shag-pile.

The whole house was so silent. Eerily so. The hushed silence of airless expectation or the respectful silence of the dead? It was hard to tell which.

There was a mobile above the cot, he remembered that vividly. Strung across, from one side to the other. Cut-out cartoon characters and a line of little bells. He could imagine the cardboard shapes rocking gently back and forth on a breeze, and the delicate tinkle of the chimes playing a random wind-tune. Except today they remained as still and silent as her future. As his past.

There was a slight smell of disinfectant. It was intermingled with other smells: the cloying humidity of baby oil and the sweet scent of cut flowers in a vase on the window sill, but the disinfectant pervaded, as though eradicating rival scent particles in the atmosphere in the same way as it cut through harmful baby germs on the hospital-clean surfaces of the nursery. There was no smell of milk. People always say you can smell milk in nurseries. But like rainbows in a thunder storm, or swallows in the summer-time, these are things you only notice when your heart is full of joy. When your mood is otherwise, you can't see rainbows for rain clouds, nor swallows for heat haze: and as for milk? It simply wasn't there.

There was a large wooden chest against one wall, stencilled with unicorns to match the border. The stencilling had been done carefully but by an inexperienced hand, and it was possible to see where several of the delicate images were smudged, or had been redone over a previous attempt below. Piled up on top of the chest was a slightly untidy pile of colourful blankets, and the corner of another patch of linen showed from beneath the closed lid of the trunk. Folded on top of the whole precarious tower of fabric was a small, yellow, all-in-one baby's jumpsuit, and a white cotton bonnet that looked like it had been thrown deceptively casually at a rather jaunty angle to the whole purely for aesthetic effect, since it didn't appear as though it could provide a practical benefit for any juvenile wearer.

All of these things he took in.

At the foot of the chest there was a small toy. Lots of others lay strewn around the room, but this one he particularly noticed. It reminded him of one he had had himself when he was little. This one was a bit nicer perhaps: the paint a little more glossy and bright, and the carving a little more finished, but the concept was the same. It was a wooden chicken - a cockerel actually, judging by the painting of its brilliant red and yellow plumage, and with its proud crested head held high and its beak half open as if in readiness to break into voice - but in place of legs it sat upon a small wheeled wooden trolley, to which a string was attached with which to pull it along. He remembered dragging his version of this poor fowl everywhere with him when he was about three, trailing it behind him unconsciously, inseparable from him as though it were a grafted on tail, rolling behind him on its wheels, or sometimes when the ball-bearings got rusty and the wheels became stiff and wouldn't turn, bouncing along, bright plumed head over mottled feathered heels, banging into walls, and knocking the paint off skirting boards. It was one of his earliest memories. He wondered whether this one had been bought with the baby in mind or whether it was one of her parent's reliving their own childhood experiences.

Close to the chicken on the carpet was a toy he had seen once before, in the window of Mothercare. It was a baby chair but it looked like it would have been more at home on the control deck of the Starship Enterprise. The baby sat in presumed comfort in a softly padded sling in the centre of the contraption, while all around, spaced out on a colourful plastic rim, were myriad fascinating distractions; enough to have baby's mind whirling by the embarrassment of rich entertainments. Should I play with the duck in the bubble of water? Or the button that plays a tune? Or the light that turns red? Or the one that turns blue? Choice? Is it a healthy thing? Aren't humans often happy when there is no choice; no dilemma as to what to do, where to do it, when to do it? No opportunity to look back and think they had a choice back then and they made the wrong decision? Doesn't choice just mean that you have no one left to blame but yourself?

He knew he had no choice. And no one he could blame.

Leaning against the wall, beside the painted box, was a folded push chair and next to that, rather incongruously, an ironing board - never an easy thing to find a place to store. And on the opposite wall, beside the door, was a small chest of drawers, painted white, with small, white plastic handles. He imagined the sensation of pleasure caused by the smoothness of the drawers moving backwards and forwards on their new, well-oiled runners.

Still the house was silent. As if the air had all been sucked out of it, except the sharp tang of disinfectant continued to hang in the atmosphere, so he knew that this couldn't be so. The baby was perhaps the stillest thing of all. A slight mound beneath a blanket the only indication of its presence. No sign of the usual minuscule movements of somebody comfortably asleep: a fluttering of the eye-lids or the shallow, rhythmic rise and fall of the chest, nor even the jerky, reflex twitches of the restless slumberer, and certainly no noise at all: no gentle snores or happy baby gurgles. Silence. The behind-closed-doors, sleepy soft furnishing, padded silence of suburbia.

That was when he killed her.

- - - - - - - - -

Diana looked rather ashen-faced, 'I wish you hadn't reminded me of that. What a terrible time.'

'It's over now,' her husband tried to reassure her.

'Those nightmares you had then. It was horrible.'

'I know.'

'Let's hope they never put you through that again.'

'They?' David questioned.

'Why the Force of course,' Diana looked puzzled. 'Who else?'

'No,' David sounded distracted, his memory once again returning him to the first time he had entered the infant's nursery, 'of course, the Force. Who else.'

Chapter Twenty Five

Julie found Daniel before Daniel found Julie.

'Hi there.' she called out, as she saw Daniel's long-striding approach across the field, 'I was hoping to see you last night. You remember you asked if there was anything missing from the shore office after the window was smashed, well I've just discovered that there is.'

Daniel had caught up with where she stood now and rather impatiently took her arm, carrying on walking at the same time, 'I know. I know. And I think I can show you where it was taken.' he said. 'Well come on,' he continued, as Julie showed some reluctance in being guided where he was trying to lead. 'And we'd better grab a couple of strong-arm helpers on the way. Do you think any of the lads working down on the cliff road would be game?'

'For what?' asked Julie. 'You'd better tell me what you have in mind first.'

It was a delegation of four that stood in front of Big St John's cottage three quarters of an hour later. The one-time farm building had now been split into two detached holiday properties, both tucked away on a sheltered plateau, overlooking the St John's Valley and, on a clear day, with fine views east, out over the sea to distant Devon. Not wanting to be party to yet another island break-in, this time Julie had come equipped with a master key to the quarters, and without so much as a knock of advanced warning, had opened the front door of the property, letting it swing open inwards on its hinges. She waved her hand in the fashion of a bowing invitation towards Daniel, 'Over to you, I think.'

Everything was silent within and Daniel entered alone, signalling for Julie and one of the workmen to stand by the front door, and for the other to keep watch at the rear of the building. Was he about to enter the house of a murderer? Would there be a particular look to the place by which it was possible to instantly identify the perverse psychology of its inhabitant? Chairs spaced too far apart? Cutlery in too orderly rows? Covers not matching cushions? Carpets clashing with curtains? Daniel knew that rooms, like faces, could not be read so easily and did not usually give up their hidden story without detailed examination, but in the same way that you may distrust a stranger's appearance at first glance without any more justification than a vague sense of unease, so Daniel felt this cottage would reveal the saga he wanted told.

The front door led straight into a spacious hall area, off which there was a small cloakroom to the right, and, to the left, a kitchen, separated by a low, dividing wall. Further doors led off left and right, both of which were shut. Daniel opened both in quick succession, confirming that the one-storey bungalow was empty.

The lounge was a pleasant room, brightly lit, even on such an overcast day as today, by the presence of two large picture windows facing out over the sea, and a third window looking towards the approach to the village. A table had been set earlier for breakfast, and a single cup and empty cereal bowl had still to be washed up and cleared away. A solitary hard-backed wooden chair was pushed back at an angle from the table. The opposite corner of the room contained a large floral-patterned sofa, neatly folded on top of which were a navy sleeping bag, a woolly blue blanket, and a thin, misshapen pillow, indicating that the divan also did part-time service as a bed. A slender book lay open on top of the pile of linen. Daniel read the title: *Birds of the North Devon Coast*. He picked it up and saw it was open at a page of colour plates illustrating varieties of terns. Beside two of the pictures was the scribbled, handwritten word 'seen' followed by a date and time. Daniel quickly flicked through some of the other pages and noted that many were similarly annotated. One page had its top corner folded over, and a big photograph of a Peregrine Falcon circled with the words 'must see' written beside it. Daniel read the brief description of the bird: *This fierce and extremely fast raptor catches birds in mid-flight by approaching them from high above and diving to take them by surprise. In the final stages of its dive, or stoop, it has been recorded as reaching speeds of 250mph. Peregrines are widely distributed, typically nesting on rocky ledges and cliffs. The rugged coastline of north Devon and the island of Lundy are among the birds most favoured haunts in the British Isles.*

Beside the sofa was a small pile of women's clothing,

and tucked away out of sight behind the furniture was an empty and folded rucksack and a small toilet bag, which contained the barest of essentials: a flannel; a toothbrush; a bottle of unperfumed shampoo; a container of wet wipes; one lipstick, crimson - the only nod towards vanity; and a half empty, blue-wrapped pack of Tampax. Daniel crossed to the other room.

Here there were two single beds, separated by a small wooden cabinet and a barricade of shoes and clothing. Daniel was secretly relieved to discover that he was not the only person who chose to live in squalor. Indeed, he wondered how the two occupants of the room could ever have coped with sharing together: one bed was neatly made, its sheet and blanket stretched taunt and uncreased across its surface, like a calm sea undisturbed by the slightest ripple; the other was a jumble of bed-clothes, hastily flung back in a pile towards the bottom of the mattress, spilling like a magnificent rising wave from a Hokusai painting, just waiting to fall, crashing and descending down upon some unfortunate beneath. Each side of the room was similarly different: the one minimalist - practically devoid of personal possessions; unreadable - the other, a clutter; a life spread out to be sieved and analysed.

Daniel turned from the regimented austerity of the right hand bed to the happy detritus of its verso counterpart. He picked up a half-eaten chocolate bar from where it lay on the pillow and placed it on the bedside cabinet, next to a CD Walkman and a small pile of CDs: Hotel California, the Housemartins. On the unmade bed itself there was a large A4 pad, open, a cheap biro lying across the blue-lined paper, the top couple of sheets of which had been roughly torn out and were missing. Daniel flicked through the rest of the pad, but the other pages were all blank. He held the uppermost sheet of paper up to the light of the window to see if any of the writing that had been done on the missing sheets had made an impression below, but there was no visible indentation on the page. It was probably of no consequence anyway. There was a paperback novel too, half caught up in the tangle of sheets at the foot of the bed - *Birdsong* by Sebastian Faulks. Inside the front cover was written the name James Brewer and the date August 1998, presumably when it had been purchased.

Julie entered the bedroom just in time to see Daniel fling off the remaining bed-covers and, sprawling lengthwise across the mattress so that his feet hung over one side and his head over the other, peer underneath the mass of hard springs. He disappeared still further as he felt for something just out of reach, before hauling himself back up and sitting upright on the bed, a look of triumph on his face and a tight bundle of items held in his hand.

'Is this what you were going to tell me was stolen from the office?' he asked, holding out his new discovery.

Julie took the creased and dirty, red rain-hood and the solid chunk of grey metal that had once formed the shaft of a Stanley knife, and nodded grimly, recognising them as the items that Mark had handed in to her several days earlier. 'How did they get here?' she asked, rather unnecessarily.

Daniel's reply was interrupted by a shout from outside and the sound of urgent footsteps from the adjoining room. The head of the workman who had been standing guard at the front of the cottage appeared at the door.

'They've taken off,' he said anxiously, 'I called out, but they'd already spotted me. Just coming around the path to the north they were. They've run back the same way, but you should catch them if you're ...'

Daniel was already on his feet and racing for the door, pushing Julie to one side in his haste.

'... quick.'

They were already out of sight by the time that Daniel emerged from the cottage and into the fresh air again. He suddenly realised that he had no idea even how many people he was pursuing. Not one, that was for sure, the alert sentry had definitely said 'they'. But two? Three? Surely, not more? No, not unless he was completely mistaken in his assumptions, and every thing had proved him correct this far.

The weather that had started off miserably had deteriorated even in the short time that Daniel had been in the cottage, and he was surprised to feel a few cold drops of rain on his face as he followed the grassy track northwards, leaving St John's and the neighbouring, low-lying bunker of Government House behind, and came upon one of the tunnel-like entrances through the thick tangle of rhododendron branches, leading down and along the eastern slopes of the island. There was no sign of human life, fleeing or otherwise, along the open expanse of the cliff top, and so with no more ado, Daniel ducked his head beneath the first entwined clump of branches, and entered the dark tunnel of flora.

It was proving difficult now to keep up the speedy progress he had made across the open ground. The path descended, albeit gently, but was littered with stumpy, protruding roots and rotting leaf debris which combined to make a treacherous surface. Daniel's only comfort was that his quarry would be finding the going equally awkward, although he was only too aware that the trapped beast has little thought for fear if it sees some small chance of escape. The path through the dense bushes suddenly levelled out and Daniel was able to increase his pace again, although in his haste he continually snagged his clothing on the rough undergrowth, and twice felt an out-hanging twig dig painfully into his cheek, causing him to jerk his head backwards, too late to prevent the wood creating an ugly raised weal across his face. A month earlier and the rhododendron would have been in full bloom, a mass of purple and red flowers; now their evasive advance was hacked back, leaving a gloomy forest of stunted shrubs and truncated boles. In the dark catacomb of boughs and limbs, Daniel sensed rather than saw the mass of the looming banks to his left; saw just the occasional flash of blue of the sea on his right. Bent almost in half to duck under one particularly low branch, now skipping up to vault a severed stump. Was it his mistake, or did it suddenly look slightly brighter ahead? The light at the end of a tunnel had seldom looked so dim.

It was only as he came out into the open again, and was able to completely straighten up after his hunched progress through the interminable bower, that Daniel realised he was not alone. Hot on his heels, and looking depressingly more energetic than he was feeling himself, was Julie.

'Where now?' she said, hopping from one foot to the other, both to keep her muscles warm, and judging by the look of happy excitement on her face, out of the pure childish anticipation of the thrill of the chase. Daniel would have sent her back to the village for help, but he realised that she was not going to be put off so easily and that a delaying argument now was the last thing he needed. Instead he looked across the short clear plateau, halfway up the sloping eastern perimeter of the island, ahead to where a pathway picked up again through the short green bracken, and then disappeared out of sight around the next headland. There was still no sight of anyone ahead of him on the track, but his only hope was that a longer stretch of the coastline would come into sight around the next bay and he would be able to make out the people he pursued somewhere in the distance.

'Onwards. Where else?' he answered, and not looking around to see if Julie was following him, set off at a quick jog across the clearing, enjoying the luxury of a flat and open piece of ground while it lasted. He knew from his previous walks around the island that not all of the eastern side was so accommodating.

The rain continued to fall, slightly more heavily now, and the wind swinging in off of the sea lashed the drops forcibly into Daniel's eyes, making visibility even harder. The track was well defined though and relatively straightforward to follow, and unless his quarry had deviated from the path which seemed unlikely since their progress would have slowed dramatically, or had hidden in the dark canopy of the rhododendron bushes and managed to double back somehow, which secretly Daniel admitted to himself was a distinct possibility, there was only one way they could have gone. It would be nice to see a sign though.

Quarry. It was a strange word. It was at the island's stone quarries that Daniel now found himself, but it was with thoughts for the protagonists ahead of him that Daniel thought the description more apt. Shakespeare used the word to describe a pile of corpses, or a heap of dead game, but it was also the term for the reward a falconer gives to his bird after a successful kill.

Daniel stopped again briefly to better survey the route ahead. Still nothing. By his side, Julie seemed to realise his anxieties. 'It's lots of little headlands from here right up to a point just under the Halfway Wall.' she said. 'We stand a better chance of seeing them after that. There's a long broad section of exposed incline with little more than ankle high bracken to conceal a person. If they're ahead of us, we'll see them then.' she added, optimistically, and then in an attempt to raise their rain-soaked spirits, she took the lead along the path, picking up the tempo once more, 'Come on then.'

The eastern slopes were ablaze with towering, purple foxgloves, rising from the hillside like so many waving banners, cheering on the side of good. Underfoot the bracken glistened a radiant green, each fern-like frond dripping wet with perfect tiny droplets of rainwater. And above on the summit, great monoliths of granite: irregular, grey columns reaching up to an equally grey, forbidding sky.

'Around the next point and we should see Halfway Bay.' Julie called back to Daniel. 'We should spot them as soon as we reach that rock at the end, there.' She pointed to a large, rounded boulder, which at one time must have proudly crowned the top of the rise, but which had since become dislodged and found a new resting ground close to the course of the path.

Daniel didn't know why he was so surprised to see them. It was almost as though chasing phantoms for so long he had forgotten that there was a flesh and blood reality behind this pursuit; that his targets were real live people, not abstract creations. There were two of them, a man and a woman as far as he could tell, although the distance and the continuing drizzle made a positive identification impossible. They were red anorak one, and bright blue anorak two. Red anorak - the larger of the two - was some little distance behind its companion, and looking back, briefly held up a pointing arm in Daniel and Julie's direction, before, head down, returning its efforts to the task of flight. Julie judged them to be not more than two hundred yards distant as the crow flies, but once the meandering bends of the path had been negotiated the distance over the ground was effectively double that.

'We must have been slacking,' she said, 'To allow them to get such an advantage over us.'

Daniel who had taken the opportunity for a pause, and was standing bent over, his hands resting on his thighs, gasping in great lungfulls of air, and wondering if he wasn't just about to throw up from his exertions, flashed her a withering look, before regaining his composure and pushing past her to lead the way along the trail. 'No time to lose then.'

The two specks of colour had once again vanished from sight by the time Daniel and Julie had crossed the slight valley that subdivides Halfway Bay and were well on the way to the next coastal landmark, the rocky promontory of Tibbetts Point, with the outlying chunk of Gull Rock isolated in the sea at its foot, and with the two craggy islets known as Knoll Pins just discernible in the distance where the waves spewed out white around their bases. The rain had momentarily stopped, but the water below still looked stern and uninviting, reflecting the atmospheric mood it sensed around it.

'There! Can you see them again.' It was Julie this time pointing. 'They're right down by the sea at Brazen Ward.'

Daniel looked in the direction she indicated and could clearly see the two figures moving across the large flat shelves of rock by the water's edge, helping each other across the wider ravines; steadying each other on the slippery surfaces, as little by little they drew ever closer to the waves that raged and battered the foot of the cliff and threw up great plumes of spray into the air.

'We've got them now,' Julie continued excitedly, 'There's no way out down there except back the same way they've come. If we're quick we should head them off before they can reach the summit again.'

It was her haste that was her downfall. Racing forward in her eagerness to cut off the fugitives, Julie's leading foot came down on a patch of compacted grass made wet and slippery by the morning's downpour, causing her leg to slide forward in a long skid, and eventually upending her so that she landed in an inelegant heap on her back. She grasped the base of her spine instantly, her face contorted in pain. Daniel hurried over to her and helped her back to her feet but it was obvious that she was in some distress.

'It's the small of my back,' she said, 'I think I jarred it when I landed. Oh, how stupid.' She made a hesitant attempt to straighten up fully and took a few tentative jogging steps. 'I'll try to run it off. Oh, ow.'

Daniel looked from Julie to the two figures way down

on the rocks below. 'I'm going to have to run on ahead to stand any chance of overtaking them. You stick to the path along here and keep up as best you can. Try to keep them in sight and make sure they don't double back. I'll make my way back along to the cliff top where the ground is a bit flatter and see if I can get ahead of them.'

'There's not another path back down the cliffs again until Gannets' Combe,' said Julie. 'It's about half a mile on. It runs alongside the river valley, so you can't miss it.'

'Where does it come out?' asked Daniel.

'Gannets' Bay. You know, where the large rock stands in the sea.'

'Yes, I know it.'

'And that really is the end of the track. Unless you are any good at walking on water?'

'Let's hope it doesn't come to that.'

Daniel took one last look at red anorak and blue anorak, as they continued their determined progress across the treacherous rocks far below, and then turned away and began to follow the grassy path which lead back up the incline to the top of the island.

- - - - - - - - -

David was looking eager, 'What are you stopping for? It's almost the finish.'

'I know. I just feel tired.' replied Diana.

'Because you are carried along with the excitement of the chase? Does it almost feel as though you are there, running beside me?'

Diana could feel her eyes closing and her head nodding. She would have liked to have just turned off the light and finished reading tomorrow, but she realised that the simplest course of action would be to humour her husband and press on to the end. She smiled, 'Something like that.' she agreed.

Chapter Twenty Six

The heather on top of the rocky, flat plateau at the northern end of the island was not the springy mattress that is so often described in travel accounts of the Scottish highlands, instead it was a coarse, sparse shrub, grimly hanging on to existence in scattered, sheltered pockets; weather-beaten and cowed against the prevailing wind. But as an antidote to the winding path that Daniel had previously been following, through the tall bracken with its perilous drop to the sea beneath, this terrain made a pleasant and speedy remedy.

Two goats, startled by the sudden appearance of this running intruder across their normally tranquil landscape; interrupted from where they had been peacefully grazing on the plants growing in the grikes in the stony ground, reared up their heads and took to flight, only to stop again and watch with continued bemusement from a safer distance. Daniel did not even notice them. His eyes were fixed firmly on the ground in front of him, insuring that he did not turn an ankle on a loose stone or snare himself on a trailing plant, as he hastened across the uncharted surface. He also tried to keep a lookout towards the sea. He could not hope to see red anorak and blue anorak from where he was, on the cliff top, but he wanted to make sure that he did not run past the distinctive natural edifice of Gannets' Rock, rising from the sea like a jagged, giant shark's tooth, and the landmark by which he was required to turn right in order to outflank the fleeing duo.

The wind whipped about him and howled like so many wailing banshees across the exposed plateau, but even above this cacophony of sound the sweet singing of a single Skylark could be heard. Up, up, Daniel's eyes followed the direction of the trilling note until he spotted the small brown shape fluttering high above him in the grey sky, rising all the time ever higher, the sound of its voice becoming increasingly indistinct, until the tiny bird was all but out of sight, swallowed up by the vastness of its auditorium. Gone. And then it was back again. Knowing how to tantalise its listeners, the lark had dropped like a stone almost down to the level of the heather, and, now starting off with a new song from its repertoire, began spiralling upwards once again, singing as it climbed. Despite his urgency, Daniel could not help himself be momentarily distracted by the small chaunter's antics: spiralling up, plummeting down, spiralling up, plummeting down, spiralling up ...

The bird came from nowhere. Like a Blitzkrieg bomber out of a sunless sky, targeting its own avian version of Guernika for destruction. Daniel felt the rush of air and brush of feathers pass so close to him that he ducked instinctively and then threw himself spreadeagled on the ground, looking up only just in time to see the dive-bombing raptor cut off the performing lark's song in mid-note, and disappear back up into the clouds with that unfortunate entertainer neatly skewered on one trailing talon. Music critics in the bird world have sharper and more incisive claws than the pens of their human counterparts. A Peregrine Falcon - it reminded Daniel of the immediacy of his own prey.

Standing, he rubbed his hands on his trousers to remove the wet dirt they had acquired in his tumble, and involuntarily shivered from the coldness of his now drenched clothing, before resuming his progress along the cliff top. On his right hand side he could now see the black, pointed summit of Gannets' Rock, emerging from beneath, where it had previously been hidden, the artificial horizon of the island's edge, like a strangely subdued sunrise, portent of a dark, joyless day. Daniel hurried on ever quicker, as he realised, with the sighting of the rock, that the finale of the chase was almost upon him. He stepped across one tiny brook, a mere overflow across the heather, barely noticing it, never breaking stride, before pausing momentarily at a second, following its noisy, burbling course up to the point where it plummeted vertically downwards to the sea, in the hope that from this viewpoint he could get his bearings as to where he too should shortly make his descent. He hoped also to spot the reassuring signposts of two multicoloured anoraks, but the bay below him was devoid of movement; devoid of life. Something else that gave him even greater cause for anxiety, was the apparent lack of a visible path down the cliff side. Julie had talked about a way down at Gannets' Combe, but now that he stood in sight of that valley, he realised that Julie's idea of a path was in reality a plant-choked battle along an erratically descending river course, the one advantage of which was that it offered a somewhat gentler incline than the instant-impact verticals of the cliffs themselves. There was no other choice. The only good news was that Daniel could see that the river valley followed a route that would eventually bring him out directly by Gannets' Rock, and he knew from his own experience that there was no way past that landmark, even for two determined fugitives. Only supposing they hadn't double-backed, of course? Don't even think it, Daniel.

The first part of the river bed looked fairly well defined and Daniel thought that he would be able to make reasonably swift progress if he kept precisely to the course of the sparkling clear, ankle-deep, cold waters, and the hard, stony ground beneath them. He was thwarted in these good intentions almost immediately though. The actually waters were soon swallowed up in an increasingly dense tangle of plants and reeds, and the solid ground beneath him was replaced by soft, springy vegetation, which gave way at every step, such that he seemed to be continually walking on air. Each footfall was into a quagmire of the unknown: would he step on a hard root; a cushion of flora; or into a giant, bottomless pothole direct to the island's shore. Once or twice he deviated from the most direct downwards route because the ground to left or right looked more secure, but each time he was deceived, only finding equally unwelcoming terrain, similarly clogged by weeds, and in the end he vowed not to be seduced from the most direct course, bad though it might be. At points he was able to stand almost atop the vegetation, to keep in sight the goal of the rock ahead, at other times it swallowed him up so completely that he was physically fighting with the plants, like the gallant knight trying to reach his Sleeping Beauty, breaking branches and frantically tearing at lassoing shoots that threatened to permanently bind his limbs to the spot and engulf him totally in a sea of greenery. He was cut all over and battered and bruised, but there could be no escape other than onwards.

He recognised the onset of panic, but could do nothing to prevent its march. The snagging plants at his feet were no longer plants, but clinging, crying children, holding desperately on to him as if to their mother's coat, more and more of them, dragging him down with their increasing weight, filling his ears with their incessant screams; relentless, demanding, untiring. The branches that hemmed around his waist and cut into his stinging cold cheeks were no longer branches, but the accusing, jabbing fingers of blame and guilt and failure; failure above all. Pointing at him, mocking him, slapping him across the face, as they had done all his life; a forest of obstacles where others walked so effortlessly. Faces leering in on him from all sides, left and right, pressing up to him, faces, faces ... A face. There in the bushes straight ahead: two big brown eyes, staring directly at him as if out of a Rousseau painting, looking every bit as surprised to see Daniel as Daniel was to see the deer. He could see its nostrils flare and a thin trail of white breath show distinct against its frame of emerald bushes. Long super-model eyelashes and a black button nose. It twitched its ears back and forth once, and then with a single bound had turned and was heading off at speed in the very direction that Daniel wanted to follow, down the slope. The spectacle brought Daniel to his senses. He could just make out the retreating brown back of the small deer, as it hopped and leaped through the verdant jungle, and he hurried forward, anxious to reach the point he had first spotted it. If a deer was here, the chances were there would be some sort of path it had followed, albeit, Daniel realised, it might be a fairly indistinct one. Still, he reasoned, indistinct was infinitely preferable to the impenetrable avenue he was currently failing to carve out.

The track, when he found it, was better than he could have hoped for: the taller plants were swathed back entirely, and although the ground underfoot was still very soft and squelchy, the undergrowth had been sufficiently well trampled and compressed to form a reasonably solid foundation. The deer had vanished by now, and for the first time in what seemed like hours, Daniel's' mind returned to the idea of pursuit rather than of escape. He was actually nearer the end of the valley than he had realised, and in clearer ground now, so that he once again had an unobstructed view across and down, towards Gannets' Bay on his right and the headland that reached out towards the water-locked chunk that was Gannets'

Rock immediately in front of him. This really was the end of the track: the rocky buttress was impassable except by sea, and the only way off the sea-washed stones of Gannets' Bay was either back up the river valley, or otherwise around the coast to Brazen Ward and into the arms of Julie and, hopefully by now, some willing reinforcements. The end of the track, and yet there was no one here, save him. Daniel sank down both in exhaustion and despair.

The bay and the constantly agitated and roaring sea were still some hundred feet or so below him, and although a well defined zig-zag path showed a clear route down the final steep section of cliffs, from his lofty vantage point it was only too apparent to Daniel that neither red nor blue anorak were anywhere on that exposed stretch of shore, and a final descent seemed rather pointless. Instead he scrambled on all-fours several metres up and around the great monolithic peninsula of the headland, aiming to sit on top of a large, flattened altar of stone which commanded a magnificent position, jutting out over the sea, high enough above the water such that even the most determinedly ferocious of waves were unable to splash any would-be upstart king who had pretensions to claim this natural throne.

He saw them instantly. The moment he rounded the flat rock. Couldn't miss them really: they were less than six feet away from him. He took in what had happened instantly too. It was a snapshot scene he was never likely to forget - like the slow-motion inevitability of a car crash or an action replay on the TV, the minute details of a seconds' exposure were to be indelibly printed on his subconscious memory.

Red anorak - the man - was hanging perilously over the gaping drop to the sea below. His torso was precariously supported across a sloping expanse of smooth rock but his legs and feet hung free in mid-air, where the cliff dissolved away above the void. One hand gripped, white-knuckled, to a small pommel of rock, the other clasped the forearm of blue anorak, who was stretched out full-length, horizontally along a narrow cliff ledge, her right hand scrunching up the plastic material of his jacket, continually trying to gain a firmer grip, while all the time trying to maintain her own delicate balance. Upon hearing Daniel's approach, red anorak's eyes turned towards him and said in a desperate, strained voice, reduced to almost a whisper with fear, 'Oh thank God. Won't you help me please.'

Instinctively, blue anorak turned her head too, and Daniel saw it was the young woman whom he had first noticed on the boat, whose offered handkerchief, those brief few days before, had been the final evidence that was needed to wrap up the Twitcher case. Now, for the first time that he could see the two fugitives so close together, their two faces upturned towards his own, Daniel could see the similarity between the two of them: the rather broad nose; the large, appealing eyes. The similarities that exist between brother and sister; between twin brother and sister; James and Teresa Brewer.

Daniel also noticed another element in the frozen tableau: a seemingly bizarre and incongruous additional prop in this theatrical denouement. The bird's nest. Dislodged from the safety of its cliffside crevice by one or other of the two siblings, it now teetered, as precariously balanced as James himself, just within reach of both brother and sister, on the very edge of the fatal drop. Inside the nest, Daniel could see two dark-hued ovoids, rolling backwards and forwards, as the wind see-sawed the nurturing cradle of twigs and moss, like a mother rocking its child to sleep.

Daniel imagined the scenario must have been such: brother and sister desperately fleeing, succeed in traversing the rocks at Brazen Ward and manage to cross the boulder strewn expanse of Gannets' Bay, only to be stopped in their tracks by the unsurmountable bulk of the headland by Gannets' Rock. They consider an ascent of the river valley, but catch a glimpse of a grim Daniel making his slow but ever determined descent down that concourse, and loath to retrace their steps, instead decide to chance their luck to a dangerous climb in order to circumvent the rock buttress. Only a matter of seconds into their enterprise though, one of them - James probably - steps too close to the nesting bird, which flies up surprising him and causing him to lose his footing on the rock, at the same time dislodging the nest and its contents. Teresa manages to steady things with a lunging, supporting arm, resulting in the finely balanced triangle that Daniel was now witness to.

James' voice sounded once more, 'For pity's sake. Help.' He shifted his body slightly across the sloping incline, attempting to gain a more secure position, although his manoeuvre only resulted in dislodging a few small, loose stones and sandy scree, which plummeted downwards; the noise of their splash lost among the continual roar of the sea below. 'Please.'

Was this justice? A murderer and a lethal drop? Centuries of similar criminals had met an equivalent hangman's fate, and most without the benefits of such an aesthetic end. A lifetime of prison or the hope for a quick death - Daniel had no opinion on the subject. He also knew that he was no judge. It was not his decision to take. He moved forward with helping hand outstretched, when fate - was it fate? Could he truly swear so with absolute conviction those months later in the witness box? - took control.

It was a sudden gust of wind, more violent than any previous. Daniel felt it as he went to move forward in his standing position. It bowled him backwards, forcing him to take a step back in order to regain his balance. Teresa felt it, and her blue anorak billowed and ballooned, as she lay prone on her rock ledge, and James felt it, pushing his flailing legs harder underneath the dreadful overhang, making him reach up and cling on ever more limpet-like to the safety offered above. Most affected though was the old bird's nest, which rose on the air current like a mini hovercraft, momentarily hoisted into open space, depositing each of its two precious charges into free orbit; two fragile globes of life-to-be, propelled into the sky, like a juggler's set of balls, only to be neatly caught again. One, two.

Teresa's face was turned towards Daniel's. He would always remember that look of momentary exultation as, clasping one in each hand the two eggs that had been so impremonitorily thrown from their nest, he saw her smile transform her normally unemotive face and for the first time an expression of such unbridled childish glee light up her features, whilst below her brother tumbled to his death. Teresa's later statement about the incident went against her with the jury: 'I just remembered his accusing eyes. So big. So black. Watery, like great deep puddles, they were. Staring at me. Accusing. As if I could have done anything. But it was too late, do you see. They were already dead by then. His babies. I didn't knock the tree. I didn't cause the nest to fall. That was her and her stupid baby in her stupid push-chair. But I could see it in his eyes, that he blamed me. All the time that he was perching on that fence, watching me, chirping, he was blaming me too. That's why I had to save the eggs this time. Do you understand? No one could say that I was to blame this time.'

She wouldn't let go of the eggs as Daniel took her by the arm and led her off the ledge and back to the safety of the valley floor. She rolled them around in her hands and gazed into them as though they were precious stones, reflecting back the wisdom of ages: a vibrant red brown colour, they could have been mistaken for huge rubies freshly dug from the muddy earth, mottled and flecked with patches of colour, each one as unique and as identifiable as a fingerprint. Teresa still maintained the same expression as if on a joyful high, gazing at the priceless bounty in her grasp, but now the smile was frozen, like a corpse's dreadful rictus, or like the twisted gaping grin of a bird of prey.

Daniel guided her slowly down the zig-zag cliff path, neither speaking, until they eventually reached the smoothed slabs of stone on the sea shore, at the foot of the outcrop, closest to the point at which James had fallen into the toiling water, when she suddenly held her arms outstretched towards him, her palms facing upwards, and as she let the two eggs roll slowly and deliberately over her hands and between her taut and straightened fingers, such that Daniel had to spring forward to prevent them from falling and smashing on the rocks at her feet, she said, 'I saved these for you.'

It was then that Daniel felt fear: worse than the subconscious terrors of the lighthouse ascent; worse than the physical panic of being ensnared in the quagmire of plants, or the discovery of his cottage violated; this was a quiet terror that gripped his guts and blinded him to reason. He did not know what he would have done had not Donald stirred him from this glimpse into the dark unknown. The old man had appeared from nowhere, but there was no mistaking the urgency in his voice.

'You're wanted, son.   Quick.   Now.   Back at the Old Light.'

- - - - - - - - - -

Diana was feeling more mentally alert again, 'So your job was done for you then?'

'How do you mean?' asked David.

'No trial.   No judge.   No jury.'

'Perhaps it was the best way.'

'You mean with the lack of witnesses or material evidence, it might have been hard to prove in court?'

David sounded rather flustered, 'No, I mean, the sea provided its own justice.'

Diana gave her husband a sideways look, and continued reading with a 'Hmmm.'

Chapter Twenty Seven

'I can fly. I can fly.'

There was already quite a large crowd assembled at the base of the Old Light by the time that Daniel and Donald arrived with Teresa in tow. Daniel had been amazed by the old man's stamina during their cross-country journey from the northern shore; also by his knowledge of the island, pointing out tracks and short-cuts that Daniel would never have noticed. Teresa had dragged along between the two men in what appeared to be a waking dream, insensible to her surroundings or situation.

'Watch me, I can fly.'

High up on the open-air balcony at the summit of the lighthouse tower, the third occupant of the ill-fated Big St John's cottage, Martin, was running back and forwards in a state of high excitement, flapping his arms wildly up and down as he ran, in a grotesque parody of a giant bird.

'See me fly. See me fly.' he cried.

Daniel went up to the villager Tom, who appeared to have appointed himself as being in charge of the spectators, and who was currently in heated debate with the young school teacher Drew about the behaviour of one of his children. Daniel caught the younger man's wagging finger in mid-flight and ignoring him turned to Tom.

'What's going on? How long's he been doing this?'

'Best part of half an hour,' Tom replied. 'We've all tried to talk to him, but anytime someone approaches the tower he puts his leg over the balustrade see, and makes out to jump.'

'And no one has tried going up the staircase to reach him?'

'Same thing. He'd be over the edge before anyone got half way. Seems to think he's a bird, or something equally daft.' Tom concluded by way of explanation.

'So what do you think you can do now you're here then?' Drew butted in, accusingly.

Daniel looked up at the figure high on the tower above him. Good question, he thought. Just thinking about that heady climb made him feel dizzy again. He asked of Tom once again, 'Does anyone know why he's behaving like this?'

The shop-owner shrugged, 'Search me. Perhaps he heard you was after his two friends.' He nodded his head towards the rest of the assembled gathering, 'After all, we all heard that something was up.'

Daniel surveyed the sea of expectant faces about him, eyes all upturned despite the still drizzling rain, not wanting to miss any minute details of the events developing atop the lighthouse balcony. The scene would have drawn an interested crowd even in an apathetic inner-city; in a small island community, more accustomed to having its wildlife hit the headlines than its inhabitants, the drama would be the thing of pub-gossip for years to come: 'Where were you when the birdman was up the Old Light?' Only two people seemed slightly remote from the fascinated group: one was a young woman, stooped over looking at the ground, sobbing and sniffing loudly in equal measures, occasionally dabbing at her eyes with a rain-sodden tissue that had all but disintegrated into papier-mache; the other was Lex, who comforted the other woman, one arm wrapped around her shoulders Her eyes though remained piercingly fixed upon Daniel. More than Drew's words those eyes asked the scathing question: 'So what do you think you can do?'

The rain had turned to a thin mist, hampering visibility, and giving the illusion of so many white whirling dervishes rising up from the grassy moor, tapering upwards until they joined and merged with the descending blanket of clouds above. The view, that on a clear day seemed to encompass the whole island to the north and the whole sea to the south, was suddenly compacted to an area no larger than you could play a game of tennis on, and as the mist came down so the village disappeared; first the church and its tower, then the barn, and finally the nearest cottages. Stone that had stood for generations, dispersed in fleeting seconds. One by one the gravestones in the old cemetery were enveloped in an unearthly, ethereal haze; a rolling fog across the landscape, which spared not a sheep, not a blade of grass in the field, not a bird in the sky, nor a wave upon the sea. Daniel, though, was not aware of this loss of vision. For him the mist was a spotlight, obscuring that which was unimportant, focussing in with profound intensity on that which was: he was the actor about to take centre-stage; the audience dimmed and hushed about him; the other actors waiting silently in the wings, awaiting their cues to enter. He sensed their expectation; the murmured anticipation from the half-light. But this was his moment. Where the apprehension of Teresa had been a lonely triumph, this would be a glorious opportunity to bask in the accolades. The mist which for others was a curtain closing on a performance, was for him a curtain rising: act one, leading man enters, with ... With what? Props please. Props! Props! Words. What was the opening line again? How could he have forgotten it now. Of all times. The spotlight on him, alone on an empty stage. All eyes looking his way. No props. No words. Alone with no excuses.

'Don't fancy it much, do you?' Donald lay a hand on Daniel's arm, and nodded towards the tower.

'Not much.'

'Didn't think you did. Remember I saw how green you looked climbing up last time.'

'Have you any ideas yourself?' Daniel asked.

'We might get to the door at the bottom of the tower without him seeing under cover of all this mist, but I don't know about then. He could hardly fail to hear us coming up the staircase. You particularly, if you make as much lather as you did before. What could any of us do up there anyway? He'd have us all over, as well as himself, soon as not.'

Daniel knew what the old man was saying was good sense, but his position of responsibility weighed upon him to act, even if to do so ended up making the situation worse.

The top of the lighthouse tower was intermittently obscured by waves of the enveloping gloom, which was only pierced by Martin's wild cries, now sounding as though they emanated from a disembodied aerial spirit, circling somewhere high above.

'Perhaps the girl might help?' It was Donald's suggestion. Both men turned to look at where Teresa sat, cross-legged on the damp grass, rocking gently backwards and forwards, her head bent over, as Donald continued, 'You never know, if perhaps he were to see her down here.'

'What? A friendly face.' Daniel said rather

sarcastically.

'I've got no other suggestions.' Donald reasoned, 'Have you?'

'No.' Daniel admitted. 'OK. I'm prepared to give it a try.'

The two men helped Teresa to her feet and then Daniel led the young woman falteringly towards the stone perimeter wall which formed part of the lighthouse enclosure. The gallery at the top of the tower was now completely masked by the thick, wet mist and it was impossible to discern the man above, his head, now quite literally, in the clouds.

Daniel called, 'Martin! Martin! Can you hear me?'

The sound of the wind across the grass was his only answer. From above there was a suspicious, eerie quiet. In the pockets of mist about him, the crowd of spectators were hushed, scarcely drawing breath for fear of breaking the spell of silence that suddenly presided. Daniel tried again, 'Martin!'

'Perhaps he's on his way down?' Donald whispered, close by his shoulder.

'Perhaps.' Daniel answered, sounding unconvinced. He gave Teresa a tap on her arm, and then seeing the look of surprise and incomprehension on her face, tried to explain the situation to her, speaking as though to a small child, 'It's your friend, Teresa. He's up the top of this tower and we want to get him to come down. Give him a call. Let him know that you're here. Let him know there's someone wanting to see him down here.'

Teresa continued to stare, unblinking into Daniel's face, and so Daniel tried to coax her, 'Go on. Shout "Martin". "Martin". As loud as you can.'

The force of the shout when it finally came surprised everyone, Daniel most of all since he was standing just two paces away from the young woman: a long drawn-out, wailing, 'Mar-r-r-tin.' It was answered almost immediately from out of the murk above, 'Teresa. Teresa. Watch me. Watch me fly.' followed by a terrifying, loud scream of high-pitched terror, culminating in a loud, sickening thud somewhere on the ground on the far side of the lighthouse tower from that where the onlookers were all gathered, their eyes staring heavenward.

Daniel was racing towards the point where as near as he

could judge from the sound the impact must have occurred. Nothing. The mist was still proving disorientating, and he scoured around frantically, one way then the other, round and round, like a dog chasing its tail, in his indecision which way to turn next in his search. It was Donald who eventually made the discovery.

'Over here.' The voice was very close at hand and yet in the fog completely without form. It called out again, guiding Daniel to it, 'Here.'

Little by little Daniel began to make out the shape of the old man from behind the shifting wraiths and spectres of the water-logged air. He was standing silently, looking down at something on the ground. Daniel braced himself, his mind already creating a mental image of the wrecked body of the unfortunate Icarus. It was only by approaching nearer still, that imagination and reality suddenly took divergent paths. It was Donald that put his sudden confusion of thoughts into words.

'He's gone.'

The two men looked down at the smashed and splintered frame of the red and white striped deck chair.

They hurried back to the entrance of the lighthouse, of course; they checked the spiral staircase; and Donald climbed up to the lamp room, but it was too late. As Donald remarked, 'The bird has flown the nest.'

Daniel was secretly relieved. He had his prime suspect dead; the killer's sister, herself now facing a probable charge of manslaughter; the last thing he needed was the suicide of the final member of their holiday trio. True, Martin's bizarre behaviour might disguise a guilty knowledge of some of his friend's atrocities, but, from his own reading of the case, Daniel considered him innocent of any more serious crimes, and felt sure he would come forward as a witness when he had had time to regain his sense.

'Unless he did what he said he was going to.' It was the school teacher Drew Dance who made the facetious comment.

Daniel was rather slow on the uptake, 'What do you mean?'

Drew laughed and flapped his arms, 'Flew away.'

Daniel ignored him. Suddenly he felt intolerably weary. His every limb ached and the enormity of his morning exertions hung heavily upon him; muscles that had performed so well now felt ready to collapse, and mentally he was exhausted. He was cold now too. And wet. His clothes felt damp and clammy around him and he shivered involuntarily. He zipped up his jacket and stuck his hands deep into his pockets, where he was momentarily surprised to encounter two smooth round objects. The bird's eggs! He had forgotten all about them. Amazing that they had survived intact during the journey across the island. He drew them out to examine them properly.

No sooner were the two orbs revealed to the world from the secrecy of their surrogate downy hollows, than Daniel felt a rough push in the back which sent him sprawling, and the two precious parcels were wrenched from his hands. By the time he looked up again, he saw the strange spectacle of Drew Dance pinioned on the ground by one of the large, local men; the young school teacher putting up a frantic struggle, kicking out with legs and feet, butting his head, trying to push off the considerable weight of the villager with his own body, fighting maniacally with every resource open to him, except that is for his hands, which all this time maintained their possessive clutch upon the two bird's eggs, protecting them as fiercely as any brooding mother, holding them as far out of harm's way as was possible. It was a battle he was doomed to lose, and through simple attrition all the fight was worn out of him, and he was eventually helped to his feet by a posse of local men and a confrontational-looking Julie, who still limping, had just joined the scene. She took the two eggs from his possession, and with a single look of anger and disgust, turned her back on the beaten man. Still restrained by two villagers he screamed after her retreating form, 'Have you any idea what those two eggs are worth?'

So incensed by the words, Julie returned to face Drew, her answer like venom spitting in his face, 'Have *you* any idea of what those two eggs are worth?' She held up the two specimens. 'Peregrine's eggs. As you know only too well. You can't measure their worth in terms of money. You can't even measure it in terms of the time, and the love, and the energy, a lot of people have put in to try and create the right environment for them to nest, and to hatch, and ...' Her voice was so filled with emotion that she stumbled in her speech and was unable to regain her train of thought. She looked at the figure of the egg-thief with contempt, 'I don't know why I'm even bothering to try and explain to you. You wouldn't understand.'

As Drew was led away in the opposite direction, he remembered the fleeting moment when he had held the two red eggs in his nurturing charge, and a tear welled up at the corner of his eye, as he whispered to himself, 'I would.'

The crowd was dispersing as rapidly as the mist, and Daniel was left watching Teresa being escorted back in the direction of the village by two local men under the supervision of Donald, who was enjoying his role as officer-in-situ. Behind this group slunk the woman he had seen crying earlier.

'Sonya.' It was Lex, standing at his side, and indicating in the direction of her retreating companion. 'Just in case you suspected that she was just make believe.'

'I never thought that,' replied Daniel. 'She seems to have taken things badly.'

'Yes.'

'Holiday romance?' he asked, tactlessly.

'Something like that.'

'You know I ...'

'No, you wouldn't.' Lex completed for him.

'No. Perhaps I wouldn't.' He let out a long, tired sigh.

'You look knackered.'

'You know sometimes when you get to the end of a long journey it is often something of an anticlimax?'

'Yes.'

'Well I feel like I have been on a very long journey.'

Lex smiled mischievously, 'And just when you think you've reached the end of the journey and you couldn't feel any sicker ...'

'What's more? What do you mean?'

Lex cocked her head. 'Don't you hear the sound of the

Oldenburg's fog horn? You've still got to make the boat trip home. *Bon voyage*, sailor.'

- - - - - - - - -

Diana turned over the final page of A4 paper and made an exaggerated display of looking for further continuation sheets. She then looked across to where her husband lay next to her in their large double bed, an unmistakable expression of 'Well?' written across his face.

'Is that it?' she finally asked.

'Yes. What do you mean?'

'Aren't there one or two loose ends?'

'Loose ends? Such as?'

'Well what has happened to the bloke on the cliff?' asked Diana.

'Who?'

Diana turned back several pages of the manuscript, 'Here it is. Mark. How can you say "Who?" You leave him hanging on a cliff edge by his fingertips and all you can do is go for a gentle ramble in the countryside. What happened to Mark?'

'Dead.'

'Just dead?'

'What more do you want? You know that I can't go into specifics about an investigation.'

'So what's the point of all this then?' Diana shook the loose sheets in the air, Neville Chamberlain-style fresh back from Munich.

'That's different. That's a story.'

Diana sighed patiently. 'OK. Hypothetically then. Supposing that Mark hadn't been a real person in your actual investigation, how would you have had him die in your story?'

'We presume ... or rather, he was, pushed from the cliffs in the way that I described because his body was discovered washed up in one of the rocky coves several days later, still with his climbing ropes attached. He hadn't drowned. He must have been dead before he hit the water. He had a terrible injury to the side of his head which suggested he had struck a rock as he fell.'

'Or been hit before he fell?'

'Whose story is this, yours or mine?' David grinned.

'Talking of which,' his wife continued. 'Just what did take you to Lundy in the first place? You've never mentioned having a friend called Mickey Wragg before. And it seems rather too convenient you just turning up out of the blue on the same dot in the ocean as the very killer you'd been hunting for in vain all those previous months. I don't mean to sound critical, but you always used to complain that coincidence was the greatest crime a thriller writer could commit.'

'No coincidence. I went deliberately. They were my prime suspects after the house-to-house enquiries following the Hannah Croft killing. I may have been officially removed from the case, but I wasn't going to let them out of my sight. It wasn't hard to keep tabs on their movements.'

'All the way to Lundy?'

'It seemed so out of character. The woman in particular I had been told hadn't been out of the house for a year. It had to be followed up. Unofficially. Come on then, tell me. What do you think?'

'Hold on. I've still got plenty of questions. In fact the more I think it through, the less I can make much sense of any of it. Like Martin for instance. What happened to him after his vanishing trick on the lighthouse?'

'Presumed dead.'

'How so?'

'We doubt he made it off Lundy. He could have lived rough for several days but he would have had to reveal himself eventually. We watched the *Oldenburg* crossings for several weeks of course and he never returned to the mainland on any of them. A few other boats do occasionally anchor off the island, but they are all carefully registered and none of them reported anything unusual, and of course it is far too far to the mainland to swim.'

'So what do you think happened to him?'

'My guess is suicide. I doubt his body will be found now. The sea does not always willingly give up that which is returned to the sea.'

'Why kill himself though?'

'I don't know. Perhaps he had discovered what his two

friends had done and thought that he would be imprisoned too. He certainly behaved like a trapped animal up on that lighthouse. I'm not so sure he wouldn't have been looking at a few years if we could have proved he had been withholding information. Personally though, I think he was a minor player. Just another victim caught up in the twins' deadly web of deception.'

'Deception?'

'Yes.' David stopped himself short. 'Oh, but of course, I never explained how this thing all started, did I?'

'Does it have anything to do with the break-in at your cottage, and the knife, kagoul hood and skeleton on the cliffs that you have also conveniently forgotten to explain?' asked his wife.

'Yes, everything.'

'OK. You can carry on then.'

Chapter Twenty Eight

'It was Teresa who told me the full story during one of our prison dialogues. Strangely enough, it all began on Lundy, so perhaps it was appropriate that it should end there too.'

'When was this?'

'What, when she told me?'

'No, when did the story begin, but yes, since you ask, when did she tell you?'

'Almost immediately after her arrest. At the same time as she gave me her account of her year spent in her brother's house in Kings Street, leading up to the murder of Hannah Croft. She seemed willing to talk then. Shock and fear I suppose loosened her tongue. And so we just let her. I don't think we would have found out so much now.'

'Oh?'

'I haven't seen her for some time, but I understand that she has become very introspective. Except for her birds, of course. Maybe it's just her way of surviving inside.'

'So tell me how it all began.'

'It was almost exactly a year before. In the April actually. It was a cold month and very few people were staying on the island at the time.'

'God yes, last April was cold wasn't it? Do you remember, we were due to travel up to see Eileen in Glasgow, and you had to cancel at the last minute because that case came up in ... where? Kent, was it?'

'Kent. Yes, that's right.'

'I was so glad we didn't go. Eileen said that she hadn't seen snow like that in years. Even her pipes froze.' Diana looked across to where her husband was patiently waiting to recommence his story. 'Sorry. Do go on.'

'OK. So we can agree it was a cold month. As I was saying, there were very few visitors to the island, but two people that did brave the conditions were our deadly siblings, James and Teresa.'

'So the Goth wasn't mistaken about having seen her there before?'

'Yes, that's right. And moreover the two of them were not alone.'

'Oh?'

'No. They were accompanied by James' wife, Laura. They all stayed up at the Castle.'

'And Teresa told you all this?'

'That's right. But that's just the start. What should have been in no way more dramatic than any normal family holiday, instead ended in tragedy. Laura fell from the cliffs and died.'

'Fell?'

'That's what she said. I tend to believe her too. I really think it was just a dreadful accident.'

'So how does this tie up with all that followed? Really, David you are a hopeless storyteller. A typical man, you boil down all the meat of the intrigue and end up giving me just the bare bones. Tell me it the way Teresa told you. In full.'

'OK. So there they were, the three of them. Husband, wife and grown-up sister. James was a keen bird-watcher, perhaps Laura was too. Teresa joins them, who knows why. Perhaps she always did? Reading between the lines though, I suspect that James and Laura's marriage was hitting a rough patch, and perhaps she accompanied them as mediator. Whatever, where better then to spend a peaceful vacation than Lundy? Fresh air. Tranquillity. Birds galore. Lovely. And so indeed it seems it was until towards the end of their week. Like myself, they spent days wandering the island, along the cliffs, up and down the central path; even though the weather was cold, it didn't stop them all enjoying themselves. Until the Friday that is. Two days before they were due to catch the boat and go home.'

'Is that when she fell?'

'Now who's cutting the story short?'

'Sorry. Go on.'

'Anyway, yes, that was the day she fell. It sounds as though it started off like any other day. Teresa had gone out early and had walked to the far north end of the island before anyone else had stirred. She said that she had wanted to watch some of the seabirds on the cliffs above the Devil's Slide before they headed out to sea for their day's fishing. She had gone prepared to spend the morning there, only the weather had turned unexpectedly bad and instead she had thought it more sensible to head back to the sanctuary of the village, rather than risk being caught out in a storm in such a remote spot. It was coming back along the west cliff path, just above Jenny's Cove, that she saw James and Laura heading towards her, evidently with the intention of making sure that she was OK, now that conditions had turned so nasty. She said that the wind had been howling ferociously by this time and sheeting rain had begun to make visibility difficult. She said it was just appalling bad luck: she had called out to the two of them to let them know she was all right, Laura had looked up, raised her hand to wave, and taken a quickened step forward, when at the same time a particularly strong gust caught her off balance, and she stumbled and was over the cliff before either herself or James had a chance to react. She said it happened that quickly. One moment she was there, the next she was gone.'

'What did they do next?'

'Teresa said that she was just frozen to the spot. Stunned and powerless, she said that she had never felt more helpless. Before she knew what James, though, had started to descend the cliff, presumably in the hope that Laura had not been killed, but perhaps in a desperate attempt to just do something. Teresa said it was terrible to watch him, scrambling like a madman over the rough rock surface, impervious to the danger he was putting himself in, beaten by the continual rain, his jacket billowing out in the never-ceasing wind. She wanted to call out and tell him to come back but all she could do was watch, horrified and fascinated. There was a narrow fissure in the cliff face, and she remembers being exalted when he reached that because it offered some protection from the elements, but also so alone and frightened because once he entered the fissure he disappeared from view completely from above. She said the next quarter of an hour was the longest of her life: not knowing if he had plunged to his death somewhere unseen beneath the rocky outcrop, in which case she was waiting for a spectre, or whether his head would suddenly emerge from beneath the crevice into which he had vanished; the spot from which her eyes never once left. Of course, we know he did reappear. He was cut and he was bruised and his rain-jacket was badly torn, but Teresa thought it was only the pure mindlessness of his bravado that had brought him back in one piece; any sane, reasoning person would have been gripped by fear at the climb James had just made, and a doubt on that cliff-edge would have been death.'

'And so did he reach Laura?'

'Teresa said that he could not speak at the time, but that she found out later, back in the Castle, that he had seen her body, well out of reach on a ledge below, but that it was only too obvious from where he was that she was dead. I think even then he had tried hard to get down to her, but the hood of his kagoul snagged on a jagged rock and he had had to use his knife to cut the material and set himself free. He cut himself in the process, and I think it was probably at that point that some realisation of the perilousness of his own situation dawned on him, and he gave up his attempt of a rescue and thought about saving his own skin.'

'So why didn't they report the accident? I presume they couldn't have done, for the body to have lain undiscovered for so long.'

'Teresa was rather hazy upon this point. She said they both just panicked. Lost their heads altogether and just wanted to get away. They went back to their cottage in the Castle, packed their bags, and caught the next boat back to the mainland. She said that at the time their only thought was to put as much distance between themselves and the tragedy, I suppose in some misguided belief that it would ease the pain.'

'That seems rather suspicious.'

'Well, so I thought too, and so I did a little checking. It turned out that Laura Brewer had accused her husband of assault only four months before the Lundy trip. She had made the report at her local nick, only to retract her statement a few hours later when she spoke to the officer on duty. It stood in the files, but of course no charges were ever actually brought. Perhaps James knew about this and thought he wouldn't be believed if he said that his wife's death was an accident.'

'And perhaps it wasn't an accident?'

'Perhaps. Although I am still prepared to believe Teresa on this point.'

'I really don't see why you put such faith in her

account.'

'Call it instinct. You just had to be there.'

'OK. Another mystery to clear up then.'

'What's that?'

'Brad.'

'Well, that's the final part of the jigsaw. Mark was killed to prevent him from retrieving Laura's body. His fellow climber Brad, similarly, had to be got out of the way so that James could gain access to the accommodation in the Castle he had stayed at the fatal year before, and so remove the pages in the cottage's journal that revealed the written proof of the threesome's earlier sojourn. In the same way, once he discovered that I was a cop, James broke into my cottage in the hope of reclaiming the handkerchief I had been handed on the boat, but thank goodness I still had it on me, and that same night he burgled the shore office and managed to acquire the recently discovered hood and knife handle, which might also have been able to tie him to having been on Lundy before.'

'And so Brad was killed too. How senseless.'

'We presume so. Forensics have matched the blood on the floor of the cottage to his group, but his body has never been found.'

'Oh?'

'My guess is the sea claimed another sacrifice. I doubt that we will ever know for sure. It seems likely, though, he was clubbed down as soon as he opened the door, that evening he staggered back so drunkenly from the tavern. He was a big chap, and not someone you would have wanted to have squared up to, unless he was at a serious disadvantage.'

'And what about poor Leo?'

'Leo?'

'The bird-watcher. One moment he is peacefully watching shearwaters in the dark, the next he's confronted by a night-time wraith. So did he survive, or is he too lying in some shallow moorland grave?'

'God him. I'd forgotten all about him. He wasn't in the actual case, you see. I just threw him in for a bit of local colour.'

'That's all very well, but you can't just throw him in

without revealing what happened to him.'

'But I don't know.'

'Don't know! You're the author. Of course you know.'

'OK then. He survives if you like.'

'How come? None of the others survived. So why does he?'

'Are you saying you want him dead then?'

'No. What I'm saying is that I just want to know. If he survives, how come? Why wasn't he killed like all of the others?'

'Um. What about because he was recognised as a fellow bird enthusiast and the killer took mercy upon him.'

'Not very convincing, but OK. So where's he been then? He didn't return to the campsite in the morning and rejoin Oliver. If he's not dead where's he been all this time?'

'Right,' said David, warming to the topic, 'He was left unconscious, bound and gagged.'

'Where?'

'Um. In Benson's Cave. You know the little hole in the cliff beneath the castle which used to be used for prisoners. And he was discovered safe and well when the case was wound up. Satisfied now?'

'Strangely enough no. You've just made all that up.'

'So? That's what fiction's all about, isn't it?'

'Perhaps. I suppose I prefer my authors to show a little more ... well, authority.'

'Meaning?'

'I like the idea that the truth is set in stone, or in this case, written in black on white. It seems too God-like to witness it being invented before my very eyes.'

David joked, 'You sound like me when I am complaining about an imaginative prosecutor in court.'

'No, really. I'm serious. I feel like Alice in the shop in *Through the Looking-Glass*, when every shelf that she looked directly at was empty, and yet every shelf that she saw out of the corner of her eye was full.'

'Things flow about so!'

'Exactly. The truth included, so it would seem. How can you even say that a case is closed when the truth is so malleable?'

Annoyed, David swept up the scattered pages of his manuscript, knocking the edges of the collected bundle against the top of the bedside table to square up the sheets. 'The case - like this manuscript,' he thrust the loose papers into a drawer of the cabinet and banged it shut with a flourish, 'is closed when I say so.'

'Really?' persisted Diana. 'So if I were to show you that you'd got the wrong man ...'

Part Five

_____

The Case Is Altered

Chapter One

'I love you.'

'No you don't. We've been through this before.'

'Why do you deny it? I love you.'

David pushed back his chair and stood up. He took two paces across the room so that he stood facing the wall, took a deep breath, and then turned and took two paces back to return to the woman facing him across the table. 'Shall we start again. Where is Martin?' he asked.

Teresa's eyes flicked from David to the guard standing, quiet and motionless, beside the door. 'What are you asking that for? Why are you doing this?' she whispered hoarsely.

David had intercepted the glance that Teresa had thrown towards the prison officer, and ignoring Teresa's questions moved over to the silent sentry. 'Do you want to take a break, John,' he said, more a statement than a question, following it with a coaxing, 'Don't worry, I'll be fine on my own.'

The young warder started to protest, 'It's not strictly regulation, Sir.'

'It's not a strictly regulation enquiry.' David answered. 'Really,' he continued, 'it's OK. I'll be fine. She's tried and convicted. I'm not taking an official statement. This is just to settle a few questions I have myself. You've heard her,' David nodded his head towards Teresa, 'she's not making any sense, in any case.'

The young man still looked doubtful but David persisted. He drew out from his pocket his own personal Dictaphone machine. 'I'll be recording the whole interview. I'll send in a transcript of anything she says, if it makes you happier.'

John shook the bundle of keys on his belt. 'Ten minutes. Then I'll be back.'

Chapter Two

Diana sat smugly reviewing the evidence.

'I told you, you put far too much faith in that woman's original story.'

David sat on the edge of the bed and took off his shoes without answering. It had been a long day. He had spent several hours at the prison conducting his interview, and then several more back at the police station transcribing the account both for his own files and to be able to send a copy to the prison warden for his records. He wouldn't have minded the paperwork so much, if it wasn't for the fact that it threw himself into a particularly poor light. The case that yesterday seemed to have been so neatly and satisfactorily concluded was once again blown wide open. And for him personally, it meant stepping down from the pedestal on which his colleagues had raised him aloft, and which he was just beginning to savour; to lose the title of 'crime-cracker', and perhaps even have to admit that he may have misinterpreted vital evidence, and take responsibility for the fact that there was still a reckless murderer on the loose. The last thing he needed right now was to hear his wife's triumphant words, but there was no stopping them. He continued undressing, pulling his sweater up and over his head, hoping that they would muffle the monologue.

'It was the beer glass that put me on to it. Did I tell you, darling?'

David resigned himself to his fate, 'Yes. But tell me again.'

'The clue of the half drunk glass of beer.' Diana was enjoying herself. 'That would be a better title for your story.'

'Yes.'

'It was in the Marisco Tavern, and that woman...' David groaned at his wife's constant refusal to name Teresa, 'was already sitting alone at a table. Do you remember? You noticed her when you came in.'

'Yes.'

'But she had two glasses in front of her as though she had a companion. There was her own orange glass and there was the half drunk glass of beer.' Diana paused for the meaning of her words to sink in, building up the suspense like a magician before he unveils his grand illusion. She continued, 'Now the only two people who we would presume to have been her drinking companion that evening would be her brother James, or her brother's friend Martin. But ...' she was now in full stream with her deductive reasoning, 'we know that James is a teetotaller, so that just leaves Martin. Now you may wonder why this is so important?'

'No, dear. You have already pointed it out to me.'

Diana was not to be distracted though, 'So I shall tell you. It means that James could have not have known that Mark was at that moment clambering down the cliff on his mission to retrieve the long-missing Laura, and if he didn't know that he was on the cliff, he couldn't very well have made him fall. Ergo you got the wrong man. Martin's the one.'

David tried to find loopholes in his wife's reasoning, 'Your argument is not entirely water-tight, you know. James could have discovered about Mark being on the cliff by any number of means. He might have heard someone talking about it around the village.'

'Like who?'

'I don't know. Anyone.'

'Except that no one knew. Apart from Julie, who wouldn't have had time to tell anyone. And Brad. And where would he be most likely to spread the news? When he was in his cups in the pub. And only Martin could have heard about that and actually done anything about it. By the time that James arrived later, they were all together in a big group and no one was seen to leave. Besides, the motive was all wrong in the first place.'

This was a new criticism, and David was keen for his wife to elaborate. 'What do you mean?'

'About the baby's death. Hannah Croft, wasn't that her name? You thought James had killed her out of revenge, because in some bizarre, twisted way, he blamed the child for the death of his precious blackbirds. And the other killings, the earlier ones, the same motive behind them too. It's a bit thin. I was never entirely convinced by that argument.'

'You never raised any doubts beforehand.'

'I never thought about it beforehand. That's your job,

not mine.'

David looked puzzled and then pleased, 'OK. So what's your motive for Martin then?'

Diana looked momentarily flustered, realising that although she may have identified a new suspect, the reason behind the slayings remained the same. 'Isn't it obvious, he was insane.' she countered weakly, following this up with, 'Anyway, what are you arguing for? You know that I am right. Didn't that woman confirm it all when you saw her today?'

David remembered back to his interview and sighed again, 'After a fashion.'

'So what next?' asked Diana. She carried on more sarcastically, 'Will you be writing a sequel? "How I Let The Twitcher Fly"? "You Can Run But You Can Not Hide"?'

David finally snapped back, 'You don't seem to understand. This is no longer just the plot of a novel for you to pick over in bed, this is my career we're talking about.' Something that Diana said though suddenly sparked a new train of thought, and he fell silent again after his brief outburst. Diana was intuitive enough not to interrupt him. Hide? Hide. Perhaps if he acted quickly enough he could conclude this story after all, without having to start a new chapter.

Chapter Three

'Problem?'

'No, I don't think so.'

'Why the worried look then?'

John looked up from the document he had been reading. The young prison warden did have a puzzled expression, although he broke into a smile as he passed the papers across for his superior officer to examine. 'Oh, it's nothing. Just the report D.I. Sutton has sent in. You know, from when he came in to interview the Bird Woman the other day.'

'Oh, yes. Anything interesting?'

'No, pretty regular stuff. Have a read if you want, it's quite short.'

'I don't know how anyone can read this awful spidery writing. They should send some of those C.I.D. boys on a calligraphy course. Have you got a magnifying glass? Look at that, is that an 'e' or an 'r'?'

'That's an 'r'. And that...' John pointed to an undecipherable glyph, 'is an 'm'. It took me quite a time sussing out that one.'

David Sutton: OK. Can we start again? Tell me about your friend Martin.

Teresa Brewer: Martin?

DS: Teresa, please. No more lies. I know most of the story already. I just want your confirmation. (for the record, there is a long silence) Tell me about you and Laura and Martin.

TB: Laura?

DS: Were Martin and Laura lovers?

TB: (for the record, TB stands) No. Martin loved me.

DS: You told me originally that it was you and Laura and James that went to the island on the occasion that Laura was killed. That wasn't true, was it? Why don't you tell me what really happened.

TB: (for the record, TB sits again) We wanted to be on our own together.

DS: Why don't you tell me right back from the beginning.

TB: We were lovers.

DS: You and Martin?

TB: No. All three of us. Although Martin liked me best. He told me so. I don't know why he brought Laura along. I think he felt sorry for her. She was having a bad time with my brother. I think she hated him. He had ignored her for years. All he was interested in was his stupid birds. He seemed to have forgotten that she existed. That was when she turned to Martin. Martin had been James' friend for years. That was how I first met him. We just wanted to get away together. The three of us. We were tired of meeting behind James' back, grabbing brief moments when we could be together, when he wouldn't know. I didn't care what James thought. I don't think even Laura did. She would have left him for Martin given the chance. It was Martin. Despite everything he really cared for James. He didn't want to see him hurt. That was when we decided to go away together. Somewhere remote, where we could just be ourselves and be alone for a short while. The cottage on Lundy seemed ideal. Martin made all the arrangements. Laura engineered an argument with James just before we were due to leave, and stormed out of the house. It wasn't unusual. They were always having rows, and Laura would often disappear off for days at a time, and stay with one of her women friends. Of course, I wasn't living with James then, so I don't think he ever knew that I had been away. And Martin. He came in and out of our lives as he pleased. He's different, Martin. Everything is on his terms. Everything. We were both in love with him.

DS: Is that why you pushed Laura from the cliffs. Jealousy?

TB: No. I never did that. It was an accident. It happened exactly as I described.

DS: Except where you told me James, it was actually Martin?

TB: That's right. He did everything he could to save her. Climbed the cliff like I said. Risked his life. He was frantic.

DS: So why didn't you report her fall?

TB: That was Martin too. He didn't want James to find out what we had been doing together. He thought he was still protecting him in some way.

DS: Or protecting himself? (for the record, there is a silence) So what did you do when you got back?

TB: You know. I've told you already. I moved in with my

brother. *I was in shock. He helped me. I think I helped him too. His wife was missing. He presumed she had just walked out on him. I never let on what had really happened. Martin had said not to. We supported each other.*
DS: *And Martin?*
TB: *Yes?*
DS: *Did you see him during this time?*
TB: *No. Martin had said it was best not to. I think he met up with James though. They would go off bird-watching together during the day. A long time ago they built a hide together in the woods, close to where we lived. I think they often used to meet up there. The first time I saw him again was when we returned to Lundy.*
DS: *And what about now?*
TB: *I don't understand.*
DS: *Where do you think he is now?*
TB: *(for the record, TB started crying) You told me he was dead. I don't understand. You told me he was dead.*
DS: *We have reason to believe that he may be. But if he wasn't?*
TB: *I don't understand. You told me he was dead.*

'Strange tale, but I've heard stranger. What's your worry then?'

'No, really Sir, no worry. It's just that ... I don't know. It's not the sort of account I was expecting. You know I wasn't in the room at the time, but before I left, the prisoner was babbling pretty wild, nonsensical stuff. She seemed pretty emotional. Saying how she loved the D.I., weird stuff, you know. This...' John held up the transcript, 'well, it all seems rather too contrived.'

'Contrived, eh?'

'Yes, you know. As though it were from a book.'

'I shouldn't worry yourself about that. I've heard the D.I. quite fancies himself as an author.'

Part Six
_____

The Case Is Closed

Chapter One

David brought the car to a stop neatly beside the curb, pulled on the hand-brake, and turned off the ignition, instantly halting the emission of clouds of thick white smoke that sailed skywards from the car's exhaust pipe as the hot fumes hit the bitter, early morning air.

He was parked on an isolated country slip-road beside a dual carriageway, the sight of which was slightly camouflaged by a sparse line of small spruce trees, gamely clinging on to their bright green foliage despite the joint assailants of the winter's cold and the traffic's pollution. Even at this hour on a Sunday morning there were plenty of fellow motorists up and about, as the occasional Grand Prix roar of diesel engines rocketing past on the main road alongside testified. Despite the chill it looked as though it was going to be a bright day. The sun was already far enough above the horizon of trees to shed a sleepy, half-light on the normally gloomy lane, and the illumination from the arching street-lamps that hung suspended, line after line to the distance, high above the cars on the dual carriageway, had already been automatically extinguished on its preset program.

David sat still in the driver's seat and took a deep breath. He sank backwards slightly so that he could feel the head-rest take his weight and closed his eyes. Another deep breath. Air in through the nose. In. Deeper and deeper. Down to the chest. Flooding the lungs with new life. Expanding. Deeper and deeper. Down to the diaphragm. Pushing the stomach out. Out. And upwards. Up, up, and out through the mouth in a noisy blast. And in. And hold again. And still he remained motionless. Eyes shut, not wanting to face the day.

Of course, he'd been on these sorts of searches before. The last time would have been ... actually, not for a couple of years, now that he came to think about it. The McKenzie case. Up on Redler's Common, over in Buckinghamshire. They hadn't found her of course, nor any sign of her. He had said all along that they were looking in the wrong place. But orders. Still unsolved that one. Never likely to be solved now. No one to care, that was the problem. Perhaps that had been the problem all along. That had been a different kind of hunt to this one though. Thirty uniformed officers spread over the search area. And later, thirty more volunteers from the public joining them. Sniffer dogs. A systematic investigation. Beaters working methodically, prodding, probing, insuring no square foot of earth went unseen; that no clue went unnoticed. The camaraderie of the group. Young Bob working just six feet away, and Malcolm in the tall bushes behind; always complaining. Shouts and calls back and forth. The mechanical click and distorted tones of walkie-talkie voices. A whistle close-at-hand from the left and an officer with his hand in the air: just an old tramp's cardigan, not relevant, but bag it anyway. And so the line moved forward, little by little, like a vacuum cleaner meticulously expunging every speck of dirt from each individual fibre of a carpet, or an army of ants stripping a landscape bare behind their unstoppable advance, until the coarse grass and short scrub of the common were left behind, their innocence assured, and they entered the woods. It was at that moment, with a sense of despair, that he realised that they would not find her: the task was just too great. And yet today, it was back to the woods he had to come. Different woods, true, but they would be equally diffident about revealing their secrets, he had no doubt, and this time he came with perhaps an even more elusive needle to unearth from this most uncompromising of haystacks.

Eyes open. The wood lay on the other side of the dual carriageway but there was an old, ugly concrete footbridge built, to ensure safe passage for walkers determined to maintain their right-of-way across the treacherous multiple-lane trespasser. David stretched, lent over to the back seat and withdrew a small holdall, and then picked up his overcoat which was strewn on the seat beside him. He got out of the car, stretched his legs once again from where they had got cramped, this even despite the relative short distance he had been driving, hastily pulled on his coat and shouldered his bag, and locked the car door behind him. He looked up to the zig-zag metal construction of the ramp that gained access to the footbridge, standing slowly rusting orange, like a gigantically unimaginative first experiment with a Meccano kit, and tried to imagine what the landscape must have looked like before such abominations. And then was saddened to find that he no longer could. He wondered if his mind had witnessed so much unpleasantness that it could no longer remember what beauty was. Or recognise it when it saw it. He also thought about Teresa.

Each breath was a visible white puff before him, and each exhaled cloud seemed a little bit harder to produce with each progressive footstep up the inclined ramp. Up one way, slowly ever rising. Turn and back the other way. And turn again, level now with the bridge. He was higher now than the trees beside which he had parked, but still below the level of the dense vegetation on the opposite slopes, into which he must eventually disappear. David stopped in the mid-section of the bridge, folded his arms across the top of the protective barrier, and paused to watch the cars pass beneath him. A sleek, long Mercedes, here and then gone, further, further to the distance; a Vauxhall or a Ford; then a white Mini phut phutting in the slow lane; a shiny blue Estate car in the inside lane; and behind a Porsche, straddling the centre line, moving one way then the next, looking for an opening to pounce and be past. Then a gap and nothing, before a lorry and then another, both painted identically, travelling in convoy. How did that song go, Rubber Duck? A small section of grey paint on the balustrade was raised and flaking where the metal beneath it had started to corrode, and David idly picked at it with his fingernail, until it eventually peeled away completely and slowly fluttered earthward, erratic in its flight like a sycamore seed helicopter, twirling this way then that, on a still summer day. And then finally, a solitary car travelling in the opposite direction: there on the horizon, a hazy red blur, getting nearer, and faster, and noisier, and bigger, and ... then gone, beneath and beyond and onwards on its journey. Time wasting. David didn't know why he was doing it. He wasn't normally an idle person. Even with an unsavoury chore, his philosophy was normally, soonest started soonest over. Why then was today so different? Perhaps it wasn't stalling after all. What if instead it was a deliberate delaying to heighten the anticipation of something pleasurable - that prolonged climax that is always better than the inevitable conclusion - David sensed the end of the case was very near; that it would end here, somehow in these woods. Pleasurably though? That seemed very unlikely.

He could even make out the registration plates on some of the cars: it wasn't easy when they were travelling so fast, but it was a skill you picked up. D345 MB ... what was the last letter? H513 ... no, it was gone. Blue BMW, T560 GH ... no. Enough, enough. Wait for that white sporty one to pass and then go. It's travelling fast. Too fast, if he cared. Almost here. Almost. And gone. OK, go. Go.

It was still bitterly cold as David left the bridge and returned to ground level on an equivalent ramp to the one on the opposite side of the roadway from where he had parked his car. Rather, though, than follow the tarmac pedestrian path, which hugged the side of the busy traffic artery with the tenacity of a fatty clog of carbohydrates, David followed the seemingly dubious advice of a slightly toppled, green sign, that portrayed a silhouette man walking briskly and jauntily carrying a broad stick, and which claimed that Lower Wass Farm was this way, 2 miles. This way pointed to a muddy narrow track, which headed steeply up the hillside for a short distance and then disappeared into the darkness of the trees. David looked from the unavoidable obstacle of the mud, down to his shoes, which sparkled black like polished metal - the result of several minutes concentrated effort the evening before - and rued not wearing his grubby trainers after all, even if the insole was hanging out of one of them. He was out of practice with this sort of game. He was dressed for the office and he was playing in the woods. And he wasn't even sure that he knew which rules were going to be applied today. David let out a long, resigned sigh. Best foot forward. Squelch.

The path petered out abruptly after the initial sharp incline, and where David had expected to immediately enter the solitude of the woods, instead he found himself once again back at something resembling civilisation. The impression of a great, dark, impenetrable wall of trees was just an illusion and whereas he could now see the wood did start in earnest only a short distance further on, the first forested barrier was clearly just a mere few metres thick, and was obviously a noise buffer and a visual screen to protect a small settlement of houses from the ugly insensitivity of the busy by-pass. Not that they really needed it. If the aesthetic of their dwellings was anything to go by, these people could give lessons in ugly.

The houses were all lined up on one side of an unmade gravel road, dotted along the length of which were a series of uneven potholes half-full of rainwater, the shallowest of which were frozen, their surfaces showing a crisscross mosaic of white lines. A short distance away a small Labrador was sniffing something on the ground which looked like an used condom. The Labrador's hair hung long and uncut, and was dirty and matted at the ends where it had trailed in the muddy puddles. It looked up briefly as David approached and then returned to its unsavoury discovery. The side of the road opposite to the houses was lined by a thin wire mesh fence and the small paddocks beyond were screened by an untidy hedge, now largely bereft of foliage, leaving a tangle of knotted branches and uncompromising-looking thorns. In the enclosed field David could see that a jumble of throw-away items had been gathered together to form a makeshift gymkhana: a row of red-and-white striped, metal oil containers stood on their ends, bulky and barrel-shaped and slowly sinking into the soft quagmire of grass, providing the supports to a collection of wooden and metal rods that lay horizontally across the expanses between them, making a fair impression of a line of equestrian fences. Boxes had been strewn around to provide further obstacles, and piles of old tyres were scattered around each jump, presumably to provide a slightly softer cushion to any jockey unfortunate enough to come a cropper. In the furthest corner of the paddock, next to a pile of dark brown, sodden-looking straw, a small horse was tethered, miserably shaking its head to try and remove the piece of coarse rope that had somehow got ensnared and knotted around both its neck and mouth, forcing its upper gums open in an awkward fashion. A long trail of sticky white, saliva hung down from the horse's mouth, occasionally dropping to the ground, only to be replaced by more. With each fresh movement the rope only seemed to fix faster, until the poor creature, realising the futility of its struggles, resignedly stood still.

David walked along to a point where there was a hole in the wire large enough to squeeze through: the churned up mud and multiple imprints of thick-tread boots revealing that it was a much-used point of entry to the small field. David wasn't particularly keen on horses, always having regarded them with suspicion at close quarters: the too-knowing eye; the sudden kicking legs; those hooves, so very hard and dangerous, but at the same time he didn't like to see an animal in such obvious distress, when by a simple intervention he could help. He had his head and shoulders through the hole before he noticed the caravan. It was a little further along the paddock and almost completely hidden from the road by a thick clump of bright red dogwood stalks. It looked deserted: the white paint was much in need of a re-coat and one window pane was smashed. It was also slightly tilted over, like the mobile-home equivalent of the Tower of Pisa, where one of its supports had broken.

The dog let David get as far as one leg and one arm of the way into his territory before it barked. It was the same Labrador that had been beguilingly ignoring David before, but now its expression of innocent detachment was transformed into that of a snarling hell-hound. David had only ever before seen a Labrador smile; it now came as something of a surprise to him to see what sharp teeth they appeared to possess. He tried to turn and reverse, in the hope that retreat would see the dog return to its amicable indifference, only for him to snag his coat collar on a sharp, rusty barb of wire, and fix fast. In the field the horse whinnied in recognition of the irony of the situation.

Rrrr-af-raf-raf-raf. Rrrr-af-raf-raf-raf.

David hadn't noticed that the door of the caravan had opened until the man spoke, 'What's all this barking? Rhett! Quiet!' The creature fell silent instantly, although continued to watch the newcomer with a respectful wariness. The next question David realised was directed towards himself. 'This is private property. What are you doing?'

'I was just ...' It was proving difficult to answer in any kind of adult fashion, from a position of such obvious disadvantage - half crouched, and pinioned. David indicated towards where the loop of metal had pierced the material of his jacket. 'Perhaps? Would you mind unfastening me? I seem to be caught.'

The man - David could clearly see he was very tall and very fat - lumbered forward, his Wellington boots disappearing up to the ankle in the soft ground with each step. He grabbed David's coat roughly and wrenched him free of the fencing with an audible renting of the fabric, at the same time pushing David back onto the road, leaving the wire as a barrier between them.

David pulled the edge of his collar around so that he could examine the jagged tear in the cloth. A two hundred and fifty quid coat ruined. The words in his head - the words he would be repeating when he retold the story - were 'What the fuck do you think you're doing?' and 'Do you know how much this coat cost me, you dirty, overweight tub of country lard?'. The words that came out as his eyes went up to meet the unwelcoming glare of the bearded giant were, 'Thanks. I was just ...'

'Well don't.' With which the man turned back to his caravan abode, accentuating that dwelling's alarming tilt by adding his own considerable weight to the two short steps up to the entrance, and disappeared inside with a bang which left the door swinging lamely on its hinges. At the unbroken window towards the rear of the van, two faces were pressed up hard against the pane, misting the glass with their breath: a sad-looking woman, her hair lank and unwashed, and an impudent looking boy, perhaps just into his teens, who stuck up two fingers in an unmistakable V-sign in David's direction, before both were spirited away by an angry command from inside.

David watched for a brief moment longer, to see if the massive figure would reemerge to pull the door to, but seeing no further sign of activity from within the caravan, and with a final look back at the still passive horse, he returned to the public domain of the road. 'Fucking Deliverance extras.' he muttered under his breath, at the same time giving the once-again-docile dog a wide berth.

- - - - - - - -

He had discovered Diana re-reading the Lundy manuscript in bed that morning, when he returned home from his night-shift. One or two questions she had said. Having difficulty separating fact and fiction she had said.

'I'm tired, darling. It's been a long shift. Can't this wait?'

She had persisted though, 'Five minutes, that's all. Let me talk these things through while they are still fresh in my mind. I was thinking about it last night, and some things just don't seem to make sense.'

'Such as?'

'Well, help me straighten out who was actually there on the island, you know, in real life, and who was just a figment of your author's imagination.'

'If it's about that lad, Leo again, I've already explained, he was pure fiction. I just forgot about him. Give me a bit more time, and I'll incorporate some more satisfactory end for him in the plot.'

'No, it wasn't him I was worried about,' said Diana.

'Who then?'

'Well John, the Goth, for one. Was he real?'

'Imaginary.'

'And Graham, the lad he befriended. And his mother. What about them?'

'Imaginary too. OK. Interview over?'

'Not quite.'

Chapter Two

'Thomas Evans. Marble and Granite' said the sign.

The yard was at the very end of the row of five houses. Number one with its wooden fence knocked down: end of terrace, never a good idea. Number two with its stone statues of squirrels on the lawn and white plaster birds above the porch. Number three - well not number three really, but 'Timande' - with its net curtains and suburban pretensions. Number four, painted bright pink: oh, how number three must hate you. And number five, empty and derelict: too close to 'Thomas Evans. Marble and Granite' to ever be desirable.

It was the kind of place you always wondered how anyone ever got to. In the midst of the countryside, seemingly with no road to speak of leading to it. And yet there were large lorries in the mason's yard. And pile upon pile, row upon row, of great slabs of stone. Marble and granite if the sign was to be believed. Left out in the open. Why here? Except this wasn't really the countryside, David had to keep on reminding himself. Instead, that strange half-way house, where the racing sprawl of the town stopped, yet where the baton was not smoothly passed on to contestants of a purely rural existence. This was not a place for a seamless merging of ideologies; this was the shunned void where magnetic poles oppose.

There has always been a fascination with margins and boundaries - the place where two conflicting bodies meet. And clash. In many ways it was what David dealt with every day. What he sought to control. Conflict. Where bad meets good. Except here, what was bad and what was good? You couldn't say that city dwellers were wrong, or that country folk were right. Sometimes things were not so clear cut. Perhaps it didn't really matter. With magnets, positive and positive repel with equal force as negative and negative. Whichever, this middle ground is forever spurned.

Who would choose to live in this no-man's-land? David couldn't imagine someone emerging from any one of this row of damp-looking terraced cottages, getting in their car first thing in the morning and driving off to their lucrative stock-broker job in the city. This was not the rural idyll that wealthy townies splashed out fortunes to buy into. Nor could he imagine someone whose livelihood came from the land, choosing to live in such a way. It was a mystery. But not his mystery.

The footpath sign indicated the right-of-way led directly across Thomas Evans' property. The main gates of the plot were securely fastened by a thick iron chain and impregnable padlock, but a small concession had been made to ramblers, by the addition of a narrower side gate, just wide enough for a thin person to squeeze through sideways-on, which although shut was not locked. The Beware Of The Dog sign was less welcoming though.

David knew all too well the problems that could arise from both the denial of, and the upholding of, the law of the right to roam on the ancient footpaths of the country. In his early days in the force, as a young constable, he recalled being called in to settle a dispute between a group of walkers and a farmer who was denying them their legal right of access to one corner of his land. He had good reason to remember the incident well. It was the first time he had ever faced the wrong end of a shot-gun. Whether Thomas Evans would be quite so inhospitable ... well, the jury was still out.

As it was, passage through the building merchant's grounds was swift and untroubled, and after negotiating a similar gate to the one he had entered from the roadway, he was back on a dirt path which had the dual blessings of being well defined and surprisingly free of mud. Someone had even gone to the trouble of laying down a thin layer of bark chippings on top of the surface soil, and there was a brand new council footpath sign, made from unstained, light brown and - the implication being - environmentally friendly timber, pointing enthusiastically along the trail. Never one to turn down an invitation, David mused to himself.

The trees were on either side of him now, but he was still as isolated from them as he had been when he had been back at the settlement of houses. Between him and their straight trunks was a newly-run wire fence, seven feet high, and made up of a lattice of diamond mesh, keeping him to the route of the new path whether he liked it or not. He could now see that this area of the wood was a plantation, neat lines of dark conifers, planted in regular rows, stretching away to the distance in street-grid pattern. It was an environment he had always been repelled by; nature and yet not nature. These were the GM crops for the lay-person. No subtlety on a microscopic scale; no scientific knowledge needed: here, man's influence was only too evident. He knew though, that his own feelings of repulsion for this landscape had a far simpler and more personal explanation; a rooting set in experience rather than in ideology. The fear of getting lost. The memory of getting lost.

It is an experience which shakes human conviction to its core; when that in-built navigation system is thrown out of kilter, disorientating as effectively as though the subconscious compass has been placed in front of a powerful magnet. It is a sensation, though, that disturbs more subtly than to provoke just simple questions such as 'Which way?' and 'Where?', it brings with it larger doubts that seep right through the normally robust fabric of humanity, like 'Why?' and 'Who?'. David's first experience of being cast adrift in a suddenly unfamiliar world, had come in childhood. He had been in a large shop, a department store, standing next to his mother, happily absorbed in looking at the colourful items on the shelves. A ceramic pot had particularly taken his eye, it was made of such a fine china that it looked almost transparent, and it had a light blue glaze, so smooth and cool, like ice. He wanted to reach out and touch to see if it felt cold, but he knew that his mother had told him not to touch anything. Although perhaps if he asked her permission it would be all right? Ask her permission. He had looked around to where she had been standing, but she wasn't there. He had looked the other way: no one. He had walked to the end of the tall aisle of shelves: nothing. And the other way: no one. He was in a panic now. He had called out, but it was though no one could hear him. He was alone; abandoned. He had sat down on the floor, not knowing what to do, the tall banks of shelves upon shelves, stretching right up to the strip lights on the ceiling, towering above him, in the same way that the great trees hounded in above him now, and he had cried; pitiful sobs, he was ashamed to still remember. She had come, of course, his mother; she had been queuing up to pay and not realised that he had wandered off. Somehow it had been his fault. She had been scared too.

He was grateful for the decisiveness of the path. It had no doubts. 'This way, perhaps?'; 'No, what about this way?'; 'Haven't I been this way before?': the path asked no questions; left no room for debate or independent thought. This wasn't the environment he was seeking in any case. Just listen. Close your eyes. Stand still. And listen very carefully. Nothing. This wood is dead.

Crunch. Crunch. He listened to the sound of his footsteps on the surface of wood chips. It was a tracker's worst nightmare to step on, and break with a crack, a dry twig or a piece of dead bark: here there was no alternative. Each footfall advertised his approach like a forest fanfare. Perhaps he should try to be more stealthful? After all he had no clear idea of what lay ahead; of what this morning held in store for him. Should he attempt to conceal himself? No, not yet. Instinctively he knew that he was not close yet. There was a long walk still before him.

The path, which had been falling ever since the builder's yard, started to rise again: a gentle, steady incline, that became noticeable to the feet and calves, and then the chest and lungs, before it had properly registered with the eyes and brain. High above David could see that it was quite light now too, a bright blue winter morning's sky; beneath the canopy of cones and needles it remained, though, forever black. These were the trees that were never destined to brighten a family home at Christmas time, never to be bedecked in baubles; hung with tinsel, nor to be a centre-piece of celebration. These trees had grown too old, and too big, and so they were left with nothing else to do but wait; and yet all the time, while no one had told them that they were never to be destined to go to the party, these arboreal Stoics continued to wear their proud finery of leaves, continued to hold their branches up high, all the time though suspecting that this was once again not to be their year; one further little drop of hope turning into bitterness, seeping down, like resin running down their trunks, until it lay like an all pervading black carpet on the floor, cast in the shade of their communal disappointment.

It was with some relief that David reached one corner of the plantation and was then faced with a choice. There was a signpost ahead. Four arrows. Four directions. To go back was obviously not an option. The left-hand path, too, seemed to turn back obliquely upon itself, and David suspected it would return him to a point just a little further along the dual carriageway from where he had parked his car. Right or straight ahead then? The path ahead was a faintly discernible line across a ploughed, muddy field. In the summer time, David could imagine the flat expanse of pasture a sea of golden heads of maize, at the moment though it more closely resembled a First World War no-man's-land: an obstacle course of boggy patches, deep furrows, and crisscrossed with such an array of wide, tractor's tyre marks that it gave the impression that two farmers had been out joy-riding their heavy vehicles. The lighter coloured line of earth, which appeared to follow a relatively straight course across the field, looked easy enough to follow from where David stood, but he knew from past experience of similar trails, that what looked like firm ground from a distance turned out surprisingly quickly to be a mire as you approached, and a path which seemed clearly marked when safely standing at one end of it, vanished altogether, leaving you stranded, as soon as you had committed yourself to its trust. Right it was then.

The path right still meant walking on the fallow field, but the route was easier to keep to, since the right-of-way followed the line where the field met the forestry plantation, such that David had open ground to his left and the line of dark trees to his right. The rigid mesh fence, that had been his companion for so long, had now vanished, and should he have desired, David could have wandered off into the wood. A drainage ditch ran the same course as the one he now followed, and although his shoes and the bottom of his trousers were already wet and muddy, he took care not to walk too close to the edge of the ditch, having no desire to loose his footing and tumble into the several inches of murky water at the bottom. Some distance away three gulls were swooping up and down, one settling momentarily on the brown soil, only for the other two to fly down upon it with a chorus of cries, causing it to squawk rowdily in return and rise into the air again; then another would try to land, only for the two remaining airborne birds to pick on it in its turn. Apart from that there was no other sign of life.

The sound of the road could still be heard in the distance, but it was already becoming a muffled noise, one that could be completely blocked out if you chose not to concentrate on it. It was a surprisingly uninspiring landscape: nature, but with the hand of man intervening at every point. Nothing seemed untouched. Or perhaps it was him that was the problem: a resurfacing of that same cynicism that had troubled him at the flyover bridge. Was it just him that couldn't see the beauty? His mind drifted back to the little island where he had hoped this particular nightmare episode had been laid to rest, only for it all to return to haunt him. Now there he had seen beauty. The beauty of nature unsullied by mankind; in the sea, in the magnificent cliffs, in the animals and the birds. An oasis of beauty: there, he could imagine that even man himself could be beautiful again, free from the ugly emotions that govern modern life. He remembered Julie's unselfish care of her natural wards; Lex's humour and forgiveness; Sonya's spirit and abandon. Teresa? He remembered the beauty of her eyes; large and owl-like, innocent and unblinking. And behind those eyes? Perhaps beauty really was only skin deep. The memory of Teresa brought David back to the here and now. He realised that he was putting a shine on a past that had never been the case: his past was as ugly and unpleasant as his present. And his future wasn't looking like an armful of roses either.

- - - - - - -

He had always commented upon how his wife would have made a good detective. She had the right tenacity. Like a dog gnawing on a bone, when she thought that she was on to something, she wouldn't leave it alone until she had discovered what was right down at the marrow.

'And Lex and Sonya. The two women,' she continued.

'I knew it,' his voice was full of exasperation. 'This is what this is all about. I've told you before. Nothing happened.'

'But they were real?'

'What?'

'Real people. Not just characters in your book.'

'Yes, they were real. But nothing happened.'

Diana looked dubious. 'Really? That would be a first.'

'What do you mean?' He tried to keep his voice calm, but he knew the question had come out sounding too aggressive. He was tired. He wanted to go to bed, before the sun rose and the room was illuminated by its diffuse rays through the curtain, after which he knew he would never be able to sleep. He didn't need a debate, much less an argument.'

'I think we both know what I'm talking about,' said Diana.

Chapter Three

'Lovely day for it.'

'Pardon.' said David.

'A walk. I said, lovely day for it,' said in the same strident, plumby voice as before.

David stopped the very activity that the new arrival was advocating in order to let the old woman pass him without having to make a detour into the mud.

'Cheerio.' She waved her stick in the air by way of salute for this act of kindness as their two paths crossed, and looked as though she would walk right past him without breaking stride, when she seemed suddenly struck by a thought and motioned him to step closer. She whispered confidentially in his ear. 'Take a word from me. At the end there. Two paths. Best take the left one. They both come out to the same place. We came the other way and Daphne is still there, squatting down over a bush. Wouldn't want to disturb the poor thing with her pants round her ankles now would you. Be a good man.' Then with a parting crescendo, 'Well cheerio.'

David viewed the route ahead with additional anxiety. He could see the two routes the woman had outlined from where he stood, both shooting off like dark tunnels through the surrounding trees. He remembered taking particular note of them when he had studied the map of the area the night before. Left or right, they were both essentially minor forks from the straight-on path, and after diverging for a matter of only a couple of hundred yards, they rejoined each other to form a single track again. He had paid particular attention to them because this was the place where, for the first time, he would be forced to enter the woods proper. There was no alternative. The wide open spaces of the deserted fields were to be left behind. As if to reassure himself, he reached inside his coat pocket and drew out the map again now. The folded sheets billowed around in the breeze, opening up, catching the air like a sail, until David turned around, and used his body as a break against the wind blowing across the fields. He punched and battered the cumbersome expanse of paper into submission, until he had finally managed to reduce it in size to a usable, if inelegantly folded, six inches square, with, much to his own surprise, the depiction of his immediate vicinity uppermost. Yes, he had remembered well. Of course the map conveyed a very different visual image to reality. On the map, the area he was about to enter looked a vibrant green space, populated by neat, clipped, miniature conifers, and the path he was about to take was marked out by an unfaltering line of little blue dashes. David looked at the scene ahead and wondered if the Ordnance Survey had a symbol for these sullen, shaggy arboreal evergreens, and a hatching that more adequately conveyed the colour of depression.

Left path it is. He had no desire to bump into the squatting Daphne. Daphne appeared to be equally diffident, and David saw no sign of her as he was swallowed up by the darkness of the wood.

- - - - - - -

It was another quality that he had always admired in his wife, that she always managed to maintain perfect control over her emotions. She had not let the potential argument sidetrack her from her original train of thought.

'Hermione and Gemma. They must be real. You couldn't have invented them?'

'Well that's where you are wrong. Pure imagination.'

'Wherever did they come from then?'

'What do you mean?'

Diana explained, 'Are they drawn from life? I mean, are they based upon people you know? I can't imagine you bumping into too many Hermione-types in the course of your job.'

'Just people I see around.'

Chapter Four

The dead fox was lying on its side, on the incline of the short muddy bank running down to the stream. David could see it from where he stood on the tiny footbridge. One front leg was outstretched as though the animal had been flexing its limbs, the other was folded up under its body. It looked very peaceful; a small, almost serene, smile seemed to be playing around those long jaws, as if it was still enjoying the moment of realisation that death was not going to be so bad after all. It looked as though it could have only died very recently too. It was perfect. Totally undisturbed. David wondered how it could have died. Did animals die of natural causes? For a creature like the fox, which is so traditionally associated with images of hunting and violent death, it seemed so unlikely that one individual could have seen out the whole of its natural life and ended its days in such peaceful contentment. And yet there were certainly no obvious signs on the small, orange-furred body to indicate that it had died of anything other than encroaching old age. And so what happens to it now? No grieving relatives. No chance of a decent burial. David half considered clambering down the bank and trying to effect some modest internment himself, so beautiful did the animal look that he didn't like to think of it being defiled by opportunist rodents or desecrated and turned into a piece of carrion by scavenging birds, but the mud by the river bed looked soft and treacherous, and he seemed to remember reading that foxes were often thick with fleas, and so he thought better of the idea, contenting himself instead by preserving his perfect memory of the fox, untainted by harsh reality. Perhaps to be remembered favourably is as good a legacy as anyone can reasonably expect. Besides he had a job to do.

And yet still he lingered. The small dead body held a strong spell over him. It's vulnerability. It's loneliness. It's beauty. How far had humans strayed from what is true nature. What David wanted was to protect this frail corpse; to see it warm, safe, to say some words that gave its life and death some meaning, some explanation. How artificial is that? When to leave the useless carcass of meat, to forget it, let it rot and be eaten, undignified and unspiritual, unexplained and unremembered, would allow it to pass on the only gift that death can bestow: life to another. That was nature. Perhaps he was just deferring again. Counting cars, musing on life, it was bringing him no closer to concluding the case.

A big, black beetle, heavy-bodied, its long, jointed legs making the faintest of impressions across the squelchy surface, scuttled purposefully from the shelter of the grass, across the exposed muddy slope, and disappeared underneath the wispy cover of the fox's brush. It reappeared, now walking brazenly along the length of the reddish hued flanks; cocky, already with the assurance of ownership: almost slipped as it tried to descend the white fluffy belly, but managed to right itself, its rear leg desperately clinging on to a tuft of hair as it hung perilously in mid-air, finally to disappear, burying down beneath the still warm flesh of the tucked up front leg, not to reemerge. It was a start.

The stream provided a natural boundary for the plantation on one side and the wood proper on the other. David was glad to see that the line of the footpath on the map followed the course of the stream along its right hand bank, providing a break from the oppressive conifers. He took a deep breath. He could almost feel the fresher air. Or was it just relief. Here the trees were the usual English deciduous hotchpotch, spiky branches and gnarled trunks, leafless limbs and stark silhouettes at this time of year. It was lighter here too. The sun was able to penetrate the denuded canopy and patches of blue sky were once again visible overhead. There was bird song too.

He was getting closer.

The stream accompanied him with its tinkling music: delicate harps and clear, crisp chimes, a purity of note it was impossible to reproduce; a bubbling, boisterous enthusiasm, endless and unfaltering, such as to have a thousand natural conductors rapt in an ecstasy of unnecessary baton-waving. The orchestral sound of running water, over protruding stones, round twists and turns, rushing, gurgling; submerged plants and fronds joining in the dance, swaying, waving, unable to resist the mesmeric quality of the clear water's caress; faster, falling, the brook running with a purpose, as though it has a reason, an urgency, rather than the fact that it is moved by an irresistible force, on a course, to a destination, unknown to its constituent parts. David felt his own purpose almost equally uncertain, and so he was glad of the company of the water for its exuberance and carefree hope, or maybe for its blind devotion.

There was a crashing as of something large moving with fast steps and an obvious lack of any attempt at concealment in the undergrowth to David's right, followed almost immediately by a dark furry shape bounding through the bushes, which quickly revealed itself as the possessor of two big muddy paws and a warm, wet tongue.

'Down, Wally. Down.' A balding man carrying a stick, appeared from the opposite direction ahead of David on the footpath, and called to the spaniel with an apology to David for his dog's behaviour. 'Here boy. I'm terribly sorry about him. He's too friendly for his own good. It's his breed, you know. They're all the same. Come here Wally.' The old man's verbiage increased as he approached nearer, 'Named after my brother, you know. He was a great dog man. Keen yourself? On dogs. Wally! Will you put those paws down. The nice man doesn't want you making his clothes all dirty.'

David brushed himself down as the boisterous animal rushed back towards its owner and then scampered short steps back and forward between the two approaching men in an excitement of indecision as to which one looked likely to provide the best entertainment. 'That's OK.' he said.

The spaniel had bounded up to David again, and he bent down making a half-hearted attempt at displaying friendliness towards the dog by patting its head, while at the same time trying to stop it putting its dirty feet up on his trousers again. The man had joined him by now.

'He's a fine fellow, isn't he?' The old man stooped down, placing his own face close to that of the animal's, and ruffling the dog's long, floppy ears. He continued talking all the time, but whether to David or Wally it was unclear. 'Yes he is. Yes he is. He's a fine fellow, isn't he.' The unfortunate dog eventually made its escape and disappeared into the bushes again.

David's mind went back to the fox on the river bank. The direction the newcomer was walking it was inevitable that he would cross the footbridge and so pass the small corpse and, even if he did not see the body himself, he could not imagine the playful spaniel not sniffing out the helpless fox. It would snuffle up to it, cautiously at first, suspicious that it wasn't really dead, not wanting to risk a painful bite if the creature was only play acting. Then it would get bolder, it would snarl from a distance and bare its teeth and gums; run in closer and experimentally pull at one of the limp, hind legs, before retreating. And then once certain that it would encounter no resistance, it would growl and then bark joyfully, and take the creature in the grip of its jaws and shake it. Too heavy, it would be forced to drag the lifeless body, while its owner looked on shouting its name, unable to intervene. Blood on its teeth, still warm, and a primeval stirring it barely recognised in itself from soft days spent asleep on a warm sofa and cold, tinned meat served straight from a can.

David once again felt protective of the poor, defenceless animal he had left to the mercy and indignity of such an end. Although perhaps his feelings of protection were no longer for the flesh and blood corpse itself, that responsibility he had since relinquished to fate, now he felt possessive of that Platonic snap-shot image of perfect, peaceful beauty he had taken away with him from the scene of the encounter and which he now felt was his own. His private special thing. And yet how so easily it could be taken away.

Like everything else he had ever valued.

As a policeman he always thought it was something he would get used to. After all, it was his job. While there were people that had valuable things, there would be people that would want to take those valuable things away. And his job - a large part of his job - was to stop them. He would have expected, with experience, with years and years of experience, that he would have learned how to hang on to what was important. That, if nothing else. And yet the things he had always held most dear, trickled through his fingers like so many drops of water from the babbling brook.

- - - - - - - -

He had seen that she had marked the manuscript in several places with a red biro: specific references that she had questions about; notes that she intended returning to.

'And Donald? I don't remember you being assisted by such an able-bodied pensioner. You didn't give him credit at the trial, in any case. What's the story with him?'

'No. He is another invention. You know, I'm beginning to regret I ever started writing this case up. I would have been better off sticking to fiction.'

Diana was scornful, holding up the pages of writing, 'And what are you calling this? Fact? The more I read, the more I'm not sure it isn't all pure fiction from start to finish.'

Chapter Five

He could hear the woodpecker but he could not see it.

As he walked, all the time, he kept his eyes open for fish in the stream. The water was so shallow and so piercingly clear where the sun sparkled on its surface and illuminated the depths below, that David felt certain that he must spy a fish. There wouldn't be trout here of course, not like in the Cotswolds or the West Country, where he had seen dozens of the fine-tasting fish in the rivers there, but perhaps a stickleback, or a little minnow darting for cover, or even a big old tench or perch. Like from his childhood. He could barely draw his eyes away from the hypnotic glistening surface. He remembered one summer when he had been a boy, with a friend he had built a den down by the riverside, many miles from here, where his family lived at the time. The whole long summer holiday they had played there, close to the water, inventing names for the fallen logs and natural hiding places around them, daring each other to balance across the river on the big branch, spying on passing people from their secret lookout, watching the fish. Not fishing. Just watching. Did lads today still do this? He felt old just entertaining the thought. But did they? Their mothers would probably argue that it wasn't safe for them to be out on their own any more. You don't know what sort of people are about these days. But then wasn't that his job too? And had it really been any different when he was a lad?

That summer, all those years earlier, had been the first time he had really learned to appreciate the countryside. Except that it hadn't really been the countryside, not really, not like that described in the fiction that he read at the time, not the smuggler's dens and deserted farmhouses, nor the unspoilt mountains and haunted forests. It had been the park and the woods at the end of his road, close to where he lived, on a busy road, in the middle of a busy town, close to a major city. But his youthful imagination had filled in the imperfect blanks.

They all used to play by the river. There was a rumour that there were crayfish under the big rock on the opposite bank, but although they had repeatedly trawled their colourful string nets through the water there, they never once had seen one. Not even when Roger Wilde waded right in and lifted the rock just a fraction to look underneath, before letting it drop back with a splash. They all saw a snake once, or a slow-worm more likely, startling them as it slithered off right by their feet, pink and naked like a fat rat's tail, obscene. There was a weeping-willow tree, with pendent branches, that was impossible to climb, and which dropped large catkins on the ground which looked like huge, hairy caterpillars. And so many birds. He could remember them all. Ducks and swans on the river, and little moorhens swimming back and forth, calling shrilly. Once a big heron up in the tree top, disturbed by the youthful voices, took to flight, slow and majestic like an ancient pterodactyl from the movies. And all the little brown birds, anonymous, that used to hop and peck around the riverside den when they thought that no one was watching, and would scatter in a flapping shower into the tree branches if any one of them had come too close.

Rat-a-tat-tat. Rat-a-tat-tat. Like a machine gun, the repeated beat of beak on bark. And yet still he could not see the woodpecker.

- - - - - - - -

He had felt the adrenalin surge kick in and instantaneously relieve the feelings of tiredness. He had felt glad of the helping hand. So many body mechanisms that were outside of mental control. What was it that stimulated them? Excitement? Fear?

Diana had returned to the beginning of the manuscript. 'I marked this passage here.' She pointed to a thick red underscore. 'Something is nagging me about this part, but I just can't seem to put my finger on it.'

'Let me see. Which part?' He took the page and read, '"He looked up to see an attractive young woman offering him a cotton handkerchief". I don't understand. What is your problem?'

'How did Teresa get the handkerchief?'

'From James.'

'Don't you mean Martin?'

'Martin, James, I don't know. It could have been either of them.'

'I'm beginning to think it was neither of them.'

Chapter Six

It was part of an old country estate, this wood. The Earls of somewhere or other, he seemed to remember. It was long since disused now, and the big house had been pulled down long enough ago to no longer cause consternation in the memory of even the most fervent preservationists. The grounds had completely reverted back to their natural state now too, although just occasionally there were glimpses of past glories: the overgrown plinth of a statue long since reduced to rubble, barely discernible amidst a tangle of brambles; a rather too precise line of trees, too straight to be entirely natural, revealing the course of a now disused ancient carriageway; and the lakes. At first glance they appeared entirely genuine: one large expanse of water, bridled by two smaller ones, the result of the stream's natural drainage, created by the run off from the slopes around. Except there were no obvious slopes around, and the stream had appeared to be quite merrily running on its seaward-bound route without need to stop and linger in these large, languid pools. The little island was perhaps just too perfect too, rather too ornamental to have occurred by chance. Once again, nature crafted for the aesthetics of man.

It was a pleasing spot though. The ponds which David imagined would once have held colourful goldfish for the delight of their owners, were now clogged at the edges with a vibrant, green algae, and the mysterious, dark centres neither revealed whether they continued to sustain life nor gave away just how deep their waters ran. Trees grew around the perimeter of the lakes, forming a protective enclave and a boundary to the water, as if to say, this far but no further. Overhead the branches were less generous about surrendering their space and the canopy of dry twigs and tortuous bows still stretched out far and wide, as if trying to meet those from one bank with those on the other. On the ground the fallen leaves still formed a damp, squidgy base of russet compost and David's impression as he looked upon the scene was one of a gently golden-glowing glade.

Something felt strange though. He listened acutely, keeping still, and was aware that the short hairs on the back of his neck were standing on end. David knew that it was a cliched reaction, but he had always found it a reliable response in the past. He was close now.

It was the lack of the woodpecker's staccato drum that he now found disturbing. The intermittent percussion that had followed him through the old wood, was now silent. Even the wind through the trees had died away; not a rustle of movement in the highest branches, not a ripple across the surface of the still lake.

He knew he was being watched. He had realised it as soon as he had stepped out from the cover of the woodland path and exposed himself to the relative open expanse of the clearing and the lakes. It was a sensation he was familiar with. The unease. The unsettling experience of no longer being in total control. It was a power thing, and until he could locate and identify his silent observer, the power was out of his hands. He knew not to give in to the mind games though. The uncertainty could be your downfall.

He wondered about big cats. It didn't have to be a person that was watching him. The prolonged gaze of an animal produces the same effect, often more so, since they are generally more experienced than humans in the need for stealth and quiet, and don't give in so quickly to the temptation for exposure and action. Patience. It was something else we could learn from nature. There were always rumours of big cats, escaped from zoos or let loose from private collections, roaming wild across the tranquil English landscape. There was the video footage, hazy and unconvincing, of a black panther walking across a green and pleasant field, and the farmers in Bodmin with their reports of mauled sheep and giant teeth marks. It wasn't evidence that would stand up in a court of law, but alone among the trees, evidence didn't seem quite so important.

The silence continued. David felt the weight of standing still. How much easier it was to keep walking than to remain motionless. He surveyed the trees all around him for signs of movement, swivelling around, revolving through a complete circle.

The spell was broken by almost simultaneous noise and motion. The distant rat-a-tat-tat beat that had grown so familiar, and the movement, high up on a tree trunk close at hand. A striking pied bird, with a brilliant red abdomen and a scarlet nape. The Great Spotted Woodpecker took to flight, undulating up and down, in characteristic fashion, passing, momentarily, low over the water's surface, before swooping up again. David watching, followed its progress through branches and above bushes, at times close to the ground, sometimes high in the canopy. Deeper, deeper, into the darkness of the wood. And with every faster wing-beat, further and further away from the still reverberating echo that signalled its mate and its home.

The wind had started up again now, gripping the tallest trees and shaking them, as they called out for release, sending a cold shower of water droplets down from where it had rained in the night, and making the soft carpet underfoot ever more brown and mulchy. It was time to move on. Although still there was that feeling. A nagging doubt that he was not alone. No longer the one in control.

- - - - - - - - -

The inevitability. He had likened it to being in a car accident. How very like the one they had both been in - how many years ago was it now? Three. The slow-motion, unstoppable progression, towards an absolutely inevitable conclusion. Such was Diana's reasoning.

'I have a problem with Martin.'

'Surprise me.'

Diana continued, 'This business on the tower. His relationship with the twins. It's all a problem.'

'My only problem is finding him.'

'Really? I should think you would know exactly where to look.'

Chapter Seven

It was the crack of a twig behind him that confirmed his suspicions if ever they were required to be confirmed. He kept on walking. Ignore it. Keep alert. Let them reveal themselves first. No point showing your fear.

The path followed the right hand perimeter of the larger of the ponds, before disappearing into the trees again for a short distance. The wood ahead was more sparse than before, and David could see much further ahead another ploughed field, and beyond, atop a low ridge, the bold outline of a great stone gateway, the last remaining monument to the grand estate of old. Which way now? He needed to remain within the woods, of that much he was certain, and yet all the pathways led him away from them, back to a civilisation from which he was trying to escape. As if to reinforce this idea, there was a signpost again, the first he had seen for some time, pointing towards the silhouetted archway: Wasston 1 mile. Across the field, beyond the ridge, there was a different world order laid out: row upon row of little houses; an orderly grid of roads and streets and avenues, with regular corners and straight lines; cars and trains and buses going back and forth and back again; and people, busy people, living in their little houses, in their ordered streets, driving in their cars. Back and forth and back again.

Crack. It was another dead twig. Whoever was following wasn't very good at it. David felt more reassured. If he turned around suddenly now he felt sure he would spot his pursuer. The cover was less dense here. There was nowhere to hide. Wait. Just a little bit longer.

It was the giggling that eventually gave them away. David had decided to walk on the half a dozen or so more paces that would bring him to the edge of the woodland and then turn around and confront the stalker behind him, when the sound of a louder, closer footstep, quickly followed by a high boyish laugh and the noise of running feet revealed the identity of his shadows. David turned in time to see two lads, neither of whom could have been yet into their teens, fast disappearing into the anonymity of the trees. The slightest movement of a bush to the left of the path betrayed the hiding place of the third tail who had not had the presence of mind of his companions to run away.

The young boy cowered back, too quickly on the defensive as in one only too used to facing retribution for his actions, 'We didn't mean any harm, Mister. We were only having a laugh.' David's smile - part relief, part amusement - must have reassured him, because he continued rather more cockily, 'You know how it is.'

'Yes,' David agreed, 'I know how it is.'

The boy made to follow after his friends, but David called him back with a question, 'Do you play around here a lot?'

There was suspicion in his answer. 'Yer.' Was he yet going to be accused of something?

'Do you do any bird watching?'

'Bird watching!' There was contempt in his voice. 'That's for poofs. What would we want to do bird watching.'

David continued, 'So you wouldn't know if there was a hide in these woods? You know, a sort of shelter that bird watchers might use.'

The lad was cagey again. This time trying to judge if his knowledge could be used to his advantage, or if it was another ploy to trap him. 'Might do.'

There was a silence, before David said, 'Is that a might do, yes, or a might do, no?'

'Might do, yes.' Then realising that he might have convicted himself unduly, he hastily added, 'But we don't ever go there. I mean we know where it is, but we don't ever go there. Not inside. Jack says the bloke who goes there is a nutter. We'd never go inside.'

'You've never seen him then? This bloke?'

'No.'

David changed his line of questioning, 'So where do you live then?'

The boy nodded his head as though indicating a point beyond David, 'On the estate. Over the road.'

'The dual carriageway?'

'Yer. Can't you hear it? It's only just over there.'

The distant roar of the traffic was indeed apparent if you listened hard again, and David realised that he had come close to rejoining the same road that he had originally parked by, except some considerable distance further along its length.

'How do you get across. There's no bridge there.' He knew, he'd checked long and hard on the map the night before.

'No, we run. It's fun.'

'What's your name?'

It was a question too far, and one the young boy must have recognised as so often preceding recrimination, 'What is this? I'm out of here.' He made to tear away, but David managed to extract one last piece of information from him.

'So which way is this hide?'

The lad pointed back into the uncharted trees to his left, as he turned his back and showed a grubby pair of trainers' heels to David, 'That way. By the secret pond.'

- - - - - - - - -

Was this how they all felt? He had interviewed enough suspects in his time - innocent and guilty alike - to recognise the irony of being on the receiving end of an interrogation. You looked for a slip-up: one wrong word that gave them away; one loose statement that conflicted with an earlier one.

'I never did understand why you didn't reveal your true self.'

'How could I?' he sounded puzzled.

'All that knowledge you have. Everything you had learned. I never did understand why you never let on. It was as though they were your words, but being spoken by the wrong characters.'

'What do you mean?'

'I mean, why wasn't the Daniel in your story a bird watcher, when the David I know is such a fanatic?'

'A bird watcher?' he said, relieved, 'I thought ... no, nothing.'

Diana continued, cutting across her husband's explanation, 'Which got me thinking, if you can lie about one thing ...'

Chapter Eight

The fungi on the tree was a vivid orange, and formed a diminishing spiral of embracing loops around the smooth, silvery bark. On the ground, in between the protruding roots, sprouting erratically from the disintegrating leaf mould, were small toadstools. David recognised the obvious white fluffy balloon of a puffball, but the other stringy, spidery growths were unknown to him. He touched one suspiciously with his shoe, and it exploded into a cloud of white powder.

The 'secret pond' had not proved as elusive to find as its name had suggested. Fifty yards of battling to try and carve the semblance of a path through the spiky shrub, and several scratches and snags later had brought David to the edge of a quiet pool of water, skirted by rather limp, bedraggled reed beds. The wooden hide, which in the summertime, would probably have been completely overgrown by plants and weeds, stuck out, exposed like a beached hulk of a boat, close to the far bank of the pond, underneath the cover of the nearest trees.

David lent against the thick bole of the beech tree and surveyed the scene. Everything was very quiet. David closed his eyes and tried to listen to the furthest sound. Totally still. Just listening. At first there was nothing. Or perhaps just the faintest rustling of the old branches in the wind. But then out of blackness, awareness grew as his hearing became more and more acute. Reaching out further. The whisper of the breeze through the reed beds, and the faintest of splashes as a fish surfaced in the pond with a ripple and a water boatman skimmed across the shallows. The constant low hum of traffic on the dual carriageway; the purr of powerful performance cars, the heavy rumble of laden lorries, and the noisy misfirings of an ancient motorbike. And further still, a car horn sounded, jarring, in the housing estate beyond the woods. Somewhere high overhead, an aircraft. Or perhaps a helicopter? And a dog barking. A big dog, with a deep, angry bark. How far away? Miles, maybe miles.

Two ducks glided across the pond, leaving V-shaped ripples in their wake. Mallards. One male, one female. The male had a vibrant green head, shot through with an electric emerald hue when the sun caught its plumage in certain directions. It had a bright yellow beak and a narrow collar of white down. The female duck was tawny brown in colour all over, speckled with darker brown mottles. They scarcely looked as though they belonged to the same species. If the mantra, Men Are From Mars, Women Are From Venus, had a visual depiction, it would be the Mallard Duck. Beautiful birds, all but taken for granted, being the most common of ducks seen on British waters. The pair, swam side by side, silently. Seemingly relaxed and content in each others company.

David had always admired the apparent fidelity of ducks. Swans too. Rare to see a solitary swan or a loner duck. Mated for life. For better, for worst. Perhaps that was something else man could learn from nature, or was this just a particular weakness in himself? He thought back to his own vows to Diana. He had been very young then. It seemed a long time ago now. He tried to remember how she had been back then, when they had first met, but his mind kept on slipping back to the image of the round-eyed young woman in prison who had said that she loved him.

The hide was empty. It looked like it had been so for some time. There was a thermos flask of tea on a small table, but the liquid inside was cold and fermented and covered by a thin film of stewed scum. It appeared as though the small boy had not been lying, and that neither him nor any of his mates had been over the threshold of the tiny shelter: there were still too many items of potential value inside, that juvenile hands would have been only too anxious to remove before now. David let out a sign of relief. It was going to be all right after all: Martin was dead. This is where he would die.

- - - - - - - -

He had realised that there was no point in denying it. Sometimes the truth can be surprisingly therapeutic. Even if it arrives too late to effect a cure.

Diana was quite calm, 'So there was no Martin?'

'Merely another fiction.'

'Although that's not quite so, is it?'

'Oh?'

'I mean, how much of him was actually you?' Her husband's silence prompted her to carry on, 'The killings on the island? The baby? Was it you with that woman the year before? Laura,' she spat the word out.

Laura. For one brief moment there had been a chance when it all could have been so different.

Chapter Nine

'I do not want to hurt you. You will always mean so much to me, but we both knew that it could not last, and this is the only way I can think to end it.' David realised with a start that he had been speaking the words out loud as he read them on the pages in the letter. He continued reading to himself.

I am going back to continue my studies in Japan. I have been offered a post-graduate place at the university in Sapporo on Hokkaido, the north island. It is close to where my family live and it is a good opportunity for me. There is some teaching involved too. I know this will be a disappointment for you, but I hope you will understand that I have to leave. I have waited and studied for too long to pass up this chance. I hope that you can be happy for me some day.

I will always be so much in your debt for all your support during those terrible months after I was mugged. I never thought that I could feel safe after that but you made me feel alive again. You showed me how to trust again. How to love again. I can't tell you how important that was for me. I remember you saying at the time, that you would teach me how to fly again, and you did. I owe you everything. That is why it is so important that I don't miss this opportunity now, otherwise you will have given me back my life for nothing. I hope that you can understand this, my darling. We both knew that it could not last for ever. It was a fantasy. A beautiful fantasy.

Perhaps one day, when you can forgive me, you could visit me in Japan. Could you not find a crime to solve out there? I'm sorry, I don't mean to joke. I just want you to be happy for me. I am not leaving you. I am finding me.

I do not know what else to write. I leave on Thursday. Perhaps we could meet for one last time. I shall be in on Tuesday night if you can find an excuse to get away.

I will always remember you.

With love,

The letter was signed Kazumi. David put the letter back into the steel box from which he had found it, and drew out the next sheet of paper from the container. He sat back on the bench before reading any more though, his back leaning up against the wooden panels of the hide, and closed his eyes. Even with his eyes tight shut, he could visualise his surroundings as though they were still wide open: the four walls closing in upon him. And it was hot, like being in a sweat box, even though the temperature outside was still icy, out of the sun light. He felt a bead of sweat trickle down from his forehead, down his cheek, and another down his back, such that where he leant against the wall he felt sticky and unclean. Still with his eyes closed he removed his coat and let it drop on to the earth floor of the shelter. There was a smell inside the box, like that of moss or peat, an earthy odour of the soil, but not that of a snug, safe hiding-place, but more of a damp, unhealthy cell. Humid and stifling. One or two plants had managed to invade the small cracks in the tight construction between the wooden planks, but most had kept their distance, recognising that this was not their domain. It was airless. David opened his eyes and took a deep gasping breath. He wanted to open the door to the small building and let the light and air flood back in and cleanse the place of all its memories, but he realised that if he did so he would be tempted to flee the place forever, and never complete the task he had set himself. Instead he contented himself with pressing his mouth up close to the small shutter that opened up as a spy-hole on the bird life of the pond and wood, and drawing in great lungfulls of fresh air.

His view of the world outside was restricted to what he could see through an oblong frame, three feet wide and less than one foot high. It was like being in a military pill box. He could imagine the tension and excitement of waiting for the enemy to emerge from their hiding places and show themselves to his sniper's bullet. They could be anywhere: distant and hidden in the trees, or close enough that you could hear their every pounding heartbeat. They could be as near as three feet away and he would not be able to see them if they fell outside his narrow field of vision. Perhaps it was not so different with bird watching: waiting for a duck to break cover from its reed bed camouflage, or a finch to reveal itself from its concealment in the branches. It could be a tense business. Although it was exactly the opposite experience that had drawn him to the activity in the first place. It was the sense of relaxation. The excuse to spend days away in the tranquillity of the countryside: the perfect antidote to a city policeman's stressful life. David shifted back on the bench again and returned to examining the next sheet of paper from his cache. It was a list of bird names, neatly typed, each name followed by a box, in which there was either a handwritten tick, or a space where it had been left blank. Most boxes appeared to contain ticks. David's eye ran swiftly down the list, occasionally settling on a particular name, which would momentarily spark a pleasing memory. Common Kestrel, tick: that early morning on the motorway, not a car in either direction, just a long straight road ahead, and a long straight road behind reflected in the mirrors, and high above in the sky, a tiny, hovering speck, hovering, hovering, then plunging straight down on an unsuspecting mouse in the field beyond the barriers and the hard shoulder. Smew, tick: just once, on this very pond, unmistakable with its snowy white plumage and black eye patch, just passing through on its way to eastern climates. Long-tailed Tit, tick: a beautiful, late autumn day, much like today. And yet so unlike today.

Extraordinary the intrinsic value of a few modest sheets of paper. Insignificant and worthless to anyone other than the person who had compiled them - of little more than a passing competitive interest even to a fellow birder - they represented hours - years - of devotional pursuit. What David held in his hand was as real and as precious as someone's life. He folded the sheets carefully into thirds and, picking up his coat from the dirty floor, tucked them in the inside pocket.

The next batch of papers in the box appeared to be a diary of some sort. They had obviously been extracted from a larger volume, but had been removed carefully, such that the glue binding along the spine still held the sub-section of pages together, forming a mini-book in its own right. The handwriting was small and spidery, and the character that looked like an 'e' was actually an 'r', and the character that looked like a flying seagull was actually an 'm'. David read swiftly, oblivious to the deficiencies in script.

April 3rd
Sanctuary! We are alone at last.

April 4th
Raining today and so we have been reading the diary entries of the previous tenants of what is currently our Castle abode. Some were humorous. Some were action-packed. This Lundy logbook lacks for only one ingredient to make it a bestseller - Sex! (here a note had been added in a different handwriting and in a different colour pen) *And we aim to rectify that!*

April 5th

April 6th
Teresa is out walking, and so Laura and I have the cottage to ourselves. I am writing this journal while Laura sleeps. Obviously! I have never felt so free. Have I been carrying a yoke across my shoulders all these years? The yoke of responsibility and commitment and accountability. To job, to marriage, to society. Here it is as if the burden of each one has been successively removed. Perhaps it is the Lundy magic that my fellow scribers have waxed lyrical about ad nauseam? Huh! Freedom is a state of mind. I could be locked in a prison cell and yet as long as I was with Laura I would still feel as free as the birds that I see outside the window.

April 7th
What is it about this journal? It feels almost like a confessional. And so do I feel guilty? I don't know. Perhaps. There is always a serpent in the Garden of Eden, and perhaps that serpent is guilt. Or perhaps it is Teresa? She is out walking again. She still sleeps with us both in the evenings, but has taken to staying out during the daylight hours. I do not mind. It is Laura that matters. With Teresa it is only sex. We would not have brought her, except that she insisted, although I do not think she would have done as she threatened and told her brother about us. He would surely be no more upset to discover that his wife was sleeping with a

strange man than to find out that she was sleeping with his own sister! Laura has talked about leaving him. I don't know why she stays. But she says it is not that simple. It never is. Look at me. And Diana.

April 8th

Do people write diaries for themselves, or in the secret hope that they will be read by someone else one day? I don't know, I've never written one before. But I can see that it could become an obsession. Already I am keeping this logbook secret from first Teresa, and now Laura too. It is strange, and yet I am planning to leave it for a generation of future cottage-dwellers, everyone of them a stranger to me, to read and gawp over. Laura is sleeping again. I have never met anyone like her before. She has given me a new chance. For love, for happiness, for freedom. If experience has taught me anything it is that these kind of opportunities - these kind of feelings - occur perhaps once in a lifetime, and to fail to seize them now, will leave me in torment for evermore hereafter. Laura and Teresa had a row earlier. Laura thinks that Teresa is falling in love with me. She said that it would get in the way, that it would spoil everything. I do not care about Teresa. It is Laura that matters. I will talk to her again about leaving her husband. Maybe it is because the week is coming to an end and I know that we must soon return to the inadequacy of those brief clandestine meetings; maybe it is the thought that she will be sleeping with him again. It makes me feel angry. I must have her. Or if I can't, I swear that he won't either. I have ways. Within my job, I have ways.

April 9th

I think a walk is the order of the day. Well why not? We go home tomorrow and I might as well breath a bit of fresh air before returning to the city. Shame to miss out on the birds altogether too. Although I have been kept very happily entertained in other areas. If I can be allowed to once again return to my Garden Of Eden metaphor, I think any reader would agree that I, Adam, have had his hands more than full in precipitating Eve's fall!

The journal ends at this point and the very beginning of the next entry, in an entirely different handwriting, and in an entirely different style, takes up from the 3rd May, with an account of watching three seals from the east cliffs. David suddenly felt very tired, weighed down by memories. And past hopes.

The steel box had very few further secrets to reveal, but David removed the last two sheets of paper regardless. He could never be accused of not being thorough on an investigation.

Another letter. Headed paper: gothic script on pastel pink cartridge, a strangely tasteless combination, and in the twirly, hard-to-decipher lettering, the words, Susan Croft, 9 King Street.

Darling,

This is the hardest letter to write, but I think you already know what I am going to say. These last few months have not been easy for me leading this double life and I have finally come to a decision - I can no longer go on seeing you.

I have been foolish - we both have - I have a husband and a new baby that I love. It is for her, more than anything else, that I have to put an end to this affair before things get out of hand. You must see that.

I think it would be better if we don't see each other again. Please do not try to get in touch.

Susie.

David remembered back to the day in mid-May when he had first read this letter. The sun had been shining outside. There had been a gentle breeze blowing through the trees. And somewhere in the distance he had heard the sound of that unmistakable two-tone siren, taunting him, and calling him names: cuck-oo. Cuck-oo.

It felt colder inside the hide again now. David shouldered his coat and brushed off the loose dirt, and then opened the door of the small enclosure and stepped outside into the chill air. He fished around inside his pockets and, from his coat, produced an unmarked cassette tape, and from the back pocket of his trousers, a small petrol lighter. The steel tin containing all of the papers was lying, open, on the floor of the hide, close to the door. He threw the cassette, along with Susan's letter, into the secure container, and flicked the ignition on the lighter, sending a small, blue flame into the air. He bent down and applied the flame to the corner of the top letter, fanning the fire slightly so that the heat built up sufficiently to take hold of the plastic casing of the cassette, making it wrinkle and distort, twisting and turning in the agony of being consumed. The terrible agony of being consumed.

There remained just one final sheet of lined A4 paper unread. The edge of the page was jagged as though it had been torn out hurriedly from a larger pad, and the handwriting was small and scrappy, sloping dramatically from left to right, as though each line was trying desperately to escape off the bottom of the page. David held it up to the weak sunlight and read.

To Whom It May Concern.

This may be the only chance I have to communicate to you. I think my life may be at risk and I don't think I have very long before they find out. If you are reading this now I have been proved correct in this belief. Everything else you will hear will be told to you by murderers. Believe me about this if nothing else. Everything. That is why I write this testament - to shine as one ray of truth through a darkness of deceit.

It was only last night that I discovered the truth myself. Now I can marvel at how I could have been so blind. So stupid. It was only last night that I finally found out what happened to my wife. I discovered the pages from the journal under his bed, quite by chance when I was looking for something else. Should I have read them? Of course, I wouldn't have, except that I saw her name. In black and white. In front of me on the page. And then I was lost. Curiosity is such a powerful instinct. But even now, I wonder if I wouldn't have been better off if I had just put those pages back unread. Except it is not true what they say, that ignorance is bliss. Ignorance was killing me as surely as my life is finished now.

And why did I break into his cottage in the first place? It was stupid, so stupid. Except that I recognised him; recognised him as the policeman who had helped us when we had had a break-in at King Street the year before; recognised his name, as the one investigating the murder of the kiddie down the road; recognised his signature on a letter I had found at the bottom of one of Laura's drawers. What a fool I have been. I can almost laugh now, at my stupidity: to think I believed that he must suspect Teresa of this crime; that I believed she was so innocent. In the space of five short minutes, for that was how long it took to read the poisonous account, I discovered that I had not only lost a wife, but had lost a sister too.

And what of my wife? She walked out of my life over one year ago. Not a word, not a letter, not a communication of any kind, and yet I always hoped that she would come back. One day, I would hear the key turn in the door and it would be her. Never once, did I consider the possibility that she was dead. Even now I can scarcely take it in. Except that it all makes sense. Such horrible sense.

I wanted to write more, but now there are people coming down the path above me, and I fear there will not be another opportunity. If this is to be my final communication, I just want to tell you, that I loved her. Too.

Signed *James Brewer.*

David flicked the switch of his petrol lighter, once, twice, before it sparked, and silently studied the dancing blue figures that pirouetted in the gyrating flame. There was a crack of dry branches high above him, as a large, solitary Rook, vacated its lofty perch and disappeared into the distance on bat-black wings, cawing critically. A sudden gust of cold air made David shudder and blew out the hand-held fire, and David had to press the starter again to get the thing to reignite. He held the light to one corner of the sheet of paper and watched as blackness took hold of the page, spreading like a cancer, eating up words and then sentences: each inch of paper becoming as tenuous and brittle as the truth, until piece by piece it blew away. Charred fragments on the breeze. Long after the last scrap had disappeared David continued to watch, but there was to be no Phoenix from these flames.

Epilogue

The fire brigade had already been and gone by the time he had returned home.

The police had remained though. They had wanted to know his name. And he had told them. They had wanted him to confirm that he lived here. And he had told them that he did. They had told him that there had been a terrible accident. And he had asked them if it was his wife. They had said that they were very sorry. And he had said that she would not have been able to get out because she had been bed-bound since the car crash. They had said that he had misunderstood; that she was alive but was in hospital. And he had asked them what they meant. They had said a neighbour had alerted the fire brigade and they had managed to save her - 'nick of time, very lucky, Sir'. And he had asked them how she was. They had said that she was unconscious but that she would be able to speak in a day or two - 'she's breathed in a lot of smoke'. And he had said that that was a great relief. They had asked if there was anyone that he knew locally that he would like them to contact. And he had said that there was no one. They had said that they might need him to come down to the police station later - 'details, forms, you understand, Sir'. And he had showed them his identity card and he had said that he understood. They had said that they were very sorry again.

And he had said that so was he.

Author's Last Word

It's odd: having always wanted to write 'a book', I finally manage to put down a sufficient quantity of words on paper such that I have something that vaguely fits that description, only for it not to be 'the book' I had ever really intended writing. Partly, this is because it took on a life of its own in the writing process - the story frequently changing in ways that I would not have credited at the outset of the project; partly, all the 'profound and important ideas' that I thought I had to say to the world at large and wanted to include in my writing, didn't seem so very profound and important when I had committed them to paper. Perhaps, though, this is a good lesson in realising that fiction is about entertainment, not about preaching. So, 'the book', which every one of us is supposed to have lurking away inside of us, still remains bottled up within me somewhere. And if this just sounds like a plug to watch out for the sequel ... well, perhaps it is!